Real reader reviews for

MAGNOLIA PARKS

'If *Gossip Girl* and *Made in Chelsea* had a baby, it
would be this book.'
★ ★ ★ ★ ★

'Hands down the most emotional romance book I have
ever read and therefore my favourite.'
★ ★ ★ ★ ★

'Magnolia and BJ have embedded themselves into
my DNA.'
★ ★ ★ ★ ★

'This book gave drama, love triangles, toxicity, chaos
and I ate up every single moment.'
★ ★ ★ ★ ★

'TikTok made me do it, 1000% lived up to the hype.'
★ ★ ★ ★ ★

'Ridiculously addictive . . . My heart broke a
million times.'
★ ★ ★ ★ ★

By Jessa Hastings

Magnolia Parks
Daisy Haites
Magnolia Parks: The Long Way Home
Daisy Haites: The Great Undoing

JESSA HASTINGS
MAGNOLIA PARKS
THE LONG WAY HOME

DUTTON

DUTTON

An imprint of Penguin Random House LLC
penguinrandomhouse.com

Cover design by Rachael Lancaster
Cover photograph by Garrett Lobaugh on behalf of Avenir
Author photograph by Anabel Litchfield on behalf of Avenir

LIBRARY OF CONGRESS CATALOGING-IN-PUBLICATION DATA
has been applied for.

ISBN 9780593474907 (paperback)
ISBN 9780593474914 (ebook)

Printed in the United States of America

1st Printing

Winds in the east, mist coming in
Like something is brewing and about to begin.
Can't put my finger on what lies in store
But I feel what's to happen all happened before.

– Bert from that movie starring
BJ's second-favourite girl

PART ONE

ONE

Magnolia

Hipsters aren't my favourite people. They used to be my least favourite kind of person, but they've actually been usurped.

They've been replaced by—arguably—a subset of the hipster that is worse than what came before, like a mutation of a virus that's a bigger pain in the arse than the original. This subset is often a lot more grubby and, unfortunately, usually at least semi-naked. I think they'd call themselves 'free-spirited'.

I see them standing topless in fields that they're probably trespassing on because they can hardly own property by working four hours a week as an artisan barista. Their arms usually seem to be thrown up in the air, there are knots in their unkept hair, and they're probably holding sparklers as they use grainy, overexposed filters to make it look like their photos weren't actually taken on what I can only imagine is a cracked iPhone 7 but instead some old-timey camera they traded a poem for.

When I see them I just want to pop on some latex gloves, hand them a shirt, give them a good shake and yell, "WHAT ARE YOU SMILING ABOUT YOUR JEANS ARE FROM H&M FOR THE LOVE OF GOD."

I've met a lot of these people in New York, actually. Many a free spirit on the subway—which I'd never take. There's a stop by my apartment though, so I see many a miscreant pass by.

It's lonelier here than I thought, and I did think it would be lonely.

It couldn't have been any other way, I knew that—leaving it all behind. Leaving him.

3

No packing up, no goodbyes. Just the first flight out of London to get as far away from it all as quick as I could.

It's been nearly a year. Not exactly, but almost.

And everything is different now.

There's an incessant knocking at my front door.

I live on the top floor of 995 Fifth Avenue. I chose to live here because it looks like London, or about as much as a sixteenth-floor apartment in Manhattan can look like London.

The knocking is louder and more insistent than the standard knock-knock-knock a regular person would make. This is an aggressively bright and rhythmic knock. Knock-knock-knock. Knock, knock. Again and again.

It's obvious who is on the other side of the door before I even open it. What isn't obvious is why she's here or how she got upstairs without me buzzing her in.

I swing open the door and there she is—arms folded over her chest, brows knitted behind her Cartier Trinity cat-eye sunglasses in the tortoise shell which she then shoves on top of her head and glares at me.

"Took you long enough," Taura Sax growls.

"I was upstairs," I shrug. "And I wasn't expecting company." I stare down at her feet. "Do you really dare wear those Balenciaga monstrosities in my presence?"

"I know, I know," she groans.

I shake my head at her wildly. "They look like—"

"—Geriatric shoes," she jumps in. "I know."

"Have you no pride, Taura? No sense of self-worth?"

"Alright—" She rolls her eyes. "I'm wearing a shoe you don't like, I didn't sell my baby . . ."

"I might have preferred it if you did."

"They're just very comfortable." She shrugs as though she's innocent.

"So is nudity, Taus, but there's a time and a place. And for these—" I stare pointedly at her Triple S Clear Sole logo-embroidered leather, nubuck and mesh sneakers—"that place is a rehabilitation unit for the elderly after a nasty fall." I cross

4

my arms and eye her with suspicion. "What are you doing here, anyway?"

She pulls in her little Brics carry-on and follows me to the kitchen.

"I thought you'd need me," she shrugs.

I wrap my white Juliet cashmere cardigan from Khaite tighter against myself. "That's very thoughtful."

"Yes." She gives me a smug smile. "I am quite thoughtful when you don't think I'm a raging slut."

I give her a look. "You are a bit of a slut though."

She laughs brightly. "Yeah, I am."

"I'm here to fly home with you," she tells me.

I frown at her. "Why?"

"Because." She shrugs. "You haven't been back in a year, and there's the wedding, and your mother's basically a contestant on her own personal version of *Love Island*."

I roll my eyes at her, though I know it's true. My mother has taken my father marrying my childhood nanny like an absolute champion, if we consider champions today as high-functioning, trollop-y alcoholics.

"You're still not talking to Jonah. BJ's dating someone now." She watches me closely as she says this and I avoid her eyes, looking down at the checked stretch sports bra that I'm wearing from Burberry. He's dating someone new. That's the one everyone's worried about. I don't let it show, not even a flicker on my face, and you can bet your bottom dollar that the beast I've beaten, bound and buried for the better part of a year is so restrained and controlled and sedated that not even a whisker of emotion breezes across my poised little face.

I cock my eyebrow in defiance of her—she of little faith, waiting for my heart's knees to buckle at his name.

Never again.

"It's going to be a hard couple of weeks for you," she tells me cautiously. "I'm here to bring you home because that's what best friends do."

I glance over at her. "Are we best friends now?"

She perches up on the kitchen island and I hand her a glass of pinot gris.

2014 Hans Herzog. Peach blush tint. Dry but not overly tart. Refreshing tannins.

I was sleeping with a boy here for about a month whose family owns vineyards all over—Napa, Burgundy, Champagne, Marlborough.

The alcohol was an important component of the relationship.

During that time I picked up some obnoxious, sommelier-adjacent qualities which were the only real takeaways from the relationship.

"Are we not?" She frowns. "Who else would your best friend be?"

I shrug. "I don't know. Henry? My sister?"

"Sisters don't count." She rolls her eyes. Delightfully hazel. They're quite like Montana sapphires. I used to hate them, but now I'm rather fond of them.

"Why?"

"Because I don't have one, so it's not fair."

"Fine." I roll my eyes. "Besides Bridget and Henry, you're my other best friend."

"Don't tell Henry." She gives me a look which I mirror.

I could never.

I'd never hear the end of it.

The day he turned up in New York with Taura Sax I could have thrown him in front of a taxi.

I'd been here maybe five months then.

Henry was visiting me every few weeks. Still does. It was his seventh trip and I knew they liked each other by then because he'd told me they were sleeping together when I met him in Cannes and we'd had a fight over it already. We'd never had a fight before, not really. Well, besides the time he was upset when he found out that Christian and I were together, but that was a one-way fight and it only lasted the length of the drive home until I told him about what BJ had done and then it was back to regularly scheduled programming—so fighting in

6

Cannes was big. Cannes in general was big for other less-ideal reasons, so I'd left early with Rush without saying goodbye and then a few days later he turned up in New York with her. Can you believe it? He'd just brought her here with him.

To New York.

To my apartment. To stay. In my house!

I stared at him in the lobby, blinking until it made sense.

He approached me with placating hands.

"Don't freak out—" he started. "Or be a twat."

I gave him a dark look. He shook his head as he hugged me extra tight.

"I just thought . . . you two would be friends now . . ." He raised his eyebrows in hopeful expectation. "Now that you know it wasn't her who fucked Beej."

Big, awkward smiles from both of them.

I glanced over at her for a few seconds—unimpressed—then back to Henry.

"Yeah, but she did fuck BJ, so . . ."

"Yeah." Taura rolled her eyes. "But who hasn't?"

Henry froze.

I stared at her for a few seconds.

And then I snorted a laugh. Figuratively, obviously. I don't actually snort.

And that's how it happened. That was how Taura Sax wormed her way into my heart and to self-professed best-friend territory.

She jumps off the bench and goes fishing in my fridge.

It's mostly just a lot of wine and olives in there because I still don't cook, but I am on a first-name basis with half the Uber Eats drivers in this city.

Taura bleakly pulls out a jar of pickles, bites down on one. "How's Tom doing?" she asks and I scowl over at her.

"How should I know?"

She shrugs innocently. "You might talk, I don't know."

In case you don't know, here are the bones of my last few months:

I left London and I flew here.

7

Tom flew out the next day to meet me—just to be there for me, because he's like that. And then we were back together. Until we weren't.

It was hurting him. I was hurting him. We weren't just in the foxhole. He was more like a shield and a security blanket and a pacifier and bandage and a stitch for my broken heart.

I wore him like a flak jacket. He bore a lot for me, I can see it in retrospect. He took many, many bullets. Actually, I suspect that one of those bullets nicked his little heart too, the one that deserves so much more than I could ever give it.

He stopped it. It was sudden.

I didn't see it coming.

He flew in, we had sex, we had a fight, he left. It was bad, and so out of the blue.

I don't do so well on my own. I never have. And that night—afternoon, if we're being specific, because I remember the tiny bit of light bending around the blackout blinds we'd pulled down because I don't like to have sex in daylight—we fought about a film and then he just left. He grabbed a few things from the apartment that technically was just mine but really we shared—a phone charger, a watch in a drawer, his spare passport—and then Tom was gone.

Him leaving was akin to finding oneself in the middle of the Arctic Circle with nothing but a light cardigan.

Searing pain, head to toe.

It was like being back in the Mandarin all over again.

I couldn't see properly, I couldn't breathe.

Dying, probably just metaphorically, but maybe also literally?

My neighbour Lucía found me. Dragged me to a bar where I proceeded to make many, many mistakes with Rush Evans in a cloakroom.

Rush and I continued to be on and off whenever he was in town.

I don't know if it was shittier of me or him. Me, the ex-girlfriend of his best friend. Him, the best friend of my ex-boyfriend.

"Technically, Sam was my best friend," he'd sometimes say to make us feel better after we'd done it. It never worked.

He went away for a month to shoot a movie and I stumbled literally and drunkenly into the arms of Stavros Onasis, the son of the oil tycoon. That didn't last so long, which was fine because by then Rush was back. Then he left again for reshoots, and I found that vineyard boy, Dieter Van Lauers. Not much more to say than that, I don't think we lasted a month.

Briefly there was a boy from South Africa—a man, I should say—Addington Van Schoor, a school teacher at Nightingale Bamfords. Very handsome, but not much there. Just chemistry and a dead end. All of them are dead ends though. I guess that's the point.

Rush and I, we drifted back and forth as friends with a lot of benefits. He was a mess and I was a mess, we both knew it and didn't hold it against each other. We did often hold one another though. He became one of my closest friends, actually, though it cost him a dear one in the process. Rush never ordered a negroni in front of me, he once told a girl to fuck off because she smelt of orange blossom, he fought an old boy from Varley when I told him he started a rumour about me back at school, he'd take me shopping and let me dress him and he turned the other way at night times, pretend I didn't have to spray Dark Rum by Malin+Goetz to fall asleep.

Rush and I properly called it around August, a bit because it was well overdue—we started to get complicated. I think there's only so long you can be what you were before certain things start creeping in—possessiveness and feelings and stupid things like that—so we called it. We also called it because of Jack-Jack.

Jack-Jack was his housemate ways ago. We met through Rush and accidentally kissed one night while he was out of town. He was sort of cross about that, but then not really because we really were technically 'just friends', but anyway after that happened Rush said we had to be really done because

Jack-Jack is a hardcore romantic and Rush could tell that he was already all-in. Unfortunately for Jack-Jack, I'm never going to be all-in again.

"Are you ready to tell me what happened with Lover-Boy?" Taura asks with a pointed look.

"No." I snatch the wine from her hands and throw it back. "No, I'm not."

TWO

BJ

She blows air out of her mouth, nervous, shrugs it off.

Like she's about to walk into a cage fight, that's how her face looks.

I try my best not to laugh but I smirk a little. She frowns and smacks me in the arm.

"It's not funny." She glares. I smile more but it's just because of her accent. Australian. Pretty hot.

"They hate me," she tells me.

"They don't." I roll my eyes at her.

Hate is a strong word, and my parents definitely don't hate her. They don't hate anyone. Don't even think my mum could hate Mussolini, let alone Jordan Dames, the only girl I've ever brought home for her to meet besides . . . well, you know who. So Mum definitely doesn't hate her.

My siblings though . . .

"Jordan!" Mum sings as soon as I open the door and J holds out some flowers and a bottle of wine. She insisted on both. Pointless though because Mum already likes her and I can see Madeline rolling her eyes in the corner of the room. ("Kiss arse," she whispers to Dad, who elbows her quiet.)

Mum takes the flowers, kisses my cheek and walks away.

"Don't you just look beautiful!" Mum calls back at her as she puts them in a vase.

She does. She is. Black hair, blue eyes, big mouth for a white girl. Kind of like a hot Snow White.

"Sit, sit—we're just about to eat," Mum tells us.

Jordan sits between Mum and me.

Smart.

Protection on both sides.

Henry sits on my other side, nods his chin at her as a hello. He's pretty reserved with her, always has been—probably has to be, I reckon, but at least he doesn't pile on like our sisters. Not to her face, anyway.

Madeline sits directly across from Jordan though.

I pour her wine. Pour some for myself.

"Jordan." Mads gives her a cool smile.

We met through Jonah's stupid-hot cousins from Australia who came over for the dregs of Europe's summer. Two sisters, Scotland and Taylor Barnes—I'd go there if I could, but I can't. Not worth the drama though. Anyway, the girls brought Jordan with them.

We hooked up one night after Man U fucking creamed Bristol and we were on the good foot and then she kind of just stuck.

Decided to stay for a bit. Deferred her final year at university, got a job here in PR, covering for someone on maternity leave.

I didn't ask her to be my girlfriend. Heard her refer to herself once at a dinner, and then the next day I woke up and it was fucking everywhere. I like her, it's fun. Felt like a heavy conversation to tell her that I wasn't in the market for a girlfriend so I didn't have it and now it is what it is. Second relationship I've been in in my life and I fell into it.

It's good. She's good. She's easy. In the good way, not in the other way. It's easy with her. And she came at a good time, even if it was a pretty unplanned arrival. I was better when she came, but actually, that had nothing to do with her and everything to do with this article *The Sun* ran back in September.

Magnolia at The Met, BJ back in Blighty, drunk and alone.

That was the article title.

They got me half right. Definitely drunk, seldom alone though.

I knew Magnolia would have seen that article, knew she would have seen that photo of me sunk back in the chair, eyes blurry and shit. I know she knows my mouth better than anyone else ever has or ever will and I know she'd know from that photo I'd been kissing someone. I also know she'd know that I was fucked up. High as shit. Forget that Parks was on the cover of the magazine too, glistening away on the arm of Rush fucking Evans, forget that it made me sick to my stomach where his hand was on her waist; without even a word from her, I knew in the centre of myself how she would have felt when she saw me like that. I hated the feeling of her being ashamed of me, and I knew she would be. She would have looked at that article, swallowed heavy, then flipped it over and tossed it away. She probably piled it under a bunch of other magazines, trying to bury the truth of what I'd become because she'd be embarrassed to be associated with me when I was like that—and we're always associated, even when we haven't spoken in nearly a year.

I stopped taking drugs after that photo ran.

And then the therapy, I'd already been doing that a while— Bridget Parks's doing, I'd bet my life on it. She'll deny it though.

Bridge hasn't spoken to me directly since it all went down, but around June, the day after a particularly damning article about me ran in the *Mail*, ten prepaid sessions with one of London's top psychologists arrived in the post with a note that just read *Or lose her forever*.

Four and a half months of weekly therapy sessions and I can tell you this: I probably have lost her forever.

And a bit of that might always feel like a punch in the gut, but it's okay, I think.

I fucked up.

For a lot of reasons. Some of them might even be valid, some of them might even wash what I did away, but I still fucked up. No one else made me do what I did.

And I was always going to lose her with the way I was going . . .

Don't know why I kept it from her for so long. She was always going to find out, and whenever she did, there was at least always a chance that she would be done with me right then.

That killed me for a bit.

That maybe we were always going to end no matter what . . .

But when I sort of accepted that—that maybe we were starcrossed lovers, or whatever—you know, fire and powder, dying in our triumph, all that shit—I was more okay than I thought.

I started therapy to get her back, wanting to grow into the kind of person she'd want to be with, be good enough, be the sort of person worthy of a girl like Parks. I definitely wasn't before and maybe I won't ever be—even if we're dead in the ground for good, can't hurt to try to be good enough anyway.

I put my arm around my girlfriend.

My girlfriend. Weird to say. Fresh to say too.

Only been about a month since that article ran and I just rolled with it. Been hanging out a bit longer than that though. Met at the end of August and started hooking up late September.

Now here we are. Nearly mid-November and I have girlfriend number two at the ripe old age of twenty-five.

"Where's Taura?" Allison asks Henry brightly.

Henry squashes a smile, pretends he doesn't notice the stark difference between their interest in Taura Sax and their complete disdain for Jordan.

Mads has always been weird about the girls I hang out with. Allie and Jemima are usually fine, but none of them are fine about Jordan. It's like they've all been possessed by the ghost of my ex-girlfriend who lived in Holland Park and wasn't very friendly to new people.

"New York, actually." Henry nods. "Flew out two days ago."

"Oh." Dad nods. "What for?"

Henry clocks me, nervous. Licks his bottom lip. "Uh, to bring Magnolia home."

"What?" Jordan sniffs, amused and confused. "She can't fly by herself?"

And the look Henry gives her . . . If I was a better boyfriend, I'd call him out on it. I mean, fuck, if someone ever looked at Parks like that I'd hit them. But Jordan's not Parks, so I just give my brother a look.

"She didn't grow up here, Hen."

"They can be quite mean to her," Jemima says, taking a sip of wine. Jordan frowns, confused. "Why?"

"Because she's beautiful." Jemima shrugs like she's not just merrily tossing grenades about.

"My God, did you see her at The Met?" Al shakes her head.

Maddie rolls her eyes. "With Rush Evans again? She's so lucky—"

"Her dress was perfect." Jemima sighs. "Versace?" she asks no one in particular.

It was definitely Gucci—I shouldn't know that but I do. Plus, felt like it might have been for me. Not for me, at me, maybe? A solid 'fuck you', red carpet edition. I miss all her chatter about clothes. How much she loves them made me love them. She looks good, she always does though. Sometimes her photos just pop up. Algorithms and shit, you know? Also, I love her, so sometimes I peek. Bit weird, probably shouldn't, but her face is her face and it begs to be looked at.

"People can be quite cruel to beautiful things. For no real reason at all." My mum gives Jordan a thoughtful smile, but her face shifts and I can tell she's missing the same girl I'm always missing even though I shouldn't any more. Mum shakes her head, shakes it off like I should too. "Public fascination for Magnolia has always been a private burden."

"Why do people care about her so much?" Jordan asks, and I think it's a genuine question, even though Henry hears it as a sulk.

"Because she's Magnolia Parks," Madeline says. If Parks ever heard this specific sister of mine defending her she'd probably die happy. Wish I could text her, tell her, make her day. Hopefully Henry will because I know I can't. She wouldn't reply anyway. Wrote her a bunch of letters for months. Don't even know how many. Never heard back.

I top off Jordan's glass and look over at Henry. "Bit of a circus, then?"

"Of course it's a circus, BJ." Allie rolls her eyes impatiently. "She hasn't been home since—"

"—Allison," Mum growls.

"What?" She shrugs impatiently. "He knows he cheated on her. Everyone knows."

"Allison," Dad says this time.

"Are they expecting a lot of press?" I ask my brother, ignoring the rest of them.

Henry nods.

"Lots of people flying in for it." He shrugs. "You know Harley."

"Right."

"They've booked her on a BA flight, told a loud-mouth travel agent she's flying in on the Monday but she's taking the jet on Sunday."

"Smart." I nod. I want to ask if she's okay, but I can't—can't or shouldn't? I don't know—both, probably.

"So why is she coming, anyway?" Jordan asks brightly.

Madeline chimes as she pulls a face. "Awkward."

I breathe out, shoot my youngest sister a look. "Her dad's getting married."

"To their childhood nanny," Allie adds theatrically. "She used to come on vacations with our families. It's so crazy—"

"I think I caught them once," Jemima announces.

"You did not." Mum rolls her eyes at the same time the young ones collectively gasp.

"Yeah, when we were in the water and he was helping us all back up, his hand was on her behind but when they saw me see it they just laughed and said something about it being slippery!"

"Gross!" Madeline scrunches her face up.

"Anyway, the wedding's next week," Allie announces. "We're all going."

"Well," Madeline tosses Allie a bitch look. "Not all of us . . ."

"Madeline," Dad growls.

"What?" She shrugs like she doesn't know. She knows. Madeline is an A-grade manipulator. "She's not . . ."

"Thanks, Mads." I toss her a look and Jordan flashes me an uncomfortable smile.

"Anyway," Henry jumps in. "She's not staying long either way." He looks from me to Jordan, and I can't tell whether he's tossing me a line or trying to make a point. Hard to tell with him sometimes, so I drink my wine.

It's fine, by the way. I'm fucking fine.

I knew she was coming back, and Henry's right. It's just for a bit and then she'll be gone again. Then everything will go back to normal.

Or at least go back to this—whatever 'this' is, I guess.

Parks is gone. That's normal now.

Jordan's pretty quiet for the rest of the dinner after that and we don't stay for long, a bit because my sisters keep hounding Henry for every shred of information he has about Magnolia and Rush, and he won't tell them so they're getting more and more annoying, and I don't want to hear it anyway so we thank Mum for dinner and leave pretty quick.

We walk a few houses down before Jordan stops on the street and looks up at me, squinting. "Why aren't you taking me?"

I give her a look. "It's my ex-girlfriend's dad's wedding. I can't bring my new girlfriend."

She shakes her head, annoyed. "Then why are you invited at all?"

"Because," I shrug, "it's London high society and shit. I wouldn't be completely surprised if her mum was invited."

She gives me a look, but I think she sees my point. Hopefully, anyway.

Her face softens a bit. "Why didn't you tell me?"

"Because it's not a big deal." I shrug dismissively.

That's a lie. Can feel it in my chest as I say it.

Jordan rolls her eyes. "Sounds like she's always a big deal."

"Yeah?" I slip my arms around her waist. "And how would you know?"

She gives me a look. "Everyone at my work asks about her all the time, like I'd actually know about her dating whoever that guy is in those stupid movies . . ." She rolls her eyes.

By those 'stupid movies' she means the highest grossing film franchise in the world, but yeah, 'stupid movies' works for me.

It annoys her, all this. A bit because she doesn't get it and that's hard, and a bit because at least once a week we'll be out and about and some little sixteen-year-old will come up to me, ask Jordan to take a photo of me with them and then usually they'll ask me if Magnolia and Rush are really together. The press releases say they're just friends, and Henry says that's true. I think he's telling the truth. Don't know why he'd lie about that.

I asked him once if they're sleeping together and he said nah, but I don't know—that photo at Cannes with Rush's hand on her waist, there was something about it. So maybe he's covering for her in a way I don't think he would for me.

Jordan sighs quietly but I hear it.

"Look, Jords—" I shake my head to placate her. "She probably won't even talk to me. Avoid me like the plague."

She looks hopeful. "Really?"

I nod.

"She hates me," I tell her. I even manage to deliver the line without the *Super Mario Bros.* death sound effect playing out across the universe.

This relieves her, I can see it on her face.

"And Hen's right—she'll be in and out. You won't even know she's here."

This is also an obvious lie but it works for me because Jordan's never known a London where Parks and I exist in it at the same time.

She doesn't know. Doesn't get it. Doesn't know about the eyes and the photos. Doesn't know what we're like if we're in the same room. How we're magnets, how we look at each other, how we find each other.

She doesn't know that I'm a wolf and Parks is the moon whose name I've howled since I was fifteen.

Jordan doesn't know how me and Parks are.

Were.

I mean were.

She smiles more, relaxes, takes my hand in hers. Kisses it. I press her up against my car. Kiss her. It's conscious but I don't think of Parks when I kiss her, if you can believe it.

Don't think of Parks when I sleep with Jordan either. Try not to, anyway. Harder to do sometimes than others—like now—when we've been talking about her.

Let me be clear: Jordan's so hot.

Probably easier that she's nothing like Parks too, even in the dark. Their bodies feel so different. Jordan's athletic, boobs and butt and curves. And she's cool and approachable and easy-going. She's fun. Level-headed. Drinks beer. Wears denim. Puts her hair in one of those girl buns on top of her head.

She's no fuss.

She trusts me.

Guess I haven't given her a reason not to trust me though.

I'm kind of nervous about seeing Parks if I'm honest.

Nervous she's going to fuck me up a bit. Don't tell me she won't, she always does—even if it's in ways I like.

It's just easier dating someone who doesn't rip your heart out of your chest all the fucking time. And Parks always will. She can't help it. One look at her stupid eyes and I'm undone. Or I used to be—I shake my head at myself, staring at my girlfriend.

Not any more.

For fuck's sake. Please, not any more.

THREE
Magnolia

My sister flings herself into my arms as soon as I walk through the door.

I see her all the time. She flies to me or meets me somewhere in Europe for my work trips, but it's been a bit more than a fortnight since the last time we've seen each other.

She picks me up off the floor even though she's shorter than me.

"You're home!" She lets out a squeal of excitement and I peel her off my body, frowning a little.

"That's much too much emotion, Fridget. And you're crushing my dress."

Ballerina Style Tulle Dress from Miu Miu with the cut-out flower pumps from Dolce & Gabbana.

My sister rolls her eyes and smacks me in the arm. "How was the flight?" She pulls one of my suitcases inside and throws me another look. "How many of these are there?"

"Hmm?" I look over at her mindlessly. "Oh. Twelve perhaps?"

"You're here a week." She blinks.

"Actually," I glance from her to Taura, "I'm here just under three."

"Oh." Taura schleps in another bag before we all give up and leave them in the courtyard. *Is this not what fathers are for?* I wouldn't know, I suppose. Mine's been terribly useless thus far.

"Three weeks?" Henry asks, poking his head out of the study. "What for?"

"Couple of work meetings." I shrug and it's a bit of a lie but what else can I say? December 3rd?

They'd never understand, not even Henry.

I skip over into his arms and he wraps them around me as he kisses the top of my head. He sniffs me. "Your hair smells weird."

"Oh." I frown. "It's the Philip B White Truffle shampoo—do you not like it?"

He gives me a look. "Why would you want your hair to smell like a mushroom?"

"It's very expensive." I frown at him.

He shakes his head. "That doesn't answer the question."

"I use Clairol Herbal Essences—" my sister announces.

I give her a look. "Don't brag about that, Bridget."

Henry grabs her by the waist and sniffs her hair. "Brag away, Bridge. You smell like a fucking meadow."

I link my arm with Taura's and glare over at them—my sister specifically.

"This is what you wear for my big homecoming, you terrible wench?"

She looks down at herself in her matching green tracksuit and then back up at me, frowning. "I have those stupid puffy Chloé slides on you bought me."

"I like it." Henry throws a defensive arm around my sister.

"I'm quite sure you would." I eye him in his Wild Thang tee from Golf Wang with the black logo-print track pants from Vetements. "Tell me, did you two make some sort of tracksuit-wearing pact to lower morale or has everything just fallen entirely to the wayside in my absence?"

My sister tries to kick me and I swear at her in Russian, dodging her dumb, gangly leg because I don't want my white dress to get dirty.

"Where is everyone, anyway?" I'm semi-miffed that my sister, my lifelong best friend and my new best friend are the only welcoming committee for my big London return.

I don't know who else I was expecting. Christian, maybe? I haven't spoken to Jonah since. Having Marsaili out here with some flowers and a banner would have been nice though, don't you think?

"In here." She nods at the dining-room door, then stops. "Dinner's on the table. You're almost an hour late—so typical of you."

I shrug, unperturbed. "Harley should have sent me the G700 then and not the Bombardier, and that's just a consequence he's going to have to bear."

Taura stands in front of Henry and he slips his hand under her Get Back printed cotton-jersey jumper from the Stella McCartney x The Beatles collaboration.

"And what consequence might that be?" She blinks. "The potato gratin gets a bit cold?"

I frown at her playfully. "What's a potato?"

Henry slings an arm around me. "It's where vodka comes from."

Bridget looks across all of us, blocking the path.

"So look, on the other side of this door is a lot of family drama . . ."

I roll my eyes. "Great."

"Bushka isn't talking to Marsaili—"

"—Why?" I interrupt.

"Because Marsaili won't let her be a bridesmaid," Taura tells me.

She spends a bit of time with Bridget, I'm told. That's nice. I'm glad they have each other here in my absence.

"Mum's new bottom's here—"

"Bridget!" I poke her in the ribs. "If you insist on creating an acronym out of Boyfriend Of The Month, I beg of you, please, don't say it phonetically."

Henry starts laughing.

"Dad hates the BOTM . . ."

Henry tilts his head. "Interesting."

"Keeps asking why he's here—"

"Seems fair," Taura considers.

"Then Mum is angry because Uncle Aleksey's hurt that he's not invited . . ."

22

"Your mum's brother is angry that he's not invited to her ex-husband's next wedding?"

Bridget shrugs, helpless. "I'm just here with the facts."

"Wow." I blink. "I really was the glue around here, wasn't I?"

"Yeah." My sister gives me a glib look. "That's what it is."

And then Henry pushes through the door.

My mum is first up.

Hands on both my shoulders, kiss-kisses each of my cheeks by bumping them with hers.

"Welcome home, darling."

"I'm not home." I smile at her politely.

My father stands, gives me a hug that's rigid and uncomfortable for us both.

"So glad you're home, darling."

"I'm not home," I say again with a curt smile.

Marsaili touches my face with her hands and smiles tenderly before hugging me.

("Welcome home, Magnolia," she whispers. "I'm not home," I whisper back. She gives me a look. "Yes, you are.")

I sit between Henry and Bushka, squeezing her arm hello.

"Where you been?" She gives me an annoyed look.

My face falters. "New York."

"Since when?" She frowns.

I glance around the room uncomfortably. "A year almost." I give her a little look. "You visited me last month? We drove to Bedford to visit Martha Stewart? She made you special Moscow Mules?"

Marsaili gives me a look. "Perhaps one too many?"

"To be fair," Taura shrugs, "she's got a heavy hand, that Martha. Loves a good pour."

"Who doesn't?" Mum nods appreciatively. "Oh, Magnolia, darling, Henry—this is Enzo." She gestures to her BOTM who's just been sitting there, smiling pleasantly.

Just chuffed to be here, old Enzo.

Sort of handsome, I suppose. If you like Euro-trash and bratwurst. I don't know exactly what I mean by that, but it is apt.

"Magnolia," he sings my name in a thick Italian accent. "Isa great pleasure to meet the famous tree girl—"

("What?" I whisper, blinking at my sister, who shakes her head, rubbing her ear. "He's not excellent at English.")

Enzo stands to hug me but I hold my hand out to stop him.

"Oh, no, no—" I shake my head as I instead pat his arm gingerly. "Thank you, Enzo. We don't need to hug. But I'm very happy to meet you—here. Now. On my very first night back in London, at an intimate dinner with my family and best friends." I give him a cordial smile.

He does a little bow.

Marsaili and I catch eyes.

"Enzo's number . . ." my dad starts, counting off on his fingers.

"Harley—" Mars growls.

"ВОСЕМЬ," Bushka says at the same time Bridget says, "Eight."

Mum drinks her wine with tall eyebrows and flaps her hand once to dismiss them all.

"So, have you heard from BJ, darling?"

"I have not," I tell her, my nose in the air. "Nor shall I."

Bridget rolls her eyes but I catch it.

"What?" I scowl. "I haven't. And I won't. And I hate him and, actually, our love is dead—"

"—Oh!" sighs Mum's BOTM remorsefully.

"No-no, Enzo—" I shake my head at him, flashing him a quick smile. "It's not a sad thing, it's an empowering thing."

"Is it?" Henry tilts his head and I elbow him quiet.

"I'm very empowered. It's like that part in that film, with the love fern? And it dies. And she's fine. Relieved, even—"

"Your plant die too?" he asks, a bit devastated.

Taura shakes her head. "Doesn't she go mental when the love fern dies in the film?"

I shoot her a look.

"Uh—no. No, everyone listen. I, metaphorically—" I try to clarify just for him—"dropped the—metaphorical—plant of our love into the desert and willingly abandoned it there.

24

So, to just elucidate—not sad—" I give Henry a stern look. "Very empowered."

I give Taura an exasperated look.

Bridget thinks for a few seconds. "Out of curiosity, what sort of plant was it? Your metaphorical love plant?"

I blow a raspberry and shrug off her stupid question before giving her a stupid answer. "I don't know—something super boring like an ugly shrub. Like a . . . like a Sprinter Boxwood. Super ugly."

"Oh." She squints over at me. "You mean an evergreen? The plants that never die?"

I look up at her, alarmed.

"What?" I shake my head. Hen glances at me, amused. "No! I mean—no, that's no—I understand the implications of that and no." Fuck. "I've changed my mind. It's an English rose. Very fragile, stupid flower. Can't survive shit."

"Oh." She nods sarcastically. "So the metaphorical plant of your love is only the most iconically beautiful flower . . . ever."

I blink at her.

"What the fuck, Bridget? Are you a fucking botanist in your spare time now?"

Taura starts laughing.

"And also no . . . Even though yes, but no." I give my sister a stern look. "Sure. Maybe it's very pretty on the outside but it has a lot of thorns. Very thorny. Also it's in the desert now. Where no one can see it. Or water it. No chance in the desert. It's done for out there, for sure. One-hundred per cent dead. And there's no such thing as rose ghosts, so that's great."

I drink my wine quickly and then Henry's too and keep my head down for the rest of dinner.

My room is how I left it.

Preserved perfectly and it feels like a hundred paper cuts all over my heart for a second—all the ways my room makes me think of him—and then I throw back some more wine and it washes those feelings away.

Or drowns them out.

Bridget lies down on my bed right where he used to.

"You okay?"

I blink a few times, probably a couple too many because probably I'm not, but I lie anyway because it's easy.

"Grand." I nod.

She nods back and I know she knows I'm lying.

And then she smirks. "Rose ghost . . ."

21:52

Henry

You feeling okay about seeing him?

Who?

. . .

. . .

Let's not do this

Agreed

Just answer my question

No, I am not feeling okay about seeing him

Is he feeling okay about seeing me?

Don't break the rules.

Sorry.

I'll see you tomorrow.

It'll be good.

FOUR

Magnolia

I helped plan a lot of the wedding from afar.

The colour palette, the flowers, the dresses—Marsaili has two sisters, both are bridesmaids as well—the older one who somehow managed to secure the title of maid of honour over me has the style of Christopher Walken and is about as visionary as a brick. The younger one—or 'the shit one', as Bridget and I have come to call her—is also useless.

Bridget is too. She tried to be helpful, but she suggested roses and ranunculus in the same bouquet so she was obviously an absolute and immediate dead end.

But all the planning was good for me. Kept me busy. Because as it turns out, I used to spend a lot of time with my friends in London, and in New York I didn't have that many people who were around all the time.

There was Rush whenever he was in town. And Lucía Nieves-Navarro, my whacky telecom-heiress neighbour from Mexico who shared my floor with me. Then there were others I met throughout the year, but New York is so transient.

I still travelled a lot for work—I was busy, I had things to do. I guess I just hadn't consciously realised how much of my time I had filled with BJ and Paili.

She's living in Spain now, I heard. I'm pretty sure the Spanish Flu is fairly under wraps now, but if it's not, I do hope she catches it.

Anyway.

28

The wedding's at St George's. Obviously. Like there's anywhere else to get married in London besides St Paul's Cathedral, but that's where I want to get married so I made sure to steer Marsaili away from that venue.

We arrive in Hanover Square twenty-five minutes after the wedding was supposed to have started but that was barely my doing and was primarily on account of London's hideous traffic and also just a little bit because Bridget decided to 'do her own make-up'. If you've ever seen her try to do her own make-up, you'd understand why we're late and you too would have wrestled that dark fuchsia, high pigment travesty from her colour-blind little hands.

Marsaili's dress is gorgeous.

From Pronovias's SS2022 The New Oasis Collection—the Kufra dress.

Asymmetrical neckline with one long sleeve, one sleeveless, a form-fitting mermaid cut with some light beading and a subtle but rather lovely train.

The maid of honour is in a dusty-blue ruffle-shoulder embellished gown from Marchesa that on my mother would look like an Oscars gown but on this lady it's just sort of a mess. Like she's going to the Yule Ball at Hogwarts.

The Shit One's in a simple silk cape gown from Valentino that's very classy, sort of a subtle . . . I don't want to say lilac because lilacs are stupid, but not *not* lilac.

I wrangled Bridge into this gorgeous baby-blue Tony Ward gown with a flowy tulle skirt and these gorgeous puff sleeves and coerced her into the Anilla 100 crystal pumps from Jimmy Choo and, to be honest, she looks a bit like Cinderella and I'm nearly jealous but I can tell she feels beautiful so my jealousy simmers at a healthy 30 per cent.

And me? A dress from the Elie Saab Spring 2011 Couture runway that I asked him to recreate for me. Nice, pastel, bright purple. Sheer, lace paneling, figure hugging, subtly belted with draped silk crystal organza that I've paired perfectly with the Carrie Crystal Bow Mule 75 from Aquazzura.

We're all holding hydrangeas, lavender and white rose bouquets and the colour theme for the wedding is to die for, if I do say so myself.

I'm nervous, standing out there, waiting to walk in.

Bridget first, then me.

I know I'm going to see him. I know he's going to be here. It was a big thing—a big discussion in our family. Everyone flew over to talk to me about it.

Took me out to Nobu to butter me up. Bridget thought it was deeply inappropriate that he be invited. My father and my mother both said he had to be invited because they were inviting the rest of the Ballentines, and then my father said my mother needed to bugger off and what was she doing here anyway? And then Bushka said he has a great arse and to pass the rock shrimp tempura. Marsaili said it would be rude not to and that if I'm as over him as I tell everyone I am, I should be fine with him being there, but that if I insisted he not come, she'd insist it too.

So they invited him because I couldn't tell them that actually he is the drain in the centre of me where all the happy things fall through and that I feel his absence in everything. Everything. Breakfast time, cups of tea. Bumblebees. Honey. The stars. Gucci. The Discovery Channel. Long drives. Driving in general. Willow trees. Uno. Old Skool Vans. Tiffany's. Maserati's. Boys with tattoos.

And now here I am, standing on the steps of St George's with a thudding heart in my throat and eyes that don't know where to look because I'm afraid they'll find the thing they're dying to see.

Henry and Taura appear at the top of the stairs and then he jogs down them, throwing his arms around me.

"How good is it having you here in London?" He picks me up off the ground, jostling me around.

I give him a wry look and straighten his bow tie. Blue and cute from Tom Ford. I know, I picked it out. Giorgio Armani classic tuxedo suit, little blue crescent moon and star cufflinks with Elkan Penny Loafers also from Tom Ford.

"Well, you mustn't get used to it," I tell him as Taura curls her arms around my neck.

Sky Rocket Maxi Dress (The Vampire's Wife) in oxblood. Very classy.

If she wasn't (apparently) my best friend and if she wasn't sleeping with my actual (other) best friend, I'd be insecure about her.

She looks me up and down. "Are you trying to kill him?"

I put my nose in the air. "I don't know what you mean."

She ignores me. "Nervous?"

I look over at her, my eyes flick from her to Henry, and I nod.

She slips me a little bottle of vodka.

"Drink this one now, and this one," she slips it into my bouquet, "after."

She gives me a little wink as she backs up the stairs. "We're on your dad's side. Middle-front-ish. Towards the left."

"I don't care—" I lie.

"He didn't bring her," Henry calls as he walks backwards up the stairs.

I pause. "I still don't care."

He raises an eyebrow and points at me. "Bullshit."

Then they dart back inside.

"Well, that's interesting," Bridget says, sidling up next to me.

"No, it's not," I tell her quickly.

She glances at me, annoyed and intrigued.

"No girlfriend?" she repeats.

I ignore her.

("Very interesting," she says under her breath, but she's a mouth breather so it's very loud.)

The music swells. 'Ave verum corpus'.

Bridget starts walking down the aisle.

Then me.

And my eyes are frontward. They do not veer left, they do not veer right. And still, I can feel his eyes on me—he's to the right of the church, not just because the right side is traditionally the groom's side, but because I just know it.

That pull we have, the undertow of the universe always dragging us back towards each other, it has to mean something, don't you think? That great magnetic force I've spent the better (or worst) part of a year fighting and defying and I feel it still, my legs trying to walk me back into his orbit—I think it means something.

Or maybe it doesn't and I just want it to because that would give all our pain a purpose.

I don't listen to much of the wedding sermon.

They're all sort of the same, don't you think?

Love is patient, love is kind. It does not envy, it does not boast, it's not proud. It doesn't dishonour others, it's not self-seeking, it's not easily angered, it keeps no record of wrongs. Love does not delight in evil but rejoices in the truth. It always protects, always trusts, always hopes, always perseveres. Love never fails.

But it's shit. It's all a lie.

We weren't any of those things but don't you for a second try to tell me we weren't in love. I loved him more than anything and at the end of everything, it's all we had and it did not persevere. It failed.

The reception's at the Royal Hospital Chelsea—beautiful, of course.

I make the rounds—put in some face time with my godfather, as well as Bridget's. (Graham Norton. I know, I'm jealous of that too.) Lots of people flew in from America. Chris Martin, the Timberlakes, Usher. The whole thing's shamefully star-studded, but Marsaili and my father look pleased, so that's good, I suppose. If we insist on looking on the brighter side, I suppose it's good they're happy . . . They're just gross old people in love now. They don't like it when I tell them that though. "Save something for the speech, darling." My father gave his new bride a look.

"Oh, I'm not giving a speech," I say. "The Shit One is."

"Would you stop calling her that?" Marsaili huffs. "That's my sister."

My father gives her a look. "She is a little bit shit though . . ."

"Harley!" Marsaili growls.

"Question—" I interrupt, giving them both a look. "Arrie Parks is here . . ."

I stare over at my mother who is dressed in the brightest outfit at the whole reception: two-tone pink floor-length dress by Carolina Herrera. Marsaili gives me an impatient look. "That's not a question, Magnolia."

"Bit of a sticky wicket, her being here, no?" I glance between them.

"No," Marsaili says at the same time my dad says, "Absolutely."

We all stare over at her arse being squeezed by Enzo like it's a fucking lemon in the back corner of a reception there's no doubt in anyone's mind that he shouldn't be at.

Marsaili waves her hand through the air. "It would've been rude not to—"

"Would it?" my father and I say at the same time and I don't care for the synchronisation.

And then there's a tap on my shoulder.

I'm nervous to turn around but I do it anyway because I'm brave like that, but I should have known from the tap it wasn't him.

I'd feel it if it was.

It is someone else I love though.

"Well," Gus Waterhouse grins. "If it isn't my favourite heartbreaker . . ."

I frown at him playfully. "Mean."

He gives me a look. "True."

I roll my eyes at him.

"You holding up okay?" he asks tentatively.

"It's not my best day." I shrug breezily. "It's not my worst either though—"

Gus nods. "Seen him?"

"No."

He tilts his head. "Intentionally?"

33

I give him a look because he's annoying like this. "Yes."

He gives me a small smile, pleased his assessment was correct. I take the drink from his hand and sip at it. "How's Tom?"

"Good." He nods. "Yeah, good. Better."

This makes me happy. He deserves to be good. "I'm glad."

"He loves Hawaii."

"He would." I smile as I think of him. "All those mountains to climb, the surf—"

"—The girls." Gus gives me a pointed look. I think he's trying to make a point, to make sure I know that Tom is fine without me.

I never thought he wouldn't be. Tom is Tom England. The most wonderful, whole, beautiful man to ever grace the planet. He never needed me and I was never under the impression that he was lucky to have me; I always knew it was the other way around. What happened after he left proves that I was right. My eyes pinch at Gus because I think it's rude he's hitting me with a softball at my own father's stupid wedding.

"You haven't visited me in a while," I tell him and he tilts his head and cocks his eyebrow. "Hawaii calling?" I guess.

Gus breathes out through his nose. "He is my best friend . . ."

"And what am I?" I frown, offended. "Chopped liver?"

"Nah—" He shrugs coolly. "Just the girl who broke his heart." He flicks his eyebrows up. "And fucked his heterosexual best mate."

Ouch.

I deserve it, I guess.

I did and it's true.

Clara helped (with the breaking, not the fucking), but it was a lot of me in the end, I think. Me and BJ. Me and Rush.

"I should get back to my date," he tells me, nodding his head over towards someone I recognise who gives me a small, overwhelmed wave.

"Jack Giles?" I blink. He's so gorgeous—chocolatey eyes that are always smouldering like he's wearing eyeliner even if he isn't, sexy pushed-back brown hair and a sensational jawline

—he makes me wish I were a gay man. Or he were a straight one. "I didn't know . . ." I shake my head. "When?"

"It's recent." He nods, blushing a little. "Let's get a drink before you fly back out. I'll catch you up—"

He kisses my cheek.

After that, the speeches are spoken and there's a father-daughter dance that I dodge by hurling my sister into my father's arms and making Henry dance with me instead. I stick close to my Safe Three because everyone in the world wants to talk to me about New York and Rush and why I disappeared in the dead of night the way I did.

Like they don't all already know. Everyone knows.

It was everywhere. The whole of the Rosebery heard it. There's videos of it on the internet. Do you have any idea what it feels like to have everyone see your maybe worst moment, where your heart broke on your face in front of the entire world for all to see, only to have them then use it for small talk at parties when the conversation lulls?

I make my way to the bar.

"Can I have a Martini, please?" I ask the bartender. "Vodka."

And then I feel a body saddle up next to me.

Feel it.

Even though he's not touching me at all, I feel it in my bones. A curious, deep ache and a mild episode of SVT.

He leans against the bar.

"How's the weather, Parks?" he asks and I don't turn to face him.

I can't. My heart's going too fast, it's run up into my throat. I try my best to steady my breathing.

I take a long sip, don't look away from my glass. "Do you remember Geostorm?" I reply coolly.

He sniffs but I think it's a laugh.

"Yeah, you walked out of it."

I still don't look at him. "Well, it was terrible."

"You're avoiding me," he tells me, looking for my eyes.

"Yes," I say. And now I look at him.

35

Oh my God. He's beautiful.

It hits me in my chest, spreads through me like a spider web. He looks different but the same all at once. Older, I think. But healthier, maybe?

Some new freckles.

More scruff on his face than when I last saw it. Just a tiny bit.

My favourite forget-me-not bow still on his thumb.

I fight the old urge to push my hand through his perfect hair—an urge I thought I shook but I guess you can't ever really, not with a boy like him.

And his stupid pillow mouth rips at the seams of my resolve not to love him how I worry I always will, and my mind falls through an infinity of memories I've had with him and thought I'd have with him and worry I won't ever have with him again.

I swallow. Count to three, breathing through my nose.

I won't let him know he does this to me still. I'd sooner die.

"I am." I look up at him and nod slowly. "Thank you so much for respecting my wishes and not approaching me—"

He smirks and goes "hah" and I miss him.

"Come on," he chides with a half-cocked smile. "Had to say hello. Rude not to . . ."

I take a sizeable sip of my drink. "I suppose."

Peak-Lapel wool suit and the Pre-Tied Silk-Satin Bow Tie, both from Tom Ford. White Formal Button Up Shirt from Dolce & Gabbana with the Jordaan Horsebit Gucci loafers. I love him in a suit.

BJ licks his bottom lip and tilts his head to look at me. "Oi, are you in lilac?"

Fuck. I purse my lips for a second and then roll my eyes.

"I didn't pick the colour palette." I shrug demurely.

"Yeah right," he scoffs. "You're gonna tell me Marsaili picked out this monochromatic masterpiece on her own?"

I get the feeling he's trying to flatter me but I roll my eyes anyway because I don't want to make anything easy for him.

He nods at me playfully. "What'd you call the Pinterest board?"

"Nothing," I tell him, my nose in the air.

"Tell me—" he presses.

"No." I cross my arms over my chest.

"Violet Supernova?" he guesses.

I squint at him, equal parts amused and annoyed.

"Amaranthine twilight," I concede.

His face cracks wide into a smile.

I frown, not feeling like being teased by anyone today, least of all him. "I look good in lilac."

His face softens a little. "Yes, you do."

Our eyes hold.

"I know," I tell him, my nose in the air.

He goes "hah" again and the years whistle around our ankles like leaves in the wind and we're lovers in autumn under a tree raining orange and regret, and in that moment we're still each other's and time wraps around us in the infinity we thought we had but we don't anymore because he broke us.

He smiles a little, watching me closely. "You good?"

"Yes." I give him a glib smile. "I'm simply thrilled to be here celebrating a love birthed in the canal of infidelity."

He laughs and for some reason it sounds like I'm ringing the doorbell of the home I grew up in.

"Here for long?" Not letting go of my eyes.

"Just a few weeks."

"You staying till—"

"—Yes," I cut in.

He nods, I nod. I feel dizzy. I grab my drink, take a few big sips to steady my jitters.

"So," I take another drink, "I hear you've got a girlfriend."

His face pulls funny. Strained. Uncomfortable? Remorseful? Disappointed? Frustrated? Maybe none of the above—maybe he's just sorry for me.

He nods once. "I do."

Have we lost touch? I wonder. The thought makes me feel panicky. Has a year apart changed our channels? I don't think I can hear his thoughts anymore.

"She's not here." I glance around.

37

He shakes his head. "Felt like that might be inappropriate—"

"—And yet, here you are." I give him a curt smile as though I'm not hanging on to every word he's saying.

"I was invited." His eyebrows flicker in defence and he shrugs a little. "Mum made me," he lies.

And I can tell he's lying—his mouth falls at a particular angle when he's lying. I don't even care that he is, I'm just glad I can still tell. Glad to have not lost him completely.

"Besides," he shrugs again, "I didn't want Mars charging down the aisle and tackling her. The society papers have been surprisingly drama-free in your absence," he tells me with a look.

I roll my eyes.

"Are you seeing anyone?" he asks and I wish I could say yes. I wish I had a boy I could wear like a hard hat for my heart, but I don't.

"I was," I say because it's fractionally less pathetic than a plain old no.

"What happened?"

I give him a cool look. "None of your business."

He nods once. "Do I know him?" he asks after a few seconds of silence.

I think about it for a second—everyone knows Rush, but that's not who I've been dating. Not for a while, anyway. If you were going to call what we were doing 'dating'—which I wouldn't, though my grandmother might. Rush and I, we've let them think that we're together because people always talk and sometimes it's easier to have them talk about the wrong thing. It gave me a minute to work out if the other thing was the right thing, but it wasn't. He wasn't. I don't think anyone else will ever be. It doesn't matter anyway. I shrug with both my shoulders and my mouth.

"I'm not sure—I don't know. No, probably."

He nods again, relieved a bit, maybe, and my eyes snag just below his right thumb.

I nod my chin towards it, which makes me feel strange because once upon a lifetime ago I would have reached over to touch him just so I could touch him. "Is that a tattoo of two dead bees?"

He looks sprung and covers it with his over hand, flashing me an apologetic smile and my shields slide on up.

"Yeah." He shrugs like it's silly and not callous.

I nod once. "Right."

He peers down at it, mouth pulling a bit strangely. "Someone told me once that they'd never go extinct—" He looks over at me. "She lied."

I give him a curt smile. "She wasn't the one who killed them."

His eyes fall and he swallows, breathing out of his nose.

"Anyway," I sing brightly as I spin my Jennifer Meyer flower diamond ring around my finger, "I should get back to bridesmaid duties." I tell him this quickly—I don't know why—maybe because even though he's figuratively killed the metaphor of us and displayed it permanently on his body, I still don't think I could bear the thought of him leaving me first.

He presses his lips together as he nods. "Yeah."

I take a step away from him.

"Bye—" I do a weirdly passive non-wave but almost wave.

His mouth twitches, amused at it. "Bye."

I turn away.

"Hey, Parks—" he calls after me and I look back. "Can we meet up before you go back? Have a chat?"

My heart starts racing.

"Yeah." I nod very, very casually. "I guess . . . We can do that."

"Okay." He smiles a little. "I'll call you."

"You don't have my number anymore," I tell him just because I want to, I don't know why.

"I'll get it from Hen," he says, not letting go of my gaze.

I nod again and walk away, ignoring all the eyes on me and him—I haven't missed this, the fishbowl effect—but I don't care because it's BJ and something about him will always be worth it.

39

I slip into the toilet, lock the door and lean against it as a terrible revelation dawns on me. It's like the morning sun when you forget to close the curtain—it's my fault, I should have closed the curtain, I knew the sun was there, I knew the sun would eventually rise again, but I didn't close the curtain and now this invasive, bright, shimmering light wakens me from the slumber I was using to avoid it.

I still love him.

FIVE

BJ

"How was the wedding?" Jordan asks the next day.

We're getting breakfast at a café by her house in Fulham. She likes it here. I don't.

The coffee's always shit and the eggs are overcooked, but it's across the road from her so she calls it her local.

Bit of a sad local.

Sadder for me than for her, because she drinks coffee with milk in it but I drink it black. Milk covers a lot of sins when it comes to burnt coffee.

I stir in some sugar because the brew is particularly shit this morning.

"Yeah, fine—" I shrug.

It's a necessary level of downplaying how the wedding actually was.

Fucked. That is how the wedding was. For me anyway.

God, she's beautiful—that's all I keep thinking. Parks, not my girlfriend, unfortunately. And in the lilac? Fucking shit of her. Did that on purpose she did, I know it. Know her. That's the kind of shit she'd do to pull the rug out from under me.

I'm fine finally, I'm doing good, she comes back and wears fucking lilac, the twat.

"Did you see her?" Jordan asks, watching me closely.

Makes me feel more shit.

I look up at her, try to smile in a way that will make her feel good.

"Yeah." I shrug again. "Just for a sec—"

She asks, chin in hand. "Did you talk?"

"Yep—" I take a gulp of bad coffee then nod. "A bit. Nothing major."

That's a lie and I know it because that bit of conversation with Parks was the most exhilarating thing I've done in the last ten months and it was about the literal colour purple.

Jordan grinds her jaw absentmindedly.

"She's leaving," I remind her—pretend the thought doesn't feel like a tackle.

"Right." She swats her hand. "And it's not like you're going to see her again . . ."

I squint uncomfortably. "Actually, we'll probably see her around a bit for the next couple of weeks. Like . . . at Christian's thing in a few days."

She sighs. "Great."

I scratch the back of my neck. "We have all the same friends—"

Jordan shakes her head. "Yeah but she left—"

"Yeah, because I fucked her best friend."

She shifts, uncomfortable.

Don't know whether it's because I'm a cheater or because I'm defending my ex-girlfriend.

Both options are shit.

"Also," I say and then grimace a bit. She gives me a dark look. Swallows. "I'm going to meet up with her."

"What?" She blinks. "Why?"

Nice eyes. Crazy blue.

I shrug. "Because I need to."

"But why?"

"Jordan—" I shake my head. "Me and Parks, we've been friends since I was six. And we were together for—how many years?" I shrug. "And I've hurt her more than anyone. I need to talk to her."

She folds her arms over her chest. "What about?"

"We just need to sort out our shit."

"You have shit?" She blinks, put off. "What shit?"

42

I look over at her, annoyed. More annoyed than I mean to be. "Of course we have shit."

She breathes out of her nose, stares at her plate. Fruit salad. Parks would never order that. Too many things touching each other.

She sighs after a few seconds. "Do you have to?"

I nod. "Yeah, I do."

Her eyes pinch. "I thought she was leaving?"

"First week of December."

That's another eyeball from her. Warranted, I guess. "You know her flight details now?"

Yes.

I pull a face.

I do, but not for a reason I could explain to her.

And you know what—I do feel for her. Jordan, I mean. She's on the back foot here. All girls are on the back foot when it comes to me and Parks.

"Why would she come to Christian's? I thought she hasn't spoken to Jonah in a year?"

"She hasn't." I rub my temples without realising. "But Christian and her are close."

I steel for the grimace my face naturally wants to pull, even though I know it's different now and I don't have a fucking leg to stand on.

Their closeness, in context, is still a kick in the dick.

"Visits her with Henry sometimes," I shrug.

I deleted Instagram whenever they went. Safer that way.

"Yeah, but he's your best friend." She sounds annoyed for me, which is sweet of her, I guess.

"Yeah—" I sigh, shoving my hands through my hair. "But he was hers first." I give her a quick smile. Don't know why I'm defending her—habit, I guess. "Her and the boys were in the same class since nursery."

"Oh." She nods but she doesn't get it. Not her fault. Jordan didn't watch us grow up like the rest of London did, all in each other's pockets and shit.

Parks and her family have been in the papers since she was tiny. Comes with the territory with what her parents do, I guess. For me and the boys it didn't start till later, but it did start. And it's always had its pitfalls. There's a lot of shit to be said about being watched in some way or another all the time, but one of the redeeming parts (usually) is that I don't have to explain very much. People just know.

But Jordan's not from here. She grew up on a horse ranch in the outback. From money too, but not from money like us. And it's different there, with the society pages and shit. So she says, anyway. People might know who you are there, but it's un-Australian to give a fuck about it, so no one cares.

Jordan hasn't seen me and Parks together, doesn't get the connection we have . . . Wish I could say that in the past tense, but the wedding showed me that I can't.

So this, here and now, Jordan all weird that Parks is close with my friends, weird that me and Parks still have shit between us—it's just a fracture of understanding, that's all.

Jordan did go to boarding school though, so probably could have propagated her own experience if she gave it a whack, but I guess I get why she doesn't want to. Being the girl I'm with who isn't Magnolia Parks has to be a bitter pill.

Jordan swallows, looking nervous again. "Is she nice?"

Feels like a trap. Scratch my neck again.

"Depends," I sniff.

Her face flickers. "On what?"

I bang my fist absentmindedly on the table. "I wouldn't be banking on you two being best friends, Jords."

"I don't want to be her friend," she says with a scowl. "She hurt you."

I nod, throw her a small grateful smile. "I hurt her first," I remind her.

She shrugs. "Yeah, well, she and I aren't sleeping together so that's harder to give a shit about."

SIX

BJ

Jonah is shitting himself about seeing Parks.

Shitting himself.

Texted me all morning.

She took him knowing hard. Hasn't spoken to him since. He tried. Called her, wrote her, even flew out once.

She wouldn't see him.

She's a difficult person to be on thin ice with.

There's something about Magnolia—it's as annoying as it is fascinating—even when you fucking hate her, even when she's being the biggest twat in the world, you want to be in her good books.

Like there's something holy about being in her light or some shit.

Me and Jo, we've been cast in the shadows since last December and he's fretting about her being at lunch.

Christian's bar launch today—Verona. Italian summer all year round, that's how it's supposed to feel. Box Set, minus the two that none of us speak to anymore, plus Taura and Jordan—so are we even the Box Set still?

Jordan takes forever to get ready this morning and I know it's because Parks will be there.

She wears some black and white collared dress she got from Balmain that I know she loves.

Feel sad she's wearing it. Don't know why.

Her dressing to impress some girl she's never met because of me. It's fucked, but I do it too. Wear a denim jacket from Balmain that I reckon Parks would fancy me in.

I hold Jordan's hand as we arrive. Fingers interlocked. Real couple shit.

The boys look up.

"Ey." Jonah smiles, kisses Jordan on the check, smacks me on the arm, hugs me as he whispers, "she's not here yet."

Don't know if he's whispering it for me or for him.

I roll my eyes at him, then look from him to Henry.

"Where's Taurs?"

Never know who to ask. Pretty high-stress situation these days—both Henry and Jo act like it's not, but it is. They're both sleeping with her. They both like (more than like, in my opinion) her. And she likes both of them. It's a fucking mess.

Most of that mess is under the surface, lurking. Pops out when one of them gets shitfaced or she overtly favours one over the other in public, but she tries her best not to.

"She's coming with Parks," Henry tells me.

"Did you say Parks is here?" Jonah whips his head around, looking for her like a fucking maniac.

"Calm down, man." I give him a look.

He rolls his eyes, continues freaking the fuck out.

I frown at him. "What's the matter with you?"

Don't know why I say that—I know what's the matter with him.

I've been there.

It's the worst feeling. When she's not talking to you, it's like living in the shade.

He's been living out of the sunlight for a year.

But join the fucking club, mate.

"Don't pander to it," I tell him and also a bit to myself.

"Beej, man—" Jo shakes his head at me.

"It's been a year!" I tell him.

"Yeah." He shrugs. "And she's still not speaking to me for it." I roll my eyes.

"And okay," he shrugs again, "in the scheme of it, gun to my head, you're my boy, I'd do it again, but . . . there wasn't a gun to my head and I still did it so she hates me for it."

I frown at him. Feel sad for him though. Feel a bit responsible. He shrugs like he can't help it. "She's been one of my best friends since I was what—fifteen?" Looks sorry at me, like he's being a bad friend to me by wanting to make things right with her. He swats his hand through the air. "Plus, you know what she's like when she's pissed . . ."

I roll my eyes. "I am familiar, yeah."

He gives me a steep look. "Fucking scary."

"You're a gang lord," I remind him.

Jonah shrugs but not exactly indifferent. "Not my favourite term, but sure."

"A gang lord," I repeat. "Just want you to think about that for a minute."

He nods.

"And I want *you* to think about how grateful you are that I'm the gang lord and not her." He drops his chin, lifts his eyebrows. "Imagine London if it was Magnolia ruling with an iron fist."

I sniff, amused. "And what kind of fist do you rule with?"

Christian walks up behind us. "Compared to her?" He clocks his brother. "Aluminium, at best."

I hug Christian. "Good turnout, man—"

"Yeah." He grins, pleased.

He's here with Vanna.

She leans over, kisses me on the cheek, ignores my girlfriend.

"Vans, you remember Jordan." I give her a bit of a look. "My girl friend."

Jordan smiles at her.

"Of course." Vanna smiles back with only her mouth. "Love the dress."

And then there's a ripple through the bar like how wind hits grass on a field and it scatters over it, fanning out.

I know she's here before I know she's here because I can feel that every eye is on me. I look over towards her because I feel like it'd be weirder not to.

She's in this mini red and white tartan top with a little black bow tie, a black coat, a green bow in her hair and these black

47

boots that make her legs look stupid long. She's so fucking hot I want to neck myself.

It's so Magnolia, everything about it. If I let myself be caught off guard here I reckon I could choke up.

Parks skips over to Christian, jumps into his arms, and wraps herself around him like a fucking koala bear.

He's not into her anymore—he's with Vanna—but still I look away.

Jordan's sort of frozen up. She's watching Parks how you watch Olympic gymnastics—a bit of awe and this underlying fear something's about to be broken. I squeeze her hand. She looks over at me, flashes a grateful smile.

Parks kisses my brother on the cheek and then her eyes fall to me. They flick from me to Jordan.

Her eyes stay on Jordan a beat too long for it to be comfortable. Reading her, watching her, taking her in. Honestly, I don't know what to expect.

I've met Magnolia's new boyfriends billions of times, but I've never had a girlfriend before. New territory for us all.

Fuck. This could go sideways.

Magnolia extends her hand to Jordan and—boom—megawatt smile.

"You must be Jordan." She tilts her head, smiling. Like she means it too. "It's so wonderful to meet you."

Jordan's jaw gapes. So does mine.

"You . . . too." Jordan frowns a tiny bit, confused. She catches herself, corrects her face, forces a smile. "W-welcome home," Jordan stutters.

Magnolia shakes her head at Jordan like she's being silly.

"I'm not home, really. Just for a minute—" Then she gives her another warm smile. "But thank you."

She turns to me.

"She's beautiful, Beej—well done." She leans in. Bumps my cheek with hers. And that's when I feel it on her—the lie. It's a lie. She hates those kinds of kisses. They're fake. Her mum does them. Drives her mad.

48

Magnolia pulls away from me, her eyes locked on mine. "She's a keeper."

Don't know why that feels like a slap, but it does.

And then she moves away from me and plants herself between Taura and Jonah—which happens to be directly across from me—she's not looking at me though, she's looking at Jonah.

He gives her a big, nervous smile.

"If it isn't the worst friend I've ever known." She gives him a curt smile.

". . . Wouldn't that be Paili?" Taura asks, poking her head in, and Magnolia snaps her head in her direction, scowling.

"Sorry, sorry—" Taura shakes her head and looks at me, pulling a face.

Parks looks back at Jonah, eyes flicking up and down him. "And you're not wearing all black—" She eyes his white trousers. "What's happened?"

"You always wanted me to diversify my wardrobe." He gives her a hopeful smile and she meets it with pinched eyes.

"I'm sorry," Jo says. He means it.

Magnolia folds her arms over her chest. "I should think so."

He lets out a tired laugh, bit of relief mixed in there too.

"What can I do, Parks?" He tilts his head at her. "To make it up to y—"

"—o Torino?" says Jordan and I suddenly realise she's talking to me and I haven't heard a fucking thing.

Shit.

I shake my head, clear it. "Sorry, Jords, what?"

She frowns. "What's in a Milano Torino? Have you had one?"

"Um—" I try to think. Focus on my girlfriend, not on what Parks is saying to Jonah. "I don't know. I've had one, yeah—"

Her shoulders slump a little, annoyed. "Do you think I'd like it?"

I frown. What's the matter with me. "Um—"

"It's Campari and sweet vermouth," Magnolia tells her with a glance. "Bittersweet. I personally think it's yuck."

"Oh."

Jordan nods. "Thanks."

Magnolia turns back to Jonah and they keep talking, and I lean in towards Jordan. Force myself to focus.

The waitress asks for my order.

Negroni.

Parks catches my eye, amused. Maybe relieved that something hasn't changed.

"And you, Miss?" the waitress asks Jordan.

"A Milano Torino."

Magnolia's eyes flick back over to mine and they catch.

I lick away an amused smile.

Jordan sees, glares at me a bit.

And then a shadow casts over our table.

I look up.

Julian Haites.

I grin up at him to say hello but he doesn't even register that I'm there. His eyes are locked on Parks.

"Oh shit—" he says, watching her as she looks over at him. "Here's trouble . . ."

Her mouth drops into a delighted smile.

He gives her a small scowl. "Come on—get up and give me a squeeze."

She bounces up into his arms and I know at least a bit of it's for show. Trying to deflect my arm around my girlfriend by spring-boarding herself into the arms of another man in a fucking leather letterman jacket.

Vintage Parks.

Julian's touching her how he's always tried to. She's always liked his attention, even when we were together.

Can't blame her for that, I suppose—he's just that kind of person. Never bothered me before because I knew it meant nothing and she'd never. She'd still never now, I know that. He's a fucking gang lord, but still . . .

Watching him here, I want to punch a fucking wall because his hands fall down her in a way that would have made her skittish before but now she's just letting him feel his way down her body all playful and shit and I wonder how many ways New York's changed Parks and if all of them are going to make me feel like dying.

He plants her back on the floor, grins down at her.

"How's New York?"

She takes a breath and smiles up at him. "It has its perks." Bats her eyes.

Why does my stomach feel like a sinking ship?

"Like what?" He cocks his eyebrow—looks past her to Ed Bancroft and the girl he's with, sitting next to Taura.

He cocks his chin at them, wordlessly telling them to move.

They do. Quickly. That impresses her. I can see it roll over her face.

She likes feeling powerful. He's powerful.

Julian sits down. Pulls Parks down next to him.

I look away, feel a bit naff.

"Like New York paparazzi don't give a shit about me—" she starts.

I can't look at her, I'm looking at Jordan, who is looking at me looking at them.

I feel lightheaded.

Fuck.

I lean in to kiss her.

She kisses me back more than she needs to, but I'm grateful for the distraction.

"—horse-drawn carriages," is where I tune back in. "—My completely ridiculous neighbour, Lucía. Fifth Avenue. Central Park at midnight—"

"Central Park at midnight?" Julian frowns and my brows go low. "You got a death wish?"

Parks laughs it off like it's nothing, but I'm angry at her for it. Why would she—I shake my head.

How annoyed I am snaps me back to focusing on Jordan, who's being socially carried by Jonah at this point.

"How is it?" I nod at her drink.

51

She scrunches her face a bit. "Pretty gross."

I try my best not to laugh, nearly do anyway, so I just kiss her again.

Happy to kiss her again.

Not just because she's my girlfriend and we're together, but because it's a good reminder to myself of what I should be focusing on.

Parks isn't staying. She's just prattled on about all the things she loves about fucking New York. She's done with London. Done with me.

And that's all good, because I'm with Jordan now.

I hold her hand, squeeze it.

I lean over the table to get Parks's attention. She pretends she doesn't notice straightaway, but her eyes give her up.

I smile at her, squinting. "Heard a lifelong dream of yours actualised while you were over there—"

She beams. "Vagina steams with Gwyneth?"

Jordan's jaw drops. "Gwyneth Paltrow?"

Magnolia can hardly keep it together, she's so smug about it.

I snort a laugh. "Everything you hoped for?"

She nods once. "And more."

"Did you say 'vagina steams'? With Gwyneth Paltrow?" Julian butts back in.

"Who else would you do that with?"

"Who else would I do it with?" He emphasises the I in that sentence, then cocks his head towards my ex-girlfriend.

I'm going to be sick watching how Parks eats that up. Her cheeks go pink. Fuck. Maybe she's keen on him?

"What do you talk about when you're getting your vagina steamed?" Julian asks curiously.

Fair question, if I'm honest.

"I mean, what don't you talk about?" she counters. "It's all already on the table—"

"Are you on a table?" Jordan asks.

Parks sniffs a laugh and catches my eye. "I'm sorry to say you didn't fare particularly well during the vagina monologues."

Jordan lets out a small laugh and I shrug, guilty. "Can't imagine I would have."

Jordan shakes her head, staring at Parks, now a little starstruck. "How do you know Gwyneth Paltrow?"

"We're new-ish friends." Magnolia shrugs demurely, as though it's not been one of her main manifestations since she was eleven.

"My father's worked with Chris a lot over the years, so I've always known her—but I think she took pity on me because I was a bit of a lost soul over there."

"You're welcome." I give her a courteous nod that's mostly met with an amused glare.

"Right." She gives me a glib look. "Thank you for that."

I poke my tongue out at her.

She pokes hers back.

Jordan stares at me, and I can't read her face. It's not sad, but it is something.

"Who's her dad?" she whispers.

"Every good song in the last twenty years that smashed? He wrote about half of them."

"Oh." She frowns like that was an annoying thing to hear. I guess it might be, so I throw my arm around her again and she leans in, kissing me. At the tail end of the kiss she lingers and I can tell she's going to try to have sex later. Hope I don't think of Parks.

"Heard you picked up golf in my absence?" Magnolia says, holding my gaze.

I nod. "Yeah, without you holding me back I've thrived—"

"Held you back?" Jordan asks, frowning between us.

I tip my head in Magnolia's direction. "Didn't have a lot of patience for it."

"It's such a long game for so little payoff." Magnolia rolls her eyes. "Two million pounds in the pot is hardly chump change."

"Oh—" Magnolia nods sarcastically. "Playing the PGA now, are we? God, you must be good."

I look over at her more tenderly than I should, feel an old kind of missing her in my chest that I wish would just die but it can't seem to take its last breath. Every time it takes one it takes another and another, and it's never a last breath. Loving her like this is a kind of breathing that feels like dying.

"You could probably be better if you wanted to be," I tell her. I shouldn't have because that was a deep cut. Parks's eyes go round. She looks just like the four-year-old she was the day we met twenty years ago and I feel it in my chest—old flames that never died anyway, the kind that have never needed stoking a day in their life. The over-the-shoulder restraints lower down over me and I'm locked in.

I'm on the ride whether I want to be or not.

"So, when're you heading back?" Julian asks, nodding at Parks.

Shits me how much he's focusing on her, but he's a shit talker so I know it means nothing.

Parks glances over at me, our eyes catch for less than a second.

"I fly out December 5th."

"Maybe I'll come visit you," he tells her.

I throw back the rest of my negroni. Do my best not to watch them.

Parks smiles up at him with playful eyes.

"You should," she tells him. She doesn't mean it though.

"I think you could show me a pretty good time," he tells her, smirking.

Magnolia throws back her Martini in one gulp. "Oh—I don't think you could keep up."

Julian lets out one obnoxious laugh, and I'm done now.

The wheel of the ship's spinning out of control and why the fuck is it that when Magnolia Parks is in my life I am all riddles and nautical metaphors?

I lean into Jordan, cock my head towards the door and whisper, "Let's get out of here."

She nods, ready. "Nice to meet you," she tells Parks.

Magnolia watches her for a couple of seconds. "Yeah, you too."

"See you around, Parks." I nod at her.

Jordan walks towards the door.

'I'll text you,' I mouth to Parks.

She gives me a tiny wink and then I'm gone.

23:56

Parks

> Oi

> It's BJ.

I figured.

The only person on the planet who greets me with 'oi' and lives to tell the tale.

> Hah

> Julian Haites hey?

Nothing to worry about, Ballentine . . .

> Hah.

> Still keen for that chat?

Yep :)

> Tomorrow good?

Sure

Where?

> Dunstans?

4?

Okay x

x

SEVEN

Magnolia

"Julian Haites couldn't get enough of you," Taura says to this month's issue of *Vogue*, which her nose is buried in.

She and my sister are lying on my bed as I'm sifting through all the clothes I left behind here to see if there are any worth bringing back with me. My pink dress. This should probably be in a vault, not my closet. It's far too important.

"He's just friendly." I give her a look.

"No, he's not," Bridget clarifies. "You're just leggy. And he thinks you're the one who got away."

I scoff. "I am not."

"Are too." Taura glances up. "Daisy told me."

I peer over at her, curious. Though I'd never go there. With Julian I've always known I could, but also, I couldn't.

For one, BJ would be so angry. And two, he's dangerous.

Handsome though. Like, painfully so.

Dark blue eyes. Really dark blonde, almost brown hair. Scruffy beard. Very serious eyebrows—the kind of man you double-take.

Apparently he's the most dangerous man in every room so you'd double-take him anyway out of fear for your life, but you'd mostly just do it because he's beautiful.

Taura's watching me closely. Her eyes pinch, amused.

"He's a ledge in the sack," she tells me.

Bridget shakes her head adamantly. "Magnolia, do not even think about it—"

I roll my eyes. "I'm not."

"He is though," Taura insists.

Bridget's eyes pinch. "Well, so, how good?" Taura gives her a look. "Good."

"What makes him so good?" I perch on the edge of my bed.

"I don't know." She shrugs. "He's just good?"

"Better than BJ?" Bridget asks nosily.

They both glance over at me, Taura with some discomfort and remorse, Bridge with the annoying indifference only a sibling can sport.

"On par," Taura considers. "Probably better—a bit."

That surprises me because BJ is . . . BJ. Everything about him oozes sex appeal. He's accidentally romancing the pants off of everyone at all times—he's practically fabled.

I press my hands into my cheeks absentmindedly.

I'm nervous about meeting up with BJ, I don't know why. You'd think I'd want this . . . the 'sorry' I assume I'm getting. For him to clear the air, make it better.

I do, but it makes me nervous because either way, it means something.

Either he's clearing the air because he's moving on and that's how you do it, or he's clearing the air to move forward, he and I.

I think he might tell me he still loves me . . .

Right? Surely. After how he was watching me at Christian's bar launch—I knew he was. I was his eye kink for the entire afternoon.

I felt high from it. I've missed the feeling of being his focus. There's nothing quite like it in the world, that's my conclusion at this point. And I can be angry at him, I can be hurt by him, I can be scared of him, and even with all of that still, I can want all of his attention.

Which I do.

All of it. I want all his attention, all his time, all his wandering eyes and lip bites. I don't want to share those things with that Australian girl, I want them all.

I wonder if we'll kiss.

Would he kiss me? Would I let him? Of course I'd let him. I hate that about myself a bit, but I would.

The butterflies in my stomach at the thought of being somewhere alone with him, being at Dunstan's with him, they're prehistoric in size. Like bats flying around in there. Ill with jitters and nerves.

"Nervous about tomorrow?" Bridget asks as I hold clothes up against my body, deciding what to wear when I see him. I'm in my head about it, because either way I want it to hurt him when he sees me. If he's leaving me for good, I want him to remember me perfectly, and if he's starting things over, I want him to remember me perfectly then too.

Dark green and navy single-breasted tartan coat from Miu Miu, probably the navy Intarsia-Knit, some sort of white polo underneath it . . . a pleated white mini skirt. The one from Recreational Habits, I think. Maybe some black Horsebit pumps from Gucci? Mid-heel probably. He's already so much taller than me, but I like it best when he feels like a tower.

I suppose he's always towering over me in some way or another. Is that a good thing?

I look over at my sister and shake my head at her like she's crazy, but I think she knows I'm lying.

"No, I feel fine—looking forward to it, actually." I shrug breezily.

Taura smirks. "I bet you are."

EIGHT

BJ

I've thought about what I'd say to her a thousand times.

I'm nervous as shit.

Needed to tell her for too long, should have told her forever ago, probably.

It's more for her than for me now.

I'm okay.

Talked a lot about it all with Claire, the psychologist I've been seeing since the ten anonymous sessions.

She thinks it's an important part of me moving on, telling Parks, but I'm worried about it. For a bunch of reasons. Some selfish, some not.

I don't want her to think of me differently, want to preserve what's left of me up there on the pedestal in her mind—but I think she needs to know.

She's standing there under our arch, leaning against the limestone.

Big tartan coat, short little white skirt under, black heels, white socks.

It rolls through my mind like a thundercloud how in another lifetime I could have just walked over to her, slipped my hand behind her head, and kissed her real good up against the wall.

But in this lifetime I just give her a little nod.

"Hey." I temper the smile I want to give her.

She looks nervous, wringing her hands like a wet towel. "Hi."

"Good coat," I tell her.

"Yours too," she says with shy eyes.

I cock an eyebrow playfully. "What is it?"

Without skipping a beat, "The Giant Damier Laces Windbreaker is Louis Vuitton—obviously." She nods at it.

"And the jeans?"

She squints at me for a second, takes a step closer, slips her finger through a belt loop and spins me around once. "Acne Studios."

I let out a single laugh and sidle myself up next to her.

"She's still got it . . ."

She peers up at me, smiling a little.

"Oi." I nod at her, frowning a bit. "Do you really go to Central Park at midnight?"

She drops her eyes like she knows she's about to be in trouble. Looks out over the grounds instead. "Just sometimes."

I breathe out through my nose. "Why?"

She shrugs. "It's quiet."

I give her a look. "It's dangerous."

She stares at me defiantly for a few seconds. "Only in an obvious way."

I shake my head, annoyed. "What the fuck are you talking about?"

She gives me a small, indifferent shrug and glances away. "After what happened with you and Paili, nothing really is scary to me anymore."

I hang my head, let out the breath in my lungs.

Sounds like it wounded me.

Did a bit.

I gnaw down on my bottom lip, look over at her.

"Right. So about that . . ."

She goes nervous again. I take her by the wrist, pull her over to the bench we always sat at when we were kids, and I sit us down.

"I have to tell you something—" I swallow. "And it's going to be hard for you to hear, but I need you to know that I'm okay now . . ."

She frowns. "Okay?"

I take a breath, steady myself.

"When I was fourteen something happened."

It was Jemima's eighteenth birthday. My sister's always been pretty tame, but some of her friends could be wild. They'd gone out dancing, came home—our parents were out.

She had this friend, Sadie Zabala—super hot, eyes kind of like a cat.

I thought she was cool in that older girl way. She'd play FIFA sometimes with me and Hen, sneak us beers and shit.

The night of Jemima's birthday, she came into my room with a bottle of vodka, sat on my bed.

Poured me one. First time I'd had vodka, actually. Poured herself one, then me another.

Started pouring doubles.

I don't really know after that.

Came to a little while later, no clothes on. She was next to me, the same.

Just watching me—she gave me a proud little smile, pushed her hand through my hair.

"Good job." She kissed my cheek, rolled out of my bed and never spoke to me again.

Parks is blinking a lot; her heart's breaking in her eyes as I tell her the story.

"Beej . . ." she whispers quietly.

"And I didn't say anything to anyone." I nod to myself. "Kept quiet, tried to forget it. But the night I slept with Paili, I saw the person who did it for the first time since . . . And I just—I wanted to . . . not feel how I felt?" I shrug and look down at her.

She's just watching me. Eyes wide, mouth shut tightly.

She nods.

"I wanted to feel in control. Needed to. I wanted to happen to things, didn't want things to happen to me—and so, yeah—I saw her. Went downstairs, Pails followed me—it happened. I told you. Then you broke up with me and—"

62

"Oh my God," she whispers. She's gone pale.

I touch her face. "It's okay."

She shakes her head. "No, it's not."

I duck my head to meet her eyes. "I still have more I need to say, if you'll let me."

She nods, avoiding my eyes because hers are all wet now.

"After we broke up, all I could do was feel it, what happened to me. I wanted it to go away, and it went away every time I had sex." My eyes drop from hers, feeling a bit embarrassed —but her eyes don't flinch, they stay on me.

I clear my throat.

"Became a coping mechanism, I guess. It was never about you, Parks—" I shake my head. "Ever. It was about me. Me trying to deal, me trying to process. And last year, after . . . you know—we got back together, finally, and then when you left—I mean—I fucked around a ton, did what you'd think I'd do. Partied too hard, lost myself more, and then I bumped into Bridget once, and she was so angry at me—" I laugh thinking about it.

Parks musters a weak smile.

"Told me I was a loser and a fucking idiot and I was so gutted because it was so brutal, but she was right and I knew it." We both laugh now. "And then these prepaid psychology sessions turned up in my mailbox not long after—" I give her a small smile. "So I went. And I'm different now."

Trying to be, anyway.

She stares at her hands, nodding.

I nudge her with my elbow, missing her eyes on me.

"I'm still me, Parks," I tell her once I find them. They're round and afraid. Sadder than I want them to be. Sadder maybe than I've ever seen them. "It happened before we were together. The only version of me that's ever been with you had that happen to him—" I give her a small shrug. "You just didn't know."

"I'm so sorry," she whispers.

I shake my head at her. "You don't need to be sorry."

63

"Yes, I do. I—"

"Parks—" I squeeze her hand, shake my head at her. "I'm telling you because I know for you, the who and the why were big deals, and I couldn't tell you before. You knew the who. Now you know the why." I nod once before shaking my head. "I'm not shifting the blame. It was my fault. I did it, I fucked up. Paili didn't come on to me, I came on to her —it was me." I nod. "That's on me. That time I told you I did it because I wanted to—" I shrug. "It was as close as I could get to explaining it. It wasn't that I wanted to, but that I kind of needed to?" I purse my lips, thinking. "That made what happened less bad in my head, I think. If I wanted to have sex with other people, if it was on my terms, under my control—I don't know. It was never about you—that's all I'm trying to say. I just wanted you to know that."

She nods quickly, swipes at her face to brush away a tear.

And then she starts crying. I mean *crying* crying. Proper sobs. Shoulders shaking, chest heaving. And I don't know what to do except pull her onto my lap.

She curls up into me. People could be watching but I don't care. How sad she is about it does something to me or in me —shifts some of the weight I've been carrying or something— and I quickly realise that I should have just told her years ago.

I know I wasn't ready then—Claire and I have talked about that—and there's no point in dwelling on the should haves in life, but I can tell I should have.

Parks wouldn't have cared, wouldn't have looked at me different, wouldn't have felt differently about me—she might have yelled at me less, if anything.

Wouldn't have liked that though—I love it when she yells at me.

But she's not yelling at me now.

Her face is buried in my neck, her hands are balled into fists, clinging to the neck of my shirt.

She's crying for me in a way I've never done for myself and I love her for it.

I shift my head to look down at her for a second.

Our eyes catch. Hers are like crystals—the blue, green, grey now lit up by the red from her tears.

I want to kiss her—that's what I want to do. And she leans in, watching my mouth. Her little chest taking staggered breaths. She wants to kiss me back too—I can see it on her. Our noses graze and . . .

I remember Jordan. Fuck. Jordan.

So I clear my throat instead and it snaps Parks out of it.

She pulls back reflexively, moves away like I slapped her, takes a weird, staggered breath.

"I've got to go," she says, standing suddenly, brushing her face with both her hands.

"Go where?" I frown.

She looks around frantically like she's lost something, but she hasn't—just me, maybe. "To the airport."

I frown more. "I thought you were here till next week?"

I nod my head towards nothing but we both know what I mean.

"Um." She shakes her head. "In Europe. Not here. Till then. Leaving here now—soon. Soon, now—" She's panicking. "I've got to pack. For where I'm going. Are you p—you're not coming—" She shakes her head once.

I stand, reach for her. She shakes her head at my touch.

I sigh. "Are you okay?"

"Of course, yeah—" She's shaking her head, pushing her hand through her hair. "No. Yeah. This is fine. I'm fine. This doesn't change . . . anything. We are . . . we're good." She nods. "Are you good?"

I nod cautiously. "Yeah."

"Perfect. Then—" She presses a shaking hand into her mouth. "This is—"

"Parks . . ." I reach for her again.

My chest feels tight.

She pulls away from me, jerking back like my touch burns her. Fuck. I should have kissed her.

"No, I'm good—I'm fine. And who gives a fuck if I'm fine?" She laughs glibly. "None of this is about me. I'm fine. I'm so fine, Beej—I'm just so—" She sighs, stops in her tracks, her chest still heaving. "I just . . . wish you would have told me."

I breathe out once, shrugging. "I didn't know how."

She nods. She's crying again.

I stare over at her, shove my hands in my pockets, and ask her the question I know I shouldn't, ask her the question that might undo all the shit I've done trying to move forward.

"Would it have changed anything?" I clear my throat. "If you knew?"

She stares back at me; her breathing is ragged. I think she's crying more than she realises. New York's undone her a bit. Unrefined her or something—or maybe not?

Maybe it's me. Me undoing her, because we do that to each other.

I don't know whether that's a good thing or a bad thing, but she's all raw emotion.

She says nothing. Her eyes don't move from me. It's just me and her alone in the universe, how it used to be, how it's supposed to be in all the lifetimes. Maybe even this one.

Yes, is the answer.

She doesn't say it with her mouth, but it's written all over her, everywhere else.

And then she turns and leaves.

NINE
Magnolia

I walk away from him as fast as I can, breaking into a run once I'm out of his line of sight.

I can't see properly.

I think I'm having a panic attack.

What did I do?

How could I have left him how I left him all those years ago?

A wave of nausea rolls through me and I push past someone to throw up into a rubbish bin.

I don't know where I am when Gus grabs me by the shoulders, frowning in my face.

"Magnolia?" He shakes me a little. "What are you doing?"

"Nothing." I blink. "I'm fine. It's not about me, everything's fine—"

He wipes my face with his hands.

"Are you drunk?" He tilts his head, looking around for clues.

I shake my head.

"Taken something?"

"No." I stare off into the distant past, peering through all the ways our lives might be different if I had known.

Then Gus puts me in his car and I'm home.

Bridget and Taura are sitting on my bed, waiting for me—half expecting me to waltz in with a ring on my finger, I think —or at least a smile. I can't say I blame them. It wouldn't be completely off brand for he and I after these last few years to just be together again in a heartbeat without a second thought.

Making it forever with him on a whim.

Once upon a time it would have strictly had to be him down on one knee in the prettiest place in the world with a rock the size of the moon, and now I don't know how it would happen. If it even could . . .

Maybe after he backs into the front of my car and he tosses a diamond at my head. Maybe after he cuts me wide open for heart surgery, he'll ask me through the anaesthetic.

Maybe never.

Probably never because he's never not kissed me before. He's never not kissed me ever in the existence of time.

His little head duck from me speaks a thesaurus of dead-ends and rejections and what the fuck is the matter with me?

Why am I thinking about this when he just told me that?

My chest starts to feel like it's choking me again. My breathing goes.

That's why.

Because I can't think about that. Can't think about what happened to him, how I left him.

My sister's and Taura's faces each quickly slip into despair when I'm guided through the door by Gus Waterhouse.

Bridget launches off the bed to hug me. I let her but I don't hug her back.

"I found her wandering dazed through Tower Hill," Gus tells them.

"What happened?" Bridget asks him.

He shrugs.

"Magnolia?" she presses.

I shake my head.

My sister frowns. "Tell me."

"I don't want to talk about it."

Taura stares at me in disbelief. "What did he say to you?"

"Nothing—" I shake my head. An obvious lie. I look from her to my sister. "I can't—"

They both nod at me, barely, then exchange glances.

"I'll make you a tea—" Bridget moves towards the door.

"No," I tell her and she stops.

Her head tilts, sad for me. "I'll put in a million sugars."

"I don't want a tea—"

She stands in front of me. "What do you want, then?"

"I want to leave." I tell them.

"Leave where?" Gus frowns.

"London."

Bridget shakes her head. "Magnolia, you can't just—"

"—Now." I shake my head to silence her. "I need to go now. I told him I was leaving town, I need to go."

"But you're supposed to be home for another week—you can't just run away every time something happens."

"I'm not running away." I shake my head. "We're done. There's nothing to run from."

My sister tilts her head. "Magnolia, it's not—"

"—Booked us on a flight to Paris," Taura announces with a glance between us after she looks up from her phone. "It's in three hours."

"What?" Bridget frowns.

"I have a job," Gus tells us.

"You work for her dad." Taura rolls her eyes. "I think you'll be okay." She looks over at me. "Should I go home and grab a bag or would you rather me stay here?"

"Go home. Airport is good—I'll meet you—I'm fine," I tell her but I don't really tell her, I tell my bookshelf.

She looks over at me and squints. "I'll stay. You go," she tells Gus. "Eight p.m. at Heathrow. We'll meet at the BA counter."

Gus frowns at her, a bit impressed. "Very bossy."

"Right?" scowls Bridget.

"Great boobs though," Gus says, walking out my door. "See you in a bit."

Taurs looks over at my sister. "What are you standing here for? Go on. Go pack." She shoves Bridget towards the door.

"And get changed," she calls after her. "They'll never let you in first class in those pyjama pants."

Bridget looks down at herself then back up to Taura,

frowning. "These are just my pants."

"Oh." Taura grimaces. "Then don't pack. We'll just buy you a new wardrobe in Paris."

11:33

BJ 🐝

Who knows?

No one.

Just you.

Okay

I probably don't want anyone else knowing either

No one will.

Thanks x

Does Jordan know?

Just you, Parks

Okay.

I'm so sorry Beej

I'm so so sorry.

I'm okay, Parks.

I'm good now. X

TEN

BJ

"I told her," I tell Claire.

She's nice. Older, gives off a mum vibe.

Don't know whether she has kids or not though.

She's Welsh, been here a while, long enough to know who I am and what we are, but it's not gotten in the way. Helpful if anything . . . less to explain.

I felt weird about it at first, going to see someone. I wouldn't have gone if the note wasn't attached.

'Or lose her forever.' Wasn't going to chance it. Glad I didn't.

"Did you?" Claire looks pleased. "How did she take it?"

"Yeah—" I lick my bottom lip, shake my head. "She's shattered."

She nods thoughtfully. "I thought she might be."

"Cried more than I've ever seen—"

She frowns a little. "Did she?"

I nod, play with the smokey quartz ring from Tom Wood. Parks got it for me a while back. I wear it all the time still. Mostly because it's sick. A bit because I just want to.

"I think it changes everything," I tell Claire without meeting her eyes.

She crosses her legs the other way.

"Did Magnolia say that?"

I glance up. "No."

But yes. Not out loud, but still yes.

We have a whole language between us in the things we don't say. Don't need her to say a fucking thing to know what she means.

71

Claire purses her mouth, thinking.

"When you came to me at the start of your sessions, your main priority was becoming good enough for Magnolia. Do you feel like you've arrived at that place?"

I frown a bit at the question. "I don't think she cares anymore."

"Really?" She tilts her head.

"No." I shrug. "I think she might want me either way—"

"So you don't care anymore?" She scribbles something down quickly. "Because she doesn't seem to?"

Shove my hands through my hair. "That's not what I mean."

She glances down at her pad, looks back up at me. Thinks for a few seconds.

"Did she ever tell you that you weren't good enough for her?"

"No."

"Then why do you think it?"

"Because I'm not."

"Why?"

"I'm just not—" I shrug, defensive. "If you knew her, you'd get it."

She nods, puts her pen down.

"We've talked about this before, BJ, but let's talk about it again. How are you defining 'good enough'?" She gives me a long look. "What do you think that means to her?"

"I don't know." I shrug. "Just being a good guy. Trustworthy . . . and trying to be honourable and shit."

She nods. "And do you think you are those things?"

"Maybe." I lift my shoulders. "I'm trying to be . . ."

"Good." She smiles. "In what ways are you trying?"

I lick my bottom lip, look off into the corner of the room.

"I'm done with drugs. I'm done with lying, covering shit up. I'm honest about how I'm feeling, what I want."

Claire nods. "They're all great things."

I look back at her. "I think I should maybe just call it with Jordan. Give it a crack with Parks again?"

"Hmm," she says.

It's not an encouraging sound . . . though not entirely discouraging either. It's observational. Annoying if anything.

"Do you think that would be the honourable thing to do?" Her brows fold. "End things with your current, rather new girlfriend, because your ex-girlfriend is briefly back in town?"

"It's not like that." I shake my head at her for not getting it. "Jordan and I have been dating for a month—"

"—I know."

"Wasn't even on purpose."

"I know, but you decided to stick with it anyway," she reminds me.

"Yeah, but that was before—"

"Before what?"

Magnolia came back is the answer, but I'm not going to say it to her.

"Me and Parks . . ." I sigh. "It's a different beast."

"'Beast' is an interesting way to put it."

"Is it?" I frown.

"Isn't it?"

I shrug. "It's wild, untamable. Kind of amazing. Kind of terrifying. It hides in your closet, under your bed. It's bigger than you are, you can't outrun it—"

She nods. "Explain that to me."

And I can't. Not really. Not all the way, anyway.

Can't explain what I need to to make it make sense.

I know I could tell her because she's a therapist, it's her job to keep secrets. But we said we'd never, so I won't.

Claire takes my silence as a chance to dive in.

"You and Magnolia have a history of making co-dependent decisions, but you need to start making decisions just for you based on the information you have at hand. Right now that information is: Magnolia lives in New York. She left. She's based there now. She has a flight out of London in a week. She's not staying here. With that knowledge being the only concrete information you have, do you still feel like you'd make the decision to end it with Jordan?"

73

"I don't know." I sigh, shrug a little. "No, I guess—but isn't that shit of me?"

She smiles, a bit amused. "Why would it be?"

"Because I love Magnolia still."

"Sure." She nods.

"But you're saying I should stay with Jordan?"

"I'm not saying that." She shakes her head. "I'm suggesting you don't end your current relationship because of an old one without really considering all the facts."

I look at her with pinched eyes. "Even though I still love her."

"You might always love her in some capacity, BJ. Even if you aren't together."

I roll my eyes. "Well, fuck—"

Claire laughs, tilts her head, gives me a gentle look.

"BJ, you can love someone and not have it rule you, not have it dictate your every waking thought and decision. You can love someone and still retain your power and autonomy. You can love someone and have it just be there, a part of you, and still have a completely functional life—" She pauses and gives me a long look. "Even if it's a life without them."

Doesn't sound much like any life I'm interested in, actually.

ELEVEN

Magnolia

I cried the first couple of days.

Didn't leave the hotel room.

Terrible company for Gus.

According to Bridget, we should each have our own, which is something she declares loudly at breakfast every morning of the trip when she comes to eat breakfast on my bed.

("You two are not economical people," she told us with a convicting finger. "Magnolia, I've literally seen you blow your nose on a twenty-pound note." I frowned over at her. "Well, I didn't have a tissue—" But the truth is, we're sharing rooms because I don't like to be alone.)

We're staying at Hôtel de Crillon. Poor choice on Taura's behalf—Beej and I used to come here all the time.

She wouldn't know that though, because I was too busy shunning her at the time for being the girl he cheated on me with—which she never was—and none of that matters now anyway, not in light of everything.

They're all worried about me, I can see it in the way they move around me. How they frown when they watch me, how my sister picks at her nail mindlessly while she's next to me.

I'm not speaking, not really. Not eating, not shopping. Just sleeping and drinking.

Taura's wish came true though. With me down for the count, she got to take Bridget shopping for that whole new wardrobe like she was her very own snarky, reluctant, noncompliant little Barbie doll.

The fact that I didn't jump at the chance to give my sister a makeover doesn't placate anyone's concerns either.

But I can't help it.

My mind's poring over the last ten years, trying to see any clues I might have missed, any ways he might have tried to tell me without telling me that I was too selfish or too stupid to see.

I think about the night he cheated on me constantly, and for the first time since it happened, it hurts me. Not for myself, but for him.

To have seen the girl? I'd kill her. If I ever see her, I'll slit her fucking throat.

But if I knew—that night—if he'd told me . . .

I think I would have understood? I hope so. I understand now, so I don't know why I wouldn't have then. I would have been sad and it still would have hurt me, but I think I would have understood it—maybe?

Or maybe it's just that now I'd understand it in retrospect, after years of not understanding, not knowing all the facts. Like I'd been trying to do a puzzle in the dark.

I'm mourning, absolutely. For him. For me. For us.

I don't want to make it about myself because it's not about me—not at all—and I guess that's a bit the point. Because I thought it was . . .

He told me he slept with someone else because he wanted to—do you know how that feels? Thinking for years that the person you loved more than anything, trusted more than anyone, did a thing to hurt you—even though they knew it would hurt you—for no other reason than because they wanted to do it.

Do you know what that does to you?

It strips you away, makes you feel unsafe in the world, makes the edges of love feel sharp and dangerous. It poisons all the good that might come next and paints over all the things that used to make you happy before, because it's a different sort of betrayal when it's a conscious, coherent decision. It was him choosing him over me because he wanted to.

I've thought about BJ fucking Paili because he wanted to do so almost daily since I left for New York. It was the part of it that was irreconcilable, the part that stuck out like a sore thumb, because nothing about BJ till then led me to believe that he would fuck everything between us up just because he wanted to. That was the hardest part to accept, and actually, I think I did accept it. After Tom and I finally ended properly, and I started speed-dating through the boys in Page Six. I think I accepted that he hurt me just because I was hurtable, and thenceforth I only let boys in so far.

That's what happened with Jack-Jack.

"Are you okay?" Gus asks, lying down on my bed two nights before we leave.

I roll in towards him, my face blank. I pull the blue and lilac textured-finish button-fastening cardigan from Dolce & Gabbana snug against me.

"No."

He pours rosé and hands it to me. "Want to talk about it?"

"Yes." I flash him a weak smile.

"Okay." He nods, sitting up. I shake my head. "—But you can't?"

I nod once. He nods back.

"Is it bad?"

I purse my mouth. "Very."

"Are you okay? Like, are you hurt?" he clarifies.

"Indirectly."

He sighs, reaches over and picks some lint off my Cashmere in Love cropped polo shirt I've got on underneath.

"I'm sorry." He grimaces. He means it.

My eyes go teary again. "Me too."

He rubs his chin. "Could you talk around it? How can I help? You look like shit."

I sniff a tired laugh.

"You really do. It's weird." He shakes his head. "So unnatural. I hate it. Can I brush your hair? It looks like a squirrel's tail—"

"August." I smack him with a pillow and he laughs.

I reposition myself, hugging my knees. "You may not ask why when I say what I'm about to say—"

"Okay." He nods cautiously.

"But I should have never broken up with him." My voice chokes up a little.

He blinks a few times. "Even though he cheated on you?"

I nod back solemnly. "Even though he cheated on me."

I think back to Clara England, what she said to me that night at dinner with Tom and his parents . . .

That there are worse things than cheating.

She was right.

TWELVE

BJ

Out for a bite at Shack Fuyu with the Lads and J. Get the Yuzu Margaritas, trust me.

It was supposed to be a date, but I asked Jonah to come, which turned into Christian coming, which meant Hen was coming too.

I just didn't feel like being on a date with my girlfriend who I feel like I should dump. Feels disingenuous. I wanna do the right thing, not just by myself, but by her too.

And Parks.

A lot of balls in the air I don't know how to catch, but I feel like I need to fracture a bit of the romance—even if it's just for my sake. Dilute it with my rowdy best friends who sap the tenderness out of everything. She's a big fan of them though, thinks they're fun. They are. They're not all mad on her though, if I'm honest. It's not her fault, not her doing either.

They like her enough—don't get me wrong—couldn't not like her, she's cool and hot and chill; she watches sports, she drinks beer, eats burgers and shit, and if Magnolia wasn't this ominous presence in the back of all our minds, if she didn't have these crazy expectations of loyalty, I think they'd like Jordan more.

She is happy to leave early though, they don't like that. Always wants to take me home with her.

"She's domesticated you," is what Jonah says about her.

Parks and Paili, they slotted in with me and the boys easily. Probably because we grew up together, but Taura and even

Daisy both slotted in pretty seamlessly too. Happy to stay up all night, happy to sleep all day.

"It's past our bedtime," Jordan declared once at 11 p.m. on a Saturday.

Christian was fucking horrified.

"Bedtime?" he gawfed. "Who do you think he is? Tiny fucking Tim?"

I snorted a laugh. "It's fine—it's fine—" Swatted my hand. Told him I liked going to sleep early now.

"Because we get up for 7 a.m. coffees," Jordan told him with a big smile.

Henry made a face over her head that she couldn't see and I hit him in the stomach for it, left them laughing.

It's bullshit though.

I hate those 7 a.m. coffees and not just because they're at that shitarse café by her house, but because I don't like going to sleep early. Not now, not ever.

I don't even go to sleep. I just lie there, on my iPhone. Read a book. Try not to look at photos of my ex-girlfriend on the internet.

I don't do that last one. Don't let myself.

I think about doing it most days though. Fight the urge.

The urge has won the last few days.

She looks happy in New York.

That scares me.

She seems to have fallen in perfectly with a bunch of people she'd think are real fun.

Dinners with the Timberlakes (Justin's an old friend of her dad's), shopping with the main girl from *Sex and the City*. At bars with the loud girl from *The Hunger Games*.

Fuck.

That's what I was thinking last night once Jordan had fallen asleep and I was lying in bed looking at photos of a girl who isn't her. That she looks okay—and I want her to be—but she looks okay without me.

Fuck.

"Where's Taura?" Jordan asks brightly, dispersing her glance evenly between Henry and Jonah so as to not cause a disturbance.

"In Paris with Parks," Jonah says first.

"For that last-minute trip they took," Henry adds.

I look over, curious. "It wasn't planned?"

Henry sniffs a laugh, shakes his head. "Nah. Tausie called me on the way to the airport, said they decided to go. Parks wanted to get out of town."

I swallow once. Ignore the punch in the gut, avoid a maritime metaphor.

"Ah." I nod, offer him a casual smile as I throw down my drink. Order another.

"She's left here early, then?" Jordan asks, sounding pleased.

"Don't know. I guess so. Maybe." Jonah shrugs. "Makes sense. Why would she come back here first to fly home?"

I don't fucking know, to say goodbye to me?

I shove my hands through my hair, breathe out of my nose. She just left?

"Well, good for her." Jordan smiles, more chipper than she's been in weeks. "Paris in the winter's so nice, don't you think? It's so dreamy—" She glances at me. "Take me?"

"What?" I blink a few times, processing what she's said to me because I'm not thinking about her at all.

"Sure. Yeah. We'll go in the summer—"

Jordan sniffs, can't tell whether it's amused or hurt.

Jonah tosses me a look.

Don't care.

I can't believe she just left? Again.

Without an actual goodbye. Again. Even after that? That almost-kiss on my lap—her in my neck, crying for me. And before December 3rd.

I shake my head at the dinner table. Fuck her. I mean it. It's good she's gone. Now everything can be normal again. Easy again.

Amazing how she can be home for a fortnight and manage to toss my entire life into fucking chaos and then just fuck off again.

I look over at Jordan, ruffle her hair and lean in, kissing her cheek.

"Paris in the winter, Jords. Noted."

Subject:

███████@condenast.com
to me ▼

Magnolia darling,

Hope this finds you well.
Loving having you back in the home office.
Was hoping you'd be able to find the time to have a little chat sometime in the next week about a role that's opened up that we love for you.

Long story short, Sophie's moving on and you're the unanimous pick to replace her as Style Editor.
I know you've been loving New York, I don't want to pressure you—it's been working, you there, travelling for the pieces, we can keep down that path, but between us —this is where you belong.
In London, in fashion.
Mull it over and let's meet up next week.

Can't wait to hear about your steam with Gwen.
RD. x

+

THIRTEEN

Magnolia

It wasn't until the day before we were leaving Paris that I actually began to enjoy it, but isn't that ever the way?

They all tried to convince me to stay longer but I said I couldn't . . . That I had to get home for a meeting. That surprise little email from RD last week, making an honest woman out of me.

It wouldn't have mattered either way. I would have lied to get home for December 3rd. Not even wild horses . . .

I didn't tell anyone about the email, by the way.

I didn't tell anyone I took the meeting this morning when we flew in from Paris either. I didn't tell anyone he offered me the role. I haven't told anyone I accepted it on the spot.

I want the first person I tell to be BJ. I don't know why—I'm not staying for him. I'm not *not* staying for him though. I love him. More now than ever, I think, somehow.

And I want to make this work. So when Rich offered me the job today, it felt like those crafty old Fates were at it again, weaving the tears in the tapestry of us back together.

Please, God, let them be weaving us back together.

The drive down there is tender and familiar, even though it's long.

It's especially so on my own—but it often starts like this.

Us arriving apart and then leaving together.

It's our tie that binds, draws us in close, regardless of how far we've drifted. No matter what, or where we are, we've never missed December 3rd. Not even the first year we broke up, when I was (secretly) with Christian, and BJ and I weren't talking. Even then.

It's our little pilgrimage back to each other, a slow crawl towards the only proper home we've ever had.

My mind trickles back to last year, how long we'd waited, how badly we wanted it, how perfect it was. My heart starts stomping at the thought of his hands on my body and I wonder if it'll happen again.

Whether he'll be standing there, waiting under the tree—of course he's under the tree, where else would he be? I just don't know that he'd think it's on the table.

And maybe it's not on the table because he has a girlfriend.

Except maybe they broke up while I was in Paris? They could have.

It doesn't need to be on the table.

I'll just be relieved to see him, relieved to tell him I'm staying, relieved to see my relief mirrored on his face.

I pull into the estate's driveway and take the long way down into the garden.

I pass sweet Mr Gibbs and his two Irish wolfhounds. I give him a small wave, he gives me a big one. I park my car and look around.

He's not here yet.

I check the time.

A bit past three.

I guess he's still on his way up.

I climb out of my car and straighten myself out—the black and white sequin-embellished pointelle-knit wool mini dress from Gucci with the black LV Detail Maxi Cardigan from Louis Vuitton.

I wander down the cobblestone path towards the tree.

It gets prettier every year, and if you were looking for it, you'd see it sticks out like a sore thumb.

For the most part, the grounds of our Dartmouth house are typical for the garden of an estate. Very English. Hedges and ivy and pastel roses.

But the path to our tree is all wild and busy flowers. Tended to, of course. Nothing unkept about it. An intentional mess. He's a sweetheart, Mr Gibbs. I think he's the only person in the world who might know what happened, besides Jonah's mum.

I get to the tree and my heart sinks like usual.

To be expected, all things considered.

I look around for him, hoping he's just a moment away. My eyes trace the tree, find our initials carved into it.

All three of ours.

And then my eyes fall down the trunk to the stone we lay to remember the tiny baby girl we lost that no one even knows we had, and there are magnolias laying there and I know he was here.

He was here and now he's gone.

I feel like someone places a vacuum over my mouth and sucks the air right out of my lungs.

I lose him again and I lose her too for the billionth time in my life and I feel like the world is ending again.

Is it horrible or miraculous that you can feel that feeling so many times throughout your life?

Miraculous you survive, horrible you live to feel the world slipping out from under you again.

The world's slipping out from under me.

"He drove up just before dawn," Mr Gibbs tells me quietly from behind.

I don't know where he's come from, how long he's been there.

"Oh," I say and I nod, but it comes out strangled and foreign.

I stumble backwards from the tree a bit.

"Are you okay, Ms Parks?" Gibbs asks, I think. It's hard to tell because of that sound.

What's that sound?

"Yes." I nod, my eyes have gone funny.

That's such a strange sound. Where's it coming from? I glance around. It's like a wounded animal, like something's being ripped open.

Mr Gibbs is watching me carefully.

"I'm fine," I reassure him.

I touch my face. Is it wet?

I look up. When did it start raining?

He reaches for me. I don't know why.

And there's that sound again. That gut wail and that rushing sound.

What is that?

"It's okay," he tells me gently. He tells me I'm okay how you tell a lost child you find in a grocery store. "You're okay," he tells me again and the edges of my vision start fading.

Everything's fading to black. I really wish that sound would stop. BJ always makes things go to black for me, but this is different. It's not just me and him in all the world and the world falling to silence as he and I blast to stereo—it's not that sort of fading. I'm fading.

What the fuck is that sound?

My legs are going out from under me.

My heart is racing.

I can't see.

Am I falling?

I think I am the sound.

FOURTEEN

Magnolia

I didn't notice for the longest time.

I'd never been one of those girls with a spectacularly regular cycle, so if a month came and went without me getting my period, that was fine. When a second month came and went without me getting it, it still wasn't completely unheard of . . . Around that time Bushka had bypass surgery, so life at home was swirly and I didn't even really have time to notice as my mother managed to make her mother having surgery into a big theatrical experience we all had our parts to play in. There were a lot of dinners, flowers, an interview in *Marie Claire* that required a photoshoot with the entire family as well as a public appearance at a museum (for why?), and I remember being in the museum toilets, using the loo, and thinking, should I have my period? But then my mother accidentally set a curtain on fire and we were all evacuated and I forgot to follow up.

So then another month went by and then I realised: still nothing.

It was a Sunday night when I caught it.

Beej and I were going to go get a late dinner at Circus and then I was going to stay at his house to drive up to school the next day, but as I was putting mascara on in my bathroom, my eyes caught on a box of unopened tampons that I realised I hadn't had to use now for months, and I froze.

I did the maths in my head, pointlessly, because I knew I was late beyond late beyond late.

I remember thinking that probably I wasn't. I remember hoping I was just malnourished. A weird thing to hope, but I could have been. It'd happened before.

And I remember rationalising that's what it was, probably. Because it'd been fashion week recently, I'd walked a couple of big shows—I went full Miso for a little bit—it felt likely, actually, that that's what it was.

But there was a nag. So I threw on a coat over the pyjamas I'd been in all day, pulled on my black Hunters, and bolted to my car. Into the pharmacy, bought two of each brand of tests, bought them with sunglasses on—just to be safe, because you never know. I ran back to my car and called Beej on my way home.

"Hey," he said on the second ring. "Just about to leave mine to come grab you, you ready?"

"Uh—" I stuttered. "No."

I don't know why I called him, I didn't want to tell him over the phone. I didn't want to tell him before I knew anything either.

I called him by default. If I was ever worried about anything, I'd just—it was an absentminded call.

"I can't come tonight," I found myself saying suddenly.

"Oh?" he said, surprised. "You okay?"

"Mmhm!" I lied. "Mars is on the war path after that C+ I got in Mandarin."

"Oh. Should I come over, then?" he asked brightly. "I'll climb through the window."

"No!" I said, a bit urgent.

I could hear him frown. "Okay?"

"No—just. No, because. I've been vomiting as well." Which was true. I had. In the morning. Once that day and once three days before. But sometimes I did that anyway, and then my stomach could be funny with foods.

"Are you sure you're okay? Want me to bring you something?"

"I'm fine. Completely!" I added enthusiastically to do my best to release him. I cleared my throat. "You go out! Go with Paili and Jo. Have fun. I'm fine, I promise."

"Okay . . ." he said, unsure. "I'll call you later."

"Okay!" I hung up without saying love you or bye, which was weird of me and I knew he was bound to notice that, but I was holding myself together by a thread.

I burst through my front door as Mars and my sister were coming out of the kitchen.

"Are you okay?" Marsaili asked, looking at me, eyes discerning.

"Fine!" I nodded, giving her a tight-lipped smile.

She squinted at me in suspicious disbelief.

"Magnolia—" she started, but my sister interrupted her, that beautiful little brat.

"What's in the bag?" fourteen-year-old Bridget said with a pointed nose.

"Condoms!" I yelled and then darted up the stairs.

"Magnolia!" Marsaili growled after me. "She's fourteen!"

"Yeah! Don't worry! No one's going to want to have sex with her anyway!" I yelled back, semi-proud of myself for not allowing my present circumstances to inhibit my ability for a zingy one-liner.

I rushed back into the safety of my room and locked the door behind me.

About seven months earlier, Marsaili took the lock off my door because she thought BJ and I were having sex (we were) but my mum went out and got a lock and put it on herself, so she claims, saying that I deserved privacy if I wanted it. Part of that story was most certainly embellished, but I didn't question it because I was just pleased to have a lock back.

I gulped a ton of water and then systematically peed on all twelve tests.

Every single one of them came back as positive.

As those two pink lines appeared on my last test, I dropped my head in my hands, took a deep breath and dug my nails into my hands. I still have a little crescent scar on my palm now from where a nail broke my skin. BJ used to trace it with his finger whenever he could.

I've always liked that scar, actually.

It would be strange to have no marks left on me after all that. I don't have many other ways of knowing that any of what happened was real.

I needed a blood test, I knew that.

Even though twelve at-home tests was fairly damning, I wasn't ready to be damned all the way without a doctor telling me I was.

I scooped all the evidence into a turquoise Moschino handbag I never used anymore, grabbed my coat again, and skittered back down the stairs.

"Staying at BJ's tonight!" I yelled to anyone who was listening and ran out the door to call a cab.

A street away, I stopped the cab to throw the bag into the bin (sorry Jeremy) and asked the driver to take me to St Thomas's. It was late by then. About 11 p.m.? Later, maybe?

I marched straight over to the front desk and smiled curtly at the woman behind the counter.

She looked about forty-five, very skinny, quite mousey.

"I need to see a doctor."

"Okay," she said, smiling at me. "Why?"

"It's confidential," I told her and she peeked up at me curiously.

"If you tell me why you need to see a doctor I can prioritise you faster," she told me, possibly trying to be helpful, but it wasn't too long before this that the papers had begun to garner a bit of an interest in BJ and I.

Imagine that—following around fifteen- and sixteen-year-olds and selling their photos.

Someone from school filmed me taking something at a party a few months before this. They told everyone it was Molly but it was valium. I get nervous sometimes.

Mum said she'd rather everyone think it was MDMA, so they didn't correct the rumours, and I didn't really care either way.

I hadn't experienced negative attention before. This was my first dalliance with it and it was a doozy. It made me look at the world differently and it made me trust people less.

"I can't tell you why," I said.

The mousey woman glanced over at her co-worker who wasn't paying attention to us.

"I can tell you though, this wing—" I pointed down the corridor to my left—"is named for Linus Parks. My name is Magnolia Parks. Someday soon my grandparents are going to die and they'll leave me millions. And I'll have to give some away as a tax offset. My father likes St Thomas's because he was born here, but I like Great Ormond Street because of Peter Pan," I told the woman without blinking. "And I will remember this."

She looked at me for a long moment.

"Please?" I sighed, and I think my eyes must have looked some kind of desperate.

She nodded once and led me to a little side room.

"Wait here." She closed the door behind her.

About an hour later, a doctor walked in. She was young, pretty, with long blonde hair tied back in a ponytail.

"Hello." She smiled, folding her hands over her chest. "Hi," I said to her, sitting on my hands nervously.

She read the room, read my face I suppose, and sat down next to me on the bed.

"I'm Sarah, I'm a third-year resident here. What's your name?"

"Magnolia Parks."

"Okay, Magnolia. How can I help you today?"

"I need a pregnancy test." The words tumbled out of my mouth.

"Okay." She nodded and stood up to fetch one.

"But not a stupid bathroom one—" I called after her. "They don't work, I need a blood one."

"Have you taken some of the bathroom ones at home?" she asked gently.

I nodded. "Twelve of them."

Her face pulled.

"Magnolia," she said after clearing her throat, "how old are you?"

"Sixteen."

"Are you here by yourself?"

I nodded.

"Where are your parents?"

"Um—" I shrugged. "Singapore, I think?"

"Does anyone know you're here?"

"No!" I shook my head quickly. "I told my nanny I was staying at my boyfriend's."

"Is he here?" She glanced back at the door.

I shook my head. "No."

"Is there a reason you're by yourself?" she asked, leaning in.

"I don't want to tell him till I know, and I won't know til I have a blood test—" I shook my head. "I can't tell him without knowing for sure. He has a big game this week."

"I don't think you should do this on your own," she told me gently. "And I won't," I told her firmly. "I just need to know definitively first."

An hour and a half later, she walked back into the room with a file in her hand and a serious look on her face. She sat down across from me and looked up.

I knew the answer before she said it.

I knew it before I came.

Twelve tests don't lie, and neither did my blood test.

"You're pregnant," she told me.

"Okay." I sprang off the bed I'd been lying on.

"Magnolia, wait—" Sarah tried to stop me.

"Thank you." I turned back to give her a grateful look.

And I was grateful, truly, but I had about forty seconds left in me before I lost it.

I cried the whole drive home.

I crept back into my house, but bumped into Marsaili passing in the hall.

"Magnolia." She shook her head. "It's three-thirty on a school night—"

"—I'm sorry," I barely choked out.

"Are you crying?" she asked, reaching for my wrist.

"No." I flinched away from her.

"Did you and BJ have a fight?" she pressed.

"No." I shook my head again. "He's just vomiting so I came home."

She watched me, looking for a reason to doubt my story.

"I smell like vomit." I shook my head. "I need to shower."

I locked the door. I showered. I cried until morning.

FIFTEEN

BJ

Today's always rough.

Weird mix of emotion.

An old kind of grief for someone I've never even met. Someone I wanted to meet though.

Someone who's changed my life anyway.

Maybe it's more the mourning for a life we imagined.

It's gotten easier over the years. Funny with pain, how it propagates itself, grows into you, becomes a part of you. Shapes you a bit.

It kind of hits different for Parks, I know—the D&C fucked her up for a while. Broke her more than she said, I could always tell.

I'm always grateful for the tree. Something to point my grief at.

There's no ceremony to December 3rd, but maybe the ritual is we'll always find a way to hold each other.

Sometimes it's overt—she'll just take my hand in hers, kiss it.

Sometimes she'll come and lean her head on my arm. Won't say a thing.

That's what she did the year she was fucking around with Christian. Just wordlessly leaned against me.

We steadied ourselves against each other how we've done all our lives.

The tree's a bit of a hard reset for us.

I'd be a liar if I said a part of me hadn't wondered whether Paris was just a cover and she came up here early—that's the kind of shit she'd pull to be alone with me. I know it is because I'd do it too to get her to myself for a day or even a half of one.

I thought about it, just coming up early in case she was there, in case she was waiting for me and she didn't just fuck off all over again without a word. Hard with Jordan though, she'd ask questions. Fair enough I suppose, she should be allowed to ask them. But whatever she'd ask, there's nothing I can tell her that won't just prove to her that I haven't changed at all, that won't let her down, because I will. I'd let the whole world down to keep Magnolia afloat if I had to. Or I would have before. Not now, I tell myself. But I know it's a lie. Try to convince myself for the two hundredth time this week that Parks is nothing except the hardest habit I'll ever have to break.

Jordan's going to have questions about today as it is. I just left. Told her I couldn't stay over last night, felt sick.

Up at 6 a.m. and gone.

Pretty eager of me, even though I was angry at Parks for leaving early, no goodbye and shit. That embarrassing part of me thought she still might have been there.

Wasn't, obviously.

Cried a bit on the way home, not at the tree. She isn't buried there anyway.

It all happened so quickly and we were so young, we didn't know what to do. As soon as she was in the clear after the operation we just left. She's always regretted that part.

We don't talk about it much, but when we do she usually just goes quiet about it.

Quiet is her way of talking about it.

Jordan's called me a few times today—ignored them— because what do you say?

It's why I've never told anyone, not even Jo.

At this point it sort of all just feels like a fever dream that's tied us together for the last nine years.

I pull up outside me and Jo's place; it's evening now. I'm ready to crash out for the night. Sleep it off. Sleep off losing the only girls I've ever loved.

Can you love someone you've never met? I think about that sometimes. Probably just love the idea of her, love the idea of a tiny Parks I helped make bossing me around forever, driving me mental. It's all for naught now, these thoughts, but I'll think them tonight as I drift off to sleep anyway.

I open my front door and Jordan looks up at me from the couch.

Fuck.

I didn't ask her to come here. I don't want her to be here.

"Hey—" I force a smile.

"Hi." She stands, walks over to me, drapes her arms around my neck. "Where've you been?"

I do this weird laugh that sounds mostly like breathing.

"Work—" I nod. "Had a work thing."

From across the room, Jonah's eyes pinch. Knows I'm lying. Girlfriend doesn't though, thank fuck.

"Oh." She smiles. "A shoot?"

"Yep." I nod.

"For who?" she asks, looking up at me with bright eyes.

I lick my bottom lip, not thinking fast enough.

My brain's not in working order. Fuck.

"Neuw," Jonah says, catching my eye and nodding at my jeans.

She nods. "I can't wait to see them."

I kiss her cheek. "I'm just going to grab a shower, yeah?"

She gives me a smile and sits back down on the couch, changing the channel.

I head downstairs to my room, leave the door open because I know Jo's followed me.

Stands in the doorway, watches me.

Nods his chin at me. "Were you with Parks?"

"No, man—" I flick him a frown. "She's gone."

He looks confused. "Gone where?"

"Back?" I shrug. "To New York."

He gives me a look. "No she hasn't. They just flew back in from Paris yesterday morning."

96

"What?" I blink.

"Yeah. Tausie said she had a fight with a man at the luggage carousel because he called her shoes kitsch and . . ."

I'm not listening.

Shit. I rub my mouth absentmindedly.

I should call her. Should I call her?

I can't get back up there now. What if she thinks I forgot? The flowers I guess—she'll know I was there.

My heart sinks like a stone.

"You alright?" Jo's frowning as he watches me.

"What?" I look up at him,

He shakes his head. "What's going on with you?"

"Nothing." I toss him a look like he's the idiot. Pull off my shirt, toss it in the laundry.

"I'm fine."

He's not buying it. "You sure?"

I give him a tight smile. "Yep—"

And then I close the bathroom door.

SIXTEEN

BJ

Never saw it coming. Ever.

Wouldn't have believed you even if you told me.

That morning I remember I was all in my head about a rugby game against Westminster.

Been training for it for weeks.

It was a Monday. I remember her standing there, a few metres away from me, just watching.

Eyes looked a bit funny. Tired, glassy.

"Hey." I gave her a cautious smile as I pulled her into me.

Loved her in that school uniform. Little tartan skirt, knee-high socks, a buttoned shirt with a tie. Pretty much my every dream. Still love her in plaid.

I pressed my mouth against hers, tugged on her ponytail playfully. "You good?"

She forced a smile and I could tell something about her was off.

"Are you okay?" I asked, craning my neck down so we were eye to eye.

"Can we talk?" she said, barely more than a whisper.

"Yeah." I frowned a bit. Felt a bit nervous, if I'm honest. Checked the time. "Now?"

"Can you?"

I wobbled my head around, thinking. "I just have that big history test this period."

"Oh, I forgot—" She shook her head. Her cheeks went pink but her eyes looked teary.

"I can miss it?" I offered, trying to keep her eyes on mine.

Back in those days I could read her best if I could see her eyes. Don't need them anymore. I can read her with both our eyes closed and my hands behind her back.

"No." She shook her head fervently. "Definitely don't miss it."

"Okay?" I nodded, feeling confused. "Everything okay?"

"—Yes."

The pause she did was the giveaway. She was lying.

We never lied to each other.

I took her hand in mine. "Walk me to class?"

She said nothing the whole time, just wore this tense little frown and bit down on her lip.

"You sure you're okay?" I asked her when we got to my class.

Everything about her was weird, all of her was uneasy and I had the same urge then that I still have now: If something's wrong with her, I've got to fix it.

"Yes," she said mechanically.

"Right." I nodded, flashed her a quick smile as reassuring as I could and walked into the classroom.

"Miss," I called to the teacher.

Miss Platt was her name. Young and uppity, pain in the arse. Loved history more than she loved the kids she was teaching it to.

"Yes, Mr Ballentine?"

"I'm skipping class today."

She gave me a dry look. "You are not, Mr Ballentine. We have a test. Sit down." She gave me a stern look. "Now."

"Actually," I tilted my head at her apologetically, "wasn't a question. Just letting you know."

"If you skip this class you won't play on the weekend." She glared at me, obviously annoyed that she was being challenged in front of the class.

I gave her a little grimace. I was well known as the best player in our first 15's squad and Varley's a rugby school.

"Come on——" I gave her a look. "We both know you can't make that call——"

"Mr Ballentine, if you walk out of this classroom, you will have a Friday detention."

I nodded once.

"Yep, sounds fair!" I smiled. "Too easy. Pass it on to Jonah, would you? He'll give it to me later."

And then I walked out of the classroom, closing the door behind me. Looked down at the girl I love, lifted my eyebrows up even though they already felt weighed down. "Let's talk."

I offered her my hand, led her down the hall.

She didn't say anything for ages, not till we'd walked aimlessly to the car park.

I looked at her expectantly, waiting for her to say something. I remember I felt something coming. It was just on her, this nervous energy I hadn't seen before.

"Are we breaking up?" I asked quickly.

She paused. It was a long pause. "I hope not."

I reached over and pushed some hair behind her ears. "Parks, what's going on?" I lifted my eyebrows impatiently, a bit over it.

"I'm pregnant."

I remember there was a red robin in a tree by us, twittering. That's the sound I hear when I think of that moment. And the wind moving through the air. The way the leaves blew around the tyres of the car. The air was sharp.

Her face, staring at me, waiting for me to say anything more than the fuck-all I was offering her.

My mouth had gone dry.

I cleared my throat. "Are you sure?"

"Yes."

She nodded once.

"How sure?"

"Very," she said quietly.

"Oh," I said, like the vowel. Like an arsehole.

Notice that neither of us wondered how we got pregnant.

She knew how. I knew how. We were so careful almost all of the time. I'd say in general, we had a 5 per cent margin of laziness, and that laziness turned into cockiness when it was continually met without any sort of consequence.

A few months before all this we'd had a party up at the Dartmouth house.

It was parent-less, huge and loose, and I don't know what it was about that night, but I remember standing in the kitchen, me and the boys, shotgunning beers. I drank mine first, dropped the can to the floor, walked over to Parks, hand behind her head, kissed her hard against the wall. The whole room cheered. Slipped my hand onto her face, holding her cheek as I kissed her more. The room thought I was doing it for show, but I was just doing it for me. That's how I kissed her even if no one was watching.

I smiled at her as I pulled away, walking back to the boys, leaving her breathless against the wall, her eyes wanting me in an obvious way.

Me and Parks spent most of that party apart because sometimes it felt fun to do that, play hard to get with each other. We'd stare at each other from across the room, tension building, eye fucking like mad.

Every now and then if she felt like another girl was chatting me up a bit too much she'd shoulder her out of the way.

"Which room should we stay in tonight?" she asked loudly, even though it was her house and Lacey Talbot skulked away, put in her place.

I laughed, slipped my hand in the small of her back, lower than low, and pulled her into me, kissing the top corner of her lip. "The master." I grinned down at her, loving every chance to power play her dad. I pushed some hair behind her ear. "You good?"

She nodded, smiling. "Are you?"

I nodded back, pressed my lips against hers and she wandered away.

An hour and a bit passed and I hadn't seen her in a while.

Missed her, felt like holding her. I was ready for everyone else to fuck off home so I could have her to myself again.

I went for a wander, looking for Parks. Found her sitting on the bed of the master with Pails and another girl from school they were all close with because Henry fancied her. Romilly something.

Parks sat up a little straighter on the bed, cheeks pink as soon as she saw me.

I walked over to her; my eyes didn't flinch. I just wanted to be with her.

"Can you girls give us a minute?" I nodded at her friends without looking at them.

Romilly sniggered and rolled off the bed, but Paili just sat next to Parks, frozen.

"Paili?" Romilly called to her, but Paili was watching me weirdly.

In retrospect, that's probably the day I first worked out she had a thing for me. Kind of fucked up when you think about it—didn't give two shits about it at the time. All I could see was Parks.

"Paili—" Romilly called again.

I remember Parks looking at her best friend all confused.

"Pails, fuck off—" I laughed.

"But we were—" she started and I pulled my T-shirt up over my head.

"Oi, listen—I'm going to have sex with my girlfriend, Paili, so either you leave, or we're heading to the closet."

She let out an embarrassed sound and scurried away.

I shook my head as we watched her leave, and then I locked the door behind her.

"Fuck, she's weird."

Parks gave me a look. "She's my best friend."

"Thought I was your best friend?" I slipped my arms around her waist.

"And what might your intentions here be, Best Friend?"

"Ahh," I grinned down at her, "I'm glad you asked."

Slid my hand under her little pink dress, felt her up.

She unbuckled my jeans and I stepped out of them.

I turned her around to undo the back of her dress and just as it was falling off her body was right when fucking Thatcher Hendry's drunk arse stumbled into the room.

"Ey! What's going on here!" He grinned over at us. Parks started laughing, embarrassed.

I ran over, shoved him backwards out the door. Re-locked the door. Tested it to check it was locked. It wasn't. Tried to lock it again. Didn't work.

Parks had caught the full-blown giggles by then, and I was looking back over at her, frowning and laughing, telling her to shut up.

"It's a standard-issue lock—" She rolled her eyes.

"From fucking 1821!"

"It's very easy to use, you just turn the key—"

"—It's a broken—"

She marched over to prove me wrong and I grabbed her and kissed her, lifted her off the ground, pulled that dress off her that's still in her closet today, I bet. She'd never get rid of it.

Then I grabbed the quilt from the bed, took her hand and led her to the window, nodding my head towards the garden.

We were on the second floor and she took my hand without a second thought.

We scaled down the roof, me first, then her.

The shit we did to be alone together back then . . . Fuck, the shit I'd do still to be alone with her now.

I wrapped myself around her and the quilt around us both —smooth moves, even for me—walked her backwards towards the tree, banged her up against it.

Got her bra off with one hand—felt proud of myself because those things felt like Fort Knox back then and from there it was a quick escalation to the good stuff.

"Wait! Fuck—" She pulled her face away. "I can't remember whether I took my pill today."

I bit down on my lip. "Shit."

"Do you have a—" Her question trailed off breathlessly into my ear.

"No. Fuck." My head dropped in dismay. We hadn't used them in forever. Not since she started using the pill.

And that night, I don't know—something about the combination of pure teenage arrogance and straight lust clouding all smart decisions—I was already inside of her by then—she was biting down on her lip and there was that ache you get in your bones sometimes, to finish what we started. Consequences were abstract up till then; she was and I was and we were invincible.

And then Parks's husky little voice whispered, "I don't care."

I grinned down at her. "I was hoping you'd say that."

I remember thinking about that while she stood in front of me in the school carpark, changing my life forever while I said nothing back.

Nothing.

You ever told someone that you're pregnant and then have them just stare at you? For fifteen seconds. I counted. Because I was an arsehole.

I didn't say anything, I didn't move a muscle.

"What are you going to do?" I eventually asked. Stupid.

I was nervous. I'm never nervous.

She looked at me like I'd hit her. Face went slack. I could see it—all sad and weighed down in disappointment. She was also frightened—that one hurt me, even then. Even then when I was fucking paralysed by it all, her looking frightened smashed me to pieces.

But mostly Parks just looked indignant.

Like up till then we'd carried the world split between us two, and then I just went and dropped my side.

"What am I going to do?" she repeated back.

"Yeah." I swallowed once.

She let out a small scoff.

"Well, I suppose I don't know what I'm going to do." How she emphasised it as she began to slowly back away from me is one of those memories that I lie awake at night thinking about, feeling sick over, wishing I could crawl back through time and make her not feel alone in that moment. But you know what? I didn't.

I just watched her. Didn't move. Didn't click into gear, didn't try to stop her. Just stared at her.

If you'd told me then that there would come a time in our lives where I'd hurt her again, more than I did in that moment, I honestly wouldn't have believed you.

She got in her car. Drove away.

I freaked the fuck out. Got in my car, drove too. Drove nowhere. Screamed in my car. Hit the steering wheel. Got angry at her, got angrier at me. Pored over all the ways my life was fucking done now. I wasn't even eighteen yet and my life was fucked.

I wanted to travel the world with Parks, more than we already had. I was going to play rugby for the country, she'd be my little WAG on the sidelines, cheering for me. Stay up all night and watch National Geographic, kiss her as much as I could in the ad breaks. I was going to marry her, build a life with her and shit . . .

And then I realised all my plans had her in them anyway.

And a kid would have been a part of the plan eventually, so it was just arriving a bit early?

The only plan I'd ever had for my future was Magnolia Parks, and I'd just let her drive away by herself after she told me she was pregnant with my baby.

And then I freaked the fuck out again, differently this time.

Drove as quick as I could back to London. It's about an hour's drive from Varley to Kensington.

I didn't use the front door—didn't want to raise any eyebrows, we should have been at school—so I scaled the drainpipe instead and climbed through her window—pretty hard to do with the pink and blue balloons and a giant teddy bear, but I had to make it up to her.

She was standing there, hands on her hips, staring down at the biggest fucking flow chart you've ever seen.

I landed on my feet and looked over at her with apologetic eyes. Held out the balloons, but she didn't reach for them. I let go of the balloons and walked over to her, dropping my backpack at my ankles before I took her face in my hands.

"I'm the fucking worst, Parks," I told her. "That was so shit of me. I'm sorry. I just needed to think."

"About what?" she asked defiantly, and I loved her for it. I deserved it.

The balloons bobbed up on the ceiling.

I gave her a casual shrug. "About what our life would look like."

"And what would it look like?" she asked, nose in the air.

I looked for her eyes, found them pretty easily.

"It'll look like whatever you want it to, Parks."

She looked at me cautiously. "What do you want your life to look like?"

I shrugged, indifferent. "I just want one with you."

"I'm not getting an abortion," she told me, resolute.

I grinned down at her.

"I was hoping you'd say that!" I reached into my backpack and pulled out a Dolce & Gabbana bag. "Did you know they did baby clothes?" Pulled out a tiny rose-print dress. "And look at these!" I pulled out a pair of baby Timberlands.

She smiled over at me reluctantly.

"Beej." She put her hand on top of mine. "This is a big deal . . ."

"Not really, Parks." I shrugged. "Because we're sorted. By the time we're twenty-one, between us we'll have a bit over a billion dollars in liquid assets." She rolled her eyes but I kept going. "I'm pretty sure most people live on less than that all their lives. I can work for my dad—he'll be stoked—we'll always have money, it'll be fine."

She said nothing. Instead she looked at me with a suspicious hopefulness.

"What are you smiling at?" She shook her head. "We're fucked."

I sniffed a laugh.

"Yeah, but that's kind of what I want—to be fucked. By you, with you, over you—" I shrugged. "Forever."

Got that wish, didn't I?

"Beej, that's a very romantic thing to say, but you're not really thinking about the . . ." She shrugged. ". . . I don't know? Details?"

"And neither should you! That's not the important part!"

"It's definitely the important part—"

"No." I shook my head as I poked her stomach and grinned at her. "That's the important part."

And then she was lost to it.

"We'll make a plan tonight," I told her as I draped my arms around her. Clocked the flowchart properly for the first time. "Woah, this is detailed." I glanced down at her. "Where do I fit in this plan?"

"Oh. You don't." She grimaced. "I thought we broke up."

"You thought wrong."

SEVENTEEN

Magnolia

Tobermory was the plan.

We were going to move up the coast, away from everything back in London, from the eyes and the opinions, and live on a big property up there. Neither of us were going to work because we didn't need to. Instead we'd just make good investments and raise our baby together.

Get married.

We were always going to anyway.

My twelve-week scan (which actually took place on my fifteenth week of pregnancy) was integral because after it we would have those ultrasound photos. With them in hand, we thought we'd tell our parents.

We wanted to prove to them that we could do it by ourselves.

It was my biggest fear that they'd think that just because I still technically had a nanny that I wasn't capable of raising a baby myself. I needed to prove to them that we had this under control, that I didn't need anyone at all except for BJ, and that we were going to be fine.

Beej convinced me we needed Jonah's mum's help.

Rebecca is her name. Rebecca Barnes.

He said she had a doctor friend who would do things privately, quietly and with discretion, which meant looking the other way about me being sixteen. And a Parks.

Beej said we could trust Rebecca and she'd keep our secret forever, and to her credit, she has.

Christian has no idea. I know he has no idea, because if he had an idea he'd never have dated me.

The doctor had a private practice up down in Bristol. Jo's mum offered to come, but we thought we'd be fine. Beej and I left school early on a Wednesday morning. Nearly a four-hour drive.

We spent the whole morning talking about where we'd live and how we'd live and maybe Beej would flip houses because he's always liked houses, and me taking cooking lessons, and he'd finish school, but would I? Maybe I'd go as far as I could and we'd get a nanny for the first year to live at the house with us so I could do long distance and graduate, and then we'd be set.

Our eyes were so starry about everything.

It wasn't a lot of waiting around, Anne was her name—the doctor who looked after us. She took us to an ultrasound room. I lay down and everything felt light and buzzy and exciting.

"This'll be cold." She smiled at me warmly as she squeezed the gel on my stomach.

On the screens in front of us, all black and white, was a teensy baby.

Looked like a baby too.

Not an alien, not a bean, but a proper tiny, little baby. With a fat stomach and little legs and arms.

Beej grabbed my hand, squeezed it all cute and excited, his eyes glued to the screen.

She wriggled the wand around. "Here's the head." She smiled. "And its arms . . . and let's find that heartbeat." She smiled over at me and moved the wand around.

She moved the wand around again.

"Hm." That was the quiet noise she made, and it was only when I peeked over at her that it occurred to me that maybe something was wrong. "I'll be right back."

She gave us a reassuring smile that I didn't trust and then she ducked out.

BJ looked over at me and I know the creases and lines of his face so well—he smiled at me, but it was forced. He felt it too. Something was off.

A minute later, another doctor came back with Anne.

"I'm Doctor Lewis." He smiled warmly, shaking BJ's hand. He glanced up at the monitor, then back at me. "How are you feeling?"

"Fine," I said quietly.

"Any cramps?"

"No."

"Bleeding?"

"No."

I shook my head.

He pursed his lips together before picking up the wand and moving it around slowly—but by then I already knew.

There was no movement.

None at all.

The doctor turned around to face us. "I'm sorry," he said.

I shook my head quickly. "You don't need to say it."

Beej flopped his head back, looking up at the ceiling.

My heart was racing, palms were sweaty. Suddenly it was like I could feel it. Something dead inside of me and it made me sick.

"How?" BJ asked, eyes glassy.

The doctor gave him a tight-lipped smile. "These things just happen sometimes. It's—"

The doctor pulled BJ to the corner. They spoke but I couldn't track what they were saying. I didn't care anyway. My brain was swirling. I thought I was going to faint.

"There are two ways we can proceed," the doctor told me cautiously when he and BJ came back into view. I glanced at Beej, his hand pressed into his mouth. "We can induce you or we can do a D and C."

"People often find inducing gives them more closure," Anne offered.

Beej looked over at me and I shook my head quickly. "Just get it out."

That hit him like a train. I saw it on his face. He'll deny it, say it was up to me, that it was my choice, my body—blah, blah, blah—but I saw it kill him a little that I said that.

But I couldn't do it any other way.

In the few weeks since I'd found out that I was pregnant, I hadn't learned an exceptional amount about labour but I knew enough about it to know that I didn't want to go through that to have no baby at the end. The women who can do that are braver than I was.

After that choice, everything happened so quickly.

They took me away, put me under a general anaesthetic, and then four hours later, our lives—once again—were entirely different than we'd planned for them to be.

Anne was with me the whole time. I don't remember much else.

I remember she helped me get dressed, walked me slowly back out to BJ in the waiting area, him with his red eyes. He was wearing a grey hoodie, I remember that. It hung on him so big, and as he walked me out to the car, his whole body engulfed me in a way that made him feel like he was my hood.

He put me in the car, walking quickly to the driver's side.

"Parks?" he said quietly, watching me closely. "Whatever the fuck you need."

"I don't care," I said, barely.

He nodded, started driving. I cried the whole way back. The whole way.

I didn't even know where we were going.

He laid my car seat down as I curled up and cried. He combed his fingers through my hair and drove and drove.

I don't know why or how, but we ended up back at Dartmouth.

Back to where we made her.

It was a her, by the way. They told us that.

He pulled in, leaving me for a minute to find Mr Gibbs. I don't know what BJ told him, but Gibbs took one look at me, opened the house, put on the fire and the kettle and then left us.

Beej carried me into the house, up the stairs, and into the shower.

He stripped us both down gently and slowly and turned on the water and I remember looking down at my body and everything feeling foreign.

My now empty stomach, like it was all a dream plucked out of me.

The next thing I remember is being in bed.

I don't know how I got there, I don't remember getting there. But I remember a quilt swallowing us both whole, him holding me from behind, and us staying like that for nearly two days.

The morning I first got out of bed after everything, BJ wasn't with me.

I called for him but he wasn't in the house.

And then I saw him out the window. He was lugging a big, flat piece of sandstone and laying it under the willow tree. He lifted his shirt to wipe his face and then covered his mouth with the bend in his elbow, and I saw him take a big, staggered breath, then another, then another. He wiped his face and his tears with his wrist, gruffly, the way boys do when they aren't just wiping away their tears but their feelings as well.

I didn't know what to do when I saw that, or how to comfort him.

We were so spectacularly in over our heads.

I didn't know what to say. I didn't think I was supposed to see what I saw. I just sat on the bed, waiting for him to come in. He did eventually, and we took another shower, and then we went back to bed and stayed one more night.

As we were leaving and Mr Gibbs was sending us off, I turned to him.

"We were never here, do you understand?" My voice was sharper than I meant it to be, but it wasn't sharp with rudeness, just desperation. "Please."

"Yes." Gibbs nodded.

"And that stone he laid," I pointed over to it. "It never moves."

Then Mr Gibbs nodded again, quickly, and even if he didn't know, I knew he understood.

BJ slipped his hand in mine, put me in the car, buckled me in then kissed my nose.

We drove back to London in silence. It was a Saturday night when we arrived home. And holy shit, were our parents mental. Marsaili was practically deranged.

When I arrived on the front steps with BJ standing behind me, she opened the door, yanked me inside and physically body blocked BJ from following me in.

"Leave," she said with a pointed finger. "Now. I don't want to see you near her. Skipping school! Running away! Unacceptable. I'm calling your mother." She slammed the door in his face. "I cannot beli—go to your room," she growled. "Do not speak to that boy, do not call him. Do not sneak him in through your window. I'm nailing it shut. Magnolia Parks, do you hear me? Do not—" Marsaili gave me the darkest eyes she's ever given me—"even dream of contacting him. You will be lucky if you ever see him again."

The thing was, the moment I was in my room, all I did was cry. And not my normal crying. Not crying to get my way, not crying out of insolence or because I was drunk—it was different crying and they could all hear it because I was crying like my heart was broken.

"Magnolia?" Marsaili asked, standing over me. "What happened?" she asked gently, her tone suddenly quite different upon realising that I was different.

But I couldn't tell her. I shook my head as I cried in a way that didn't sound like it was coming from my body.

"Magnolia, darling, are you hurt?" my mother asked as she stroked her hands through my hair and I fought her off.

"Darling, sweetheart," my father whispered, "I want you to tell me what's going on. What do you need?"

"BJ," is all I managed to choke out because even then I knew it was true. He is what I need.

That got Marsaili flared up immediately. "I am not," she

growled. "Am not calling that boy. She can't disappear for half a week and run away with him and have a tantrum when she doesn't get to see him—"

"You think this is a tantrum?" my mum yelled at her—one of the only times I've heard her defend me. "Look at her! She is a shell of who she was when she left here Monday morning."

"Then obviously something's happened!" Mars yelled. "Magnolia, did he hurt you?"

"He would never," my sister whispered from the doorway.

They all kept tag-teaming and trying to get me to calm down, but I'd thrash away from them if they ever got too close.

After a few hours, probably—retrospectively—of being very deep into a very serious panic attack, someone (my money is on Bridget) called BJ.

Lily drove him over and he ran up the stairs, Lil close behind him. I could feel him moving through the house, hear him, before I could see him. He pushed my father out of the way, pulled his sweater up and over his head, discarding it on the floor and just climbed into my bed, pulling me back into him.

Our parents stood at the doorway watching us, so completely baffled at what was happening and why—how we started the week as two separate people then came back at the end of it fused as one. He lay with me, breathed loudly into my ear till my breathing slowed to match his, and then he stayed. Stayed till Monday morning when we went back to school where we lied about our week. Told all our friends we snuck to Cannes to get away from our parents. He went along with it—whatever the fuck I needed, even before that was a thing, it was always our thing.

I thought it always would be.

EIGHTEEN
Magnolia

I'm awake in my mind before my eyes can open—does that happen to you? Where your consciousness runs ahead of your waking, and something in you knows you don't want to be awake, that you shouldn't be awake. It tries to keep you down in the safety of sleep, but waking life is so loud, even when it's quiet it pulls you forward into the light of life even if there is no light, even if all the curtains on all the windows in the whole world have been drawn shut forever.

My eyes blink open eventually.

I don't immediately recognise where I am. In a bed. What room is this? I jerk up.

Then I realise I'm in the master bedroom of the Dartmouth house.

I glance around, panicked.

My sister's sitting on a chair in the corner—mixed knit wrapped cardigan from Alanui, Anine Bing Denver alpaca-blend turtleneck sweater underneath and the Journey cashmere-blend track pants from Extreme Cashmere—her legs tucked under her, cup of tea hugged to her chest.

"Hey." She gives me a gentle smile.

I blink at her a few times. "What are you doing here?"

She puts the cup down.

"Mr Gibbs called me," she says with a frown.

"Oh." I nod once.

She walks over to me, perches on the edge of the bed, looks at her hands. She fiddles with the tip of her index finger, mulling over the words I can tell she wants to say.

She looks over at me. "He said you blacked out."

"Did I?" I try to sound confused. "I must have forgotten to eat breakfast."

"For how many days?" She frowns.

I shake my head. "Not like that—"

"Then what the fuck is going on with you?" My sister shakes her head, annoyed.

"Oh." I wave my hand through the air, let out a tiny laugh. "I'm just a bit scattered—jet lag, you know?"

My sister's eyes pinch. "He said you were hysterical."

I roll my eyes. "You know how I get when I don't sleep a full nine hours."

I'm going to cry. If she keeps pushing me, I'll cry.

"Magnolia."

"What?" I blink a lot.

"Tell me the truth." Bridget's face is serious. "Don't lie to me. Please."

I take a big breath. "Okay."

"Okay?"

I sit up a little.

"But you mustn't tell anyone." I give her a look. "This stays between us, forever."

"Okay." She nods again. She looks nervous. I'm nervous.

I've never said it out loud before except to BJ and that didn't go particularly well. At least not at the start.

I clear my throat once.

"When I was sixteen, BJ and I got pregnant." I give her a curt smile.

She blinks at me.

"Accidentally," I add as an afterthought.

My sister stares over at me. "Oh my God."

"We were going to keep it—"

"Oh my God—"

"She died at around fifteen weeks."

I give my sister a tight smile, restraining all my tears behind it.

"She?" Bridge blinks. Her eyes have gone glassy.

I nod.

"I had a D and C—"

She puts her hands on her face as she stares at me. "Magnolia—"

"It was the weekend we told everyone we went to Cannes, remember? And we got in so much trouble—" I sniff a small laugh at the memory. "And Marsaili said I was forbidden from seeing BJ and—"

"—And you couldn't stop crying." She nods.

I nod. "And you called BJ."

"Well." She shrugs. "You needed him. I could tell."

I nod.

"And who the fuck could get to sleep with all your stupid crying?"

I let out a snotty laugh.

My sister climbs onto the bed next to me, links her arm with mine, leans her head on my head.

"You never showed."

"Yes." I nod. "Apparently I have something called a tilted uterus."

She snorts a laugh. "Of course you do." She peers over at me, flicking my arm absentmindedly. "No one knows?" I fiddle with my earlobe. "No one knows."

Bridget goes quiet for a while. A good few minutes of silence follow, neither of us saying anything. It's nice, actually. Having someone else know and sit with me in it.

She breathes out loudly from her nose and nudges me with her elbow.

"Not to make this about myself—" She gives me a little look. "But I did say trauma bonds with you two, didn't I? Called it a mile off."

I start laughing. It's tired but it's genuine.

And then Bridge gives me an exasperated look. "Holy fuck."

I give her a tiny, tender smile.

"Yes. It was."

NINETEEN

Magnolia

Telling Bridget does something to me. It unlocks something.

A lot of things, actually. Ranging from relief to grief to freedom and sadness, maybe even a bit of capriciousness that probably shouldn't be there.

She says she'll drive me home that afternoon.

I recline the chair of my father's Brabus G63 that I took without telling him back as far as it will go and curl up, facing my sister.

She glances down at me then back at the road.

"Why didn't you ever tell anyone?"

I purse my lips.

"Keep a secret long enough and it keeps you."

She nods, checks her rearview mirror.

"Probably at first we thought we'd be in trouble, you know? Like, they were so cross that night we got home."

She sniffs a smile.

"Marsaili especially. And I didn't want her to do anything dramatic or say we were bad for each other or something. Which she would have done. But we weren't bad for each other—" I purse my lips. "We were just . . . for each other."

"Are you upset he didn't come?" She watches my face closely.

I shift my position, let out a breath I didn't know I'd been holding.

"Yes." I sigh. "I mean, he was there. He left the flowers. Mr Gibbs saw him. He just didn't want to see me, I guess."

She shakes her head. "Can't be."

"He has a girlfriend now, Bridge." I shrug. "Maybe he's moving on."

"From you?" She blinks then shakes her head once. "In no world."

I look out the window.

Wonder how to unlove him.

If I even could.

I'll wear it like a badge of honour forever that he loved me first, that he loved me at all. Have you ever had a love like that? I always felt like the luckiest girl to have his eyes on me, his hands on me. And his mouth. I love that mouth.

I think I need a drink.

"What's she like?" Bridget asks.

"Who?" I look over, grateful for the hand up from the quicksand of my brain.

"Lizzo," she deadpans.

"Oh." I frown then shrug. "Yeah, I mean she's pretty fun. Bit overzealous with the flute the way woodwind musicians tend to be, but a great time nevertheless."

"His girlfriend, you absolute twat."

"Oh!"

She gives me a look.

"Oh, she's fine."

"She's fine?"

"Yeah." I shrug. "She's fine."

"Pretty as you?"

I pick something out of my eye and look at it. "Don't be ridiculous."

She smirks.

"She sort of gives me the energy of a person who would voluntarily dine in a coffee shop named something stupid like 'Eggshellant'." I shake my head at my own assumption. "And I can't help but wonder what that says about a person. I mean, that's not just manifesting eggshells to be in your food but I dare say it is in fact demanding it."

"That's your read on her?" Bridget blinks. "Bad coffee-shop vibe?"

"Yeah." I shrug a bit helplessly. "Bit tasteless."

"Okay taste in boys, though—"

"BJ isn't taste in boys, he is boys." I roll my eyes. "Everyone who likes boys likes BJ."

"I don't." She gives me a curt smile.

"Firstly, you absolutely had a crush on him your first year at school—"

"Definitely did." She nods. "He was so hot." She pauses to think on that. "Yuck!" She pulls a face. "Why'd you remind me of that?"

I roll my eyes.

"Are you threatened by her?"

"Well, she's the only person he's ever dated besides me, so yes, I suppose . . ."

Bridget stares at the road for a few seconds before asking ultrabrightly, "So why do you think he likes her?"

"I don't know." I shrug.

"Maybe she's wild in bed."

I give her a look. "Bridget—"

"I'm serious. Someone like him, that's probably a consideration."

"What do you mean 'someone like him'?" I frown defensively.

"Oh, I mean a big old slurry."

I chew down on my thumbnail without thinking. "Was he bad while I was gone?"

She makes an exasperated sound with her mouth as she shoots me a look. "You'd think he was trying to break some kind of record."

I scrunch up my face. I feel sadder again, like I'm losing him more. I don't know to how many different people and in how many different ways I've lost him, but the feeling is familiar. I've been feeling it in some way or another for the last almost-five years. Sometimes I think it might feel like falling down a really deep well. Every bump and stone I hit on the way down is a different person and mistake we've made—he's made—and I never seem to hit the floor of losing him. I just keep falling further away from the daylight of our maybe-one-day.

"I wasn't very wild in bed," I tell the window.

"You don't say," she tells the road sarcastically. I glare over at her but she doesn't seem to notice.

"Maybe she's just a really great person," Bridget offers.

"Maybe." I nod, a bit deflated.

"She's from Australia, right?"

"Yeah."

"Guys love Australians because they're super chill, easy-going, which has got to be at least a little bit of a relief to him, because with you, you're a h—"

"Bridge—"

"What?" She looks over at me and recognises the despair on my face. "Fuck. Sorry—" She flashes me an apologetic look. "You are though."

"Bridget." I sigh.

"You are a handful, Magnolia, but he'll love you forever anyway."

But he might not. Those magnolias on the stone. With him and me, it's never just been just any old reason to touch me, but any reason to see me and to be around me and to hover by me. He had a reason and he passed on it.

"I need a drink," I tell her.

She gives me a look. "Actually, I think you need several."

And that's how I end up at Buckley's (one of Jonah's clubs) with my sister a few hours later.

Schmammered.

Me, not her. Bridget's not much of a drinker. I've only seen her drunk a few times. We all do our best to keep her sober because Bridget full-blown drunk is very honest—scathingly honest. She got so drunk Christmas Day last year in New York and she told Harley that she thought he'd 'sexually regret' divorcing our mum but emotionally he'd probably made the right choice. She told Tom that he was the better man but she hoped he was prepared to play second-fiddle forever—delivered it to him like she was telling him the weather outside, so matter-of-fact.

She doesn't take hostages. There are never any winners.

She tried to buzz BJ up into my building when he flew in to win me back. Harley body blocked him from coming inside. I think they had a fight?

Sober Bridget would never do that, so just as a safety precaution for us all, no one ever over-serves Bridget.

I have been over-served though. I've over-served myself.

I am completely plastered.

And I don't know how we ended up at Buckley's, or why she agreed to take me—it's probably the baby thing.

The baby thing is why I'm drunk.

And the BJ thing.

But aren't they actually—when you think of it—one and the same?

We've been here I don't know how long, because before we were at a bar.

I look very pretty—obviously. We went home first. I'm wearing a yellow and pink tweed off-shoulder minidress from Oscar de la Renta and Bridget said it was too cold to wear it so I definitely wore it, and even though I paired it with the double-breasted brushed wool and cashmere-blend coat from Sergio Hudson, I didn't put it on because having a sister is weird and I wanted to spite her even if it was at the cost of myself, and during the five-second walk from the town car to the club I thought probably I was about to die from hypothermia.

I look great. It doesn't matter that I look great, it's just me and my sister, but I can't not look great in case of photos. There aren't a great many things I can control in this lifetime —I'm learning this now at the ripe old age of twenty-four. I can't control how you see me, but I can control how I will be seen. And you will only ever see me very put together. You don't need to know about the parts of me that aren't.

I have a distinct feeling that were the public to know about my weaknesses they would be used against me. I watched it happen last year when everyone found out about Paili. You'd think people might be respectful or even just considerate of how that might have hurt me. Listen to me: You must never read the comment section of a photograph you post of yourself and a boy who isn't the boy the world wants you to be with.

You should probably just never read the comments.

Bridget let me dress her but she refused to wear a dress. Fucking typical. But I did what I could—Francis colour-block merino wool cardigan from Alex Mill, the white Lucien cotton-voile shirt from Khaite, black Palace fit trousers from Philipp Plein and Dolce & Gabbana's leopard-print open-toe sandals.

Time goes slippery for me the way it goes when you've had too much, and halfway through my third fight with a complete stranger, Bridget calls for back-up.

I see Taura first, gliding over to me with the speed, grace and dexterity of what—to me, in this moment—feels like an Olympic figure-skater, but to a regular person might just be normal walking.

"Tausie!" I beam up at her in her bright pink Hailey open-back chainmail minidress from Fannie Schiavoni.

"Babe!" She blinks, looking from me to Bridget. "Wow."

Bridget gives her an exasperated look and I frown at her. Then my sister looks past Taura's shoulder.

"Oh, God—" Bridget rolls her eyes. "You brought the whole cavalry?"

Taura sighs, annoyed. "I tried to shake them. Someone—" she gives my sister a pointed look that goes over my head—"who I think was attempting to be subtle actually made it very clear he felt it necessary he come."

"How does someone's girlfriend feel about that?" Bridget asks under her breath.

"Not good." Taura gives her a look.

Taurs holds my face in her hands and smiles down at me. "How are you feeling, baby girl?"

I open my mouth to say something but then I see him behind her—my heavy head drops to the side, peering at him. Our eyes catch and he buries a smile as he walks over to me a bit gingerly.

"Heard you were on the lash." He smiles down at me, amused.

"That feels like it might be a rude thing to say to someone as fancy as I am." I blink up at him and he sniffs a laugh.

Brown YMC Military buttoned shirt over a plain white tee from Visvim, black Cutoff Cargo Pant from Dickies, and the Golden Brown and True White Old Skools. He looks so handsome and I want to touch his face but I shouldn't, so I drape my arms over Henry instead.

"My favourite Ballentine in the world," I say and give BJ an intense glare. He just rolls his eyes. "And Christian! And Jonah! And—" I spot Jordan. "Oh."

And then I frown. Fully frown. Right in her face. I don't mean to, but my social filters have gone to shit.

Henry buries a smile.

"Parks," BJ grabs my eye, holding it with his own. "You remember Jordan."

"Mm," I say, flashing her a quick, annoyed smile.

She gives BJ a sharp look.

Jonah tosses an arm around me, pulling me towards the bar. "So, you like me again?"

I bobble my head around. "You're on prevention."

"You mean 'probation'?"

I shrug. "Could be."

"You mean do? Could do?"

"Corrections shan't help you."

"Noted." He nods once. "Can I get a round of shots, please?" he says to the bartender (and mouths "water" over my head, pointing at me).

"How do I win you back, Parks?"

"You could find me a time machine and go backwards in it and stop your stupid best friend from being stupid infinity times and stop yourself from being a trickster liar." I give him a short smile.

"I could try." He grimaces. "Or could I not just buy you a bag or something?"

"A bag?" I stare at him, horrified.

"A car," he says quickly.

"You used to buy me a bag every week on Baggy Tuesday —that's why you called it that."

"That—it actually wasn't—that was something else that you hijacked."

"Hijacked!" I growl.

"Made better!" He shakes his head. "Made so much better. Your bags are . . . better. Healthier! For me. Maybe not on the cows—"

I frown at him, confused, and Jonah nudges me. "Go on —be my friend again."

I move in close to him, right into his ear and whisper, "Do you like her?"

He pulls back a little, looks at me amused. "She's alright." He shrugs, indifferent. "Nothing on you though."

Jonah carries the shots back to our roped-off area and we all drink them, but I drink two because I know Jonah's tricks —he's been ordering me water shots since I was fifteen.

BJ's girlfriend is sitting as close to him as she can get without actually being on his lap. She's touching him—his wrists, his hands, his hair—and each one tears me up a little—the only okay part is the part where his eyes are just on mine.

She's whispering things to him, and he's looking at her quickly, acknowledging what she's saying, nodding, barely paying attention, I think, because he's paying attention to me.

I give him a little smile from the other side of our table.

He licks his bottom lip. Smiles a tiny bit back. Swallows nervously. Glances back at his girlfriend.

She slips her hand onto his lap and catches me looking at him.

I glance away quickly, casting all my attention instead onto Henry.

"Why are you this drunk?" he asks, amused.

"Bad day," I tell him. "Bad week, actually—"

He tilts his head, all sad for me, my old best friend. "Yeah? You want to tell me what happened?"

I give him a tired smile, because I think I'm tired of all of it now. "I can't."

"You can't tell me?" He sniffs a laugh. "Magnolia, you tell me everything . . ."

I shake my head at him. "Yes, except this one specific thing because BJ and I said we would never tell anyone, literally no one, which even means you, did you know? Which was very difficult for me as I'm sure you could imagine because I am a blabber mouth to you—"

"Yes, you are." He nods, curious.

I give a big shrug. "But a promise is a promise, isn't it? And I promised, even though it was the worst, which was good of me I think, don't you?"

He nods, barely concealing a smirk.

"But then—" I consider. "I guess he breaks promises a bit, doesn't he?"

Henry nods. "He's been known to . . ."

"I suppose there was no outward promise that he wouldn't cheat on me, but in my naivety I just assumed it was a tacit agreement."

"Your naïvety?" he repeats, amused.

I shake my head at myself. "Should have got it in writing . . ."

He shakes his head again. "No, you shouldn't have."

I blink a lot and Henry's face falters, curious.

"Oi," says my favourite voice in the world as he sidles up next to me, eyes bright.

"Hi." I grin up at him. "Where's Australia?"

"Southern Hemisphere." I roll my eyes at him because that was terrible. Even I know that was terrible in my current state. "The bathroom."

126

"Oh—" I give him a look. "So she's coming back, then?"

BJ smirks, liking the attention. "Yep."

He takes a step closer to me, holding my eyes. "Thought you flew out?"

I shrug in a manner that to me feels demure, but in real life I'm sure looks a bit like I'm having a stroke. "I didn't feel like it."

"Why?" BJ asks.

I hold his eyes. "You know why."

He shakes his head. "No, I don't."

I sigh. It's big and loud and annoyed and dramatic, and the words that follow are said louder than I really mean to. "Because it's our worst day."

He glances around us, a bit self-conscious now, but his eyes soften. "Are you sad, Parks?"

I lean in close to his ear, so close my mouth is against it. "I'm always sad, Beej."

He shifts a little—our faces are so close-—-I wonder how it looks to everyone around us. Does it look as intimate as it feels?

"About that?" His gaze flickers from my eyes to my mouth to my eyes.

I nod once, decidedly. "And you," I offer as an afterthought.

He pulls back a little, gives me a sad smile. "And me?" I give him a big, single nod. He tilts his head. "What about me, Parks?"

"Oh, everything about you . . ." I sigh, drunk. "What we were . . . What we aren't . . . What we made . . ."

His face flickers in surprise as he glances over his shoulder to see if anyone heard. They didn't. "Hey—" he whispers, brows low.

"Hey." I smile up at him with bleary eyes.

He swallows and his eyes look worried now. "Are you okay?"

Jordan's back now. She's trying to play it cool, not hovering on us exactly, just hovering adjacent. I stare at her for a few seconds. My eyes might be starting to fill with tears. "I'm—I am good. I'm sensational. Fine. I'm totally fine—" I nod. "And I'm actually good! Are you?" I look at him, waiting for an answer, but he's just frowning at me. "Do you like my dress?"

He glances down at it. "I do," he says quietly, quiet enough that the girlfriend can't hear him.

"I thought of you when I put it on," I tell him.

A little smile rolls over that mouth I love. "Did you?"

"Yes." I stare up at him, unflinching. "And I thought, 'I wonder if I wear this if he'll think about undressing me'."

He swallows. "Oh."

"Did it work?" I beam up at him.

His eyes drag down my body like I wish his hands would. They stay low for a few seconds then they flick back up to mine, pressing his thumb into his mouth.

Yes, is the answer his mouth won't say.

He breathes out, shoving his hands through his hair. "Parks, how drunk are you?"

"Oh." I shrug airily. "Like, not very. The good amount. But very not very." I pause and look at him. "Hey, do you want to have sex later?"

Henry spits out his drink and I turn to look at him, surprised. I didn't realise he was listening.

"Henry Austin," I scold. "Pull it together."

Hen starts laughing and I'd actually forgotten anyone else was in the room. I forgot that we were in a room and not on the secret island BJ and I live on in my imagination where we're all alone and no outside forces endanger our tenuous, impossible connection.

BJ laughs. "Wow!"

Henry's still sputtering away in his half-laugh, half-choke. I frown a little. "What?"

He gives me a crooked smile with tall eyebrows. "I have a girlfriend, remember?"

"Oh—" My shoulders slump. "Right."

"Right." He nods.

128

"But do you really though?" I frown up at him.

"Yeah."

"Really?"

"Yeah." He nods his head at Jordan who is—regrettably—listening rather closely. "That's her."

"Oh, hello." I re-notice her. "Again."

She glares over at me. You know how when you're sober and you're with someone drunk, they're particularly annoying? I imagine it's directly like that except for infinity times worse because I'd imagine she'd find me particularly annoying at the best of times.

("She's just drunk," Beej whispers to her. "No shit." She rolls her eyes. "That's not the problem." BJ crosses his arms over his chest. "What is the problem?" Jordan stares at him like he's an idiot, then waves her hand in my direction. "She wants you." But BJ shakes his head. "Not really, though," he tells her. And I don't know whether he knows how untrue that really is.)

"I like your dress," I tell her to throw her off my scent.

"I'm wearing jeans," she tells me, unimpressed.

"Oh." I cringe. "Great jeans."

("Doesn't she know denim is the working man's material though?" I whisper (unintentionally) too loudly to Henry, who gives me a long-suffering look.)

Jordan rolls her eyes at me and walks away. BJ gives me an exasperated look and goes after her. I frown, hating that I have to watch him go after anyone but me. It's just me. It should be anyway. I plonk down onto the couch. Pour myself a vodka and vodka.

"You good?" Henry nods at my glass.

"Hm?" I stare at him a bit blankly. "Oh, this? No, yeah—I'm great."

"Yeah?"

"Mmhm."

"That was a lot of alcohol for a girl who swears she got drunk off of chocolate liquors once."

"I think actually I was hypoglycemic."

Henry shakes his head once. "You weren't."

"Could have been—" I shrug but Henry shakes his head again. "Couldn't have been."

"Does he love her?" I ask loudly.

Henry glances over at his brother who's a few metres away and having an obvious row with his girlfriend, who I think is probably a bitch, because no one gets to growl at him but me.

"No." He shakes his head.

"Do you love Taura?" I ask equally as loud—loud enough that both Jonah and Taura glance over at us, as I keep going. "It's okay if you do, you can tell me, I won't even tell—" then Henry laughs nervously as he clamps his giant paw of a hand over my mouth to silence me.

"What the fuck—" He gives me a 'shut up' look. Then he shakes his head and scoffs. "You're a little wrecking ball tonight, aren't you? Holy shit," he tells me as he nods back towards BJ, who's walking towards us now, with no Jordan in sight. "You good?" Henry nods.

Beej gives Henry a misplaced glare before he sits down next to me. "You're a fucking pain, Parks." He sighs as he throws his arm around the chair behind me.

"Where'd she go?" I blink innocently.

"She left."

"Oh." I sigh, pretend-sad. "Why?"

"Because we're having our first ever fight, thanks to you."

I feel clever and not one bit guilty. He can tell so he digs in more.

"Do you know how hard it is to fight with someone that chilled out? And then three words from you, and it's fucking bedlam."

I shrug because I don't care because now he's here just for me all to myself.

"Whatever happened to that Bible proverb?" I look between them brightly and Henry shakes his head, confused. "You know the one, um, 'Always let the sun set on an argument'."

"Not a proverb." BJ shakes his head.

"If it was good enough for Jesus—" ("It wasn't," Henry clarifies)—"it's good enough for me!"

"That actually explains a lot about our last year," BJ says quietly to his brother, thinking I can't hear him but I can, except I don't even know what he means so whatever.

"Well, if you aren't going to listen to the Bible, just go after her, then," I tell him lightly.

BJ's eyes pinch at my hollow dare.

"Yeah, Beej—" Henry chides. "Go after her, then."

BJ gives his brother a long look that if I were sober, I'd know was very much about me, but I'm not looking at how BJ's looking at other people, I'm just looking at his mouth like it's a piece of steak. Beej nods his chin at Henry. "Why don't you just fuck off for a little bit, good for nothing." Henry chuckles and turns to talk to Jonah.

Beej watches after him for a second, I think maybe assessing the level of our aloneness. I wriggle in towards him, tossing a leg over his. He stares at it for a few seconds—maybe counting in his mind all the lines we're crossing to be how we're being—then he moves himself in closer to me.

"Why are you this drunk?" he asks me, resting his hands on my legs in a way I don't think is absentminded.

"You know why." I frown. "You didn't come."

He gives me a gentle look. "I did, we just missed each other."

"But we never don't do it together." My mouth sags.

"Do what together?" Jonah asks brightly, leaning in towards us.

"Nothing," BJ says quickly at the same time as I say, "December 3rd."

Jonah pulls back, curious. "And what's December 3rd, Parks?"

"Nothing." BJ shakes his head dismissively, but I lean over him to speak to his best friend. BJ's hands move with my body, from my lap to my back.

"It's just the most important date in our relationship mythology." I give him a drunk smile.

131

"Oh." Jonah smirks, catching his best friend's eye just to shit him. "Tell me more."

"Parks—" Beej whispers, his mouth right up against my ear. I look at him.

"We could tell them," I whisper.

"Tell them what?" Jonah asks, but we're ignoring him now. My eyes are locked on BJ's. "I told Bridget."

("Told Bridget what?" Jonah grumps, but Beej shoves him away without even looking at him.)

His face has gone quite serious. He ducks his eyes down to mine so we're level.

"Did you?"

I nod.

"How come?" he asks gently.

I stare at him for a few seconds, suddenly feeling a bit drunker than I'd like to be.

"Because I blacked out at the tree so Gibbs called her and then I had to."

He blinks a couple of times. "You blacked out?"

I say nothing; his eyes wander over my face, brows low. If I was sober I might have been able to see it—everything between us, all the ties that bind, our two smashed-up hearts on the floor and we can't even tell our pieces apart anymore but we're the only glue we need so it doesn't matter anyway— maybe if I was sober, and I could see it for what it was, I would have felt the rustle of the universe telling me everything is going to be okay.

"Were you drinking then too?" he asks.

"No, just crying." I shrug.

His heart breaks a little on his face right there in front of me. "Parks—"

I lean on his shoulder. "Will you take me home now?"

TWENTY
BJ

She was a little hot mess tonight, and I mean that in every way possible.

I probably should have gone after Jordan—didn't.

Probably shouldn't have come home with Parks either—did.

Felt like I had to a bit though.

She's a mess because of a mess we made together, and I should have been there. Should have known she'd never miss it too.

Parks starts throwing up when I get her home.

"You can go," Bridge tells me as she watches Magnolia throw up in a £50,000 Qing Dynasty vase.

I let out a dry laugh and nod towards her sister.

"Bridge, I think this is going to require the touch of a professional."

She smirks, gives me a dry look. "You are a professional at touching my sister."

I squash down a laugh, remind myself that I have a girlfriend and the night can't go how I wish it could.

Bridget starts walking up the stairs, then stops midway up and looks back at me.

"Are you okay?"

I look up at her. I know what she means, what she's really asking.

"Yeah." I nod. "Thanks."

I give her a small smile and then Magnolia starts vomiting again, fracturing the moment.

Bridget laughs as she jogs up the stairs. "Good luck with that."

I scoop Parks up in my arms. "Come on."

Carry her up the stairs. I love these stairs. I've missed these stairs. I have a thing for her and stairs, don't know why.

Actually, I do. I used to think about asking her to marry me on the Spanish Steps in Rome about a hundred years ago when I was allowed to think about marrying her.

Back then, I thought I'd have married her by now, but instead I'm carrying her to her bathroom so she can throw up again because we still haven't sorted our fucking shit out.

I place her down by the toilet. She grabs the bowl, starts chucking up again.

I kneel behind her, hold her hair back till she stops.

She rests her head on her arms on top of the toilet, all exhausted and shit—hair's a mess, eyes are smudged.

She stares over at me.

I tilt my head. "How are you feeling?"

She blinks a couple of times then musters a smile. "Like the prettiest girl in the room."

I nod once.

"In every room, Parks," I tell her but she won't remember.

That chuffs her a bit.

Pushes herself up off the ground, walks to the sink and starts vigorously washing her face.

I walk over, take the face cloth from her hands and wash her myself. Laser-focus on those cheeks of hers I used to know so well and graze so often. My finger lags behind the cloth, tracing the hollowing indent of her cheekbone, and I wonder if she's okay or if this is a thing again.

She watches me, quiet. Eyes big. Looks like that deer I love.

I can't look at her though because if I do I'll kiss her and that's not who I'm trying to be anymore.

You're with Jordan, I remind myself.

You're with Jordan and none of this is real. She's leaving in a few days.

134

Magnolia reaches out, touches my face with her hand.

I find her eyes, kiss her palm twice and lock this moment away in my brain forever in case it's a dying breed.

I wake up the next morning with Magnolia peering down from her bed at me on the floor.

"What are you doing down there?" She frowns.

I rub my eyes, tired.

"I, um—" Clear my throat. "This felt like the safest option."

"Safer how?" She sits up quickly but immediately grabs her head in pain, closes her eyes again.

"You right there, booze hound?" I ask as I sit next to her on her bed.

She glances at me. Repeats the question. "Safer how?"

"Safer like, you're the most handsy girl in England when you're drinking Sambuca."

Her eyes go wide. "Oh no."

I let out a dry laugh. "Turns out," I clear my throat again, "drunk you still remembers all my—" clear my throat one more time—"buttons."

Her mouth makes an O shape before she snaps it shut, embarrassed.

We sit there like that for probably a minute, and I'm fucking living for it, swanning around doing the backstroke in it.

Because I never get to be the one who didn't fuck up, didn't do the embarrassing shit, and she's sitting there dying over it all because she's the one who came on to me.

"Do you still remember my . . . buttons?" she asks quietly before looking up.

I press my mouth together, squash away a smile that shouldn't be there.

"Nah," I lie as my eyes touch all the places that are seared into my mind.

Her cheeks go pink and then she looks down at herself—checkered full-length pyjamas—then back over at me.

"The Thelma and Leah Gingham cotton pyjamas." Her eyes pinch, curious. "Interesting choice."

I give her a shrug. "Didn't want you to think I was being opportunistic."

She gives me a playful look. "Are you saying you don't think I look sexy in this?"

I tuck my chin, eye her back. "No, I think you look sexy in everything," I tell her even though I shouldn't. She swallows and goes back to looking nervous.

I turn towards her.

"Parks, listen—" I swallow, a bit nervous. She looks over at me, curious.

Tucks her legs up under her. "Last night, in front of everyone, you were doing a lot of talking about . . . everything . . ." I trail off.

She frowns at me, confused.

I tilt my head. "Like, what we've been through and shit. December 3rd. 'We can tell them', that kind of thing." I breathe out, glance at my phone. The boys are nagging like old ladies to tell me what the fuck she was going on about. "You said it enough times that they're all asking questions."

Her face crumples up, a little gasp.

"Oh God—I'm so sorry." Hands fly to her cheeks. "Are you so cross at me?"

"No, Parks." I shake my head, take her hand in mine. "Not at all. I think we've kept it to just us for long enough. We can tell them now." I nod at her. "Should, probably."

She looks far away in her mind as she nods a little.

"Are you going to tell Jordan?"

I grimace.

"I mean—I probably should, shouldn't I?" I shrug.

"I beg your pardon?" She scowls at me. "Tell some girl we've known for like a day and a half our most secret thing in the world?"

I give her a look. "I mean, I've known her more than a day and a half."

Her face is dark, glaring at me, but it's not just angry, it's nervous.

I lick my bottom lip. "You don't want me to?"

She shakes her head and something about how her face goes reminds me of her when she was sixteen with that kid of ours growing inside of her and I remember again that the truth is—for me—when it comes to her, it's always going to be whatever the fuck she needs.

"Okay." I nod once.

Her face softens and she blinks a few times. "Do you promise?"

I nod again, giving her a quick smile.

"Yeah, I promise."

She leans in, kisses me on the cheek.

"I'm going to book The Bingham Riverhouse for five. We'll tell them then, yeah?" She nods obediently and I stand up. "Where are you going?" she asks, again with those big eyes.

I wipe my mouth with my hand, feeling the urge to stay— she wants me to; I could. I should, maybe.

But nothing's different, she's still leaving tomorrow so I'll still leave now.

"Yeah—" I give her a bit of a grimace. "I've probably got some smoothing over to do with Jordan."

"Oh."

She nods.

"Especially if I'm about to have to tell her I'm having dinner with all our friends and she's not invited." I sniff a laugh and Magnolia cringes apologetically.

"Go well, then." She gives me a little frown.

I nod at her, fight the urge to kiss her.

"I'll see you tonight."

I head straight from Parks' to Jordan's.

Ring the doorbell. She buzzes me in. She's shitty as hell, but she lets me in anyway.

"Hey," I say, closing the door behind me.

She folds her arms over her chest. "Hi."

"You okay?" I slip my arms around her waist. Don't really know why? I just do it and she lets me. She's so much easier than Magnolia is. Gets over shit quickly, doesn't make me work for it—something I kind of like about working for it though.

"No." She rolls her eyes.

I lick my bottom lip. "I'm sorry."

"You didn't call me," she tells me.

That's true, I didn't.

"You didn't call me either," I tell her.

Which I was grateful for. Couldn't have juggled them both last night.

Jordan looks up at me, eyes big and worried.

"Were you with her?"

I swallow, nod. "Yes."

She glares up at me, holds me tighter.

"She needed me," I tell her.

"I needed you!" she yells.

"Why?" I frown at her. "For what?"

"For what?" She blinks like I'm an idiot. "I'm your girlfriend. Do you know how embarrassing it was to stand there watching your ex falling all over you and you just lapping it up?"

"Jords." I give her a look. "She's my oldest friend in the world."

She looks at me, obstinate. "She's the love of your life."

My jaw sets and I don't know what to say.

She said it, not me.

I don't correct her either, know that I probably should, and it flags me as interesting that she doesn't even flinch when I don't.

I shake my head. "I can't explain it—"

"Try." She shrugs, unmoved. She crosses her arms and I sigh. "We have so much history. Too much—" I catch her eye to soften the blow, try to make it sound like having too much history with Magnolia Parks isn't the mounted deer I'll hang in the hallway of who I am, like loving her isn't the first thing you see when you walk through the door of me.

"Just . . . there are parts of it all that are catching up to us, and it's hard for her," I tell her, catch her eyes, give her

138

a look I know makes Parks weak at the knees. Give it a go here, see if it puts me in the clear. "For both of us."

Jordan's face softens and she sighs.

"There's just one more thing we have to tie off—"

Jordan rolls her eyes at that.

"We're going to do it this afternoon—"

"This afternoon!" she says, exasperated, but I shake my head at her quickly.

"This afternoon, and then it's done and she'll be heading back to New York."

She lifts a suspicious eyebrow. "Really?"

"Yep." I nod, and she doesn't notice when the fucking lorry drives through her living room and runs me over. Or is that just how it feels when I think about Parks being gone again?

Jordan's eyes pinch at me. "And we'll go back to you asking me to say swear words in my accent?"

"Yep." I smile as I slip my arms around her waist and pull her in towards me, remind myself there are worse things.

She lets out a big sigh. "Fine. Can you at least tell her that her dress is last season or something?"

"Fuck no—" I snort a laugh. "I don't have a death wish."

TWENTY-ONE
BJ

I knew she'd be nervous so I wait out front for her to arrive.
She gets here late.

I reckon she was probably hoping she'd get here and I'd have already told them, but I want to do it together. Felt important.

She looks like a kid again climbing out of that town car. My sweater hanging off all loose on her body—this Gucci navy and red jumper from a few years back that was big on me—fucking swimming on her—little navy skirt, a coat in the same colours as my jumper and bright red shoes.

I nod my chin at her—try my best not to read into her wearing it—give her a big smile, try to make her feel braver.

"Wondered where that went."

She gives me a quick smile and I feel like she's wearing it as a shield.

She tugs my jacket together, doing the buttons of it up—frowning—undoes them again. Touching me just to touch me.

"Logo-embroidered varsity jacket. Saint Laurent," she says to no one in particular.

I tilt my head at her. "How's the weather, Parks?"

She breathes out a nervous laugh. "A bit choppy."

Don't know why, but I'm a bit nervous too. They're our best friends.

"They can't ground us." I nudge her playfully.

She looks up at me all grim.

I turn, hold her by both shoulders, stare down at her. "We don't have to do this." She nods a little. "Only if you want to," I tell her.

"Do you want to?" she asks, eyes big.

I sort of nod and shrug at once. "It's time, maybe?"

She nods again. I offer her my hand. She looks at it for a second but takes it anyway.

We walk over to our table—the boys and Tausie—all of them staring at our hands in each other's.

"Holy shit—" Jo blinks, staring at it. "Are you two?"

"No," Magnolia says quickly, looking embarrassed. She snatches her hand back.

Fucking Jonah.

She sits down next to my brother, I sit next to her.

If we weren't about to deliver some soul-crushing information to them I'd be laughing at them. All four of them sitting there, staring at us, confused.

Parks looks over at me.

"Me or you?"

I chuck her a small smile. "Me."

I put my arm around her chair. Around her, if I'm honest, but we're calling it the chair because that'd go down easier with the girlfriend if this ever came up. It won't.

"Right, so—" I glance over my shoulder, make sure no one is listening who shouldn't be, then clear my throat. "In high school, me and Parks got pregnant."

All their faces freeze.

"By accident!" Magnolia adds like that changes anything or makes it better. I throw her an amused smile.

"It wasn't planned—" I give her a little nod. "I was seventeen nearly eighteen. She was sixteen. We were going to keep it. We lost it."

"Fuck," Henry says, blinking a bunch and looking between us.

She gives him a weak smile. Not telling my brother was hard for her sometimes, I could always tell. Unnatural for them, really.

"We lost it a bit along—about fifteen weeks. Parks had to get an operation. It was a bit of an ordeal." I can't help but look at her proudly. "We told you all we went to Cannes."

"Oh, shit—" Jonah nods. "I remember that."

Christian has his hands on his face, looks a bit sick as he glances up at me.

"Fuck, man—if I'd known—"

"No, I know." I nod. He doesn't have to say it. "It's good. We're good."

"Do you know whether it was a boy or a girl?" Taura asks delicately.

Parks smiles. "A girl."

"A girl," Jo coos, face all mush how you wouldn't think a gang lord's would be.

Henry's pretty still and Parks's eyes are on him, big and round.

"Are you angry?" she asks quietly.

His face is tight and he doesn't say anything at first, just blinks twice.

"A bit." He folds his arms, looking between us. "Why didn't you say anything?"

Parks glances over at me then back to my brother, her bottom lip turned down.

"It wasn't really a very easy thing to say."

"Right." He nods once, still frowning, but picks up her hand with his. I feel jealous of him, if I'm honest. Touching her so freely, not having to jump through hoops and make up shit about chairs to do it.

"Oi, but this is inner-circle shit. We're not telling anyone."

"—Please," Magnolia tacks on.

"Only people in the world who know now are you all, Bridget and actually," I flick my eyes from Jo to Christian, "your mum."

"What the fuck?" Jonah frowns.

"It turns out when you run a particular kind of business, you have to know a particular kind of doctor who might be willing to look the other way for particular sums of money," Magnolia says very delicately.

"Ah." Jonah nods once and gives me a look over her head. Don't know whether Jo's ever known that she knows. "So just us, Mum and Bridge, then?"

I nod.

"No Jordan?" Taura asks curiously.

Parks shakes her head. "No."

Jo and I catch eyes.

"Why are you telling us now?" Christian glances between us.

I shrug. "Felt like time? Plus—" I nod my head at Magnolia. "Blabbermouth over here last night practically told you all anyway."

Henry shakes his head, face all pinched. "This actually fills in a lot of blanks."

Christian nods. "Yeah, it does."

"I would have found your 'lost years' a lot less annoying if I knew about this," Jonah announces.

"And what, pray tell," Parks leans forward, chin in her hand my brother isn't holding, "are our 'lost years'?"

Jo gives her a wink. "You're in 'em, baby."

Parks rolls her eyes; I catch them at the end and give her a quick smile.

"Did you have any names?" Tausie asks as she smacks Jo.

Parks and I look at each other, and her face lights up a little. It's nice. Watching her get to unfold nine years of thoughts in the open light.

"We talked about it . . . before . . . before when—" She swallows. "We never decided anything. But—" She glances back at me. "I know what I think her name was. Do you?"

I lick my bottom lip and lift up my shirt, flashing tattoo number nine, the name in tiny writing running along one of my ribs.

"Billie?" My brother grins.

Parks nods once, her eyes all soft, her whole face just a giant beating heart that I want to keep inside my chest.

"Why Billie?" Taura tilts her head. "I mean, I love it, but—"

"Our first date," Parks says, just looking at me. "It was at my grand parents' anniversary. We danced to Billie Holiday."

"I'll Be Seeing You." I'm just looking at her.

I can't believe she's leaving tomorrow.

I force a weak smile because I worry what might happen if I don't.

Henry catches my eye then holds up his glass. "To Billie."

Everyone says, raising theirs, "To Billie."

Magnolia presses her face into my shoulder for a second, and I wish no one was here and it was just us, how it should be, and we're talking about her finally how we never really got to do, just around her, like we're scared to say her name —I guess we have been. Then I hear Parks sniff before she pulls back and smiles at them all brilliantly, cheersing them all.

"I'll see you at home." Jonah nods his chin at me once we're winding up. He walks over to Parks, kisses her on the cheek, then walks away.

Everyone else has gone. I nod towards the river.

"A dander?"

She nods. I shove my hands into my pockets because it's all I can do to stop myself from holding her. "Happy with how it went?"

She nods.

"You were very brave," she tells me in a way that makes me broader and I wish I could kiss her.

"You have a good trip?" I ask her instead.

She nods again, cheeks pink. From the cold or me, I don't know.

"So you're probably heading off then, right?" I ask, trying not to grimace. "Tomorrow?"

She takes a few quick steps in front of me, turns on her heel and walks backwards, facing me.

"Um—" She lets out a single laugh. "Actually, no."

"What?"

She clears her throat. "Dennen offered me Style Editor if I stay."

"Oh." I blink. "Fuck." She looks taken aback. I shake my head. "I mean—wow." I lick my top lip, frown more than I mean to. "Congratulations—?"

144

She looks up at me, confused. "Thank . . . you?"

I say nothing. Just stare at her, face tight.

Fuck.

Fuck! What am I going to do?

She watches me close.

"Is this a problem?"

"What?" I blink. "No—yeah—"

"Yes?" Looks like I've smacked her.

"No—" I shake my head. "No, it's—your home. So. No. I just thought you were gone. Like, for good, you know?"

Her head pulls back. I've hurt her. Know the look, know the face. Done it too many times not to.

She takes a step away from me. "Well, I'm sorry to disappoint you."

"No, Parks." I sigh. "It's—you're not—I just—"

"You have a girlfriend. I know."

I give her a look. "Not just a girlfriend, the only girlfriend I've ever had besides you."

She throws daggers at me with her eyes.

And I don't know what I am. Annoyed a bit. Confused. Relieved? Fucking thrown for six.

She's staying? I can't believe she's staying.

"Yeah, I know—that's great." She nods. "Message received."

"Parks . . ."

"Actually—" She shakes her head, points a finger at me. "Do you know what? Fuck you. All tender and touchy, and sweet with me these last few days—"

"We were dealing with a decade-old trauma."

"Sexy in everything". She shakes her head at me. "All while thinking that I was leaving?"

"You were leaving," I yell.

"Well, now I'm not." She shrugs, defiant.

"Great." I nod.

She nods back. "Great."

She backs away from me and the back of my neck gets hot.

"You have a great night with your girlfriend, Beej," she spits.

I watch her walk away for the billionth time in my life and I sigh. What the fuck am I going to do now?

TWENTY-TWO
Magnolia

I hadn't expected that.

Not after the last couple of weeks, but especially the last few days . . .

I thought maybe we'd turned a corner. That maybe we'd work. Maybe the Fates weren't sleeping on the job for once in their stupid existence, that the stars were going to align, and that when Beej heard I was staying, he'd run home, break things off with that stupid Australian, and come to my house, kiss me and the end.

Instead, he's staying with her. And he's displeased I'm back.

I don't even know what to do—it feels too embarrassing to tell anyone, though I suspect that all of our friends already know, what with me looking at him like a lovesick school girl for the last week. I know Henry knows. He's too decent to say it, of course. Still, he's been around extra for no real reason, acting like he's been coming to all the real estate showings for his own enjoyment and not just because I need him.

A tiny reprieve in the drama of all this is my uncle is in town from Russia.

He's big and burley like Harley is but he's scarier than my father because even 'I love you' in Russian sounds terrifying.

"Uncle Aleksey!" I skip into his arms.

I always try to get the leg up on Bridget with him because I get the impression that he's the executor of his mother's will.

"Mark-nolia," he says in his thick Moscow accent. He gives me a hug. "So beautiful. Wonderful to see you."

He pulls my seat out for me and I sit down next to him at the dining table, straightening out the short black jersey dress with multi-coloured embellishment from Dolce & Gabbana. I keep catching on things. Bit annoying. Definitely worth it.

"You remember Henry, of course." I gesture to him and Henry gives Aleksey a smile as bright as his Grow Up oversized logo appliquéd cotton sweater from McQ.

Aleksey nods. "Boyfriend, da?"

"Boyfriend's brother," I clarify. "And no—he's not—not my—BJ isn't—no boyfriend!" I smile brightly.

Uncle Aleksey elbows his mother. "Is stroke?"

My sister and Henry start laughing.

"How's my inheritance coming along?" I ask, laying my napkin over my lap.

"Good." He takes a sip of wine. "We are diversifying."

"Into what?" my father asks.

"Zoloto."

"Oh, good! I love gold." I nod. "Always chic."

"And gases."

"Less chic." I adjust the Five Flowers Headband from Louis Vuitton.

Aleksey shrugs. "Is worth almost £5 billion."

"Well," I concede, shrugging my shoulders brightly, "a girl's gotta eat, so . . ."

Bridge and Hen trade looks. I glance up, look across the table to see a man I've never seen before.

Short black hair, fair skin, nice enough eyes.

"Oh." I blink at him. "And who are you?"

"Magnolia, darling—" My mother swans in. "This is Eric. My boyfriend."

I drop my chin to my chest and stare at my sister.

"Hello, Eric," my father says dimly. "So glad you could join us."

Henry offers Eric his hand, then Eric extends his hand to me.

I stare at it for a few seconds but don't take it. "Charmed, I'm sure. Quick question." I glance up at my family. "Considering you don't live here—" I point to my mother. "And she's your mother—" I point to Bushka. "And he's your brother—" I point to Uncle Aleksey and then to Eric. "And he's new . . . why are we having this dinner here?"

"Thank you." My father waves his hand in my direction. "I'm not running a halfway house here, Arrie. You have to stop letting yourself in."

"You could just change the lock," I tell him.

"Magnolia!" my mother and Marsaili say at the same time in surprisingly similar tones.

"You should probably at least stop throwing dinner parties here, Mum," Bridget tells her gently as she rolls up the sleeves of her deconstructed zebra pattern jumper from R13.

"But, darlings—" She sighs. "The wallpaper in my dining room makes me look fat."

"Wallpaper does not make you look fat," Bushka starts. "Fat makes you look fat."

Henry snorts into his napkin but turns it into a cough.

I point to her, nodding. "That is actually very infallible logic."

Eric looks like he's struggling to keep up.

"Anywho, all dysfunction aside, it's convenient for me that you're all here as I have an announcement to make." I give them a polite smile, fold my ankles demurely, though none of them can see that. Which is a shame because my shoes are cute.

"As many of you know—"

"There are seven of us here that aren't you," Bridget interrupts.

I repeat myself louder. "As many of you know—"

"Seven," she repeats.

I stare at her silently, waiting for her to behave.

"I am no longer returning to New York and instead will be residing in London where I belong, in my dream job."

"Congratulations," Mum's BOTM tells me.

"Thank you, Eric." I nod appreciatively. "Thusly, as of next week, Bridget and I will be moving out."

"What?" says Marsaili.

"What?" My father blinks.

"Sorry, what?" says my sister.

I nod at her. "We're moving out. Henry and I found our new house this morning."

She shakes her head. "I don't want to move out."

I roll my eyes at her. "Well, not absolutely everything has to be about you, Bridget."

Mars eyes me. "Magnolia . . ."

Bridget waves her hand towards Henry. "Live with him."

"No, thank you," Henry says with a polite smile and I frown at him.

"We'll be circling back to that later—" I eye him and he grimaces, before I cross my arms over my chest and glare at my sister impatiently. "Don't be such a big loser. You can't live here forever."

(Henry leans in towards me and whispers, "That's not what we practiced.")

I breathe out annoyed but flash the room a demure smile before trying again.

"Just a quick hop and skip over to the best grocery store in London."

"You don't hop or skip," Marsaili tells me and I ignore her.

"A casual ten-minute dander to F and M."

Bridget stares at me. "That is not a grocery store."

I clear my throat. "I believe you will find it is technically and literally a grocery store."

"Who shops there for groceries?"

"Me."

"You don't know how to cook," Henry chimes in. I flash him a look before looking over at my sister.

"Queen Charlotte, then."

Bridget blinks. "As in . . . House of Mecklenburg."

"Mmhm." I give her a tall glance.

Bridget flicks me a look. "You going to double down with that? Hitch your star to that wagon?"

"It's in Mayfair." Henry jumps in. "Great ceilings, very light—your room has a study nook, Bridge."

"Mayfair." Her eyes pinch. "Interesting."

"Not interesting," I tell her, nose in the air.

"Oh." She nods. "You mean right around the corner from the man you love?"

"Paul Walker is dead, Bridget." I put my hands on my hips. "And I would appreciate it if you would let the memory of the man I love rest in peace."

("He was so hot." Bridget nods appreciatively. "So hot." I nod back, looking at Henry for him to also affirm Paul's hotness but he doesn't.)

Bridget crosses her arms over her chest. "Where on Mayfair, then?"

"Not even Mayfair really—like technically, yes, Mayfair—but literally speaking, it's more Grosvenor Square." I give her a defiant look.

("Which is in Mayfair," Henry whispers to me and I shush him.)

"Where exactly?" Bridget breathes out through her nose.

"Upper Grosvenor. Park Street end." I give her a hopeful grin.

I look back up at everyone else in the room.

"So if everyone here wouldn't mind clearing their schedules for the next hundred and sixty-eight hours, that would be fantastic."

They all laugh like I'm joking.

I lean over to Bridget.

"Will you come?" I give her a big smile. "You, me and Taura. It'll be a blast."

She rolls her eyes, pretending to be reluctant about it.

"Fine."

TWENTY-THREE

BJ

Jordan took Parks staying better than I thought she would.

Better than I wanted her to, actually.

I think a bit of me hoped we'd get into a fight, she'd get angry and call it off but she didn't.

Henry says it's because she wants to be an influencer and I'm good for her profile, but I kind of think she's just alone in London.

Which makes it shittier and harder to do what I think I want to do.

"So," Jonah stands in my doorway with his arms folded. "Parks staying in London. Bit of a spanner."

I glance up at him. Been pretty quiet about it. "Did you know?"

He shakes his head.

"Bullshit." I cock my chin at him. "Tausie didn't tell you?"

Shakes his head again. "She didn't know either. Apparently Parks said she wanted you to be the first person she told."

I flop my head backwards. Fuck.

"I haven't spoken to her since," I tell him.

Feel guilty about it, but I don't know what to say. My reaction was bad. I'm fucking chuffed she's staying. I want her to stay, she's my best friend. Bit of an understatement, I suppose . . . I just thought everything was off the table.

Or, nah, I think I hoped that everything was still on the table but I just thought I had more time to get the table ready . . .

I'm not ready, I don't think.

It was such a mindfuck for me to get around the idea of dating anyone who wasn't Parks and I finally did it and now I'm with someone else—and I don't know what to do. It should be obvious, I know. Me and Parks are never obvious though; even when we're crystal clear we manage to find a way to convolute things.

I'll hurt her, she'll hurt me, I'll do something back, she'll do something worse—it's just how we are now. And I wish I could stop it, but it's like we're stuck on a fucking track. At least we're on the track together, I guess.

I look back up at Jo. "What the fuck am I going to do?"

"I don't know what the fuck you're doing as it is, Beej." Jonah shakes his head at me. "This is Parks we're talking about."

"Yeah, but I'm with Jordan."

He gives me an impatient look. "So end it."

He turns and walks out of my room.

I trail after him up the stairs, shove my hands into my track pants. "It's not that easy."

"Why?" He frowns.

"Because I'm trying to do the right thing." I sigh. I'm trying to be good enough for her.

He looks at me like he doesn't get it. "Okay?"

"And it'd be kind of shit of me to finally decide to date this girl and it be this big deal, then only date her a month, and dump her because Parks is back."

Jonah sighs, leaning back against the kitchen bench. "Would it?"

"Yeah. It's such a shit vibe," I tell him. "And I don't even know if Parks is like, you know—if she'd—"

"Oh, fuck—" Jonah holds his forehead. "I forgot how annoying you two are."

"Like, why the fuck has she come back?" I shrug my shoulders. "I thought she was happy in New York. She was hanging out with the Paltrows, for fuck's sake—"

"Oh." Jonah sighs, pushing his thumb into his temple, and stares at me for a long few seconds. "I'm going to have to start taking Ashwagandha." He nods to himself, moving towards the tea cupboard.

"I mean, what's in London for her anyway? It's like she has this radar, and it's like, I'm fine—for the first time in like, fuck, I don't know, years? And she smells it on me and comes back to fuck me up."

He keeps nodding, riffling through the boxes. "So much Ashwagandha."

"Do you think she's back for me?"

Jo snatches a Fortum & Mason tin from the pantry and pegs it at me. "Yes, I think she's back for you, you fucking idiot."

He bends back over the bench, hangs his head in his hands. He rubs his eyes, tired. "Beej, you belong together."

I frown a bit. "Yeah?"

"Man, how can you not know that after what you told us last week?"

"I don't know." I shrug. "Since Paili, we've never been easy. It's only been hard."

Jo rolls his eyes. "I've never seen easier chemistry between people—"

"—But—"

"—You just get off on pissing each other off." I give him a look but he just shrugs. "You do. I mean, you know me, man. I don't believe in that true love bullshit, okay?" He shakes his head. "That fucking Brontë, Shakespearean soulmates shit, I think it's a thing we say to girls to get laid . . . But whatever you and Parks have, it's what those fuckwits were writing about."

I glance at him. "By 'fuckwits' you mean Shakespeare and Brontë?"

"Yeah." He nods.

"Right." I sniff.

I squint over at him. "So end it?"

He nods emphatically. "End it."

TWENTY–FOUR
Magnolia

Everyone is headed to Mahiki tonight but Henry's doing his living best to convince me that I shouldn't come, that I should stay home with Bridge, that I won't be missing anything. Instead, I'm doubling down because I feel like I need to after how fucking indifferent his stupid brother was when I told him I was staying.

I stare up at Henry defiantly. "What do you think—the pink dress or the red one?"

"Neither." He shakes his head.

"The red." I nod to myself.

My best friend shakes his head. "No."

"Yes." I try to move past him into the bathroom but he grabs me by the shoulders.

"No." He shakes his head firmly. "You're not ready."

"I am too ready." I frown, though I might not be.

"Magnolia—" He laughs. "A half an hour ago you were crying in my arms during the ancestral song from *Moana*."

My bottom lip starts going. "It's a very precious song to me—"

"You—" He shakes his head. "Are not Samoan."

"Could be," I tell him, my nose in the air.

"Your great grandfather was born on the Mississippi River."

I cross my arms. "Says who?"

Henry crosses his. "His *New York Times* best-selling biography."

I swipe my hand through the air and dart over to the mirror, trying to assess how much work I need to do to my face to make BJ rue the day. Henry comes and stands behind me. He looks sad. "Magnolia," he says gently, "you're not ready."

I look back over my shoulder. "But he's ready, Hen—" I give a small shrug. "So I must be also."

For better or (probably) for worse, I'm steeling myself with alcohol.

Not as much as last time, mind you. That feels embarrassing now.

I can't remember what happened really, other than waking up and BJ being on the floor—also embarrassing. Because I was touching him? I could die. I could honestly die. He could have slept in the guest room, though. I wasn't the sort of messy that he might have worried I'd choke on my own vomit in the middle of the night, so he could have slept in the guest room but he didn't, and before I might have read into that, but then even after everything he wasn't even excited to find out I was staying—so maybe it means nothing at all.

That aside, how much I drank that night obviously left much to be desired, so to curb it this time, I eat a piece of toast and book a Banana Bag IV for the morning to hedge my bets.

I make sure I look extra beautiful to make life hard for him—freezing my arse off in mid-December in the water-toned floral Alexandre cut-out minidress from SIR. The Label with the navy Gucci chain-trim button-front knitted cardigan and the Gaia 140mm velvet sandals from Jimmy Choo which I take off as soon as I'm inside because I want him to see as much of me as possible so he thinks about touching me but then he can't and then his night is ruined.

"Hi," I sing to all of them as Henry and I walk in. I only kiss Taura on the cheek.

BJ stares at me how I hoped he would and it doesn't give me the high I was after at all.

His girlfriend gives me a tight, uncomfortable smile.

I glance around at them. "I hope you're all ready to help us move this weekend?"

Tausie and I give them big grins and there's a general murmur of displeasure but agreement amongst the boys.

BJ nods at me. "Where's the new place?"

I inspect my nails as though they're riveting, even though they aren't—which is on purpose. I'm a bit off whacky nail designs at the minute. Beyond the obvious facts, like they're ugly, not to mention the overt impracticalities of obscenely long nails; why everyone is trying to make their hands look like they're a witch from a Disney film is beyond me. It's rather made me not even want coloured nails. A fine French tip or perhaps, even more ideally, Nail Glow by Christian Dior. That's what my manicurist and I have been feeling lately.

"Mayfair," I tell him without looking at him.

"But really more Grosvenor Square," Taura adds because she's a good friend.

I give her a quick smile.

"Are you excited to be staying?" Jordan asks me with a smile. She didn't seem to need to muster it up or anything, I think it's a proper smile. What a psycho.

I flick my eyes over to her trying to seem friendly. "I am."

I need to balance carefully how I treat her. For one, manners are everything. And two, if I'm too mean to her, I'm worried BJ might just cut me out.

"This job is perfect for me," I offer her, trying.

"Hold on—" Christian frowns. "Does this mean no more free vacations on *Tatler*'s dime?"

"I'm afraid so."

"Fuck." He frowns. "Shouldn't we all vote on things like that?"

"Um." I give him a look. "You're not poor. I think you can fund your own holidays for a while."

He swats his hand dismissively.

"What exactly is the role?" Jordan asks, sounding genuinely interested.

"Style Editor for *Tatler*."

"Oh. Cool." She nods. "That's massive. Congrats."

I don't like her being nice to me. My eyes feel sad but I force a smile. "Thank you."

I drink my wine very fast and move in closer to Taura, who's in the very sexy, very colourful rainbow open-back chainmail minidress from Fannie Schiavoni. She's intimidatingly beautiful, Tausie is. I was intimidated by her for such a long time. Mostly because of what I thought she'd done, but a little bit because she's so strikingly attractive in the way that Eurasians tend to be. Her bone structure is completely insane and her eyes are so sparkly.

Do you want to know something crazy?

Taura knew it was Paili who BJ cheated on me with and she let me think it was her anyway. Henry told me so. She thought it would be too sad to lose my boyfriend and my best friend all at once, so she let me think it was her.

She heard Paili telling Perry about it around the time it happened, and that's when Perry started the rumour that it was Taura.

Without my knowledge, Taura Sax has been a better friend to me the last five years than almost any of my other friends have been.

I raise my hand to Taura's ear, covering it as I quietly say, "I'm whispering to you to make Jordan feel left out."

She starts laughing. Whispers back, "Cool."

"Which boy are you going home with tonight?" Me, whispering.

"TBD." Taura.

"I'm not going home with anyone." Me.

"Probably a good thing because you're in love with BJ," she whispers and I frown at her, pulling away.

I am, she's right. Very much so. I stare over at him and notice how his paisley-print short-sleeved Gucci shirt falls open over his chest as he leans to say something to Jo.

He's got a new tattoo.

I hate that he has new things on his body that I haven't seen and she has.

I squint at it, tilting my head. I blink twice, my mouth falling open.

"Is that . . .?"

BJ looks over at me, down to his chest, then back up to me. His eyes look caught and he goes quickly to close his shirt, but Jordan grabs his hand.

"Don't be weird!" She laughs. "It's not like she hasn't seen you naked before. Show her." She reaches over, undoes an extra button and flashes me his chest, grinning back at me proudly. Never mind that that alone—her touching him that capriciously, that mindlessly, like he's hers and not mine—is enough to kill me dead on the spot, but there, on his chest, is a cartoon—

"Dead baby Bambi!" Jordan grins. "Isn't that cool?"

("Weird!" Taura sing-song whispers.)

"It's my favourite." Jordan shrugs, not noticing how tense everyone else has become. Henry's pinching the bridge of his nose. Christian's shaking his head, avoiding all the eyes. Jo throws back his drink. I'm nodding. I'm nodding a lot.

"Is it?" I say, my voice breaking. "Wow."

Beej—he's just staring over at me; our eyes catch but I can't—so I turn away, look at Henry who would never dare tell me he told me so and instead slides me his Vieux Carre, which I throw back in one gulp.

I wave my hand impatiently at Christian who obediently slides me his. Sazerac. Yuck. I don't know why he likes those. Still one gulp though.

I blow out of my mouth to steady myself and wonder if my life in London will just be a series of moments where I numb myself to survive watching the person I love be with someone else.

A little bit later into the night, Beej manages to work his way over to me and Henry.

Jordan's nearby, but she's found some girls she works with and they're all watching on, staring over at us, pretending they aren't.

The way BJ angles his body makes it look like he's talking to Henry rather than me. He's trying to be covert. "Can I talk to you?" he says quietly.

I turn away a little from him and cuff his brother's sleeve. Black oversized patch-work distressed cable-knit rollneck sweater from TAKAHIROMIYASHITA TheSoloist. "No."

"Please, Parks. I need to—"

"Beej—" Henry gives him a look.

"Henry." BJ glares at him. "Don't start now. Magnolia, I just want to—"

I shake my head at him curtly and point to Jordan.

"You have a girlfriend, remember?" I raise my eyebrows at him. "You made that abundantly clear to me the other evening. You also killed me—" I can barely say it without my voice choking up. His eyes go heavy with a sorry he won't say out loud. "—on your chest. You killed me on your chest and it's your girlfriend's favourite tattoo."

"Magnolia . . ." He sighs.

"So fuck off, Beej. Go talk to her. Go plan a little day trip up to Dartmouth together—make a day of it, take a chainsaw, why don't you?"

His jaw goes tight and he gets up close in my face like he does when we're going sour. "Don't you fucking ever say that to me."

I blink as though I'm unfazed by it, as though merely uttering those words doesn't feel like a whip I'm cracking against my own back.

"Or what?" I arch an eyebrow. "You'll kill me?"

His head rolls back and his breathing is jagged as I push back from the table to get away from him.

I walk to the bar just so he has to watch me walk away from him.

And then a providential thing happens.

Surrounded by a cloud of radio presenters and London-based bands is Rush Evans.

He spots me the same time I spot him.

"Oh, shit!" He stands, grinning down at me. "Here she is!"

He folds himself around me in a hug and then pulls me down into the seat next to him.

"You're here. What's going on?" His eyes are, as always, busy like bees. "What are you up to?"

"Escaping an ex-boyfriend." I gesture in BJ's direction before glancing around cautiously. "Is my other one here?"

He gives me a look. "Which one?"

I smack his arm.

It probably wasn't worth it for how much it hurt Tom when he eventually found out. We were in Cannes and someone took a photo of us that was very hard to explain away. The papers ate it up, it was very dramatic and the entire thing—or at least a great deal of it—was unfortunately caught on various cameras. That story followed Rush and me around for a long while and even still, Rush and I didn't stop. I don't know if that makes it worse—it probably does.

I could excuse it away in my mind because Tom left me, and Rush just does what Rush wants, and he wanted me. I think he wanted me more because he knew he shouldn't. The secrecy of it made it more fun, though it wasn't really all that secretive. Rush gets photographed all the time; we were everywhere.

Tom had asked him about it before, too. I know that he did because he called Rush once to ask him if any of the rumours were true and Rush said it was all bullshit and we were just friends, and I didn't know many people here, so he was just showing me around, but I was lying next to him naked in his bed as he said it.

The friends thing—it wasn't totally untrue. We were just friends, but we also did very, very friendly things to one another's body.

Rush paid a heavy price to do them though.

"Is Tom talking to you yet?" I ask, eyebrows up.

Rush shakes his head, looks a bit sad. "Not yet."

I purse my lips in a way that implies I'm as guilty as I am sorry, and he flicks his blue eyes up at me.

"So, were you ever going to tell me you were moving back to London or were you just going to dip out?"

I poke him in the arm. "It was sudden."

"Yeah." He gives me a look. "So I heard."

"Does he hate me?" I grimace.

"No." Rush scowls a bit. "Fucking adores you, even when you pull shit like this."

"Well, that makes me feel bad." I pout.

"It should." He puts his arm around me. "Tells you he loves you and you break up with him on the spot."

"Not on the spot." I sigh.

He gives me another look. "Within the day."

I sigh again.

"Same old?" he asks without asking and our eyes catch because, actually, for all the mistakes we made together, Rush Evans became a very safe person for me while I was in New York.

I'd call him on my way home from my midnight park walks if I felt a bit afraid. He'd come and pick me up sometimes. From bad dates too. If I felt things were going sour, he'd just show up. He fought for me in a bar one time.

"How are you doing with that, by the way?" He cocks his head at BJ. "Your boy's got a girl . . ."

He looks sorry for me. I hate that.

"He does." I nod solemnly.

Rush tilts his head. "You okay?"

"No." I grin stupidly and he laughs. I'm happy to hear his laugh, actually.

"You've been in the papers a lot." I poke him and he sighs. "Are you and Montana still . . .?"

"Yep." He nods solemnly.

"No better?"

He shakes his head, gives me a steep look. "Got a bit better when you were with Jack-Jack, but no. It's back to shit."

Montana Sykes. Rush's on-and-off love of his life. Big up-and-coming actress. She was a child star but transitioned really well. Last year she won an Oscar for that film, the one with the old people. Do you know the one I mean?

"Are they saying terribly mean things?" I ask quietly.

"Yeah." He sighs, tired. "Can't get enough of us."

"Is any of it true?" I ask him. That they got back together, he cheated on her again, she found out and now she's dating her co-star who also happens to be his old housemate.

He scratches the back of his neck and looks a bit sad. "Most of it, I'm afraid."

I purse my lips. "I'm sorry, Rush."

He licks his lips. Definitely sad. "Yeah." He sighs. "Me too."

Then he looks at me and squints his big blue eyes. "We're not hooking up, by the way."

"Oh." I nod, wide-eyed. "Good. That's what every girl wants to hear."

He sniffs a laugh and gives me a little look, pinches my hand. "I don't not want to, Parks. And, I mean, forget that Tom'd kill me—again—but Jack-Jack might actually kill me."

"You could probably take him." I squeeze his arm playfully and he smacks me off him with a look.

"I don't want to take him. I want to not have sex with the girl one of my best mates is in love with. Again."

"Don't make it sound like that," I pout, because I would never. I'm not like that. "I didn't even give you a sideways glance while I was with either of them."

"Don't I fucking know it." He rolls his eyes. "Dropped me like a fucking hot potato."

"You can't have it both ways."

"Yes I can." He gives me a look and speaks in a dumb voice, "I'm famous."

I take Rush's drink from his hand and take a sip. As I do, my eyes accidentally drift back over to BJ. He's staring at me from the other side of the room and my heart hits the floor because his eyes are the only eyes I care about and the only way it seems like I can get them on me is by being with someone else.

I swallow once.

Rush follows my gaze. "Does Ballentine know you broke up with Jack-Jack Cavan for him?"

I give him a long look. "No." I clear my throat. "And I didn't."

"Yeah, right." He snorts.

I shake my head. 'He doesn't want me like that anymore."

"Oi, Parks, take it from me: just because he's fucking shit up, doesn't mean he doesn't want you." He lifts his eyebrows in this hopeless, sexy way and I remember why we kept having sex for five months even though we usually felt like shit after. "I'm completely in love with Montana and I fuck up regularly."

I put my chin in my hand and bat my eyes at him. "That is true."

He palms my face away from his. "Don't you point those things at me. We're not doing this."

I huff away, annoyed at him. I finish his drink in one go.

"Take me home at least?" I ask, eyebrows up. "Make BJ think it's something it's not?"

He cocks his chin at me, gives me a look.

"Why should I?" he asks like he's thinking about it, but I already know he will.

"Because the boy I love got a new tattoo on his chest. Of me—well—sort of. It's of the thing he's said I've always reminded him of, and I'm dead," I offer. "I'm dead on his chest."

Rush grimaces. "That wouldn't happen to be a deer, would it?"

I frown at him. "How did you know that?"

He shifts uncomfortably. "Tom got it too."

My mouth falls open.

"Yeah." He cringes. "I saw it when we had the fight. I don't know. You missed it somehow."

I press the tips of my fingers into my eyes and do my best not to cry.

Both of them? Both people I loved have gotten tattoos of

me dead on them? What's the matter with them? And perhaps more pressingly, what's the matter with me?

"Oh, fine—" Rush growls under his breath and I look up at him. "I'll give you a quick peck in front of Ballentine and then I'm dropping you straight home."

20:57

Henry 🖐

You get home okay last night

I did.

Ok and then what happened?

Hah

How do you know something happened last night?

You and Rush

Something always happens

😳

Did you?

Did we what?

...

...

Magnolia

Why do you do this?

Stop being fucking evasive. You'll tell me in 5 minutes, so just tell me now

We did.

Shit

Hope Tom doesn't hear . . .

I hope Jack-Jack doesn't hear.

🫠

TWENTY-FIVE

BJ

I lie down on our kitchen counter and groan.

Jonah sips his juice, staring over at me from the couch as he eats a bowl of cereal. "You know you didn't make that sound the whole time she was gone?"

I groan again. "Did you see her face?"

"Yeah, bro—" Jonah gives me a look. "It looked about as wrecked as I thought it would."

Another groan. "Why didn't you stop me?"

Jonah dumps his glass in the sink loudly to make a point. "Tell me you're joking." I look over at him, frowning. "Beej, I've got a chip in my chin from when I tried to stop you walking into that fucking tattoo shop."

I roll my eyes.

He shows me his chin. "You hit me."

I squint over. Can't see it. He can be so dramatic.

Jo shakes his head, eyeing me. "I believe my exact words were 'I think you're going to regret this' and you said, 'I already got so many of those, what's another?'"

I bang my head down against the marble. "She looked so hurt."

"Yeah, well, mission accomplished, then. Wasn't that the point?"

"No." I stand up, square my shoulders. "Liberation was the point."

"Well, she's not Cuba and you don't seem liberated," he tells me sarcastically and I flip him off.

I open the fridge, pull out a water and look back at him. "What am I going to do?"

Jo shrugs. "You and Parks always prattle on about a time machine?" he offers. No help there.

"I'll get it removed—" I ignore him, nodding to myself. "I'll just get it taken off."

"That's a good idea, man." Jonah gives me a shrug. "Yeah, because it'll take about three years for it to come off, which is probably the same amount of time that it'll take for Parks to forgive you."

I glare over at him, chug some water. "Do you think she went home with Rush?"

"Do I think she went home with Rush?"

My best friend tosses me a look. "Beej, we watched them leave together."

"Yeah, but like—you know—do you think they . . .?"

"Yes, BJ." Jonah nods emphatically. "I do think that. Of course they did. They have before, you know they have."

I feel sick.

Jo gives me a look. "Fuck, man, everyone knows they have. There's a photo of him with his hand up her dress on the Côte d'Azur."

"That doesn't mean that they did last night." I open the fridge again, looking for something to do.

Jonah does something on his phone and then waves it in my face. "Yes, it does."

It's a photo of her and Rush. His arms around her waist, they're kind of hugging. It doesn't necessarily look romantic.

"So?" I look from the phone back to him and back to the picture of her. "This could be from before."

"It's outside PAUL on Holland Park Avenue—" He gives me a look. "Taken this morning."

"Fuck!" My head falls back and I yell into my hands. "Why would she—"

Jo stares at me. "The dead deer on your chest couldn't have helped."

I stare over at him. "When did your comedic niche become stating the fucking obvious?"

"Around the same time your everyday choices became so ridiculous we didn't need the jokes anymore."

I give him a fake smile, he gives me one back.

"Should I help her move?" I scratch the back of my head.

Jo sighs, presses his fingertips into his eyeballs and cringes. "I can't do this sober. Make me a Bloody Mary?"

I toss him a look and start pulling out the ingredients.

"But do you think I should? Would that be a good way of letting her know I'm happy she's back?"

"Yeah." He shrugs. "Or you could just tell her you're happy she's back."

"If I tell Henry I'm getting it removed, he'll tell her—"

He points over at me, interrupting. "Oi, put more vodka in that. Bit more—" He eyeballs me. "A bit more—I swear to God, BJ, if you want to keep talking about this, I'm going to need you to pour me a real fucking glass."

"Talking about what?" Jordan asks as she walks up the stairs.

Jo and I catch looks.

"Oh. Nothing." He shrugs. "Just shit with me and Hen."

Jordan pulls a face because she thinks they're being stupid.

Me too, actually. They don't talk about it, kind of just let it fester between them. It's sort of like me and Christian, I guess. They never seem to come to blows though. Henry's too controlled. And I think Jo is scared of the fallout with me.

"You're still free on the weekend, right?" she asks me with a big grin.

Shit. I forgot we had plans.

"Oh, actually, no—I'm going to help the girls move."

Her face tugs.

"The girls?" she asks.

Jonah pulls an uncomfortable face and makes a weird sound.

Jordan squints at me. "Like, your ex-girlfriend, her sister and a girl you used to sleep with?" She frowns.

I say nothing. Feels like a trap.

"Yeah, but, like—" Jo shrugs. "Now I'm sleeping with her, so . . ."

Jordan flicks him a look.

"Taurs is a fucking legend in the sack though, right Beej?" He whacks me in the arm and I feel like we're back in school when Jo would say shit to make me laugh and I'd be fighting against every instinct not to. I mash my lips together, not looking away from Jordan.

"She's top five for sure," Jonah says, grinning.

I cross my arms over my chest, flip him off covertly as I do.

"Yep, better to not answer that one." Jonah nods to himself. "Top three?"

"Fucking get out." I point at the door and he starts laughing and goes to his room.

Jordan looks over at me and rolls her eyes at Jonah.

"She's my oldest friend," I tell her with a sorry look. "I should probably help them."

"But it's a triple double date." She crosses her arms.

"A what?" I blink.

She rolls her eyes. "Three couples going on a double date. And you know how annoying Claudia's boyfriend is—"

I groan. "Jords, I don't want to hear him talk about how he would have been cast as the new Batman if Robert Pattinson just hadn't been born. I can't do that again."

She laughs before she grabs my arm and gives me pleading eyes. "Please?" She gives me a hopeful look. "Imagine how stupid I'd look on a double date by myself, like I don't have a boyfriend or anything, when actually, mine is way hotter than any of theirs."

I roll my eyes at her.

"And Caitlin really wants to meet you."

I grimace. "The weird one from work."

"Yeah." She shrugs. "She's pretty obsessed with you."

"Great." I nod unenthused.

She lifts her eyebrows. "So you'll come?"

I sigh. "I guess, yeah."

Said I would, suppose I should.
She gives my arm a grateful squeeze and kisses me.
"You're the best," she tells me.
But I'm not so sure.

TWENTY-SIX

Magnolia

Moving day arrives and not one person has said a thing about the cropped cotton-jersey T-shirt from the Balmain x Barbie collaboration that I'm wearing which is, admittedly, very casual but obviously very cute. I think they're all angry at me, but it's mostly not my fault.

Christian's standing in our new living room, arms folded across his big chest, frowning. "You're telling me I gave up my whole Saturday to move you into your new apartment, but you hired packers, removalists and," he squints for dramatic effect, "unpackers?"

I let out a frustrated growl.

"I've only moved once before and it was without warning and in the dead of night, because your best friend couldn't keep it in his trousers." I give him a sharp look. "I walked into Sotheby's on York Avenue and said, 'I need an apartment that looks like England, is completely furnished, full of clothes because I have nothing with me, and ideally available this morning' and they said that those probably weren't very realistic expectations but they'd do their best, and I said, fine I'll go shopping, call me when you find me a house."

"What—for fuck's sake—is your point?" blinks Christian.

"I don't know!" I shrug. "I guess that I don't know how to move house?"

He sniffs a laugh and shoves me.

BJ didn't come. Not that he needed to in the end, I suppose. And I thought that he probably wouldn't, but I hoped still that he might . . . just waltz on in here, grab my face and press me up against these new walls, into all these new corners, kissing me too much until Henry tells him to stop, that it's disgusting, that we're disgusting. I so badly miss being disgusting with him.

I'm sure it's no good that that's what I think of when I'm somewhere for the first time, that he seeps in through the cracks of my every single thing. He's never been here, he's never even seen a picture of it, and still my mind plays out how it would feel to have him standing over in that kitchen making me a cup of tea and my heart flip flops into a panic because I wonder how we'll ever get there?

Be the kind of couple who make each other tea and not the kind of couple who fight in the street and *Star* spreads shit about that's both true and untrue all at once.

And then, I don't know why, but Bushka walks in. What's more, she walks in wearing a pink, cream and floral silk-twill scarf from Gucci on her head, the fringed striped cashmere-blend turtleneck poncho from Chloé and the oversized bedazzled sunglasses from Dolce & Gabbana.

"Oh, no." I pout, tugging on a fringe. "This won't do, you scarcely match one bit. What happened?"

Bushka looks down at herself. "I like. Is all in colour house."

She is correct, I suppose. It is all in the same colour wheelhouse.

"It's very busy," I tell her, plucking the glasses off her face and inspecting them. "Are these mine?"

She shrugs. "You never wore so I took."

I roll my eyes. "What are you even doing here? You have literally no upper body strength. Or lower body strength. Or strength of character."

"Magnolia," Bridget growls.

I shrug defensively. "She was a military defector."

"She defected from the Soviets."

"Yes." Bushka nods conclusively. "Bad kisser. Not good to stay."

Henry starts laughing.

"Who—" Bridget blinks. "Are—are you talking about Joseph Stalin?"

Bushka pulls back, offended. "How old you think I am?"

"Very," I tell her emphatically.

My sister's eyes pinch. "Yes or no on Stalin?"

Bushka nods.

"Would you have stayed if he was a good kisser, then?" Jonah asks, leaning in.

Bushka thinks. "Is wrong to say 'probably', da?"

"Da." Bridget blinks, hands on the hips of her bright orange crystal-embellished Ganni cardigan. She looks pretty cute for moving day. Floral-print elasticated shorts from Sandro, a cropped Alexander McQueen T-shirt, Air Force 1s that I could do without, but it's not a hill I'll die on.

"Then no," Bushka says before she wanders deeper into our apartment.

Our new place is dreamy. Even Bridget likes it, miracle of miracles. I took the master because, well, obviously. Tall ceilings. Marble accents. White walls, dark wooden floors, a billion windows.

And don't think for a moment that I'm standing at them checking the street to see if he appears on the footpath, looking lost, trying to find my building to surprise me, because I'm not. That would be so sad.

Almost as sad as the infernal racket I can hear in our living room.

I round the corner feeling incredibly intruded upon. It sounds like a—

"Oh." I stomp my foot as I stare over at Bushka. "Who the fuck gave her a whistle?"

"Me." Henry beams down at me, proud of himself.

I pull the hood of his Oregon printed cotton-jersey jumper from Rhude over half his face just to annoy him. "For the love of God why?"

He shrugs. "Because now that BJ's in the bad books she's going to have to offload that five-billion-pound steel fortune to someone."

174

"Yes." I eyeball him. "Me."

"Doubt it." He shrugs. "How many whistles have you given her?"

"Just the one I'm going to shove down your throat as penance for this fiasco."

My best friend laughs, kisses the top of my head and leaves to go to buy everyone coffees.

I'm lying on my bed an hour or so later, drinking said coffee and reading a magazine because moving is the worst— did you know?

Awful.

Don't do it.

And if you must, just leave everything behind and start afresh.

There's a knock on my door and I look over.

Jonah lifts his eyebrows, waiting for me to ask him in.

Black Les Tien garment-dyed cotton-jersey hoodie, the black straight-leg logo-embroidered cotton-jersey drawstring shorts from Celine Homme with cream socks and black suede Arizonas. I look away permissively but I don't speak.

He sits on the edge of my bed. "You ever going to forgive me?"

I glance at him. "I don't know."

"He's my best friend."

"—So was I," I shoot back quickly.

He nods once. "Are."

I look away from him. "That's a bit of a one-way street."

He sniffs a laugh, pushes a hand through his dark blonde hair.

"Do I at least get points for coming today? Wasting my Saturday for you?"

"Wasting your Saturday for me?" I blink. "Please. We all live by very relaxed schedules. It could be a Wednesday for all we know—it'd make no difference."

He nods once and looks over at me. "You're angry he didn't come?"

"I don't care," I tell him, shrugging absolutely zero noses in the air.

"So that's a 'yes'."

I glare over at him and his eyes pinch playfully before they soften rather quickly.

"He was going to come, Parks."

"And yet . . ."

"He has a girlfriend."

I groan and flop my head into my magazine. "I know! My God, just write it on a pillow already, why don't you?"

He rolls his eyes. "If I tell you a secret will you like me more?"

I have missed Jonah. Unnatural to not speak to him after all this time. It was a long year in New York without him actually. He tried hard to make it up to me, but there wasn't much he could do to undo what he helped cover up.

It was easier to be angry at him over there than it is here. Here, with him in my face reminding me of the boy who held my hair back while I vomited up half a bottle of vodka at a party he threw when I was fourteen, it's harder to remain stoic.

It's that stupid Hemmes smirk they do . . . so cute, so forgivable. Their poor mother.

"Maybe." I give him a dumb look.

He purses his mouth, hiding a bit of a smile. "I have it on good authority that the love of your life—"

"—Don't have one of those," I interrupt.

He rolls his eyes at me. I go pink. "—Is calling time on his little relationship."

I freeze, looking over at him wide-eyed. "Right now?" I ask, my eyebrows up.

He gives me a look. "Right now? How the fuck would I know? Right now . . ."

He shakes his head at me.

"But soon?" I know my eyes look brighter and more hopeful than I want them to. I don't care, it's Jonah. He's seen me at my worst and my even more worst, he can see me now at my blooming hopeful.

"Soon." He nods.

I fall back on my bed and breathe out, relieved.

He lies back next to me. "Thought you'd like that."

TWENTY-SEVEN
Magnolia

The day after the move I get lunch with Henry and Jonah at Annabel's. Just the three of us. Taura's got work, and I wouldn't much like to go to lunch with their little throuple anyway. Henry and Jonah are relatively normal when they're with us or by themselves but the second Taura's around the wheels start to fall off. Because they're both dating her, they both have proper feelings for her, and she for them . . .

She says she's just playing it out, trying to work out who to be with and what to do.

The predicament here is that both Henry and Jonah have spent their entire adult lives, for all intents and purposes, evading committed relationships. Neither has ever really wanted one until now but both are too proud to admit it, and neither wants to admit the uncomfortable truth that they're both now terribly interested in the same girl. They might even both love her. Henry does, I can tell.

The fact that he's still in it, dating her when Jo is too, even when I can see it hurting him and this friendship he's had for twenty-odd years, means that he's in deep. Henry's too pragmatic to let something like this happen under normal circumstances, so I can only assume that the norm has shifted and love is now involved.

We don't talk about it, I don't even mention her name once. Which is difficult, actually, as we just moved in together and she's a fairly central part of all our lives. Anyway, we worked around it. Chatted mostly about my mother's rampant and highly publicised dating life.

"It's the age of them that bothers me the most," I tell them as we step out onto Berkley Square. "Your age." I nod my chin at Henry. "Unbelievable . . ."

I pull out the vintage CC logo black Chanel sunglasses and pop them on. I never wear sunglasses on account of my eyes being so wonderful, but these are so adorable, it'd almost be a crime not to.

Jonah turns on his heel to face us as he walks backwards. "I mean, Parks, the honest to God truth is Arrie is well fit." I glare over at him and he gives me a little shrug as he zips up his black Fear of God quilted shell down jacket. "Like, if she wasn't your mum I would be all up in that."

Henry pulls a face and I, simply horrified, smack Jonah 12,000 times from his head to his stomach.

"Jonah!

"What?" He frowns defensively, not flinching at my hits once. "Parks, come on. Her eyes, those come-hither, fuck-me eyes . . ." He gives me a look. "Dead sexy."

Henry's face scrunches up and my mouth falls open, aghast. "WE HAVE THE SAME EYES!" I yell.

"What?" He frowns.

"My mother and I have the same eyes."

Jonah rolls his eyes. "You do not."

"Yes we do!"

"Are you stupid?" Henry scoffs. "Look at them."

I point at them wildly and Jonah leans in to inspect them.

"Oh, fuck—" Jonah leans away from me dramatically before pointing right in my face. "Yuck."

I smack his hand away. "Don't point at me and say 'yuck'." Jonah looks at me, eyes wide and completely disturbed, pointing with two fingers now. "That's fucking disgusting!"

"Stop pointing at me and saying mean things!" I stomp my foot and Henry starts laughing.

"I take it back." Jonah shakes his head. "I take it all back," he says and then does one of those involuntary shudders.

"Alright," I growl under my breath. My pace walking down the street is brisk now and fuelled by grumpiness.

"Settle down. You briefly peered into my dazzling eyes, not into Dante's inferno."

"Hey, so what's Bridget up to these days?" Jonah calls after me, cheeky grin on his face. I pinch my fingers together right up in his face.

"Paper thin ice, Jonah. Paper thin."

Both boys chuckle and it makes me feel relieved that they can still be normal with each other when we take out the pickle in the equation.

"Bridget is actually very hot, Parks," Henry concedes, fanning himself with his beige Maison Margiela shirt.

"Henry!" I wail.

"What? She's—"

And then, "Oh my God," says a familiar voice. Perry Lorcan stops us in the street. "Magnolia! Hi!" He stares at me, eyes big and wide.

As a knee-jerk response, I think about what I'm wearing in case there's a photographer here hiding somewhere, or even for when this moment is inevitably regaled back to Paili.

The crystal-embellished miniskirt from Amen, black Maddy ribbed-knit sweater and the black Dolce & Gabbana spread-collar cardigan coat. I look good. Stupid that it makes me feel some relief, but it does.

"Boys. Hey." Perry gives them an uncomfortable smile.

Jo nods his chin at him and I take a step backwards into Henry, who doesn't say a word.

"Perry." I blink a few times, glancing past him. "Are you here with . . .?"

"No." He shakes his head. "She's in Spain."

The truth is, I know that after everything that happened last year, Paili and Perry's lives changed rather drastically. And I do want to interject and say that I personally had nothing to do with it. Though it might sound as though I did, I, in fact, did not. It comes off personal and vindictive—and I can certainly be that—but what happened to them was not my doing.

After everything happened, it was so publicised, because it was caught on camera. I found out, and then a day later it was everywhere. Everyone instantly knew. It was splashed any which way you looked. FINALLY REVEALED: BJ Ballentine cheated on Magnolia Parks with her long time BFF Paili Blythe.

Paili wasn't in the papers much before that. The public fascination was focused primarily on BJ and I, and then the others by association, but they were fascinated with her for this reason. They weren't nice though. BJ made it worse.

Henry told me that he wouldn't go anywhere that they'd go. Clubs and restaurants started refusing Paili and Perry entry because they'd rather have BJ. Everyone loves BJ, everyone wants to be loved by BJ. BJ has more clout, more pull, more charisma, more weight in his little finger than Paili and Perry do in their whole two bodies combined. To keep in BJ's good graces, Paili and Perry (so Henry tells me) were unofficially dismissed from the upper echelons of British society.

"Right." I nod. "No, I had heard that . . . I thought you both lived there now?"

"We do." He flashes me a smile, extending it to the boys who are silent behind me.

"Together?" I ask. I don't know why.

"Yeah." He nods. "So, what are you doing here? I heard you were in New York."

I nod uncomfortably. "I've just moved back."

"Oh." His eyebrows go up. "Why?"

"She got made Style Editor." Henry tells him without a smile.

"Congrats, babe! That's massive!" Then he looks past me to Henry. "It's good to see you boys. What's been happening?"

Henry doesn't say anything, he just looks away.

"Really, Hen?" Perry blinks. "We've been friends since we were twelve."

"Friends don't lie." Henry shrugs.

Very bravely and somewhat stupidly, Perry gestures at Jonah. Jonah's head pulls back. "You pointing at me?"

"Hey—" Perry sniffs an amused and confused laugh. "Is it true you're both dating Taura after everyth—"

"Wouldn't finish that sentence, Lorcs." Jonah gives him a tight smile, shaking his head.

"Nah." Henry's jaw goes tense. "Finish it. Let's see how it goes over . . ."

"Sorry, boys." He shrugs. "Didn't mean anything by it. I'm sure she's great."

"She is," I tell him sternly.

"Magnolia, listen, I'd really love to catch up—you know, smooth everything over."

"Perry." I cross my arms over my chest. "There's nothing to smooth."

He flicks his eyes, a bit annoyed. "Magnolia, I—"

"—No, listen." I shake my head. "I understand that you were more Paili's best friend than mine, okay? You did the right thing by her but not by me. I don't want to see you and I don't want to catch up."

"That's bullshit, Magnolia." Perry shakes his head.

"What's that now?" Henry squares his shoulders.

"It's fucking shit, Parks. And typical you." He scoffs. "Always all about BJ."

I lift my eyebrow, waiting for more.

"You're out to lunch with BJ's best friend—" He gestures at Jonah, his eyes clouding over with resentment.

"So?"

"So, you can't forgive me but you can forgive Jonah?"

"You know that, do you?" I blink. "That I've forgiven Jonah?"

"Clearly."

"Clear, is it?" I blink a few times as I point over at Perry. "You know how I feel in my chest when I see him?" I gesture towards Jo. "Jonah, my friend since I was twelve, who not only lied to me for three years about probably the most painful and monumental experience of my life but also concealed it, covered it up, took away my closure, and let me live in the dark while

181

I floundered around in it, unable to move on, couldn't let go because no one would tell me the fucking truth—"

"—Parks." Jonah sighs, eyes heavy.

"We did the same things," Perry tells me, though he looks a bit sorrier now. "I was just trying to protect Paili."

"And who was trying to protect me?" I yell louder than I mean to. "I was the only one in that whole situation who didn't do anything wrong, and who was making sure I was fine?"

"Magnolia." Perry pushes his hands through his hair. "Darling, it was so long ago now. And it was one thing, one time, one mistake. I covered for my best friend in the world when she did a terrible thing, but I'm not the villain that you think I am—"

"—Oh, so you didn't try to convince Paili to kiss BJ while he was high that time in Paris?" I stare over at him, unflinching.

Perry's face freezes, but Henry and Jo stare over at me, eyes bulging.

"How do you know about that?" Perry asks.

"He told me." In those letters he wrote me that I ignored.

Perry pulls back a bit. "He told you?"

"Did you or didn't you?" I wait for his confession.

"Magnolia, listen, you'd been broken up nearly two years—"

"—I know, Perry." I nod. "I remember."

I remember everything about that night because it was the first night BJ got high since his overdose. It was about two and a bit years ago now. We were all in Paris, it had been such a fun trip till that point. BJ and I got adjoining hotel rooms so we could pretend that we wouldn't just sleep in the same bed. We'd been there a few days and then this one night . . . he had a shoot the next morning, he said he didn't want to drink because he didn't want to feel like shit when he woke up. So he did a bump or three, because BJ can't say no when with me or with drugs. I had a feeling by the time we were at the third club of the night—just with how he was touching me—as though we were by ourselves and not in a club with five hundred people who knew who we were

182

and had their phones out and pointed at us. I was dating one of my foxholes at the time but he wasn't there. I didn't like bringing my (arguably) fake boyfriends away with us because they got in the way of being close to the boy I actually cared about, but still I didn't want photos of BJ feeling me up in some club in Paris to be plastered all over *The Sun* so I went to the bathroom and when I walked back out I saw him. Rolled up €50 note up his nose and I burst into tears on the spot.

"Parks!" He ran after me but I ran straight to Henry.

The boys were furious. As angry as me. Angrier, maybe.

We all left him, even Jonah. The only ones who stayed with him were Paili and Perry. It turns out that after we left they all did lines together, more and more. BJ's reactive when he's sad about me—he has a knee-jerk response—makes himself feel better for a minute without caring whether it'll make him feel worse in a more permanent way. And when BJ was at his foggiest, Perry got the three of them shots, and then he put his arms around them both and said, "You guys should kiss."

BJ said he frowned, shook his head. And Perry, drunk and high too, I suppose—I hope—pushed BJ and Paili's heads together and chanted, "Kiss kiss kiss kiss!"

BJ said he smacked Perry's hand away and came back to our room to find me, that he thought about telling me it all that night but I wasn't there. I'd gone to his brother's room. I didn't talk to him for a week.

I stare over at Perry on the street, my eyes getting glassy now.

"I don't want to be your friend, Perry." I shake my head. "I'm not quite sure you were ever mine."

And then I walk away.

"I didn't know he wrote you letters," Henry says as he jogs after me.

"Yeah." I nod. "Lots." I flash him a tight smile.

"What did they say?" Jo asks.

I shrug. "Different things. Apologies, explanations, confessions, regrets. Some venting, I guess. That one about Paris and Paili, I think he was just trying to get it all out in the open."

Henry's brows furrow. "Did you ever write him back?"

I shake my head.

"Why?" Jonah frowns.

I purse my lips, try my best not to cry but my bottom lip shakes all the same without my permission. "It felt like if I responded to him, it would crack open a door I could barely keep shut as it was." I wipe my eye. Shutting it was the hardest thing I ever did, and I obviously didn't even do it very well.

Henry reaches over, brushes a tear off my face.

I sniff, try to look brave as I ask them my most worrisome question. "Do you think if I'd written back that maybe he wouldn't be with Jordan?"

Both Henry and Jonah's faces sort of pinch and frown, their mouths falling open as they try to say no. I know they think the answer is yes.

I nod without them saying anything.

Jonah takes his sleeve around his hand and wipes my nose, giving me a gentle look. "He's canning it with her, remember?"

Henry hooks his arm around me. "Home stretch, Parks."

21:42

Parks

Hey

Hi.

You okay?

The boys told me.

I'm sorry.

You didn't help me move.

I know.

Next time you move, I'll do it all

Are you okay though

Thank you for not kissing her that night in Paris.

I know I never responded to your letters

But thank you.

x

TWENTY-EIGHT

BJ

I tried to break up with her—I'll start there.

Asked her to a café, a weird shit random one, because I read that's how you break up with girls on the internet. How fucking sad is that? I'm twenty-five years old and googling how to break up with women because I've only ever dated one and she broke me.

All the other girls I just ghost or ignore or fuck again, but Jordan and I are different because we're official, so I had to end it properly, and I didn't know how.

A conglomeration of advice from Google:

Take them to a place that doesn't have emotional significance—hence the random café.

Be completely honest but not brutal.

Steer clear of false promises.

Don't hook up after.

Thought I was ready for it . . . What I was not ready for was walking into the random café and finding her already crying. It was weird. She was crying, holding a mug of coffee to her face, taking a photo of herself.

"You okay?" I asked cautiously as I sat down next to her.

"My parents are splitting up," she sniffled.

"Oh, shit—" I sighed.

Fuck.

She shook her head, leaned on my shoulder. "They said it's been a while coming. They've gone downhill since I've been here—that's what my sister said."

I nodded. I didn't know what to say—my mind was swimming, trying to find any ledge I could've grabbed onto that would have saved me from not being the biggest fucking arsehole in the world for still ending it with her then on the spot.

Don't prolong the inevitable, that's one of the things Google said. But how?

"J, I'm so sorry—"

"Actually . . ." She shook her head, wiping her face with her hands. "I have something else I have to talk to you about too."

Oh shit.

Hope my face didn't falter when she said that.

"Last night Claudia flooded the apartment. The electrics are fried, so now we have to move out for a bit." She gave me a horrified look. "Maybe for a month. Maybe longer." She looked at me and I already knew. "Do you think—would it be okay with Jonah if I stayed? Just for a few weeks while we find a new place?"

"Uh—"

"I'll pay rent," she said.

"I don't need you to pay rent, but I—" I shook my head.

"Check with Jo first." She grabbed my hand as she nodded. "But I'm sure it'll be fine. Taura always stays." She shrugged.

I nodded. Didn't say anything, I just nodded.

"Thank you." She smiled, leaned in to kiss me.

I gave her a weak smile, and then she picked up her phone, took a photo of her leaning on my shoulder. Her blue eyes still teary; obviously she'd been crying. Posted it to Instagram, wrote some shit caption about how good a boyfriend I am. Tagged me in it. Got a lot of likes really quickly.

I think I'm going to be sick.

Fuck.

Fuck!

How did I walk in there trying to break up with her and left living with her?

I was planning on ending it with her there and heading straight on over to Aquavit for dinner with everyone, probably just walk up to Parks and kiss her on the spot. Make up for it how I should have done the other day. Wear a shirt from Casablanca I think she'd like on me, think about her hands slipping under it when I'd walk her home and never walk away from her again, and now I'm walking into Aquavit with Jordan . . . who wasn't even accounted for in the fucking reservation—that's how sure I was about calling it. Didn't bother to book her a seat at dinner and yet here we are. Living together, apparently.

When we walk in, Magnolia's eyes find mine first and they fall down my body, eyeing the shirt that I wore for her and her eyes go bright and just for a second they spark up like a firefly. I know her eyes better than anything in the world probably; she'd deny it, but she knew what I was going to do, she wanted me to have done it . . . and then Jordan walks in a few steps behind me and the best eyes in the world go dim.

Parks glances over at Jonah, who's staring at me with a frown. Subtly he mouths, "What the fuck?"

I shake my head at him.

Parks turns away, pours herself a massive glass of wine, drinks it in one go. She looks back over at Jonah, whispers something sharp—I can tell it's sharp by the angles of her face and the way Jonah's subtly shaking his head. He shrugs, helpless.

"Sorry I'm like this." Jordan smiles as she sits down at the table. "I didn't know we had a dinner."

Magnolia lets out a single 'hah' and Jordan looks at her confused.

"Life. Such a journey . . ." Parks shrugs loosely. "You never know when a dinner is, who'll be at the dinner, what even the fuck was the point of the dinner—"

Jonah and I trade uneasy glances.

"Magnolia," Jordan calls from across the table, "I love your top."

Parks flashes her a quick smile. "Saint Laurent."

It's bad news how quiet she's being. Won't even tell Jordan the name of the shirt? Fuck. It's the calm before the storm.

Jordan glances at me and nods her head towards Jonah. "Did you ask him?"

"Ask me what?" Jo hears because she didn't say it quietly.

I give her a look. "Jords, we just got here. When would I have had the chance?"

"The chance to ask me what?" Jonah asks again.

"Well, my flatmate, Claudia—do you know her?"

"Intimately." Jonah nods and I roll my eyes.

"Oh." Jordan scrunches her face a bit. "Well, she flooded the bathroom. And we have to move out for a month and I was hoping I could come and move in with you guys."

There's a clank as Magnolia drops her iPhone right in the middle of her dinner plate.

Christian starts laughing and so does Parks, but I can tell she's not laughing at the phone, she's laughing because if she doesn't she'll cry. Eyes are glassy, approaching sparkly, and her eyes only go sparkly before she cries. It's one of her wiliest tricks she doesn't mean to do.

Jonah's basically a deer in headlights. Probably not the over-whelming response Jordan was hoping for because he's basically been staring at her, mouth ajar, for the last thirty seconds.

"Beej?" Jonah eventually says. He's blinking a lot. "Thoughts? On your—" He pauses for a fraction of a second—"girlfriend moving in with us?"

"Yeah. I said I'd talk to you about it later." I give Jordan a look to cast the conversation back into the ocean of topics she could have brought up instead, but she doesn't and I don't honestly know whether she's not sensing the vibe or is just ignoring it.

"No, don't be silly!" Parks chirps. "Talk about it now!"

I glance over at her with heavy eyes.

"Are you going to move in with your girlfriend?" she asks me, eyebrows up.

"Temporarily," Jordan adds as a caveat.

"Are you going to move in with your girlfriend temporarily?" Magnolia asks me again, looking me dead in the eyes.

I want to reach across the table and hold her face in my hand. I know I can't because of Jordan, but I also don't know that I could even if Jordan wasn't here because I don't know what the fuck is going on. Parks, she's a territorial girl. She doesn't like new people in general and she's never liked me paying attention to anyone else, but I can't tell why that is anymore.

Maybe she loves me. Maybe she just doesn't know how to be without me.

"Oh my God." Jordan whacks my arm excitedly. And thank fuck. I didn't know where that was going to go but I knew it'd be ugly. Me and Parks locking horns? It never ends well.

Jordan shakes my arm, nodding her head excitedly towards the door. "Is that Jack-Jack Cavan?"

"What?" I perk up, glancing around. "Where?"

"Sorry—" Magnolia blinks. "What did you just say?"

"Nothing." I shake my head at her. She won't know who he is. "He's just a skater."

"Turned model, turned celebrity," Jordan adds. "Super sexy."

Magnolia swallows. Her face is still. Weird.

Then she turns over her shoulder and looks at the door.

Jack-Jack Cavan's eyes catch hers and he nods his chin at her coolly with a big grin. Magnolia smiles at him a bit, gives him a weird wave.

And then he starts walking towards us.

"Oh, shit." My brother sighs quietly and I look over at him, confused.

What the fuck? Henry trades a grimace with Parks and then he's here—four-time Street League champion, three-time X Games gold medalist, and the second-highest paid skateboarder of 2021. Jack-Jack Cavan is standing over Parks, looking down at her, grinning.

"I found you." He reaches down, takes her hand, pulls her to her feet and into him.

She hugs him back, cautiously—maybe awkwardly. "Were you looking for me?"

"Yep." He nods and I'll say it again louder for the people in the back: What. The. Fuck.

She gives him a little look that's too playful for me to like. "How did you know where I was?"

He shrugs coolly. "Rushy's got the four one one." Then he remembers the rest of us at the table. "Hey guys, sorry—" He shakes his head at himself. "I'm Jack-Jack."

(Everyone murmurs variants of 'hey' and 'hi' except me. I say nothing and just watch.)

"Taura." He gives her a familiar grin.

"Jack-Jack." She matches it.

"Hey man." He ruffles my brother's hair, that fucking traitor, then he turns his attention back to Parks. "So, hey." He smiles at her in a way I hate.

"Hi." She suppresses a smile.

"Hi." He nods, and his cheeks could be a bit pink.

Fuck.

Parks eyes him. "What are you doing in London?"

He nods his chin at her. "Would you believe me if I said I was here for you?"

Jonah and I trade looks.

Parks smirks. "I would not."

Jack-Jack Cavan laughs then nods coolly. "The Burberry shoot . . ."

"Oh!" She nods. "Of course. I forgot. How was it?"

"Good, yeah—" He shrugs. "Would have been better if you were in it . . ."

She rolls her eyes. "That would have been both inappropriate and misleading."

"They were asking for you," he tells her and she rolls them again.

"Yes, well." She rolls her eyes for a third time. "Instagram has ruined the modelling industry now, so—" (I'm pretty sure that was a dig at me.)

"Oh fuck." Jack-Jack sighs. "Not this Ted Talk again."

I frown. How many Ted Talks has she given him?

"So, listen—" He reaches for her hand. She lets him. And here's the fucking kicker—he interlocks his fingers with hers. Interlocks! "I'm staying at the Lanesborough till tomorrow night. Can I bring you to my hotel? Give you a bunch of reasons to come back to New York with me?"

I nearly scoff out loud, maybe I do a bit and I don't realise, because Jordan's watching me real close.

But the fucking stones on this guy. Asking Magnolia fucking Parks to come with him somewhere for sex.

And then she grabs her purse—pretty sure I bought it for her. Dolce & Gabbana. Red. It has a heart on it.

She gives him a playful look. "You can try."

"Oh, I'm going to try a lot." He nods coolly.

"Yeah?" She looks up at him batting her eyes. "How hard?"

Jonah chokes on his wine. My mouth actually falls open.

He licks his bottom lip, grins at her as he hooks his arm around her neck how I used to.

"Hard as you want, London."

She laughs and looks back, catching the eyes of everyone except me. "See you later."

They're about to walk away when he looks at me and, without letting go of Parks, leans down to me, offering his hand.

"BJ, right?" I shake his hand, say nothing. "Heard a lot about you, man. It's good to put a face to it."

He gives me a little wink and then walks her out of the restaurant, feeling her up as they go.

She's laughing and squirming and swatting him off and loving it.

We all stare after her.

"So."

"So." Jonah blinks. "I guess someone's discovered sex."

TWENTY-NINE
Magnolia

A few days later, it's Christmas Eve Brunch at the Wolseley —it's a tradition. Every year since we were fifteen, except last year.

Henry warned me that the boys have gone mental over Jack-Jack, and I know I'm not going to hear the end of it.

BJ's been—somewhat predictably—very silent, but Jonah and Christian have been texting me questions around the clock.

When I walk in the Hemmes boys cheer. Not Beej though, he takes a well-timed sip of his Bloody Mary.

I roll my eyes at their immaturity and fluff the fire engine red high-waisted gown maxi skirt I'm wearing from Carolina Herrera. It's very dramatic but I felt like making an entrance. Monogrammed waistband sporty crop top from Louis Vuitton and the Carretto-print canvas clogs with bejewelled appliqués from Dolce & Gabbana to really drive my theatrics home. I am completely unmissable and entirely intentional about it. I also wear my hair up so BJ can see the hickey on my neck.

I sit down between the Hemmeses because that puts me directly across from Beej, who's Jordan-less (ee!). I turn and squeeze Taura's hand over Jonah because I haven't seen her in a few days between her being at Jo's or Henry's and Jack-Jack staying an extra night or two. Also it gives me a great reason to flash BJ my neck.

He stares at it from across the table, blinking twice. He looks hurt and it doesn't thrill me how I want it to, but I don't think I understand anything anymore.

Those green eyes of his cloud over.

I've struck a nerve.

He's never seen a mark on my body he didn't put there.

I want to reach for his hand under the table, I want to slide my foot up his leg and rest it in his lap, but I can't because he has a girlfriend he's apparently living with, so I flash him my neck again instead.

Beej shrugs off his red Louis Vuitton baseball jacket and drapes it over his chair. His stormy eyes pinch as he nods his chin at me.

"Look at you. Still here . . ." He raises his eyebrows. "Your mate didn't give you enough reasons to go back?"

I glance at him, face pleasant. "No, he gave me plenty."

His eyes go to slits.

"Alright, out with it, Parks." Jonah tosses an arm around me and I snuggle into his black Walter logo-print nylon-blend bomber jacket from Enfants Riches Déprimés. "Are you fucking Jack-Jack Cavan?"

I am loving this attention. Loving in particular how cross it's making BJ and how overt his crossness is to everyone.

"Well." I clear my throat and glance around delicately. "Not right now."

Jonah smirks. "But you are?"

I leave it hanging there for a few seconds, wanting to milk it for all it's worth.

"I was. I—we dated." I glance at Henry, who nods once. "Back in New York."

"Bullshit." Christian blinks and glances at Henry. "And you said nothing?"

Hen shrugs.

"Jack-Jack Cavan?" Christian shakes his head at us, sitting back in his chair.

"He's the shit right now—" Jonah tosses an apologetic glance at BJ who glares at him. "—Sorry. I mean—er—fuck—um, I meant—"

"So you dated in New York?" Henry says loudly even though he already knows. I nod once.

"How long for?" Christian asks.

"Oh, you know." I shrug merrily. "My usual max. Four-ish months?"

"Why'd you break up?" BJ asks, face daring, spinning the goldplated bracelet from Bottega Veneta around his wrist mindlessly.

I stare over at him, suck in on my bottom lip.

Because he told me he loves me and even then I knew I wouldn't love anyone else ever again.

It's BJ or bust.

But instead I find myself shrugging. "He was too much for me in the sack."

BJ sniffs, annoyed. Shakes his head, looks away from me.

"Alright." Jonah nods. "So give us a breakdown of your time in New York, then—"

"Okay, well, I arrived last December. My family flew over just before Christmas and we went to Whistler with Tom. Then he and I spent New Years in Hawaii with the Foster sisters, and then in January I—"

"—I meant sexually," Jonah interrupts.

Henry gives him a look as Taura glances at him.

"Bit pervy," I tell him.

He shakes his head. "No, it's just—you and casual sex? It's like watching a dog walk on its hind legs . . . like, I cannot fathom it."

Christian gestures at me. "It's pretty confusing, your time-line over there."

"No, it's not." I shake my head as I cuff the jacket of his black Dante Nubuck trucker jacket from Nudie Jeans. "I mean, after you and I hooked up then I—"

BJ's cutlery clatters and he looks over at me with threadbare eyes at the same time Christian yells, "Parks!" and slinks back into his seat. "What the f—?! Why the fuck would you—"

Jonah presses his hands into his eyes.

"Thought we decided to keep that one under our hats." Henry gives me a look.

Beej has gone dead still.

"Listen, drama queens." I hold up a hand to silence them both. "Baxter James Ballentine had P in V sex in a bathtub at the height of our relationship with the girl who used to be my best friend."

"No way." Taura gives me a sarcastic smile. "This is brand new information."

"Yeah—but—" Christian holds his own forehead, distressed. "He's gonna fucking fr—"

"It's fine," BJ tells him, but the words are empty. I seize the opportunity regardless.

"Thank you, Ballentine." I clear my throat. "I really do feel like BJ fucking Paili and then lying about it for three years gives Christian and I a little bit of leeway to have nearly had sex one night in a lift in New York."

I give BJ my politest, meanest smile.

"So why'd you two only almost fuck, then?" BJ asks, nodding his chin at me from across the table. "What stopped you?"

Christian sighs and looks away, shaking his head.

He was sad about Daisy, I was fucked up about Beej. Drunk.

I don't know how or when throughout the night we started touching each other, it was hands brushing at first then holding, his hands on my legs, then my waist, and then we were in the lift on the way up to my apartment and he pinned me against the wall, hands everywhere, big kisses like we used to, hands under clothes. I pushed the lift stop button and got to the buckle of his belt when he grabbed my hand. "I still love her," he told me.

I nodded. "I still love him."

"This would kill her," he told me.

I nodded. "I'd quite like something to kill him," I said quietly.

He flopped his head on top of mine and sighed. Did up the buttons he just undid.

And then I started crying, because that's what I do whenever Christian and I try to have sex, except this time he cried a bit too.

Mine and BJ's eyes catch across the table and I don't need to say why because I know he already knows. He always already knows. His eyes drop mine.

"How was your first day, babe?" Taura says loudly, gaining control of the conversation.

I glance over at her gratefully.

"Um—good." I nod. "Good. I just went shopping, pulled outfits for a shoot we're doing next week with Florence Pugh."

"Is she single?" Henry asks a bit too hopeful and I think he sort of says it to annoy Taura.

"I don't think so." I shake my head. "If she is though, I'd like to have a crack myself."

"Yeah, but you'll have a crack at anything these days, hey?" BJ fires suddenly.

"Oi—" Henry glares over at BJ, but I just stare him up and down.

"Not anything."

BJ shoots me a few arrows and I cross my arms over my chest. "Hey, how's your live-in girlfriend?"

"Yep, love it. Great." He nods once.

"Great." I nod back.

Jonah looks between us. "Great."

"Don't you think, Jo?" Beej eyes him. "She's great."

"She's okay." Jonah nods and shrugs while looking a bit caught in the thickets.

"She's breezy and chill and fun and easy-going and—"

"—Invites herself to live with you," Henry adds and Beej shoots him a look.

"She's the best. Can't wait to spend Christmas with her," Beej tells me, looking me dead in the eye. The table goes quiet. Henry sighs loudly, half on my behalf. We always spend Christmas together and it's obvious—if only for the briefest of seconds—how much that hurts me.

His eyes that were like daggers a second ago turn to sorry feathers and I wonder if we'll ever find a groove to exist with each other where we aren't just tearing each other apart.

I blink it away quickly, give him a small smile, gesturing to the door.

"Well, don't let us keep you. Your easy-going Christmas awaits . . ."

THIRTY

BJ

I'm reeling about New York. Sick to my fucking stomach.

Parks leaves pretty quick after I make that cut about Christmas. Feel shit about that, I shouldn't have done it, but I had to—had to one-up her after that little revelation.

They nearly had sex in New York? What the fuck?

While Jo goes and pays the bill, Christian gets up and walks outside. I follow him because I feel like picking a fight, and I can't fight with the girl I want to.

Round the corner and stop about a metre away, eying him. "Are you fucking joking me, man?" I blink. "Her I get, but you? How could you do that to me?"

And then Christian scoffs. Scoffs, that cocky little shit. Shakes his head. "Beej, for fuck's sake." He pushes his hands through his hair. "I don't know how to get this through your fucking head, but you need to understand that not everything is about you." His eyebrows arch up. "That wasn't about you."

I let out this frustrated growl as I shove my old friend into the wall behind him. "She is always about me."

Nothing sparks in his eye like it used to, he's not defensive over her how he was before. He knocks my hands off him, looking annoyed more than anything.

"Sure, Beej, I get it—" He shakes his head. "You're hers, she's yours, but I wasn't thinking of you—" He pokes me in the chest. "You didn't cross my mind once. I was in New York with one of my best friends and my heart was fucked—" He shrugs. "I was in love with a girl who I couldn't be with because she wanted something that I couldn't give her. I was fucked up and so was Parks. We got drunk and I felt her up and it wasn't about you." He stares me down. "For me anyway," he adds as an afterthought. "Everything for her is about you, but this wasn't about you for me."

I lean back against the wall next to him. "You could have told me."

"Yeah—" He gives me a look. "Because historically you've always taken shit about me and Parks so well."

My brother meanders over, looks between us. "You two sort your shit out?"

"Yeah, I guess." Christian pulls out his phone, already done with the conversation.

"You knew?" I stare over at my brother and try not to look as betrayed as I feel. "About Christian and Jack-Jack? And you didn't say shit?"

"Yeah." Henry shrugs. "Because I sort of think it's probably just time you loosened your grip on who Magnolia can and can't sleep with now that, you know, you've had an affair and have, like, a live-in girlfriend and shit."

I glare over at him, shaking my head a bit. "You know, you could take my side once."

He shrugs completely indifferent, maybe with a hint of anger too. "I might give it a crack if you weren't in the wrong most of the time."

"That's not true." I shake my head. "You're just under her thumb."

"Right." Henry yawns. "Yeah, I'm the one who's under her thumb."

THIRTY-ONE

BJ

It was a lie, what I said to Parks about Christmas

Magnolia's turned me into a fucking liar, where I just spout off shit to one-up her because I don't know what the fuck we are so I need the upper hand.

Can't wait to spend Christmas with Jordan? I'm sweating fucking bullets about it.

No denying it's a bit intense to spend Christmas Day with your girlfriend of one month, but I didn't know what to do when she asked me last week what I was doing for it. Henry was standing behind her waving his arms like a fucking oaf mouthing, "No, no," but she's my girlfriend. What was I supposed to do?

"What's the problem?" I scowled at him once she was out of earshot. "Do you not like her?"

Henry frowns. "Shouldn't you be bringing Parks to Christmas?"

"How?" I stared at him. "How the fuck would you think that's a feasible option?"

He rolled his eyes. "But don't you want Magnolia to be there?"

I sighed like he'd punched me, because it's true. I do. I want her to be everywhere. Wherever I am I want her there. That's the problem.

But I don't know what we are. Haven't for a long time.

We're something. I'm something to her, she's something to me. Sometimes I think we're in love and we've just had a bad run at it, that we're fated and shit, that our stars are on their way to aligning and maybe everything that happened a couple of weeks ago is the beginning of us working out, and then she goes and fucks Jack-Jack Cavern for forty-eight hours straight and I don't know shit.

"We always spend Christmas with the Parks," Henry added with a shrug.

Also true. Since we were kids. Harley and Dad are okay friends, but our Christmases together really started because of Henry and Parks.

Little best friends from the get-go. Her parents were always looking for a good time, always looking for ways to pay less attention to the girls themselves, so we just started going on family trips. Zagreb, Colmar, Budapest, Dresden, Vienna, Basel, Trois Vallées—everywhere with her.

Haven't had a Christmas without her since I was six till last year. Two in a row won't kill me.

We spend Christmas Day with my family—extended, Dad's side—over at my grandparents' estate in Virginia Water.

It's big and loud and I love it, usually.

If we're there, usually Parks is too. Not last year, but neither was I.

Me and the boys took a bender in Paris.

Jordan did well at Christmas today. Charmed my grandparents and my aunts and uncles the way Australians usually can. Henry kept his distance, but for the most part it was pretty good. What wasn't that good was when my little cousin, Chloe, looked Jordan square in the eye and said, "You're not Magnolia."

Jordan laughed and poked her, said, "Good eye!"

Sisters didn't behave—to be expected, I guess—and barely spoke to her, made sure to bring up Parks and Jack-Jack, which broke the news over here in the last few days. They didn't know what to do when Jordan told them that Jack-Jack's even hotter in real life and she didn't blame Parks.

Can't tell whether that was a dig at me or not.

Tried to keep myself in check with all that, did my best not to look like those hickeys on Magnolia's body at brunch weren't just fucking eating me alive.

Made some hickeys of my own on Jordan last night just to prove to myself I don't care. Didn't work.

When we get back to my place around nine that night, I tell Jordan I need to go for a run. Ate too much shit during the day, got a shoot in the new year, which is true.

None of that's a lie, believe it or not.

She smiles at me, kisses my cheek, and goes back to Instagramming her presents from bed. A bed she gets into without showering, because she's normal. She tells me to wake her up when I get home and she'll give me an extra Christmas present. I say okay.

But before I'm out the door, even before I put my trainers on, I know where I'm running to.

It's pure dumb luck she's even at the Holland Park house when I get there. Didn't know she would be. This isn't where she lives anymore and I don't know her new address.

Just feel like being near her.

I stand outside the house across the street from hers like a fucking criminal casing the joint, but this is how I feel with her these days anyway. Someone on the outside looking in.

Used to have a key here, I still do, actually. Never gave it back. Probably should.

Probably won't.

I'm there fifteen minutes maybe—glad I wore compression tights under my shorts, because I'm fucking cold out here—and it's probably a bit past ten when she and Bridget walk out the front door down towards the town car.

Maybe it's because it's an icy winter night or maybe it's just her in that dark green dress and tartan coat, but I freeze up for a couple of seconds when I see her.

Bridget spots me first, taps her sister and nods with her chin.

Magnolia looks over at me, frowning and curious.

Steady myself, swallow heavy, stand up straighter as they walk over.

"Hey." I shove my hands in the pockets of my sweater.

"Hi." She looks up at me, nervous.

"Merry Christmas, Bridge." I give her a peck on the cheek.

Bridget squints at me. "Mmhm."

I glance at Parks, nod my head down the street. "Want to go for a dander?"

Magnolia glances at Bridget, who rolls her eyes.

"Will you be okay?"

"In the town car? With our driver? Yeah, I think so." She looks down at her sister's bare legs. "Will you? You'll freeze."

I give Bridget a playful look how I used to be allowed to. "Not on my watch."

"How's that girlfriend of yours, Ballentine?" Bridget asks sharply and Magnolia smacks her.

"I'll see you at home, okay?" Magnolia squeezes her hand.

Bridge nods at her and walks away. Parks and I trade looks as she does.

"Not my biggest fan?" I give her a grim smile.

"Well." She peers up at me, gives me a curt smile. "Who is these days?"

I scoff a little at her sharpness but she remains stoic.

We walk down the street in silence, and it's my favourite night I've had since the one in the club with her. Neither of these should be my favourite nights, I know that. But she shouldn't be my favourite person anymore and she still is, so . . .

"What were you doing?" she asks eventually.

I shrug a little. "I don't know. Went for a run . . ."

She nods then says, "And you ran to my house?"

I let out a single laugh, wipe my mouth with my hand. Of course I fucking did.

"Felt like I needed to see you," I offer her, glancing down to watch her reaction, but she's too poised to give me one.

"Oh." That's all she gives me.

"I haven't not seen you at Christmas since I was six."

"Last year aside," she says and flicks me a look.

I tried. Turned up to her house, fought her dad to get to her. She wouldn't see me. Harley punched me in the face when I tried to push past him. Her mum blocked the door with her body. I saw her in there though, just for a second. I saw her and I know she saw me. I think about how she looked at me that night most days now. Catches me off guard, slips into my mind without my permission. Those round eyes more hurt than I've ever seen them, more afraid. Our eyes held and I called her name and then Tom fucking England stood between us, shielding her from me like she was his and not mine.

I purse my mouth, say nothing. Becoming a trademark of mine.

"Want me to go?" I offer because it feels like I should. "I'll get you a taxi."

"No," she says resolutely.

I nod once. Swallow. Keep walking. Use the cold to keep me in check. Grateful for it because it means my hands have to stay in my pockets; any warmer and they'd be out on the street, trying to brush up against hers.

"So," she says after a few more minutes of silence, "does Jordan know you're here?"

I stare straight ahead. "No."

She peers up at me. "Well, did you get me anything for Christmas?"

"No." I smirk at her, lying. It's in my pocket and I'm not ready yet. "You get me anything?"

She gives me a look. "I'd have thought that my having forgiven you might've been enough."

I walk ahead of her a few steps, turn around so we're toe to toe for no real reason more than I want to see all of her.

"Have you actually forgiven me?"

Her face looks sad. "I guess not."

I nod. "Fair enough."

"And now you have a girlfriend," she says brightly but her eyes are dim. "Bit of a pile on, really."

205

She steps around me, keeps walking.

I walk after her—it's what she wants me to do. Me chasing her. It's how we are now. She makes me work for it 100 per cent of the time.

Didn't used to be like this, but since I cheated on her it's like she needs me to prove to her that I want her infinitely. It's a glass that can't be full. There's a hole in the bottom of the cup where I broke her and all the ways I want her fall through it.

I catch up to her and she stands at the crossroad, arms folded over her chest. Her face is in a bit of a frown, watching the cars go by as we wait for green. She and I, we're forever waiting for green. It's always the red man.

"How different do you think our lives might be if we weren't how we are with each other?" She blinks up at me.

I clear my throat once. "How are we with each other?"

"Caught," she says without thinking. I don't know whether I'm relieved or if my heart starts to sink.

"Like those turtles—" She nods, glancing up at me—"in the plastic rings and they just grow with them stuck around them. Deformed."

Fuck. I hang my head and we cross the road.

"This is my street," she tells me, nodding down Upper Grosvenor.

Pretty near me, actually.

"Which one's your building?"

She points to it. Two-hundred metres away.

"We've got some time," I tell her and she peers over at me, saying nothing.

How much time do we really have? I don't think either of us knows anymore.

"Are you liking not living at home?" I ask her just to fill the silence.

She pinches her finger mindlessly. She's nervous. "I haven't lived at home for over a year."

"Right." I nod. "Do you like it here?"

"I like living with the girls," she tells me.

"You and Taura, it's nice." I flash her a quick smile. "Glad you've got her."

"Me too," she says as she walks up one of her front steps. "This you, then?"

She nods.

"We'll have to come visit some time."

Her face looks strained. "We?"

I tilt my head, swallow. I give her a shrug, that's all. I don't know what else I can give her yet.

"Can I walk you up?" I ask her and her eyes go round as she nods without looking at me. She turns on her heel and walks ahead of me quickly.

I don't know what I'm doing, I think to myself as she pushes the lift button.

I know what I want to be doing. Her and me in the lift— we've done it before. My hands on her hair and up her dress.

She gets out of the lift and walks to her door, standing in front of it like a guard.

"So, I lied before," I tell her, my hands still in my pockets.

"Oh?" She gives me a nervous look.

"I did get you a present." Her face lightens. "Me and Jordan were in a pawn shop the other day," I tell her.

She gives me a look. "Awful. Why?"

"P-a-w-n not p-o-r-n."

Her face doesn't change and I try not to laugh.

"Still why?"

"Because Jordan collects vintage jewellery—"

Magnolia pulls a face.

"Anyway—" I give her a look. "I found this."

I pull it out of my pocket and drop it into her hand, letting myself touch her a little longer than I should. She stares down at it, the gold twisted rope bow necklace I bought her when I was sixteen, the one she loved and lost years ago. The one that I have a tattoo of on my thumb. She stares up at me blinking, mouth ajar.

"Beej." She blinks. "I love this necklace."

"I know." I nod.

"This was the first thing you ever gave me."

"I know."

"I lost it."

"I know." I laugh. We looked forever for that fucking necklace when she lost it in a club in Greece when she was seventeen. Not because it was expensive but because I gave it to her.

"I was so sad—" She stares at me.

I nod. "I remember."

"They don't make these anymore," she tells me like I don't know.

"Enter: pawn shop," I say, trying to keep it light.

"Thank you." She swallows.

"Yeah, of course." I give her a quick smile because her eyes have gone full Bambi and I'm only so strong.

"Do you want to come in?" she asks me, eyes soft and watching my mouth. She bites down on her bottom lip. If she leans in towards me I'll be a goner.

I'll have cheated on the only two girlfriends I've ever had.

I press my hand into my mouth, barely get my head to shake.

"No," I tell her and I reckon her eyes blink in morse code PLEASE.

The corners of her mouth turn up into this smile that's trying to cover up how she feels like I've rejected her and then she nods quickly.

She turns on her heel and opens her door, slips inside without saying anything else and closes it behind her.

My head falls backwards and I sigh. Cover my face with my hands. What am I doing? What the fuck am I doing? I pull out my phone.

Call her.

"Hello?" She answers after three rings, sounding confused.

"Hey," I say.

Pause.

"Hi," she says eventually.

"What are you doing?"

She pauses. "I just got in from a walk."

"Yeah? Good one?"

"It could have been better," she says and I sigh. "I love my necklace, though."

"Good." I nod to myself. "I'm glad."

"And what are you doing?" she asks.

I give it a few seconds. "Horseback riding."

She starts laughing so I laugh.

"You didn't come in?" she asks in a quiet voice.

"No, I didn't."

"Any reason?" she fishes.

"Yep."

"Any that you're willing to disclose?"

I sigh, shake my head at myself. "I'm tired."

"I'm tired too," she tells me, but I reckon she means the other kind of tired. And it hangs there, what we're really saying, both of us begging the other to wave that fucking white flag. But then, nothing. We just fall to silent. Our phones pressed against our ears, waiting for the other to talk. But neither of us do so it sits there between us. Loud and telling. Scared and hurt. The juxtaposition of everything about us. Comfortable and terrified. Everything's old and all of it's new. Before we used to smother our silences with our bodies. Now we use them to speak all these fucking words we'll never say.

"Want me to hang up?" I ask her eventually.

"No," she answers quickly.

"Okay." I nod.

"Okay."

I mash my lips together, try to think of something to say.

"Do you still hate jelly, then?" I ask and she starts laughing.

"Yes! It's the most ridiculous food in the world. Is it a liquid? Is it a solid?"

I shake my head at her. "It's very clearly a solid."

"No, it's not!" she protests. "It melts as soon as it's in your mouth!"

"That doesn't matter, just because something changes states doesn't mean it wasn't the thing it was in the first place!"

"Yes it does!" she whines.

"No," I scoff. "It doesn't, Parks. What the fuck were you doing during your Physics classes?"

Pause.

"You."

Silence.

I swallow heavy. ". . . You said those were frees."

She breathes out a laugh that bleeds into everything between us.

"Do you remember that time we—" I start to say but she cuts in.

"—Don't," she says urgently.

"Don't what?" I ask, kicking the skirting board by her front door.

"Remember."

"Why?" My breath feels caught in my chest.

"Because," she pouts.

"Because why?" I ask her quickly, staring at her door handle.

"Because it's too hard."

"Why, Parks?"

"You know why." Her voice sounds shaky.

I swallow. "Tell me."

"You tell me first," she says, desperate.

And then her front door opens.

"I'll call you back," I tell her before I pocket my phone.

She's standing there, necklace I just gave her on her already. She swallows, nervous.

I take a step towards her, take the phone from her hand, toss it away. Left hand pushes her up against her door, catch her head with my right one.

I press my body against hers. Our faces are touching, breathing sharp and staggered. She leans her forehead against my mouth and I take a few slow and steady breaths before I find her eyes. And it's just for a second, but we can pretend that nothing happened. I didn't hurt her, she didn't fuck me up. We didn't lose a baby. She didn't run away. We're together. It's Christmas. The years spin around us like a hand on a clock. I could drown in the what ifs if I let myself—might as well. I'll be drowning in her anyway for the rest of my life. Happily, too. What a way to go. What a life.

Her eyes flicker up to mine as she waits for me to kiss her. I can't.

Because I love her. Because she deserves better than me with a girlfriend I snuck away from to see her. Because I don't know if I'll ever be good enough anymore. I don't know how to unhurt her how I did, I don't know if I'll ever know.

And then the moment breaks like her heart on her face.

"I should probably head back," I tell her.

"Right." She nods once, taking a conscious step away from me.

"Jordan," I remind her as if we both could forget.

"Right."

I nod my chin at her. "Happy Christmas, Parks."

She gives me a tiny, shy smile.

"Merry Christmas, Beej."

THIRTY-TWO

Magnolia

Boxing Day. Me and Taura are at the boys' house. And by 'boys' house' I mean the house with the boys I can go to.

There's a multifaceted fracture in our friendship group, the first and most personally prevalent of these being Jordan Dames, but the second one, while harder to see on the surface, is rather foreboding also.

Taura's sleeping with both Henry and Jonah.

They both like her.

She likes both of them.

They both know it.

They're all functioning right now by pretending it's just sex, that they're all just having casual sex the way they have casual sex with other people, but this is different.

The fact is that the older I get the less sure I am that sex is ever just casual.

Henry's had girlfriends in the past, but not in a while. And Jonah's never had a girlfriend. He doesn't really keep female company, maybe because of what happened to his sister.

Just me and Bianca Harrington—neither sexual—we're the only girls he's ever kept around. Now Taura is in the mix with the added sexual component.

I can see them all falling for each other, the boys' eyes getting stormy whenever she pays attention to the other. That's what tonight is though; she's trying to treat them evenly.

Tomorrow Jonah's organised for Tausie, me and Beej to go up for a private tour of some of the ruins up on the Isle

212

of Anglesey with a Neolithic archaeologist. This is something Taura exclusively is excited for because she's weird like that and that's what she wanted to do for her birthday.

But Jonah arranged it just for the four of us. No Henry, no Christian.

It's a recipe for disaster.

Henry and Taurs are sitting on a single-seater sofa, cuddled up, as coupley as this hideous day is long.

I mean, like, legs tossed over each other, playing with each other's hands, she's wearing his socks, all that sort of awful tripe.

I stare over at them and absentmindedly fiddle with the necklace BJ gave me last night.

"You guys are cute." I turn to Christian who's sitting next to me on the couch and we trade looks.

"It's fucking disgusting," he tells them and I smirk.

We've hung out a lot these last few weeks, me and Christian Hemmes.

And please do calm down. It's not like that, we're not going down that road again.

We're both just . . . in love with people who don't want us and/ or are with other people. He spent Christmas Day with Daisy, if you can believe it, but he said the policeman ruined it. Both of our Christmases could have been perfectly perfect and they were both hijacked respectively by a sexy policemen and an evil Australian, so we're mutually miserable and our best friends are in love and so all we have is each other. And do you know what we do?

We go to the gym. I do weight training with him, he does Reformer Pilates with me (however he flat-out refuses to come to my barre classes), we swim, we go to the sauna, we bond over how annoying Jordan is. Occasionally I say, "Fuck the police," so he feels better about Daisy Haites being with that sexy policeman she's dating. We go to his house or my house and watch a disaster film to feel better about our own lives.

Does it work? Unsure, as I'm still here in my workout clothes. Didn't even bother to shower.

Still prettier than Jordan though.

213

Anyway, tonight's pick is *The Day After Tomorrow*. Very un-Christmassy.

Not really sure why Michael Bay hasn't yet graced us with a Christmas-themed disaster film, but it is bound to come out eventually.

Christian nods at the TV screen. It's the part in New York where they're running to the library.

"Oi, hold on, where the fuck did this tidal wave come from, then?"

I shake my head at him. "It's a storm surge."

"What's a storm surge?"

I give him a look and wish desperately I knew the answer because I love knowing everything. "I don't know."

Henry nods at my necklace. "I thought you lost that."

"Oh—" I press it into my chest. "Um—"

Christian eyes it. "Didn't we tear apart a club in Athens looking for that?"

"Well . . ."

"I swear to God if you had it all this time, I'll go back to 2014 and smack you in the head."

Henry squints at him, thinking back. "Didn't you . . .?"

"Yeah." Christian nods, annoyed. "I punched a lad from Bristol for that."

"It was Manchester, actually, and I maintain he stole it."

Henry eyes it. "Where'd this one come from, then?"

I breathe out airily, shrugging my shoulders like it's nothing. "Your brother gave it to me."

"My brother gave it to you?" He pulls back, surprised but a little smug.

I nod.

Henry's eyebrows are up. "When?"

"Yesterday," I mumble.

Everyone sits up straighter.

"Yesterday?" Taura blinks. "You mean on Christmas?"

"I mean—" I frown, not liking their tones. "It was late, like barely December 25th still, but technically, yes, I suppose. 'On Christmas,' whatever that means."

214

"It means he gave you a Christmas present." Christian gives me a look.

"So what?" I wave my hand. "That doesn't mean anything."

"Your childhood sweetheart and ex-boyfriend you had a secret love-child with gives you a Christmas gift and it means nothing? Even though you're wearing it?" Henry asks pointedly.

I glare at him and know we both know it means everything to me. I just don't know what it means to BJ.

"Jake Gyllenhaal," Christian says loudly, casting me a line. "Smash?"

"Have," I tell the TV.

And the whole room stares over at me.

"Just kidding!" I laugh. "It was just a kiss."

Henry throws the remote at me. "Shut up. Really?"

I shrug.

"When?" Taura asks loudly.

"New York. I just was trying to annoy Rush." I shrug again and they both roll their eyes, but Christian's not paying attention, just sitting there stroking his chin. "Should I get a beard?"

"No. Why?" I glance at him. "Because the sexy policeman has a bit of one?"

"No," Christian scowls at me. "What the fuck did you bring him up for?"

I pull a face, look over to Henry and Taura. "Someone's touchy . . ."

"I am touchy, Parks. You know why?" he asks loudly, sounding preachy. I sigh already. I don't have to respond. I suspect he'll tell me either way.

"Because you and me are sitting on this fucking couch and the people we love are with people who aren't us."

I give Christian a disparaging look.

"I wouldn't say I love him . . . out loud."

They all laugh.

My head pulls back.

"What?" I frown.

"Did you think we didn't know?" Christian glances between the other two, before zoning back in on me. "You told me in New York—"

"That was months ago!"

They all chortle more, shaking their heads.

Taura tilts her head at me. "Babe—"

Henry's face scrunches up. "Do you want us to pretend we don't know you love him?"

I snort, indignant. "I—no. Listen, I—"

"—Love him." Christian nods. "You love him."

"I—"

"—Love him." Christian gives me a curt smile. "You've loved him since you were fourteen," he tells me. "Magnolia, you never stopped."

He gives me a look I shouldn't argue with, especially considering the implications of that sentence.

"Parks." Henry gives me a look. "We all know, we talk about it all the time."

I stare at each of them, my feet feeling sweaty. I blink, a bit horrified. "BJ knows I love him?"

And he still picked that other girl?

"Oh!" Henry shakes his head. "No."

Christian shakes his head. "I don't think he knows, no."

Taura rolls her eyes. "How could he not know?"

"Because it's tangled. They're tangled." Henry gestures to me and I get the feeling these might be his brother's regurgitated thoughts rather than his own. "Too much history. Is she in love with him or is she just attached to him?"

"Both." Taura shrugs.

I stare at Henry. "He must know I love him."

He nods. "He does know you love him, Parks. But you love all of us."

"But I'm different with him." I frown.

"You have a history with him, so why wouldn't you be different?" Henry nods once. "But just because you have a history with someone doesn't mean you're actively in love with them."

"—Which you are, by the way." Christian gives me a pointed look.

I glance at him. "Yes, okay. Thank you."

I look between them all. "Do you think if he knew for certain that I love him that he'd break up with Jordan?"

Taura nods emphatically.

I look between the boys. "Really?"

"Tell him!" Henry points at me. "He's always fought for you. What have you done? Nothing! Ran away, dated a sexy pilot, fucked his best friend—"

"For the billionth time—" I wave a finger between Christian and me—"zero penetration."

"Lot of hand work though," Christian winks at Henry.

(We do a no-look high-five and Henry rolls his eyes.)

And then Christian leans over and flicks me. "Go tell him."

I frown at him. "No." I glance at Taura. "He should tell me. I made it like, very, very clear that I had feelings for him."

"Yeah?" Christian frowns at me. "How?"

"I've done . . ." I swallow, thinking for things I could say that are quantifiable. "Well, I—I did—when I told him I was staying and he—" I clear my throat.

We've looked at each other in ways that I think mean something?

We've . . . had passive aggressive conversations?

We've held hands when we told our friends a traumatic secret?

"The clearest you were was when you were drunk and you asked him in front of all of us if he wanted to have sex," Henry tells me as he stretches his arms up over his head.

I balk at him. "Sorry—I what?"

"At the club the other night." Henry shrugs. "You were sloshed. And you asked BJ if he wanted to have sex with you."

I glance at Christian, incredulous. "No?"

"You were really drunk," Taura offers.

"Oh my God!" I fan myself. I might throw up. "And he heard me?"

"Yeah, we all heard you," Henry says merrily. "You were really loud."

My hands fly to my face.

"If it's any consolation—" Taura gives me a look. "BJ was well pleased, though it was subdued for his girlfriend's sake."

I glance from Henry to Christian. "He was?"

They both nod, smiling a little.

I jump to my feet. "I'm going to do it."

"Now?" Taura jumps to hers.

I nod, looking between the boys. "Where is he?"

"Just at home, I think?" Taura nods.

"With Jordan?" I glance between them.

"Who cares!" Henry sing-songs, too excited.

"Okay." I nod and walk towards the door.

Christian's face falters. "You're going to go like that?"

I glance down at myself.

Black logo-print cropped vest top from Dolce & Gabbana with the black side stripe leggings from No Ka' Oi. Candy-pink light polyester hooded puffer jacket from Prada and the Nike Air Max 270 React in fire pink/white that match perfectly.

"Um—" I nod. "Yep."

"I'll drive," Henry nods.

I shake my head. "No, I think I need to do this by myself."

"Don't chicken out," Christian tells me, eyes stern.

"I won't."

I might. I swallow nervously, give them a solemn nod and walk to the door.

Taura runs after me, throwing her arms around me.

"Just think, in, like, an hour you'll probably be back at our apartment, kissing him."

I nod, nervous.

"I'm going to stay here tonight. Give you guys some space," she tells me as she gives me an uncouth wink.

I swallow. "Wish me luck?"

She shakes her head as she squeezes my hand.

"You don't need it."

THIRTY-THREE

Magnolia

I run there, which helps, I think.

Running makes it harder to feel how nervous I am and disguises my presumed nervous sweats with the fact that I'm actually also just a bit sweaty.

Exercising is a bit like a panic attack, don't you think? At least symptomatically. Out of breath, sweaty, heavy breathing —I'd be all those things anyway doing this.

It makes me feel quite sad to think that he doesn't know. I always thought he knew.

Because I know he loves me.

It's been one of the great burdens of my adult life knowing that I love him and he loves me and we just cannot for the life of us figure out how to be together. Needs me? I'm not so sure, but loves me? I've always known that.

They're right in lots of ways about the history. There are those attachments—Bridget's trauma bonds, the willow tree, all the ways we've hurt each other to feel close to each other, all the ways he saved me when we were little, literally and metaphorically, the oysters, the bad men in Greece, the losers in London night clubs with busybody hands, the teachers, Marsaili, shitty boys in school with big mouths full of lies. I have all these ties to him. First boyfriend, first kiss, first love, first time, first everything, really. How he was my teacher and my partner in so many key life areas. My best friend and my family and my pillow and my quilt. Each of them are like bricks laid in the house I built to love him, but the point is really that house I built isn't a monument to a love I used to have. It's a house I want to live inside of still.

I text him.

21:37

Beej 🐝

> Can you come downstairs?

Now?

> Yes.

??

Ok.

And then I stand there, out the front of his apartment, pacing.

I'm a ball of nervous energy when he walks out the front.

I go light-headed when I see him, and not just because he's perfect. Even just in his black Maison Margiela flipped logo hoodie and logo-print track pants from the Rhude x McLaren collab, he's perfect standing over there with that low brow and a deep frown.

My bravery's knees start to buckle when I think about how once upon a time he only used to smile when he saw me.

When did that stop?

When did I stop being his happy thought? Because he's still mine. Even when I've hated him I've loved him.

On my worst nights in New York, when I was my saddest and my loneliest, I didn't go out and sleep with those boys I don't really know. I lay in my bed and thought about BJ. I wrapped the thoughts of him around my lost heart like a blanket, let them warm me up, let them tear me to pieces, let myself feel the weight of losing him. And for all the pain and all the sadness, for all the shitty things that happened, I still find myself not regretting it at all because he loved me. It'll be what they put on my tombstone, I think.

He Loved Her.

I hope that's what they'll say about me.

He folds his arms over his chest and looks at me, the familiar twinkle of concern in his eyes. "You okay?"

"Mmhm." I nod, still pacing.

He frowns more. "You sure?"

I nod, so nervous now.

His frown turns to confusion, as he looks me up and down. "Are you in athleisure wear?"

"Yes." I swat my hand. "I ran here."

His face falters. "You run now?"

I offer him a shrug. "At midnight in the park, or else it's scary."

"You could just . . . not go in the park at midnight."

"Where's the fun in that?" I give him a breezy smile though none of me is breezy.

He gives me a look. "Not dying . . . pretty fun."

I roll my eyes and the frown he has settles on me as he waits. "What are you doing here, Parks? It's Boxing Day."

I frown at him. "You came to my house on Christmas Day."

He clocks the necklace and swallows. I press it into my chest, try to remember how I felt when he gave it to me last night and channel it to make me brave.

I ball my hands into fists, dig my nails into my hands—there'll be scars tomorrow—and then I look up at him.

My heart's going berserk. I wish I could grab on to him, steady myself—he might be the only thing that could.

This is the final frontier for us, I think. The only things left that we haven't tried to make us work are honesty and vulnerability.

How obvious, you'd think—right? But it's quite hard when you don't trust each other.

It's a deep dive into the darkness, hoping I pull up into some light.

"I love you," I tell him and the windows of my heart burst open. The room fills with a thousand turtle doves and one little deer.

He blinks a lot. "What?"

"I love—I'm in love with you."

He's completely still besides blinking.

A piece of hair falls over his eye and I want to move it away from his face so I can see all of him.

He says nothing.

I say nothing.

He licks his top lip, his breathing gets quicker and louder. "Are you drunk?"

I swallow nervously, hear the sound of it in my own head.

I shake my head.

"At all?" he clarifies.

I go hot under my skin. I shake my head more.

He looks away from me, nodding. Thinking.

And then I notice my own chest moving faster, up and down, the breathing quickens and my brain begins to scramble too because this is not going how I thought it would.

I thought he'd grab me and kiss me, that he'd have dragged me behind his building to feel me up and kiss me more in secret, that his hands would run over my body and we would be close how we haven't been in a year. I think about that day all the time. The last time we were together in Dartmouth. His breath on my neck, his hipbones pressing into me so hard I bruised a bit the morning after, us against the tree where we should have been this month again. I'd forgive him for not being there then if he'd just fucking say anything now— anything at all. But he's not. He's just staring at me.

"Why are you telling me?" he asks eventually, not taking his eyes off of me.

I swat all the turtle doves away, chase out the deer, and slam the windows of my heart shut because he's not saying it back.

"Um—" My eyes kind of go strange, bleary. I can't see properly. I don't know if my eyes have gone teary or I'm

222

dizzy—am I feeling faint?—maybe something blew into my eyes. I give him a weak shrug.

"Henry said you didn't know . . .?"

"I—I didn't kn—" BJ shakes his head once. "I wasn't sure."

I nod once, wondering how different everything might be if he had known.

I frown, biting down on my bottom lip. "How could you not know?"

"I don't know?" He shrugs. "You broke up with me . . . You dated my best friend. You dated Tom . . . You dated everyone—" He considers all of this. "You moved to another city in the middle of the night. You were gone for a year."

"So?"

"So you don't do that shit when you love someone," he tells me sharply.

My bottom lip shakes. "You cheated on me when you loved me."

"Yeah, but that was different."

"Why? How?" I frown.

"Because I'm fucked up," he yells at me, a bit exasperated.

"Well, so am I!" I stare at him and then say under my breath, "Thanks to you."

He scoffs, annoyed now. I can see it all over his face. "Yeah, back at you."

"Okay, well . . . great." I nod, give him a tight smile. "Is that it, then?"

He breathes out, offers me nothing but a shrug. "What do you want me to say?"

I let out a small laugh but it's tangled with a cry.

I swipe my hands at my face; I don't want him to see tears.

I shake my head at him. "Nothing."

THIRTY-FOUR

BJ

It's unbelievable that she did that.

My girlfriend upstairs and Parks calls me down to tell me she loves me.

Holy fucking shit.

I've waited for her to say that to me since she left last December and then there she was, saying everything I've wanted to hear, and I couldn't say it back.

I don't know what happened.

I got angry. Don't really know why.

Felt indignant that she'd do this now on a whim. Casually jog over to my house late one night to turn my whole fucking life upside down. Spent the shittest year of my life trying my fucking best to try to let her go after she left me for something I did when I was twenty. After everything that happened and everything we'd been through—because we'd been through everything by then. News to everyone else, what happened, but not to us. And then she ended it with me anyway. I don't understand how I can have missed her how I've missed her and be so fucking angry now that she's here, doing and saying everything I've wanted her to the whole time.

Do I love her? Of course I fucking love her. She's everything I've ever wanted. But it was honestly only about thirty days ago that I began to accept that me and her happening probably wasn't on the cards anymore. And now she's back. Fucking everything up, fucking me up—because she's back, and that's what she does. And me? I have a girlfriend who's living with me because she has an idiot for a flatmate who doesn't know how to use a fucking bath. And she's upstairs, sitting on my couch, wearing a sweater of mine that'd look better on Parks because everything about me does, and she's waiting for me to make her a cup of tea. I said we needed milk—another lie for Parks. I hate lying, and I'm lying to Jordan all the time covering the tracks of how much I love this other girl whose sole mission in life is to fuck mine up. And what about Jordan? Did Parks even give her a thought before she marched on over to declare her love to me? When the articles started running about me and a new girlfriend, I only let them run because Parks was gone. If I thought she was coming back, if I thought it was an option that we—I never would have—

It started out purely as sex, me and Jordan.

And it was fine. I was cool with that, she was cool with that. Then we kind of just started hanging out, mostly just as friends. And it was cool, like to go to a pub to watch football and shit with a hot girl who'd just drink the beers and eat the pies, someone who I didn't have a continent's worth of broken-hearted history with, no secret stone under a tree, no infidelity, no hospital visits, no near-death experiences where I'm dying in her arms—just a clean slate.

To me, all the girls from London, in one way or another, just felt like, shitter, cheaper versions of Parks. But Jordan didn't remind me of Magnolia at all, which was exactly what I needed. To be done.

I needed to be done with Parks.

Not because I wanted to be, but because she forced my hand. How could I ever actually be done with Parks? Couldn't be. So I just pushed her from my mind. I put her in the cupboard under the stairs and played the sound of Jordan really loud to drown out the banging of how much I loved Magnolia.

Got easier and easier too. To drown her out, to ignore the sound of being with someone I'm not meant to be with.

It's getting loud again, the banging under the stairs.

I love her, I know I do. I should have told her that. Didn't. A bit out of shock, but mostly cause I'm proud. Might be the death of me. Or us. We're both proud.

I don't love anything more than I love her, but I'd be lying if I said I didn't get a high out of watching her squirm. I know that's fucked up, but that's all I had for so long. Watching her be uncomfortable about the things I did or the things I said was, for years, the only way I knew I still meant something to her.

And if she thinks she can just swoop back into my life and I'd drop it all because those Bambi eyes blinked at me—? I mean, I would, but fuck her for thinking it. For thinking she can boomerang me around like this.

"Hey." Jordan looks up and then at my empty hands. "No milk?"

I shake my head, walk over to her. What the fuck am I doing? I'm angry. I'm doing what I do when I'm angry at Parks.

"Get up," I tell her.

Jordan swallows, does it.

I pull my hoodie off her body, grab her, hold her against me. She smiles as she kisses me back.

We haven't had sex in a while, not like we were before—I wonder if Jordan knows why? Why I've barely touched her since Parks came back? Or why when we do I keep my eyes open?

I don't know what I'm doing even though I know exactly what I'm doing—done this before—no doubt that, now Magnolia's back, I'll do it again. 'Sex is not a weapon,' Claire says to me sometimes in our sessions. But she's wrong.

Parks wants to throw Jack-Jack Cavan at me and then come over a few days later telling me she loves me? Fuck her.

Jordan pulls my top off, hands running over my body. I fall backwards onto the couch, bringing her down on top of me and I make a mental note to cancel therapy this week. I don't need that lecture.

I don't want to think about it, just want to do it.

And we do.

And I don't think of my girlfriend once.

Hen

What the fuck did you do

What?

What did you do?

?

Taura was staying at mine tonight and texted Parks and now we're at their house and Magnolia's crying in the bathroom and she won't let us in because I don't know why

So what did you do

Fuck off

Did you do something?

Leave it, Hen

Did you?

I said leave it.

THIRTY-FIVE

BJ

The next morning Jo and I leave the house a little after 7 a.m.
to go grab the girls for the excruciatingly long drive ahead.

Tausie's really into old shit, so for her birthday Jo organised
a private tour of a bunch of ruins with an archaeologist he
knows through Banksy.

Just a day trip, just the four of us.

Jordan offered to come too. Jo made up some shit about
how it was an already booked tour with limited seats. Not
believable at all, but Jordan seems unaware that Jonah's increasingly off of her.

Grateful she's not coming though. Need her not to be there.
Need to be alone with Parks, feel out how bad I fucked up
last night . . .

We pull up outside their place in Jo's new Rolls Cullinan
and he texts Tausie to come outside. A couple minutes later she
appears and he gets out of the car to kiss her happy birthday.

I follow his lead, hug her, but as I do she gives me a cross
look.

"Idiot," she whispers under her breath, quiet enough for
Jonah not to hear her.

And then out walks Parks.

Huge white puffer coat, hair out, sunglasses on.

Sunglasses.

Fuck me. I could count on my hands the number of times in
our lives she's worn sunglasses. She considers her eyes 'too beautiful
to cover up' and only wears them when she's hiding her eyes.

I walk up to her, chin as low as my voice. "Hey, can we chat for a sec?"

She walks past me to the car. "No."

"Please?"

"In no world," she barely whispers before climbing in and slamming the door shut.

Didn't even clock that I'm wearing a grey hoodie. She loves me in grey hoodies.

I sigh, catch eyes with Taura, who's not happy with me either. Walk around, climb in next to Magnolia.

Jonah peels out.

"Coffees?"

"Desperate for one." Taura flashes him a smile and I get the feeling she's been dealing with the mess I made all night.

We find an open coffee shop about ten minutes away and Jo and Tausie get out to go grab them.

"Parks, listen," I start.

But she just swings open her door and walks over to them.

I lean back in my seat, let out a frustrated sound, and get out of the car anyway, because it's a five-hour drive up to Anglesey and I should stand as much as I can, I suppose. I was excited about a long drive with Parks before but now I just wish we took the plane. Taura's mapped out a little scone tour though, best scones in Britain according to her.

Jo hands me a batch brew and a confused look.

Shake my head a bit.

Can't believe he doesn't know. In this friendship group? A fucking miracle.

We start driving.

Taura's on the songs. Jeremy Zucker. More feelings-y than I want, validating Magnolia's every thought.

"You're wearing trousers," I tell her, trying to break the tension.

I poke her leg. Black leggings. Never wears black. Never wears pants, actually. And honestly, I just want to touch her.

Feel like we recalibrate when we do. Skin on skin and we'll be okay.

She knocks my hand off of her, doesn't even look at me. Fuck.

"Oi, Parks—" Jonah nods his chin back at her after we've just gotten on the M40. "You can take those sunglasses off now. No one's going to pap you in my car."

She takes a measured breath. Waits a few seconds. Takes them off and looks straight out the window, but not before I clock them.

They look like fucking emeralds, goddamn it.

Must have cried all night.

Jo catches them in his rearview—a decade of friendship, you know your friend's crying face.

"What happened?" He snaps around to look at her.

"Nothing." I shake my head.

He stares over at me, annoyed. "What the fuck did you do?"

"Nothing," Magnolia says, still looking out the window.

I glance over at her.

Jonah shakes his head. "What am I missing?"

None of us say anything. Thank God.

And then—

"I told BJ I love him," Parks announces.

Jonah swerves the car. "You what?"

Magnolia looks over at him. "I told BJ I'm in love with him."

Jo catches my eye in the mirror. "What did BJ say?"

Taura glances over her shoulder, gives me an icy look. "Nothing."

Jo looks at me in the rearview, eyes all wide and murdery.

"What the fuck?" he mouths.

I shake my head and look out the window before looking over at Parks.

"I didn't say nothing."

She turns to face me and I know immediately—immediately—I'm in way over my head, because she is ready to go.

I can see it. Battle ready. Jaw set. Tongue sharpened.

Got her emerald eyes on, which makes me weak in the stomach and kills all my resolve.

She could walk all over me, strangle me to death, and I wouldn't notice. If the emerald eyes are out then I'm dying anyway.

Shit.

"No, you're right—" She nods. "You said, 'Are you drunk?' and 'Why are you telling me this?'"

"BJ—" Taura sighs like it's her I hurt.

I give Parks a look. "Can we not do this in front of them?"

"Do what?" She blinks. "I have nothing left to say to you."

I sniff, annoyed. Look out the window.

"Actually, I do have something to say to you." She clears her throat. "Do you have any idea—" She smacks me in the arm—a good sign, that. Any kind of physical touch from her is a good sign—"how embarrassing that was? Telling you and you having nothing to say back to me?"

"Are you being serious right now? You called me in the middle of the night—"

"It was, like, eleven," she growls.

("Actually, because of Jordan, he goes to bed pretty early these days," Jonah interjects.)

"—With my girlfriend upstairs," I keep going. "And you fucked off—remember? You left—"

"—Because you cheated on me with my best friend!"

("Ex-best friend," Taura notes, and Jo shakes his head. "Probably not the time.")

I talk over both of them. "And you're standing there, in exercise clothes—"

("Bit of a weird aside, my man." Jonah nods from the front.)

"—Telling me you love me." I stare at her. "What am I supposed to do with that?"

She stares at me. Glares, actually. Her eyes pinch and a look rolls over her face, and then my favourite sparring partner arrives: Petty Parks.

"Nothing." She shrugs a tiny bit. "I take it back."

I snort a laugh. "You can't."

("This isn't going to be a good birthday." Taura shakes her head.)

231

"I can." She nods. "I take it back."

I shake my head at her, defiantly. "You can't. You already told me—"

("Oh fuck," sighs Jonah.)

"—You love me," I tell her. "I heard you. My doorman heard you. You love me, there's no take-backs."

She breathes loudly through her nose, huffing.

And my heart is racing. I love fighting with her. Love everything with her, actually. Sleeping, showering, reading, driving. But fighting? That's kind of our sweet spot these days.

We didn't fight before but now it's all we've got left. Closest thing to throwing her against a wall and kissing her is just throwing words at her.

She looks a tiny bit like she might cry, like she would if she could, but she won't. Wouldn't lose face to me twice in a row.

She sits up straighter.

"Taura," she says brightly.

"Mm?" Taura glances back, nervous.

"Remember how you asked me what Jack-Jack is like in bed and I said I'd tell you another time?"

She looks uneasy. "Mmhm."

"I'm going to tell you now." Parks nods.

Tausie shakes her head. "No, that's okay—"

"—No, it's fine, I don't mind. This is great." Parks nods.

I wobble my head around. "Seems weird that this conversation didn't organically take place already, seeing as you're flatmates and all, but go on."

"Firstly," Magnolia says loudly over me, "he's ripped. I mean, jacked. Completely. Head to toe. The perfect body. So tan. California tan—"

"—Do you want me to take my shirt off?"

("No," Taura says.)

"—I will," I keep going. "Pull over? I'll fucking bench press Jonah right here, right now."

("Sorry—" Jo looks back at me. "Do I get a say in this?")

"And do you know what I love most about him?" Parks says, ignoring me.

"Nothing?" I cut in again. "Because you love me, you told me last night."

(Jonah starts laughing.)

Magnolia keeps at it though.

"He's not a slut," she says with a stare at me. "Not slutty at all! Do you know how great it is to be with a man and not worry about catching gonorrhoea?"

"Actually," Taurs tosses a ginger look at Jonah. "No."

Jo chuckles and flicks her.

"Well, it's wonderful." Magnolia shrugs. "Very, very releasing. A weight off my shoulders, because—"

I look over at her. "You know, Parks, it's funny you're talking about sluts. I mean, how many people did you hook up with while you were in New York?"

"Oi—" Jonah frowns from the front, but I know I crossed a line.

I'd kill people for saying less to her than that. But we're mid-battle and it rolls right over her. Doesn't wear it for a second.

"Jonah it's fine. Don't be so silly—" She leans forward, squeezes his shoulder, turns back to me. I brace myself, fight the urge to kiss her. "Great question, Beej. Over the almost year I was in New York, I had sex with . . . less people than you did the week we broke up."

She gives me a smug smile.

My mouth puckers and I squint at her.

"Would you like me to tell you who they are?" she asks brightly.

I nod once. "Love you to."

"Tom."

"Yeah, obviously." I shrug like it's not the fucking blow to the head it is.

"Jack-Jack."

I nod once.

"Dieter Van Lauers. Addington Van Schoor—"

233

"Stupid name." I shake my head. "Hate him. Next."

She gets a look on her face. "Stavros Onassis."

Jonah spins around. "Heard about that. Of all the people to fuck about with, Magnolia—"

I frown.

"—Dated," Taura interjects.

"Kind of." Magnolia considers. "Loosely."

"For how long?" Jo asks and I'm annoyed that he cares.

"Like a month, if that." Parks shrugs. "It was weird, actually. I think Romeo Brambilla had something to do with it ending."

A look flashes over Jonah's face that I don't get.

"Anyway." Magnolia clears her throat. "Then a secret person I can't say."

I roll my eyes. "So, Evans."

She frowns.

"You fucked Rush Evans, Magnolia. It was in the papers constantly, you twat."

And I'm acting like I don't give a fuck, but that one annoys me because he's everywhere these days. He could have anyone and he had her.

Taura turns around from the front seat to face us, her face pulling.

"Are we still going to call it that?"

"What do you mean?" Magnolia crosses her arms. "What else would we call it?"

Tausie gives her an uncertain look. "Dating?"

Parks scoffs. "Taura, Rush was gone half the time. I dated, like, three guys in between—"

"—Yeah and you dumped them all the second Rush came back into town." Taura gives her an impatient look. "You dated him."

Parks shakes her head, all resolute. "I wouldn't do that to Tom."

I stare over at her. "You did do that to Tom," I scoff, staring at her like she's a foreign object. "You're so fucked in the head with all these little caveats and parentheses that

234

you put around everything, like—I don't know why—you're trying to exercise some control over ev—"

"—You've been in therapy for four months," she interrupts. "You don't know what the fuck you're ta—"

"—It means shit, Parks," I say over her. "It's bullshit. You fucked over Tom when you fucked his best friend just like you fucked over me when you fucked mine."

Her head pulls back a bit. Everything I said is true and I mean it—she did fuck over Tom and she fucked me over too. And I'm sure she'll fucking do it again, but that's not why I'm saying it all. I'm saying it because I'm reeling.

Try not to let it look like the thought of it all is killing me but it is. And actually, what the fuck, when she left me it was just me and Tom. Ever.

And now that's five others? Five whole other people? Who've seen her and touched her and held her . . .

And I know I'm being a fucking hypocrite. Seven? That's not that many people. Could be me on a bad week.

But she's not like that.

She's not like me.

At least she wasn't when she left me . . .

She's watching me closely now. Reading me. Seeing how I wear it, this new version of her. It feels like she's trying to prove to me that she's less mine than I think she is, but until last night I didn't know she wanted to still be mine at all. I don't know what she's waiting for. Vindication? Chastisement? Judgement? Forgiveness? I give her none of them.

I'll give her my heart for free in a heartbeat though, if she'll still take it.

She's staring straight ahead, breathing like she's coming off a high, deep and measured winding down. Tired. Wish I could pull her into my lap, let her rest, remind her I'm her safest place. I want to say sorry. Tell her I'm a fuck-up and I love her, that I'm done with the games. But I can't find the words.

She took them back.

I tap her gently and she looks over at me, annoyed.

Summon her with my fingers.

She shakes her head.

Wave her over again.

She rolls her eyes but obliges me this time.

She leans over and as she does I get a rush of endorphins. She's the greatest drug on the planet. I've done them all and I know it for sure.

She lifts her eyebrow, impatient.

I move in closer, whisper, "How's the weather, Parks?"

And I swear to God, our question does its magic. For a moment, I can see it on her—she forgives me. The inclusions in those gemstone eyes of hers begin to fade and they start clearing back up to flawless. I smile at her, feeling proud of myself for winning her back.

Then it scatters. The emeralds cloud over and her face settles back into anger.

"I told you I love you and you're asking me about the weather?" she whispers to me. Then she looks me dead in the eye. "Fuck you."

THIRTY-SIX
Magnolia

This is all BJ and I used to do—long aimless drives to faraway parts of the country. I love being in cars with him.

Locked away in our own little box, no outside forces peering in, just me and him alone in the world is how it should be.

Not this drive. I hate this drive.

I'm waving the boys I've slept with around like they're sage I'm burning, trying to ward off true love.

I do it because it hurts him, which is what I want to do. Those lips on my neck that aren't his, someone else's sweat on my body and in my mouth.

But it hurts me back because I don't know that he cares anymore. He doesn't flinch, he doesn't tell me to stop. Just looks at me like I'm a foreign object.

We get to Anglesey a little bit after ten, and I'm motion sick from looking at my iPhone the whole time, but what the fuck else was I going to do?

I'm out of the car like a light, putting as much distance between me and him as possible.

I don't know how to handle today anymore because it's Taura's birthday. Jonah brought her up here, away from London, so that they could be couple-y—he didn't say that but I know it's true. So I can't just make her be my buddy. I want to give them space, I want them to get to feel like whatever they want to feel like. Just because BJ and I are stuck doesn't mean everyone else should be.

Plus they look so cute together. Both of them in their little Moncler puffers, those cuties.

When I climb out of the car, BJ looks down at me.

"What the fuck is on your feet?"

I glance down at myself then glare up at him. "The Adhara boot from the Moncler Genius, 8 Palm Angels, Moon Boot collab. Obviously." I cross my arms, huffing at him. "And I don't appreciate your tone implying that these were the wrong shoes to wear."

Jonah and Taura hold hands and walk over to who I assume is the guide. Jonah ushers me forward to the guide-man, I think just to get me away from BJ.

"Magnolia, this is Angus Welling."

I give him a quick smile, acknowledge him but only just. And I stand there, bored already but not bored because BJ's standing opposite me, staring right at me with eyes I used to think I could read but maybe I know nothing anymore. Still even if that's true—I want to poke the bear, because I love poking the bear.

Because I love the bear.

That stupid bear, standing over there in the black balloon leg trousers from Tom Wood, a grey hoodie from Balenciaga (which feels like a personal attack because he knows I love him especially in grey) that he's wearing under the black reverse monogram puffer jacket from Louis Vuitton, which feels annoying because I'm wearing a Louis Vuitton puffer too and I don't feel like being on the same page as him like that because we aren't on the same page in any way that actually matters.

I stare over at him, hypothesising how to best make him cross or sad or annoyed or just anything more than how indifferent he was to me last night.

I look around us. We're in the middle of nowhere. We took a turn off a small road just north of Llanfaelog village. There's no one around but the four of us and the guide.

I glance back at the guide.

Tall guy, dark hair, almost black. Broad. He gives off a Clark Kent vibe. Handsome.

238

He's no Ballentine, but who is?

In a pinch—you know?

I square my shoulders, brighten my face, and walk over to him, batting my eyes.

"I'm sorry. What was your name again?"

"Angus." He smiles, a bit pleased to have my attention.

"And what is this place, Angus?"

"It's called the Ty Newydd Burial Chamber."

BJ rolls his eyes.

I link Taura's arm with mine and look up at Angus. "And why do we like the Ty Newydd Burial Chamber?"

"We like it because it's from the Neolithic period."

I glance at Taurs for clarification.

"Somewhere between 10,000-4500 BC," she tells me.

("Bit of a big margin," says BJ.)

"We think this one's from about 4000-2000 BC," Angus adds.

("Still a big margin," Beej whispers to Jo, who smacks him in the stomach.)

"And sites like this are important because they give us a glimpse into the strangers of the past. At this site, archeologists have found arrowheads, pottery, even some ancient art," Angus continues, a bit oblivious.

"It's just four rocks." BJ blinks.

Jonah gives him a look.

"Do you like history, Magnolia?" Angus asks brightly as we walk around the meadow. Tausie and Jonah are taking photos in the dolmen, being all sweet and together and I feel a pang of nervousness for Henry—for all of us, actually.

"Yeah," BJ says from behind us. "Do you like history, Parks?"

"I used to." I smile up at Angus brightly, ignoring BJ. "Loved it, actually. So much. I thought there was something so romantic about history, the ways it connects people to one another, all the ways it can speak to our future. I loved history." I flick my eyes over to BJ, whose jaw's set, watching me. "But I gave up on it." I nod. "Last night."

"Oh." Angus nods, glancing at BJ. "That's . . . oddly specific."

Angus sniffs an amused laugh and then he lets out a rueful sigh. "If you don't much like history, I'm afraid I'm not going to be much use to you."

I turn around and give him a bright smile as Taura and Jo join us.

"Now, while I don't love history, I do love an educated man."

"Do you?" BJ scoffs. "Is that why you're fucking a pro skate-boarder?"

Angus's eyes go wide, Taura's mouth makes an O shape and Jonah turns to him, head pulled back. But my face doesn't move a muscle.

My heart beats faster though, because—

Ding ding goes the bell, and a girl in a bikini walks between us with a sign that says 'Round Two'.

"I'm sorry." I squint over at him, giving him a fake smile. "I don't know what you mean."

"I'm talking about that skateboarder slash model you went home with last week."

"Oh." I nod. "You mean Jack-Jack? Who I dated for five months?" BJ bites down on his tongue. "Who you're obsessed with?" His eyes pinch. "Who has a Master's in Art History?" He rolls his eyes.

BJ nods his chin at nothing. "Fucking useless degree."

"Completely." I nod emphatically. "Hey, what's your Master's degree in?"

Jonah chuckles.

"Actually—" I squint up at him. "What do you do for work, again?"

BJ's jaw goes slack and I walk away.

We go to four or five other Neolithic sites and they're all much of a muchness if I'm honest, but BJ's fucking livid that I'm pretending to care about it, so you can imagine how I've become quite the standing-stone enthusiast over the last four hours.

I research the 'Bronze Age' and 'Neolithic' so much as we drive between locations I feel a bit like I might throw up, but BJ's getting angrier and angrier by the moment, so it spurs me.

"Now, Angus," I say, practically speed-walking over to him once the cars stopped. "Tell me what's next."

BJ rolls his eyes.

Taura looks over at me, grinning excitedly. "These are the Llanfechel Triangle Standing Stones."

"Oooh," I coo. Sounds boring if I'm honest. A stone in a field? Snore. Anyway. "What's so special about these stones?" I glance between them.

"Taura?" Angus gestures to her. "Any guesses?"

"Early Bronze?" She blinks.

"Very good." He nods. "Early Bronze or late Neolithic is the general consensus."

"What are these ones for?" I ask, looking up at them. Quite big. Two metres?

"We don't know exactly what these ones were used for, but we know stone settings like these ones were often ceremonial monuments." He glances at the boys, who are both a bit glazed over, bless them. "They were used for prehistorical rituals."

Jo perks up. "Like human sacrifice?"

"Ah." Angus laughs a little. "The Celts did practise human sacrifice, yes. And—" he gives the boys a little excited look that Baxter James Ballentine does not return—"dark humic soil with charcoal residue has been found here. That could be related to an offering. We've found no human remains though."

"So what did happen here?" BJ asks, arms folded across his chest.

"Well, isn't that ever the question?" Angus asks brightly. I think he'd make a wonderful teacher. "The triangular alignment suggests to some it might have been an astronomical monument . . ."

He's actually pretty cute. I like how he likes these rocks so much. It's very pure. He goes away from us to lay his hands on them, greets them like old friends.

I glance over at BJ who's watching me, brows low, gnawing down on his thumb.

I touch a stone and for the briefest of moments genuinely wonder whether I'll fall through it like in *Outlander*. I don't. I'm stuck on this side of time with too much love in my heart for the boy who won't love me back.

There is something a bit darling about them though, all these old stones that have seen the world through so much. All the lives that were lived out around them, all the loves they'd have born witness to.

BJ and I have a tree that proves we loved each other once upon a time and a stone in front of it that I hope stays there forever, but willow trees don't last. Only thirty years—that's what it said when I googled it.

It's already nearly twenty years old.

The great monument to our love is a withering tree and a blank stone that means the world to me and maybe nothing to anyone else.

Angus gives us a brief introduction to the last site, but he heads off at Jonah's instruction. We've gone about three hours longer than we were supposed to and he has an early lecture back in London tomorrow.

It's a burial chamber called Barclodiad y Gawres, which was built somewhere between 3000-2500 BC.

We're allowed inside even though the sun's gone down, but that just means it's pitch-black and spooky as anything.

I don't know whether it's actually spooky or I just think it's spooky because it's a burial chamber and Angus said they found the remains of two cremated males in here, but either way it's a little bit scary.

It's a scariness I love because me in danger has always been catnip for BJ. He can't help it. It happens kind of subconsciously, I think, like a reflex. As soon as I'm in there, he's hovering behind me.

I glance back at him; our eyes catch in the dark.

He says nothing, does nothing. Just stands there with me.

I walk in deeper, wanting to test him, see how far I can go with him. He follows me in, sticks closer.

Close enough that I can feel the warmth of him behind me. I move around and he follows me like a shadow.

"Careful," he tells me in his low voice. "I can't see for shit—"

And then from right in front of us, someone makes the sound of a ghoul. I scream and BJ grabs me from behind, pulling me back into him. Jonah starts cackling and Taura's laughing too, but we're not.

My face is buried in my ex-boyfriend's chest with his arms wrapped around me. His heart's beating against my face. He's not letting go, so I'm not letting go. He shifts a tiny bit so his chin's sitting on top of my head.

He swallows.

"Sorry," he tells me, but he doesn't move.

"You ready to go, Romeo?" Jonah calls from somewhere in the darkness and I swear to God BJ's grip tightens around me, just for a second, and then he lets go.

"Yep," he calls and then walks ahead of me.

He pulls out his iPhone to light the way, but rushes up ahead to Jonah.

Taura grabs my arm, keeping me back.

"What was that?" She blinks, mouth cracked open, a little hopeful.

I give her a long look and shake my head, because I have no idea.

THIRTY–SEVEN

BJ

I walk as quick as I can to get out in front of Parks and to Jonah.

I give him a look, nodding him out of the burial tomb.

"Quick," I whisper, eyes wide, ushering him towards the car.

"What?" He frowns.

I look past him. The girls aren't out yet, I think they're taking photos.

"I don't want to go," I whisper.

"What?" He frowns more.

"I don't want to go. I don't want to go," I tell him, urgent, shaking my head.

He looks confused. "You want to stay here?"

"No." I growl. "I don't want to go home . . ." To Jordan, is the part I can't say out loud though, not without being a colossal wanker, so I let it hang and give him a look.

He tilts his head at me, brows low. "Beej . . ."

"Please—please. I fucked up, Jo." Shake my head. "I need to fix it."

I look past him again, back into the tomb. I can see the light of a phone coming out.

"Fuck. Please," I whisper. I'm panicked now, about to lose it. "Shit! Jo, do something." I shove him. "Do something."

He makes an annoyed sound, looks over his shoulder, moves around me, grabs a switchblade out from his pocket and slashes his tyre.

"This car's a week and a half old," he says with a glare.

I shake my head at him. "What the fuck do you have a switchblade in your pocket for?"

"Because my best friend's a fucking idiot," he says through clenched teeth and then he shoves it back into his pocket right as the girls walk up.

"What's wrong?" Taura looks down at Jo on the ground who sighs, rolls his eyes, hamming it up.

"Busted tyre."

"Oh, shit." She frowns and moves towards him. "Do you have a spare?"

Fuck.

Jo and I trade looks.

"Yes . . ." Jo nods, thinking on his feet. "But . . . that's . . . busted too."

Magnolia looks at him, confused. "Didn't you get this car like, a week ago?"

"Yeah." Jo nods coolly. "But I took it off-roading."

"Over Christmas?" Parks puts her hand on her hips.

"Yep." Jo keeps nodding.

"When?" Taura frowns.

"Last night." He nods.

I throw him a look.

"Yeah, no—" Jo nods, doubling-down on his shitty story. "When you were with Hen I went . . . off-roading."

"Metaphorically?" Magnolia asks.

Jo shakes his head at her. "What would that even mean?"

Taura's face scrunches up.

"What?" Jo shrugs. "You wanna check the PSI on the spare? Go right ahead."

"What's a PSI?" Parks whispers and I lick my bottom lip, trying not to smile too much. Her mouth that close to me? Can't help it.

"Pounds per square inch," I whisper back. She crosses her arms over her chest, not liking not knowing the answers to questions herself.

"Well, so, what do we do?" She frowns, looking from Taura to us.

"Sleep in there?" Jo nods his chin at the tomb, grinning. Magnolia shuffles a little towards me. "Absolutely not."

"—Would it be so bad?" I whisper to her and her body tenses up and all the ways I might un-tense her later roll through my mind. "I'll book us a hotel," Jo says, pulling out his phone.

"I'll call a taxi," I tell him.

"You don't think they'd have town cars out here?" Magnolia asks with a frown.

I glance at her, suppress a smirk. "Probably not this late notice."

She swears under her breath and kicks the grass.

I call a taxi. Will take ages to come.

Jonah and Tausie go back inside the chamber but I lie down on the hood of the car, staring up at the sky.

Glance over at Parks standing there in the grass, watching me, and I wait for her to join me. She does slowly, nervously. Climbs up next to me. Leans back, lies down. Stares up.

I wonder if we'll ever not be like magnets . . . not be these two things that drift home to each other no matter what. If there is a way to break the spell, I don't want to know a fucking thing about it.

"It's cold." She hugs herself.

I don't say anything. Move a bit closer to her though.

"They make me think of you," she tells me, looking up at them.

"The stars?"

She nods.

I glance at her. "Why?"

I know why.

"Fated." She gives me a shy look. "That we're written in them. Something stupid like that."

I say nothing. I'm good at that lately.

"If you love a flower . . ." I say eventually, glancing at her. One of my tattoos, about her, like all of them are.

"—That lives on a star, it is sweet to look at the sky at night," she says, staring up at them. Holy fuck she's beautiful.

All these suns we're staring at from other galaxies that I'll never get to see except in the way they're making her eyes light up right now. Hair a mess from the wind up here, her cheeks are pink from the cold.

"All the stars are a-bloom with flowers," I say, watching her and she looks over at me.

I want to kiss her, and maybe I might, that mouth is begging for it. She's frozen still, watching me watch her, so I lean in. It's the kind of cold here where I can see our breath between us, thick and it clings to you with that Welsh cold—I'm moving in closer and closer and she swallows all nervous and then—headlights.

I pull away, annoyed.

She sits up quickly as Jonah and Taura come out.

We pile into the taxi. Just a twenty-minute ride to Tre-Ysgawen Hall so I text Jo as soon as we're driving.

20:01

Jo

> Put me in a room with her.

What are you doing?

> Use Tausie's birthday as an excuse

But what are you doing?

> Nothing.

??

> Do it

> Please

247

The hotel is actually pretty sick. Like a country manor. Lots of stone and wood and gold trim.

The girls sit down in the foyer and Jo leans over the desk to the concierge and whispers, "I'll give you a thousand pounds cash if you tell the girls that there are only two rooms available."

The man squints at Jonah suspiciously.

"Nothing slimy, bro." He nods his head in my direction. "Just trying to get the most annoying couple in the world back together."

Jo flashes the guy a thumbs-up as he snatches the wad of cash.

We walk over to the girls with the keys.

"Bad news."

"Again?" Parks blinks.

"Only two rooms left." Jo grimaces and Magnolia's eyes flicker immediately to me—quick—just for a second. Then she looks up at Jonah and awaits further instruction.

"Okay." Parks swallows.

Jonah turns to me, smacks me in the chest.

"Might put you guys in a weird position, but do you mind?"

Parks glances back at me, eyes round, questioning.

I roll my eyes at Jonah as though it's a massive inconvenience. Parks looks a little winded.

"Yeah." I shrug. "We'll be fine." I nod my chin at her. "Do you care?"

She barely looks me in the eye when she shakes her head.

"Are you sure?" Taura whispers to her.

Parks nods, kisses her on the cheek. "Have the best night."

"She will," Jonah says, hooking his arm around her neck, tugging her away.

Smacks me in the arm on his way, winks at me once.

I glance at Parks, who's just staring at her hands looking nervous.

"Should we go up?" I nod towards the stairs.

She follows me a pace behind, quiet. Shoulders in, chin low.

I open the door, hold it for her.

"It's nice." I shrug once we're inside.

248

It is. Big four-poster bed. Love me a four-poster bed. Room's a bit pink, but it's nice enough.

She nods, looks around. Sits down nervously in an armchair, crosses her arms over her chest.

I watch her for a few seconds.

"You're quiet."

"Sorry—" She glances up, flashes me a tired smile. "You didn't look entirely pleased about this arrangement."

Well, what can I say, Parks? I'm a fucking thespian.

"I don't know what to say . . ." She shrugs. "Or do."

I shrug. "No one's fault."

She gives me a little nod. I sit at the edge of the bed, look over at her.

"You still have your weird shower rules?" She glances at me out of the corner of her eye. Nods once, self-conscious. "You want to go first?" I offer her with tall eyebrows.

She eyes me a bit awkwardly. "Okay."

She finds a robe and closes the bathroom door behind her. As it closes, I think about how it wasn't much more than a year ago that she would have made me sit in there with her, talking so she didn't have to be alone, and now we're here. She's showering alone and I'm lying to be with her however I can.

She reemerges twenty minutes later, hair washed, scrubbed clean, and in a white towel robe I want to take off her.

I swallow heavy.

Leave the door cracked open.

Try to tell her without telling her that she could come in if she wants to. Stay in there extra long so she can realise she should.

She doesn't.

Parks is sitting on her side of the bed when I come out in the matching robe.

Sit down next to her. She's as far away from the middle as humanly possible without risking a tumble off the bed.

She's laid out all the minibar snacks onto the bed. Already cracked into the vodka too. Offers me some. Smirnoff. Rough stuff, but I swig it anyway. I need it for what I want to happen.

I stare over at her . . . Makes me uneasy how quiet she's been.

"You angry at me?" I ask.

She glances over, shakes her head.

I eye her suspiciously. "You're never this quiet."

She breathes out delicately. "What would you like to know?"

"Why'd you and Jack-Jack can it?" I ask without missing a beat.

The question's pre-loaded. I've wondered since she avoided answering it the first time.

She sniffs, amused, folds her arms over her chest.

"He told me he loved me."

I pull back a bit. Not what I was expecting. "Oh—" I shake my head. "I mean, so?"

"So—" She shrugs demurely and gives me a controlled look. "I'm not in the business of loving people anymore."

I give her a long look.

Wow.

Fuck.

Nod once. "Because of me?"

She nods back. "Because of you."

My heart sinks like a stone for a second and then I'm angry. Shake my head at her as I stand up.

"You know what? That's fucking bullshit, Parks." I point at her. "You fucked me up too. And I'm in a functioning relationship—"

"—Are you?" She stands, mirroring me. "Is that why you're alone in a hotel room with your ex-girlfriend?"

"No, Parks. I'm alone in a hotel room with my ex-girlfriend because we got a busted tyre and I drew the short straw."

I give her a look just to win extra, and her heart sinks in her eyes a little.

"Am I . . . the short straw?" She blinks, staring at me a bit like I'm a stranger. She breathes in and out a few times, looks crushed. Fuck.

"Being in a room with me is the short straw?"

I breathe out, tilt my head apologetically. That probably sounded more brutal than I meant it to, never mind the fact that it's complete bullshit.

But she can't know that.

I don't say anything. Don't correct her, don't dispel the lie I'm peddling.

"Well," she huffs, grabbing the pillows from her side of the bed, "I wouldn't want you having to share a bed with the short straw."

I roll my eyes at her. "There are no other rooms. Where are you going to go?"

Indignant, she wanders into the bathroom, slams the door shut.

I hang my head in my hands and then I pull my phone out to text Jordan because I should. Need to tell her I'm not coming home. Need to not tell her I'm in a room with Parks.

22:11

Jordan

> Hey - we got a flat. Won't be home till tomorrow afternoon. Sorry x

Oh shit! Everyone alright?

> Yeah, all good. Just annoyed.

Where are you staying?

> A hotel Jo found. Nice enough.

Okay

miss you.

> Same. Night.

251

<3

Same?

I'm lying to everyone these days.

I glance at the bathroom door—it's been about twenty minutes—I'm a bit impressed by her commitment to pretending she's actually going to sleep in there. But her in there and me out here isn't how I want this night to go, so I text her too.

22:16

Parks

> How's the weather in there?

Fuck off.

> Right so.

> Pretty icy then?

Fuck me.

I'm so good at blowing it with her these days.

I used to know what I was doing with her, but now I'm dead in the water.

I shove my hands through my hair, work out what to do next.

Feel like touching her or fighting with her, something that lets me be close to her—because that's what I actually want.

Actually, what I want is her. Don't know how to actualise that anymore though.

22:27

Parks

> What are you doing?

Come back.

No.

I get out of bed, knock on the bathroom door.

"Go away."

She's making me work for it. Fair enough at this point, I suppose.

"Naked?" I call through the door.

"No." She sounds annoyed.

I open the door. She's curled up in the bath, trying to make it a bed.

It takes all my self-control not to laugh at her.

"Come back to the room." I nod towards it.

"No," she says, defiant and avoiding my eyes.

"Just get in the bed."

"No." She crosses her arms.

"Magnolia," I growl. "Get in the fucking bed."

"Leave me alone." She rolls over in the tub.

I breathe out loud and annoyed, and then I walk over to the tub and stare down at her in the bath. She looks up at me, scowling a bit.

And then I reach down and scoop her up and her eyes go to full Bambi. Thank God.

I love her in my arms, how she folds up into them, how she fits. My body grew up carrying her; she slots into the grooves of me, how many people can you say that about? No one but her and still I don't know how to tell her I love her back. What if she changes her mind? What if she fucks off again?

She said last time that she was in and that that was it and she still left me anyway—her word's no good now.

She goes a bit limp in my arms and I wonder how it is that I've carried her twice in the last few weeks and I've never carried my girlfriend once.

I lay Parks down on her side of the bed, walk around to my side. She's staring straight up at the ceiling, stiff as a board. She's all clamped up, nervous.

253

I stare at her because I can't help it. More beautiful than I know what to do with.

She doesn't look at me but she knows I'm watching her, her eyes fluttering like a butterfly with no place to land.

I shift my body, rolling in to face her. She stops breathing for a couple of beats. Slow like a tide, she rolls over to face me.

Swallows nervous, eyes big.

Gives me a rush that I still make her go like this.

I've made her go like this since the first time I kissed her.

Thought about that kiss a lot lately. Don't know why. Just been rolling around my head.

The summer Parks and me started up, my parents took us all to St Barts for two weeks before school went back. And when I say all, I mean all. Me, Henry, Parks, Bridget, all my sisters, Jonah, Christian, Paili and Perry. Parks and Bridge used to come away with us most trips, that wasn't strange. Our parents were close and at the time, Arrie was going through what Magnolia refers to as the "Lagerfeld Phase" (lots of black, sunglasses, no smiling), which was also what my mum refers to as her "Lustral Phase".

I don't know why my parents did it. Honestly, it must have been pure insanity watching us all.

Everyone got there before me and Jo because we had to stay back for some rugby training shit. I'd already been in love with Magnolia since I was a kid in that stupid, abstract way you are when you're small. Not real at all, felt real, didn't know what real was back then. Never felt like I could act on it because she was so fucking obsessed with Christian back then.

Jonah gassed me up on the flight over. Told me Christian wasn't keen—he wasn't either, at least I didn't know he was at the time. So I don't know whether it was Jonah or the drinks we had on the plane on the way over, but I decided I wanted it and I was going for it this trip.

I remember walking into our living room and I swear to God, I can't think of this moment without *Mylo Xyloto* blasting out my heart. She was next to Christian on the couch. Little yellow string bikini, legs folded under her, pressed up against him, but the second I walked in she sat up straighter. I don't know why, don't know what changed. Waited for her to sit up straighter when I walked into a room since I was six.

She uncrossed her legs and it was the first time our eyes caught in that way that they do. They haven't stopped since. My eyes fell down her body before I dragged them back up to her face, gave her a shy smile.

She jumped up and bounced over to us, hugged Jonah first and then, while still hugging Jo, she turned and looked at me.

"Hi, BJ." She smiled up at me,

Pointed at myself, eyebrows up like I was offended. "I don't get a hug?"

She beamed up at me, triumphant that her little plan worked, then she tossed her arms around my neck and I wrapped mine around her waist. Lifted her off the ground to make sure she knew I was strong and she squealed a bit, squeezed me tighter.

That whole next week . . . it plays on my mind like a reel.

These long days and late nights, stupid sunsets that weren't half as good as her face was. Touched her in the most benign ways every chance I had. Put my arm around her chair anytime we were sitting at a table, bent my body around her to reach for some fruit, wrestled her for the remote even though we wanted to watch the same thing. Drank from her cup for no reason. Took her phone off her and held it over her head so she'd jump all over me to reach it. We'd play tennis and I'd help her with her swing even though her swing was better than mine and she's had professional lessons since she was five. Climbed everything in sight to impress her. Scaled the house, palm trees, cliffs, the mast on boats, anything I could as long as she was watching me. She'd yell at me to get down and I liked the feeling of her worrying about me. I threw her off the side of yachts and would jump in after her. Put her on the back of a jet ski and drove like a fucking maniac so she'd hold me tight. As the first week dripped into the second, I got braver with how I'd try to touch her. Dived into a pool and went to hug her while she was lying in the sun. Grabbed her hand in a crowd. Pulled her onto my lap when we'd watch a film at night and there wasn't enough space. There was always enough space. I just wanted to hold her.

We'd kissed before. Seven minutes in heaven a year before. We don't count it as our first kiss because nothing happened afterwards and it felt pretend. I was fourteen, she was thirteen. The seven minutes were deeply under-utilised. A closed-mouth kiss and a lot of nervous chatter on both our parts. She actually asked me if I thought Christian would be angry at her and it crushed me at the time. So, not our first kiss.

I was in my head about kissing her proper though. I knew I had to do it before we went back to school. And by that point in the trip, I was pretty sure she fancied me.

I don't know whose idea it was, but we wound up playing spin the bottle.

Jo spun, he got me straight of the gate. Pecked him and everyone laughed. Christian spun, he got Paili. Perry spun, he got Parks. Henry spun, he got Parks too—they scrunched their faces up and closed their eyes. Their mouths barely touched.

And then it was my turn. I spun it and I was praying, literally begging the heavens for the bottle to land on Magnolia, but it didn't. It landed very clearly on Paili.

"Paili," Perry jeered.

And I stood up, looked at the bottle. Shook my head. "It's Magnolia."

Paili frowned.

Christian pulled a face. "It's obviously Paili."

I locked eyes with Parks, shook my head. "Nah, it's Parks." First time I ever called her that.

I remember Magnolia looking down at the bottle to double check like she might have gotten it wrong the first time.

I walked over towards the bottle and slowly moved it with my foot until it was pointing to Magnolia. "Parks."

I walked over to her.

"Stand up," I told her.

She swallowed, stood. Cheeks were pink straight away. She was standing there, eyes wide, arms heavy at her side. I slipped one hand around her waist and with the other I took her face and then I kissed the shit out of her. So much more than I needed to. There were a few natural gaps for the kiss to wrap up but I didn't take one of them. Forgot we were in front of our friends, the genesis of it all fading to black—me and her in the backyard of our house on that island, my hand in her hair, her hands on my chest—might as well have signed my life away in the moment. Never again would a day go by where I didn't think of her, where she wasn't my very waking thought. Maybe that's unhealthy, maybe that's fucked up, or maybe I just love her how someone like her deserves to be loved. I don't know.

I'd probably still be kissing her to this very day if Jonah hadn't yelled, "Get a fucking room." Magnolia pulled away giggling and I fought off a smile. Took her hand, asked her to go for a dander.

I don't know why before when I was fifteen I could grab her and kiss her and there was nothing between us—a fortnight and a game I jigged to be close to her—and now I'm here, a full-grown man, a decade of literal love and death and everything else in between, when I know she loves me back and still, I can't stop fucking it up.

Even if I am, I'm still glad to be next to her now.

We're fucking complicated, I know that, but I always feel more with her. More . . . something. More anything. It's not always good. Sometimes it's more angry, more sad, more annoyed, but not now.

Now I feel . . . a lot. More nervous. More aware. More alive.

I'm in love with her, I can tell you that. Can I tell her that? I don't know.

"Hey." Me, softly.

"Hi." Her, softer.

I move in a bit towards her. She doesn't move.

"Are you stuck?" I nudge her as I move in a bit.

She shakes her head, looking nervous.

"Do you think I'm going to bite you?"

She smiles a tiny bit. "Fingers crossed."

My neck goes hot and I smile a bit, shaking my head at her. "Magnolia Parks . . ."

She smiles over at me, eyes going soft. "I love it when you say my name."

"Yeah?"

She nods. "I love how it sits in your mouth, like you were supposed to say it all the time."

I was, Parks. That's what I want to tell her, but I don't. Move in closer again though. She swallows, bites down on her bottom lip the way I wish I was.

She shifts towards me so we're nose to nose. Her little breaths warm my face and I feel like I've been kicked in the chest by a horse, that's the way she makes me feel.

Her eyes wander over my face, searching me like a room she lost something in.

"You grew up in a year."

"Yeah?" I half smile.

"Mmhm." She nods. "Or changed." Her eyes settle on my mouth, her eyes are heavy. "Or both," she concludes. She reaches over with her finger and traces my jawline. "Look at you with a five o'clock shadow and all—"

I'd smile at her if I could but my heart is a hammer. And she's gone as far as she'll go now, she won't kiss me first. She's waiting on me. Nose pressed against mine, nose pressed against a door she's waiting for me to open.

I'm looking for the key.

I've made a lot of progress in the last year.

I don't do drugs anymore, don't really get shitfaced. Don't fuck around a lot, don't have girls like Tic Tacs, don't use sex to self medicate—might still use it as a weapon, but . . . baby steps. I won't ever progress past her though. Ever. Even when I've hated her—and I have, and knowing her I will again—she'll be the thing I'll always come back to.

She's my Mecca.

I reach over, hold her face in my hand, hold her eyes how I'm going to hold her body in a second. "I love you, Parks."

Her eyes go round, stares at me, and a little smile grows.

I press my mouth up against hers and she kisses me back, melts into me like a candle. Wrap my arms around her, she fits how she always has. There's this thing about her in my arms that makes everyone else feel like they shouldn't be there. They shouldn't be there. I know that. She moves with my body—it's the magnet thing at its peak function.

Touching Parks is like touching no one else.

It's like coming home. Even before when I used to touch her all the time, my hands on her body would brush away the heaviest days.

I think that's what we're supposed to do for each other.

Get her the fuck out of that robe quick as I can—it's just getting in the way. Lilac bra and white knickers underneath that don't stay on her for long either.

I kiss down her body, run my hands over her how I've tried my best not to think about doing for months. My hands are busier than hers, happily remembering the familiar terrain.

Parks just grips me tight—a hand on my back, a hand around my neck—she's just trying to be close to me, I think. That's what this is.

I push into her and her nails dig into me and she makes a little noise. I do it again. She swallows heavy and every time I do this with her, at one point or another—I'm being genuine —I wonder why I do it with anyone else. She's it. This is it. This is what it's about. Everything boils down to me and her and just figuring the fuck out how to be together. We can figure this out. It might be a mess, we'll do it though. Have to. Can't not have her again.

I kiss down her neck. She bites my ear, gets me every time —buries her face in my neck—also gets me every time but different. I'll never let anyone else touch her again.

Can't really put words around it, what it does to me watching Parks when she's like this, holding her against me as her body tenses all stiff, toes pointed like a ballerina, breathing fast. I press my forehead against her. She breathes faster, her nails start to hurt my back a bit. Don't care.

I don't know when we started sitting up, but we are.

Legs around my waist, arms around my neck—couldn't get closer to me if I tried.

"I love you," she breathes out.

"I know." I smile into her ear. "You already told me."

She pinches me, laughing.

I kiss up her neck and down her cheek to her mouth. Pull back, find her eyes.

"I love you, Parks."

A giant shiver rolls through her body and she curls over me, pawing at my back, and I fall backwards, bringing her with me.

We lay there. Collapsed, panting, and sweaty.

I push my hand through her hair, staring over at her like she's a dream I used to have that just walked through the door.

I guess she kind of is.

1:11

Bridget 😊

> Sex!!!!

What??

> We had sex!!!

!!!!!!!!!!!!!!

Magnolia!!!!

How??

What

260

how??

We got stuck up here because Jonah got a flat tyre, so we had to stay in a hotel and it just happened.

What about the girlfriend?

Ending it tomorrow.

I mean, so sad for her but I'm thrilled for me.

How was it?

THIRTY–EIGHT
Magnolia

It was perfect actually, how it happened, and it happened a couple of times because I'm like a bottomless pit with him. There's no such thing as enough.

Afterwards, we lay in bed for hours, hands intertwined, me on his chest, our legs all tangled like our hearts are and have been and always will be. We're not talking about anything serious at all, we're talking about everything else.

"Pretty into rocks now, hey?" He looks down at me with a grin.

I sniff, amused, and I bury my face in him.

"Love an educated man?" he asks playfully. "Fuck, I'm going to have to go to uni—"

"So," I say and pull myself from him. My eyes scan down his body. "Do you want to walk me through your new . . . additions?" I poke one of his tattoos that wasn't there the last time we were doing this.

He grimaces. "Not really."

"Too bad." I sit up and wrap myself in the sheet so he's completely exposed. He rolls his eyes.

"New." I touch the magnolias woven through a deer's antlers.

"Just the flowers." He gives me a little look. "You know I love a flower."

"Two dead bees." I eyeball them on his right hand. "Not my favourite."

He grimaces.

"Fuck NYC." I trace over it with my finger and he just watches me with heavy eyes.

"What else?"

He flashes me the index and middle finger of his right hand.

Index finger: Carver.

Middle: Hunnisett.

Our school houses at Varley.

"Is there a reason my house is on your middle finger?" I ask, eyebrows up.

He sniffles a laugh, nods once. "Yes."

My gaze drifts over to the dead Bambi and my heart sinks I think my eyes start to well up because he props himself on his elbows and shakes his head.

"I was fucked up, Parks."

"You must have really hated me," I barely say without taking my eyes off it.

"Never." And then he points to one of his ribs on his right side.

It's the time you wasted for your rose that makes your rose so important.

"How many new ones did you get?"

He counts in his head, squinting as he does. "Sixteen? Seventeen? Eighteen." He nods to himself and I smack his arm.

"Eighteen! That's so r—" He flashes me his left forearm.

RECKLESS. I give him a bit of a glare and he sniffs, pleased with himself.

"Show me the ones I'll like."

He holds up his left hand, three fingers. On his index is a tiny storm cloud with a bolt of lightning coming out of it; on his middle finger, above the old lilac that was already there, is now a cloud with a small sun poking out behind it, and then on his ring finger is a little sun.

I press my lips together and smile. "How is the weather, Beej?" He drops his index and middle fingers down and grins at me.

"And you?" He nods his chin at me.

"Very pleasant, thank you." I nod before I wave my hand, telling him to go on. Beej rolls his eyes before he flashes me his left wrist. It's the flower under the glass jar on the moon from *The Little Prince* illustrations. I squint at the flower. "Is that . . .?"

"A lilac." He nods, proud of himself.

He shifts a little, points to his thigh, just below his left hip and I do a double take.

"Is that the lock from Dartmouth?" My mouth falls open.

He nods, not looking away from me.

"I love that lock!" I beam at him, touching it.

He puts his arms behind his head and looks at me tenderly. "Yeah, me too."

"Are the rest of them bad, then?"

"One more you'll like," he says and I lift my eyebrows, waiting. He flashes me the palm of his right hand.

On the inside of his thumb is a—

"What is it?" I frown. "I don't—"

"—It's the seed of a willow tree."

"Oh," I say softly. Then I take his hand in mine, bringing it close to my face to inspect it. I lay back down on top of him and he shifts, wrapping his arms around me. I pick up his hand again and kiss the seed and lay it on my cheek.

"I missed you, Parks," Beej says, staring at the ceiling. "Don't do that again."

I glance up at him. "Do what?"

"Leave me."

The next morning we walk downstairs to breakfast.

I'm holding his hand with both of mine, hiding behind him a little because I feel shy about it. Jonah's face cracks wide open as he jumps to his feet, pointing at us with both hands, grinning like an idiot.

"Holy fucking shit!" He claps BJ's face between his hands, gives him a hug.

Our biggest champion, Jonah. It's why it killed me that he covered for him.

Taura runs over to me, jaw on the floor, eyes glancing between us in disbelief.

"I can't believe it!" she whisper-yells. "It's a birthday miracle!"

Beej grins down at me and pulls me onto his lap, his chin resting on my shoulder.

Jonah sits back in his seat, stumped, shaking his head.

"I haven't seen you two like this in . . . five, six? Six years."

I look back at him, smiling.

He kisses my cheek.

"Sorry if this is awkward—" Taura glances between us. "But what about Jordan?"

"Depending on what time we get home," BJ says with a look between us, "I'll do it tonight or tomorrow."

"Just in time for the Veuve event we've got." Jonah smiles over at me. "You can make your public debut."

"Seems insensitive," I consider. "I'm in!"

BJ snorts and kisses my shoulder.

Taura watches BJ and me, a curious look over her face, chin in hand. She's never seen us together, I guess. Not since school, at least.

"Do you feel bad at all?" she asks gently and my head pulls back.

Do I feel bad? Sleeping with the love of my life? I should think not, thank you very much.

He was mine first.

"Yeah," Jo smirks, "you're the other woman now."

BJ rolls his eyes at him.

"Oh." I go still, it just dawning on me, really. "Fuck. I'd not—"

"You're not." BJ shakes his head quickly.

"No, I am—" I stare at him. "I'd never even thought of her, I just thought of me, and that you're mine and we belong together—I hadn't thought about the very present and overt reason why we currently are not together—"

"Magnolia," BJ holds my face with both his hands. "We're good. You're good."

But we're not good and I shake my head at him.

"I've never cheated on anyone before. I've never cheated, I've never been the . . . whorey . . . mistress."

"Actually—" Jonah pipes up again. "If it makes you feel any better, we've all felt for years like you sort of cheated on all your fake boyfriends with Beej—"

"I beg your pardon?"

Jonah uses air quotes. "Sleepovers."

Beej rolls his eyes. "I fucking told you, they were—"

"Yeah, yeah—" Jonah rolls his eyes and BJ launches into a little shut-up spiel but not me, I'm spiralling. It's quick and easy because I've never so candidly done the wrong thing like this before and it's not a good feeling. Actually, the feeling is horrendous. It swallows me whole, squashes down on me. Guilt is a giant Venus flytrap and I am the fly.

I would never want to do to someone else what BJ and Paili did to me, and the honest to God truth is, I've not even really considered Jordan a real person till this very moment. I didn't want to, I didn't need to. She was an abstract pain in my arse. Until now she felt more like a very sinewy, raven-haired phantom. Not a real person who has real feelings for the boy of my dreams who I just slept with last night even though he has a girlfriend.

I shift on BJ's lap so we're facing each other and I think it must be all over my face. I'm rife with worry.

His head tilts and his brows bend in the middle. "It's not a big deal, Parks."

I sit back a bit and stare at him for a few seconds before I move off his lap and onto the seat next to him.

"It is a big deal," I tell him solemnly.

Taura and Jonah shift uncomfortably next to one another.

Beej rubs his hands over his mouth.

"It's not—it's you and me."

"So?" I shake my head, my heart starting to pound. "We still cheated?"

He sighs. "Sort of."

"Sort of!" I yell as I stand up.

"Guys—" Jonah says, flashing us a quick smile. "I was joking."

I shake my head at him. "No, you were right—"

Jonah shrugs like he's guilty. "Parks, I was just trying to get a rise out of you."

BJ stands up and sighs, tired.

"Consider her risen," he says, then he reaches for my wrist but I move it away from him.

I stare at him and it feels like under my feet, the ground is shifting. Like I'm in an earthquake and I can't find anything to hold on to, and I definitely can't find a table to hide under. How could he think that? After everything? I stare at him not like a stranger, but actually just like he's the same boy I've worried these last few years that he might be.

"Do you really not think this is a big deal?"

"Honestly, Magnolia?" He stares at me, brows low. "I don't, no. Because I love you, and you love me and we belong together—"

"Except that you belong to someone else right now!" I yell and everyone else seated at breakfast stares over at us.

I look up at him, my eyes welling up.

I don't want to cry. I can't cry here—there are too many people. In my peripheral vision I can already see a few phones out, filming us, snapping photos.

I take a few deep breaths and feel the question bubbling up inside my brain, I've wondered it so many times. Picked it up, held him under a microscope and peered through trying to work out whether it was an anomaly or not.

Not, I guess.

"Is this what you do?" I ask him but it barely comes out. "When you have a girlfriend?"

BJ's whole body deflates. His shoulders slump, his head falls back and his heart sinks on his face.

"Stop," he tells me. He looks afraid, I think.

"Answer me." I grab his wrist, holding it tightly. "When you're committed to someone, is this what you do?"

He looks at me, exasperated. "Magnolia, you are the only person I've ever been committed to in my whole life."

I stare over at him, my bottom lip trembling. "And yet."

"Fuck—" His head drops backwards and he shoves his hand through his hair, before he looks over at me with ragged eyes. "Are you fucking joking me?"

"You don't think it's a big deal—" I wipe my eyes. "It's a big deal to me."

"Parks—" He grabs my face again. "I understand that, but you have to understand, it's not the same. Me and Jordan, me and you? It's isn't the same thing."

"BJ, you've had two girlfriends and you've cheated on both of them."

His hands drop from my face and he takes a step back from me, pushing his tongue into his bottom lip.

"Am I ever going to be good enough for you?"

He says that and he means it. The hurt is old, I can see that. A lake monster that's lurked beneath the surface till now, it wanders up to the shore and stands there between us.

Is he good enough for me? The thought has literally never crossed my mind, not once. And I don't care if he's not, I want him anyway. I don't know what 'good enough' even means. All I want from him, the only thing I need from him in the world, is to know that I can trust him.

And that I don't know.

I take a staggered breath—I don't know when exactly I started crying but I am now. I cup my hands over my mouth and nose and try to take big breaths.

Taura stands up, moving next to me, looking unsettled between us.

She's never seen us in action.

I look over at Jonah.

"I'd like to go now."

Jo nods, standing up, pulling out his phone, and makes a call. I follow after him.

"Is this it, then?" Beej calls after me. His breathing is jagged.

268

"Are you going to fuck back off to New York?"

I spin around on my heel and shove him. "Fuck you!"

"You did last night." He nods, coolly. "Kind of your thing now, right?"

I shake my head at him, smacking tears away from my face as they fall and I follow after Jonah.

"Give Rush my best," the love of my life yells after me. And you know what? Maybe I will.

THIRTY-NINE

BJ

Jo drove the girls home and I rode back with one of the boys that works for him, Ambrose. He had to drive up anyway to bring Jonah a specialty tyre for the Rolls.

He's nice enough but I'm not in the mood for chatting. My mind is fucking reeling.

I don't know how I keep having her and losing her, and I'm fucking sick over it.

The whole drive down I'm trying to figure out what to do, how I can make it right—but I don't even know if I can.

I asked her to her face, will I ever be good enough for her, and she didn't say a fucking thing. I guess that answers that.

At least it was quick, like a band-aid ripping off.

Bit unfortunate that it wasn't actually a band-aid, it was a skin graft and I wanted it there, but here we are.

The pain is unbelievable.

Thought I'd be driving home today to end things with Jordan but when I walk into my apartment and I see her just sitting there on my couch in nothing but undies and a big hoodie of mine, that old voice in the back of my head pipes up. I know it well, haven't heard it in a while but that's because I haven't had anything to lose in a while. Loving something as much as I love her fucks you up a bit, have I said that before? And maybe it's worth it, if you get to the end and there's a happy ending and shit but what if we get there and there isn't? What if I get to the end and it turns out that actually, there was no such thing as good enough for Magnolia all along, so why try? The chasm her absence creates in me cracks open wide and I only know two ways to fill it.

I'm seven months clean. I'm not using that shit again, even if I want to. Even if my dealer's name is still in my phone. Maybe this one's the lesser of two evils?

I swallow, breathe out. Scroll to his name in my phone—my finger hovers over 'Send Message'—think about it. For a good few seconds, I do. And then I delete his contact.

I blow out my mouth, relieved.

One option left. You're not going to like it.

The other—well. You know what the other one is.

"Oi." I nod my chin at her, cock my head towards the bedroom.

Jordan smiles, pleased. She stands and runs over to me, jumping up and wrapping her legs around my waist.

Probably a better way to numb it all, yeah?

And what's it matter anyway? She's technically my girlfriend. Magnolia and I aren't together. We aren't going to be. How can we?

"How was it?" she asks between kisses.

"Fucking shit," I tell her and she laughs.

"Really?"

"Yep." I nod as I pull the hoodie off her body.

It's old. Burberry. Magnolia got it for me before she left. Toss it on the bed, lay Jordan down on top of it.

She grabs me by the collar of my jumper—same one I was wearing with Parks yesterday—and pulls me down towards her.

"Hey—" I pause, hovering over her. My mind is racing.

She looks up at me, eyes cloudy with how she wants me.

"I slept with Magnolia while I was away."

Her face is hard to pick, I don't think her eyebrows even move when I say that, she's just frozen. Doesn't let go of me though, just this strange staring at me for some of the five longest seconds of my life.

I can't tell what she's thinking? Can't tell if she's about to cry or hit me or laugh, no idea where this is going. Honestly,

I didn't even mean to say it, it just slipped out. Felt like I owed her the truth at least.

Then she blinks quickly a few times and shakes her head.

"Okay," she says and then tugs me down towards her again.

"Wait—" I pull back. "Did you not hear what I said?"

She nods. "Yep."

I give her a look. "You don't care?"

She shakes her head. "Nope."

And then she tugs my trousers off.

The next night it's Jo's event. That champagne one at his club.

And I'm well in my head by the time it rolls around, because I know what happens next.

I shouldn't have slept with Jordan. Feel shitty about that. Both for her and for myself. Maybe I shouldn't feel shitty because I guess she still technically is my girlfriend—but she shouldn't be, and I do.

We need to break up, I know we do. I don't know why she didn't break up with me when I told her, don't know why she went along with it, had sex with me anyway. Grateful she did, it's what I wanted—at the time at least—now in retrospect I feel fucked in my head about it. Like I'm up to my old shit again and I don't want to be but I am anyway because it works.

It's a bit shit of me but before I call it with Jordan, I'm kind of just waiting to see where that fucking east wind blows us. If Magnolia walks into Jo's tonight with Rush on her arm, then fuck it—me and Jordan? I'll give it another go.

Managed to convince J not to come tonight . . . That took a bit of convincing and some not-so subtle bribery but I think she had a good day.

Breakfast at Chiltern Firehouse. A lot of photos there, then she practically bought out Fendi on New Bond, then Sketch for lunch. I got stopped for a bunch of photos and she posed with me in every single one. Made me feel a bit sick in case Parks sees them—who knows what she'd think? What she'd do? Hit me? Fight me on the street? Call Jack-Jack? Fuck, I'd rather take the hit.

I get to Jo's club and go find him deep within it.

Roped-off area, surrounded by girls—guess it must be Henry's night tonight? I grimace at the sight of it. Seems a mess, bottles everywhere, a girl on his lap, his hand up her dress—but who the fuck am I to judge.

"Oi," I sit down next to him.

He slings an arm around me. "Holding up?"

I nod. "She here?"

"Not yet." He shakes his head as he shifts that girl off his lap. He turns to me. "You two sorted your shit out yet?"

I reach over to pour myself a drink and sigh. Give him a look that says no without me having to say it.

"I think we're done." I give him a weak shrug. I want him to tell me I'm wrong.

He sort of does when he rolls his eyes. "You always think you're done."

I give him a look. "Actually, the problem is I never think we're done—"

"Because you won't ever be with her." He gives me a pointed look. "It's her."

"I know." I toss my drink back, pour another.

Jo rolls his head back, annoyed. "You were so close."

"You didn't fucking help—" I whack him in the stomach. "Calling her the other woman, you idiot."

Jo rolls his eyes. "Beej, never in my wildest dreams could I have foreseen that joke taking such a fucking turn."

I roll my eyes at him and he nods his chin at me.

"You end it with Jordan?"

"No." I grimace a little as I wring my hands. "Actually, when I got home I fucked her."

"You what?" says a little voice from behind me.

I swing around and there she is: girl of my dreams, standing there in a little lilac dress and a cardigan, with her heart that I just smashed to pieces in her hands.

I sigh as I stand to my feet. "Magnolia—"

And then she darts off.

FORTY

Magnolia

He didn't call me. I thought he might have—hoped, I suppose.

Yesterday spun so quickly and so chaotically in a direction I hadn't foreseen, we were together and then we were yelling at each other and then I was crying and today I woke up and the photos were in the *Daily Mail*.

"At It Again" was the title.

This part of us that I hate. The no privacy, no chance to feel our feelings alone for a minute without nosey-parkers prying. It makes all our fights feel gimmicky and cheap when for us—for me—they're real. Actual waking nightmares folding out in front of me. Cheating's not a big deal to him? Clearly.

I thought forever about what I would wear for tonight, more than usual. I knew I'd see him, thought about the ways the evening might go. And I was rather sure—or hopeful, in the very least—that we'd perhaps patch things up. That he'd tell me he was sorry and that it is a big deal and we'll work it out together anyway. I thought we'd probably be in the papers again once we were spotted kissing triumphantly because we're grown-ups now, and we love each other and we each know that now, we said it yesterday. So what, I thought—we might have some issues we need to work through, some things in ourselves we need to untangle but as I was leaving the house, I was fairly certain that I'd be returning later with him. It'd be the first night he'd stay over in my new apartment. It'd be the first time he'd see that I have a bookshelf of every *National Geographic* printed in the last five years. And I was sure that I'd remember tonight forever, because it would be the day that we finally began to sort ourselves out and make our way back to one another.

Some people remember their moments in song, I remember mine by material. The lilac crystal-embellished appliquéd cady minidress from David Koma with the Crystal Twist 105mm Sandals from Aquazzura which match perfectly, and the black V-neck oversized cardigan from Alessandra Rich. BJ would love it.

When I arrived at Jonah's club with Taura and Henry, she asked if I was nervous.

I nodded. "A bit."

Henry squeezed my hand. "Just don't toss the first grenade."

I rolled my eyes and headed over to the boys in the back.

BJ's easy to spot. He always is but especially tonight.

Green paisley-print cargo shirt jacket from Sacai, a plain white tee under it from Y-3 with the black cut-off relaxed fit double-knee work pants from Dickies. Pepper Green Old Skools, and most importantly: no Jordan.

He looked so handsome, my heart was in my throat—I was relieved. Isn't that funny? Relieved to see him. Even after our fight.

I walked up behind him—he didn't see me coming, neither did Jonah, or he never would have let him say what he said.

"Actually, when I got home I fucked her."

Oh my God.

I'm spinning. Instantly, I'm sick to my core. He slept with someone else after me the same day? That day? We did it in the morning.

I can't even count how many times and he went home after one fight and slept with someone else? Again?

I feel revolting.

I hate him. How many times can he—

BJ stands, calls my name in that familiar way he does, where it's as though he's sad he's hurting me. Like it hurts him to hurt me. Like it burdens him to make me feel this way. But he never stops making me feel this way.

I shake my head at him a tiny bit. Beg him with my eyes to please not follow me. I can't have him following me.

I walk as quickly as I can without breaking into a run to get to the toilets by Jonah's office. I make it there just in time to throw myself into a stall before my legs give way. Grief is strange, don't you think?

Because I am grieving, you can be sure of that.

Feels like the oysters, actually.

That time—remember? When I was seven, and I fell off the jetty in Capri? I hit every sharp shell on the way down. They cut me wide open and BJ dived in after me. He saved me. Who's going to save me now?

The salt water in the cuts all over my body, all over who I am.

Oh my God.

I don't believe it. I can't believe it.

The pain is shocking, actually. Like I've been hit by a meteor. A crater in the centre of me, on fire. Total destruction.

I press my hand into my mouth, clamp down the cries that are trying, trying, trying to come—

Hands trembling, vision gone.

My shoulders shake as the cries come anyway, each of them crushing me on behalf of him.

There's a bustle in the toilets.

"—This is the girls' room," someone says. I can only hear it vaguely.

It feels like my ears are under water.

I slump against the cubicle wall; my body feels like it's filled with lead.

"Parks?" Henry calls. I don't move. "Magnolia?" He knocks. "Open the door."

I don't.

He crawls under and into my cubicle.

It takes a good friend to crawl on the floor of a girls' room of a club when you're wearing white Mastadon cargo pants from Rick Owens DRKSHDW.

He sighs when he sees me, he licks his bottom lip, tilts his head sad for me.

"You had sex with him," Henry tells me.

I nod. Henry nods back at me, mouth tight.

"And now he's staying with her?"

I shrug.

"But he slept with her."

I nod again.

"Fuck." His nostrils flare as he shakes his head. "Get up."

He pulls me up off the ground even though I'm not cooperating. "Up, Magnolia. Now." He plants me on my feet, holds me steady. "Listen to me—listen! There's no one in this world that's worth Magnolia Parks sitting on the floor of a club toilet."

I barely nod. He wipes my face with his hands, and it occurs to me I fell for the wrong brother.

Henry's the better one. He's just not my one.

"Want me to fight him?" Henry asks with his chin.

He grabs a wad of loo paper, blots my face as he leans against the vanity.

I sniff.

"This is my fault," Henry says, eyeing my carefully. "I shouldn't have told you to tell him."

"No," I shake my head. "It's not. It's him—" I tell his brother and our eyes catch.

"It is him." He nods once. He looks livid. "Come on. I'll take you home."

He takes my hand, leads me out of the toilets—and there's BJ waiting for me.

Standing there, brows low, arms folded over his chest.

"Parks, can we talk?" He walks towards me, blocking us in the narrow hall.

"Get away from me." I push past him.

"Parks." Beej shakes his head, reaching for me.

"Get away from me." I shove his hands off of me.

"Magnolia—" BJ frowns, his heart looks like it's breaking in his eyes but I know it's all bullshit now.

"Get the fuck away from me." I spit at him.

And then Henry steps in front of me, shoving his big brother.

"Oi, boys." Jonah appears from behind BJ. "There are some eyes about tonight. Come on——"

Henry ignores him, ignores the flashing phones behind us, shakes his head at his brother.

Beej reaches around him for me and Henry shoves him away.

"Fuck off, man," Henry tells him in a low voice.

BJ ignores him. "Magnolia——"

"No, BJ. Stop." Henry's blocks him again, shadowing BJ as he tries to get to me. "Don't look at her, look at me—she's off limits to you now."

BJ gives him an angry look and a shove.

"Fuck off, Hen. I'm not doing this with you here."

Henry pushes him back.

"Where do you want to do it, then? Because I'm done with your shit."

"Boys——" Jonah shakes his head, trying to keep them apart.

"Don't you fucking start with me——" BJ points a finger in his brother's face, and Henry smacks it away. They never fight like this.

"What the fuck are you doing?" Henry spits.

"I swear to God, Henry——" BJ shakes his head wildly. "If you don't get out of my fucking face——"

"Can you just let me leave?" I sniffle as I try to step past him. He blocks me again, looking for my eyes.

"I made a mistake."

"With me or with her, Beej?"

He breathes out, heavy. "Parks—I wasn't thinking, I didn't think you'd even give a shit——"

"I told you I love you!" I yell.

"And then you left!" he yells back. "Like always. You ran away!" He stares at me.

"Home!" I tell him as I take a staggered breath. "I went home!"

"Yeah?" He nods, eyes like slits now. "To who?"

"What?" I shake my head at him, confused.

278

"You give Rush a call?"

I scowl at him. "He's in New York."

"Cavan?"

"San Fran." I give him a dark look as I cross my arms over my chest. "See, unlike some people, when things go astray for me I don't just fuck the first person I see."

"No, I know—" He nods, glaring over at me. "You fuck their best friends."

"Oi—" Henry growls.

BJ whacks Jonah in the chest. "Better watch it, bro—she'll be coming for you next."

My eyes go glassy and I feel about three feet tall. It's never nice to hear what anyone thinks of you if the opinion is unsavoury, but when that opinion comes from the person you love most in the world, it pierces right through to the centre of you. Poisons you a bit, makes you believe the words they're saying are true.

Words are so powerful.

I had no intention of running to anyone else. My plan for tonight was him. Yesterday after our fight I went home, had a shower and made Henry and my sister stay in my bed with me.

I didn't text Rush. I didn't call Jack-Jack.

I didn't want to do anything to ruin us right as we were about to start again.

But he did, so fuck it.

It rolls in over me like a cloud.

My eyes go dark and if there were curtains, they'd be flapping. The water would be choppy and the animals would start behaving all peculiar, frantically searching for cover. Good. They should.

BJ frowns, sensing the shift in the air.

Batten down the hatches, ring the town bell.

He swallows. "What's that face?"

I shake my head at him as I push past him to leave.

"Where are you going?" he calls after me.

I'm going to Central Park at midnight.

+44 7700 900 274

Hey

Hey.

Are you out tonight?

Yeah.

Club Haus.

Stay there.

Ok.

Why?

You made me a promise once.

PART TWO

FORTY-ONE

BJ

Julian Haites throws these legendary New Year's Eve parties.

Wild, truly insane.

Celebrities try to get on the list for them.

Kygo played last year.

I think this year he's got David Guetta.

He just has it at his house in Knightsbridge. House is underselling it. His dad bought about five houses in a row and made them into one.

This is where the party is.

I arrive with Jordan—thought twice about bringing her but I haven't heard from Parks since two nights ago so I'm going to take a leaf out of her book and dig myself a little Australian foxhole.

Boys have been off me a bit though. Henry's not talking to me, really. Probably should be angry that he's always on her side, but part of me is relieved she's got someone I trust. Rather him in her corner than Rush fucking Evans, that's for sure.

Kind of thought I'd see Parks here tonight . . . Pretty dress and stolen glances—get to spend New Year's with her anyway.

Thought she'd come around, we always come around.

Special occasion big-shit events for me and her are pretty hard to resist—I drifted to her Christmas Day, she'll drift back to me on New Year's.

I'm a bit disappointed when I walk in and she's not with the set.

Taura lifts her eyebrows as an unenthusiastic greeting—off me too, I guess.

Jo whispers something to her, she looks at him, looks a bit annoyed and then nods.

Walks up to Jordan, puts on a warm smile. "Love that dress—" Taura tells her.

"Oh, thanks." Jordan pushes her hair over her shoulders. "It's from Self Portrait."

"Should we grab a drink—" Taura links arms with her. "Jonah tells me that BJ's been a right idiot lately." Leads her away.

I watch them go—peer over at my friends.

"Oi," Jonah saddles up next to me. "We've gotta talk—"

"Is it about Parks?" The leading Jordan away was a bit of a giveaway.

"Yeah—"

"Don't want to hear it."

Christian gives me a weird look. "Yeah, you do."

I glance at him, frowning. "She hurt?"

"No—"

"Is she in danger—" Jo looks over, catches Christian's eye before he shakes his head.

"No . . . but—"

I bite down on my bottom lip, shake my head.

"Then fuck it, man—I don't want to hear about it."

Jo grabs the shoulder of my jacket. Burberry. Thought Parks would like it.

"Yeah, but Beej—" he starts and I give him a look.

"No, Jo. She fucked me over too. She might have you all wrapped around her finger because she's got the sad eyes that win out at everything, but I'm fucked up over it too. I just want to have fun, get loose, kiss my girlfriend at midnight—"

Jonah grimaces. "Sticking with that? The girlfriend?"

I shrug like I don't think it's stupid myself. "Why wouldn't I?"

Christian stares over at me, fingers pressed into his mouth, face strained.

"What are you looking like that for?" I nod my chin at him.

"You fucked Jordan," he tells me like I didn't already know. "For Parks, that was Pearl Harbor."

I frown, confused. "Okay."

Christian pats me on the arm, his mouth pulling in this funny smile like he's sorry for me. "Hiroshima is coming."

I roll my eyes at them and grab him by the shoulder. "As long as you didn't fuck her, I'm good."

Jonah grimaces. "We'll see."

He hands me a tumbler of whiskey.

"You're gonna need it." He smacks me on the arm before he walks away.

I frown after him, confused, then wander over to Jordan and Tausie by the bar.

The set-up here is insane.

Not at all how you'd think the house of London's biggest gang lord would be—or maybe it is, I don't know.

Whiter, more gold than you'd have thought. A lot of marble. Big double staircase from the bedrooms upstairs that spills down into a foyer—you'd be forgiven for thinking you've accidentally walked into a hotel. Foyer spills into one of the living rooms—there are at least four living rooms. A bar on the roof that's tended to 24/7.

Rumour has it they have a pet tiger somewhere around here but it sounds like bullshit to me—been here a few times. I've never seen it.

"This place is insane—" Jordan peers around it. "What's he like?"

"Julian?" I clarify.

"Yeah."

I shrug. "Yeah, I mean, he's a bit of a G."

"He's literally a G," Taura says, bored.

I sniff. "He's cool. Wild. Like, the stories he has, the shit he pulls. It's insane. Like straight out of a Stratham film."

"Really?" Jordan asks, wide-eyed.

I nod. "He's fun. You'll like him. Always a good time."

"Is he dangerous?"

"Yeah, I mean—I wouldn't want to be on his bad side."
I shrug, looking up at Taurs. "Actually, we should say hello.
You seen him?"

Taura gives me a bit of a weird look. "Yeah, I've seen him."
I mirror her confusion.

"Okay." I shrug. "So where is he?"

Taura looks past me, nods towards the staircase.

And then from his bedroom at the top of the stairs he walks
out with a laugh. He pauses to help tug a girl's dress back on.
I snort a little—typical Jules.

Zips the girl into her tight little black dress—she looks hot
from behind, actually.

He waits by the door for her—more chivalrous than he
usually is—and then she walks out.

Holy fuck.

Magnolia hops out of his room in one heel, reaches up and
holds on to his shoulder to put on her other shoe.

He cocks a smile at her. Looks proud of himself.

Holy shit.

She walks down his stairs, hand grazing the rail—sex hair,
sex mouth—her eyes are soft around the edges in a way that
makes me all sad and sick and jealous.

My jaw is on the fucking floor. Feels like I'm falling through
space.

She walks right by me. Not a fucking glance in my direction.
Her bottom lip's heavy like it's just been bitten.

Fuck—I'm going vomit.

Just breezes over to Anatole Storm, who smirks at her like
he knows what she's just done. Makes me want to die seeing
her bounce around people like him. Anatole Storm? One
of Julian's mates. One of the most fucking terrifying men in
Britain. Runs militias.

Julian cruises after her, cool as a motherfucking cucumber—
pauses in front of me.

Squints, cocks a smile.

Reaches over, closes my open mouth—smacks me on the face twice—technically playfully, technically hard.

"Happy new year, bruv." Gives me a shit-eating grin. My jaw goes tight.

Anyone else, anyone else on the fucking planet and I'd kill them on the spot.

But him?

He might actually kill me back.

He moves to Jordan, takes her hand in both of his.

"You must be the girlfriend?" He shakes her hand and she's blushing. "So happy to meet you. Pleasure—" He grins, catching my eye. "Absolute pleasure. You have no idea. Pleasure's all mine."

He chuckles at his own joke, then walks up behind Parks, slipping his arms around her waist from behind.

Way too familiar.

His hands on her body make me feel like something's crawling under my skin.

I need to talk to her.

I shove my hands through my hair.

Toss Jordan a weak smile. All my smiles are weak these days. Or maybe that's just me.

I nod at Taura, giving her eyes that ask her to please, take Jordan away for a minute.

She gets it. I know she gets it—me and Taurs are pretty tight, on a good jive. I know she knows why I want her to take Jordan away, and she gives me a look and mouths no.

We go back and forth

Yes—I scowl.

No—she scowls more.

Yes—my eyes go wider.

No—so do hers.

Yes!—my eyes might fall out of my fucking head.

Fine!—she mouths, eyes slits.

"Jordan," she sings. "have you seen their indoor basket-ball court? In. Sane." Taura pulls her away, glaring over her shoulder at me. "Come on, I'll show you."

287

Parks moves away from Haites over to the bar.

I go stand next to her. Stare straight ahead.

"'You have nothing to worry about, Ballentine'," I repeat her text back to her.

Her eyes pinch, sucks in her cheeks. Breathes in, out.

"'I love you, Parks'," she repeats back to me, adjusting her gold headband.

"I do love you," I sigh.

"Could have fooled me," she says as she looks up at me, eyes so dark the emeralds have turned to onyx. I lean in closer to her than I should. My eyes fall down her body.

"You're in black," I tell her. She never wears black. "That's different."

Her eyes catch mine. "I am different."

"Why?" I stare at her, shaking my head. "Because I slept with Jordan after we had a fight? You and I, we weren't together—"

"Clearly." She nods, distant and controlled.

I roll my eyes at her.

"So what?" I take a sip of my drink. "You're dating a gang lord now?"

Vintage Parks, runs off to date the first man she can find who isn't me.

"—Thank you," she says to the bartender who hands her a Martini. "Guys like Julian don't date."

I nod my chin at her. "So then what are you doing?"

She takes a long sip. "Fucking, Beej."

Back over me with a fucking truck, why don't you, Parks?

"You're fucking him?" I repeat.

"Yeah." She shrugs way too casually before she takes another sip and waves her hand through the air. "Well, I've been fucked over by you for years. I thought it was high time I gave someone else a turn."

Jaw on the floor for the second time in about five minutes. I shake my head at her.

"Parks, he's literally the most dangerous man in England."

288

With eyes as tattered as I think I've made her heart, she gives me a long look.

"I disagree."

Fuck me.

I could, might actually, literally hate myself.

I sigh. Tilt my head as I look down at her. "Magnolia—"

"Beej, listen." She touches my arm, glancing up at me.

Surprised she's touching me. Can't believe it. I'll take it—a fucking miracle.

"I just want to say, and I really do mean this with every fibre of my being—" she stares up at me before she delivers flawlessly—"Fuck. Your. Self."

I blink after her as she wanders over to Julian, snatches the drink from his hand—tosses it back too easily.

His face flickers in amused annoyance.

"Easy, tiger. That was a two-thousand-pound Scotch," Julian tells her.

She looks at him with indifference. "So pour me another—"

She turns to speak to Jonah and Julian makes this 'hah' sound. "You heard her." He nods at one of his boys, cocks his head in her direction, says to Declan, "She's going to be an expensive fuck, I can tell already—"

Parks hears him, turns around, gives him a tall look.

"Worth it!" he calls to her and she rolls her eyes, looking away.

He doesn't like her annoyed at him, no one does—one of her secret tricks that she keeps in her back pocket. Everyone wants to be in her good books. Don't know why or how she does it, but if you make her feel sad or shitty, even if she deserves it, somehow you always manage to feel like a fucking knob and you're buying her a necklace from Cartier or, like, a whole fucking florist to win her back.

I can see it on him—recognise it well, actually—how she gives him a look, it pushes him onto uneven ground and he's just fucking clambering to get back onto a level playing field.

Fuck it, I'm there now. I hate this feeling, hate being out of sorts with her, hate being at odds and even still then, I'm a bit like 'fuck you' anyway—

She's fucking Julian?

Julian?

I toss back my drink at the same time that Julian grabs Parks from behind, pulls her back against him and starts kissing her neck.

Says something—can't hear what—to the people around us.

Pushes her through the crowd, pauses in front of me.

"Heading to the bar upstairs—" Nods his head at me. "You coming?"

He leads her by the hand upstairs, then over to a lift that goes up to the private rooftop.

We all pile in. Me, Parks, Jo, Henry and Taura, Christian, Julian, Daisy Haites and her cop boyfriend, and then Jordan.

Julian's got my girl pinned in the corner of the lift—I should clarify—not my actual girlfriend. Just the girl I love.

He's whispering things in her ear and she's staring over at me with eyes that tell me she's pretty fucked, and when the doors open, I can't get out of there fast enough.

Jonah reaches over the counter, shakes the hand of bartender behind it.

Never cared that he and Julian were close till thirty minutes ago.

Now I'm fucking pissed.

Walk up behind Jo, pull him aside, say through gritted teeth, "You said she wasn't in danger."

He gives me a look. "She's not."

"He's a gang lord," I tell him and Jonah gives me this look.

Raises his eyebrows a bit. "And?"

"And he's a gang lord."

"I'm a gang lord." Jonah shrugs.

"Thought you didn't like that term?"

Jonah rolls his eyes, nods his chin at me then. "What's wrong with gang lords, then, ey?"

I shake my head at him. "He's not like you."

"How's that now?"

I roll my eyes and tip my head in their direction—Julian's mega so fucking north of her knee I want to jump off the balcony. "So, you're fine with that—"

"Beej." He gives me a pointed look. "You fucked someone else! You didn't have to! You could have called her—told her it was a big deal—"

"It wasn't a big fucking deal, Jo! It was me and the love of my life—" Jonah interrupts me with a look that tells me to speak quieter. "It was me and her. Which is a massive deal in and of itself, and it being a massive deal is why us sleeping together wasn't a big deal to me."

"I get it, bro." He nods. "I understand what you're saying. Would have backed you, actually—" He shrugs. "But then you slept with Jordan. Kind of took the wind out of your own point."

I roll my eyes. "She's my girlfriend."

"So be her boyfriend, then," he says over it all. He nods his chin at Parks. "And fucking leave her alone."

Then he walks past me, goes and sits down with them.

Leave her alone? Never. I won't ever leave her alone. Especially when she's fucking about with Julian Haites—of all the people she could—fuck.

I know that how I feel seeing her with him is indicative that I should end it with Jordan, I know that. But I won't do it anyway. It might be the bigger thing to do, could be a short-cut home for us—but we love a detour, me and Parks. And she just swerved us right off the fucking road.

I look around for Jordan. She's over at the bar talking to a celebrity DJ. Flirting with him, I can tell. I don't even care, it's not a thought in my mind. All I'm thinking about is the only thing I've ever truly given a fuck about and how she's cuddling up into the arms of the most notorious man I've ever met.

"What're you doing all the way over there, Ballentine?" Julian calls, pulling Parks up onto his lap to give me space to sit down.

He's just doing it to fuck with me but I sit down anyway, because I miss her.

Parks runs her hand over her head, smoothing it down.

"Ow." She frowns. "Why's my head bruised?"

Julian licks away a smirk. "It's called a headboard, Tiges."

Her mouth makes an 'O' shape, her cheeks go pink and I toss my drink back in one go.

"So, wait—" Daisy's policeman stares over at them as confused as the rest of us. "How long have you two been hooking up, then?"

Julian and Parks look at each other and back at him. Magnolia sucks on her lip demurely, considering this.

"Um, probably broaching on seventy-four hours now?" Parks offers.

Julian bites down on her bare shoulder.

"Non-stop."

Daisy rolls her eyes.

And it's then I remember that, technically, I still have a girlfriend. Only remember because she stands in front of me. Smiles down as she sits on my lap and kisses me.

"Should we bounce?" I whisper to her, keen to get out of here.

She frowns, confused. "It's not even midnight."

"Yeah, Ballentine—" Julian smirks, staring me down. "It's not even midnight."

Fuck, I'd love to hit him.

Clock Christian off to the side also miserable as fuck, but it's because he's watching Daisy and her boyfriend and he wouldn't bring Vanna here to her house.

Good man. Decent. Me? I'm going to move Jordan into a dark corner, try my luck getting to third and hope to fuck Magnolia Parks sees and I ruin her New Year's the way she's fucked up mine.

FORTY-TWO

Magnolia

How do you imagine a gang lord's bedroom? I can't say I'd ever given it much thought till I found myself in one.

And I know what you're thinking—Christian Grey's Red Room.

But you would be incorrect.

It's not like that at all. Neither is he, actually.

His bedroom's changed since the last time I was in it, which was probably more than four years ago now, if you can believe it. That infamous night with the pancakes and the no sex. I was so scared of sleeping with anyone who wasn't BJ, as though doing that with someone else might make me less his. Jokes on me though, because BJ's as not mine as ever and I wake up every morning to check the status of my tether to him. It's iron clad, even now.

I used to think about that night a lot. Me and Julian and what we didn't do. He's a strange person, but I sort of love being next to him. There's just this feeling you get from being by him that's not like anything else in the world.

I never knew whether he didn't say anything about the night because he was annoyed or embarrassed or he was just a better man than we all give him credit for, but it became apparent that night at his thirtieth that none of the boys knew we'd ever gone home together.

It made me look at him a bit differently once I realised he hadn't told anyone. I don't know in what way it made me see him exactly, but I suppose I've read stupid things in the papers about boys I've kissed or allegedly gone home with hundreds of times. Most of the time it's never true, but I did kiss him, and I did go home with him, and he seemingly didn't tell a soul.

Back then his room was more of a bachelor pad. Game consoles. I think there was a candy bar vending machine? Definitely a condom vending machine, I remember that. Dark grey walls, dark wooden floors. Big chandelier. Almost as though he styled it in a way he thought would be sexy in the eyes of the girls he was bedding.

But now?

The walls are a lighter grey, lots of brown and wooden accents. Huge bed. White bedding. Dramatic lamps. 1950s rococo style headboard which, unfortunately for me, is not tufted. There's some fine art—original pieces only—dotting the walls.

Actually, there are originals all over the place.

"You're rather big on art, then?" I asked him brightly the morning after we first slept together as I peered up at the most convincing print of Ernst Ludwig Kirchner's *Street, Berlin* I've ever seen.

"This is very realistic." I look at it closer.

Julian squashed a smile. "It's not a print."

I spun around on my foot, confused.

"You bought *Street, Berlin*?" I asked, feeling a tad jealous. "How much was it?"

He licked away a smile. "Cheaper than you'd think . . ."

"Huh," I said as I shook my head. "Some people just don't appreciate the value of art. Funny. I swear I saw this hanging at MOMA a couple of months ago—"

He rubbed his chin. "Don't know much about my family, do you?" He smirked over at me a little. "What we do."

I thought I did. Arms dealing. Some light crime. Probably cocaine because it's the fanciest drug. I don't like admitting that I don't know things so I pursed my mouth and he leaned down and kissed me. A lot. Far more than the question required.

"Daisy likes art."

But do you know what Daisy doesn't like? Me.

She doesn't like me. I don't know whether that's a Julian thing or a Christian thing, but her thinly veiled distaste for me is now my raison d'être.

No one doesn't like me. Ever.

It just fundamentally doesn't make sense to me. I mean, it does make literal sense in this case, as I'm sleeping with her brother and used to date the boy she loved (loves?), but that's neither here nor there.

I'll make her like me.

Don't know how. She's always holed up in her bedroom with either the sexy policeman or Julian's giant dog—and quite frankly, both strike me as a bit off-putting so I've kept my distance, but we'll get there.

She'll like me in the end, I swear it.

Anyway, I'm lying in Julian's bed, staring up at the ceiling.

It's coming up to nearly a week of this. I haven't really left his house since the night I texted him. He's funny, kind of a blackhole. There's a huge gravity about him that pulls you in and you lose time.

That night was an interesting combination of spectacular and heartbreaking, and about as alcohol fuelled as you can imagine. But that is my whole existence right now: especially alcohol fuelled.

I get out of Julian's bed and go into his bathroom, mostly because I'm not so good at being alone, not even for tiny moments. I've been filling all of them with him, but I suspect we'll wind up soon. Julian doesn't date girls, he doesn't have houseguests for days on end either, Henry told me. There's a tiny part of me that's nervous he's going to turn around one day and just tell me to leave—that would be very like him. Part of me can appreciate how forthcoming he is, but also part of me would just die if he ever did say that to me, so I brush my teeth even though I already did it while he was sleeping in bed because I didn't want him to think I have disgusting morning breath.

"What are you doing today?" Julian asks as he walks out of the shower with a towel wrapped around his waist.

I glance over at him through the mirror. "It's the Fuck Off Brunch."

He blinks at me twice. "The what?"

I sniff a smile. "It's this thing we do every year. It's actually The Fuck Off New Year's Brunch." I nod at him. "Jonah's invention. New Year's Day brunch, everyone's hungover and gross and nowhere good is open to eat anyway, and you sort of need the second to recover from how terrible the first day of the year is, but by January third everything's open, no one's hung, everyone's fresh."

"That's cute." He nods, smirking. "Annual brunch . . ."

I nod at him, ignore him baiting me, and look back at my reflection who is pursing her lips.

He watches me for a second. "Nervous?"

My face flickers. "No."

Yes.

"Why would I be nervous?" I frown at him.

He comes and stands behind me. "Because he might bring her."

I say nothing.

"Even if he does, you'll be the hottest one there," he tells me, tugging on the tapered logo-print cotton-blend jersey sweatpants from Vetements.

"Yes." I nod once, staring at myself. As though that matters, as though looking how I look has done anything for me in the ways of making BJ love me more or want me more or cheat on me less. "And then what?" I give him a shrug.

He stares at me through the mirror, rests his chin on top of my head, and wraps his arms around me. It catches me off guard, these random acts of tenderness.

"Want me to come?" he asks, tightening his grip around me.

I barely shake my head. "No."

He peers down at me, mouth rosier than you'd think. "No?"

"I know we're not—" I shrug. "I know you're not like that."

"Like what?"

"Like, the kind of boy you bring to brunch."

"Not a boy—" He gives me a curt smile. "And I'm not, you're right."

I nod. "It's fine. I can go by myself. I'll just drink a lot, it'll be fine."

"I'll come," he tells me.

"Really?" I try not to sound too hopeful.

"Yeah." He shrugs. "I don't have much on today. Pretty slow around here at the minute."

I turn to face him, "Okay."

He holds my waist, pulling me in against him.

"Are you sure?" I ask, my cheeks pink but my heart feeling relieved.

He nods once.

"Thank you." I give him a small smile, probably looking more grateful than I mean to.

He bites down on his bottom lip, grins up at me.

"As far as thanks go, Tiges, I'm not really a big words guy . . ."

I laugh. "Is that right?"

He drags my body down towards him, looks down over me. "That's right."

He raises his eyebrows instead of asking the question.

And there is no question.

It's why I'm here.

I'm here to forget.

FORTY-THREE

BJ

Haven't broken up with Jordan yet. I know, I know—don't
start. Decided against it after Magnolia's little New Year's
display. Feel shitty about that. Still shagging her anyway.

Jonah flat out won't talk about Parks and Julian—don't love
that. Says if I'm going to have a girlfriend, I have to have a
fucking girlfriend and not ask questions that apparently have
nothing to do with me. Don't love that either.

Henry swears up and down he saw Jordan give that DJ her
number. Didn't ask her about it. Honestly, fair play if she did—
it's not like I'm an overly attentive boyfriend at the minute.

I do bring her to brunch though, just to fuck off Magnolia.

I get why she did this all these years. Brought fake-lovers
with her everywhere she went, I know how I'd look at her
every time she'd wheel one of them in. I'd be lying if I said I
wasn't looking forward to seeing her face when I bring Jordan
here today.

The Fuck Off Brunch is pretty close-circle shit. We don't
bring dates. Told Jonah I had to bring her because she's my
girlfriend, not a date. He just rolled his eyes.

Wear a jacket from Isabel Marant that has material Magnolia
will need to feel to guess it. Just want to be close to her for
a second. When we arrive at IT for brunch, there's only one
seat left and Parks isn't here yet. Can't help but feel relieved
to know that she's not bringing him.

It mustn't be a thing. Julian's not a brunch guy. She'd bring
him if she could. She'd shove him down my throat, no doubt.

Here's hoping they were just a New Year's hook up.

Stretch my arm around Jordan, kiss her cheek. I'm not really listening to her story about her friends from Australia coming over in a bit—Taylor and someone else—but decide to try to listen. A good boyfriend would listen. I have the capacity to be a good boyfriend.

"Taylor and who?" I ask.

"Tim Tottle? Her boyfriend." She lifts her eyebrows. "They've been together forever."

"Oy, J—" Christian calls over to her. "Do you have any hot Australian friends you could bring here? Blow all my troubles away . . ."

"I have lots of hot Australian friends." She nods. "But all of them have already heard about Scottie and Taylor's super hot but insane cousins in England. I don't think anyone's going to blow anything for you."

I snort a laugh.

Christian rolls his eyes, annoyed, then his eyes light up a bit.

"Oi," he cheers, looking over my shoulder.

Must be Parks.

Jonah stands, opens his arms. I look over, spot her in a second, this bright orange and lilac feather dress that only she could pull off. What I fucking wouldn't give to be the one who could pull that dress off her, but it won't be me. It'll be him, the one behind her. Fucking Julian Haites.

Hugs my best friend. Reaches over, clasps hands with Christian, ruffles my brother's hair.

I feel like I must look a bit spun out, so I look around, trying to flag down a waiter.

Grab one.

"We're going to need an extra seat," I tell them.

"Nah—" Julian says as he pulls Parks down onto his lap. "We're good."

His eyes go tight as he smirks over at me.

Parks tugs his jacket how she used to tug mine. Celine Homme. Nearly bought it. Glad I didn't.

"Miss you," Parks leans over the table, grabbing Taura's hand.

"Same!" Tausie sings.

"Where've you been?" Jordan asks brightly.

Parks looks over at her with her mouth open, a little amused, maybe a bit embarrassed.

"With me," Julian answers for her. He bites down on the inside of his cheek. "I'd tell you to come join us, Taurs, but it sounds like you've got a lot going on already."

Magnolia smacks him and frowns.

"Say you're sorry."

He rolls his eyes and then something happens that fucks with my head: Julian Haites presses his lips together and says it.

"I'm joking, Taurs. I'm sorry."

Taura and Jonah sit back in their chairs, can't believe it.

"Holy shit—" Taura stares at Parks. "How good in bed *are* you?"

Julian squashes a smile as Parks uses his hand to cover her face as though she's embarrassed, as though she's not fucking living for this.

I run my tongue over my teeth and she catches it.

"Hey, Beej." She gives me her best fake-warm smile. "How's that weather today?"

Jordan glances at me, a bit confused, and raises her eyebrows waiting for my answer.

"Yeah, it's a fine day—" I scratch my arm, shrug indifferent. "What about you? Fine over in Mayfair?"

"I've not been in Mayfair for nearly a week, but it's rather pleasant in Knightsbridge." She scratches her neck to flash me a hickey. "Hot," she tacks on at the end, eyes ready to fight.

I swallow, act like she didn't just put a knife in my stomach.

"Is that Knightsbridge?" Jordan asks. "Where we were for New Year's?"

"Yes." Magnolia nods.

"Oh, I like that." Jordan turns and looks at me. "We could look for a place in Knightsbridge."

Magnolia's face falters, blinks a bunch of times.

"You're moving from Park Lane?" She looks at me. "Together?"

I let it hang there. Watch her squirm. Half conceal a smirk but not all the way. I want Parks to see it, to see what I can still do to her. I look down at the sleeve of my jacket. I fucking miss shopping with her. Dressing yourself isn't all it's cracked up to be.

"No." Jordan laughs, shaking her head. "Me and my housemate."

Parks swallows. "Oh."

Her eyes drop; she looks embarrassed.

I keep staring over at her, happy to have made her feel like shit for a second.

Julian's phone rings. He looks at it, looks at Parks.

"Be right back—"

He excuses himself, darting out of the restaurant quickly as the waiter brings over our drinks. Parks takes an extra long sip of hers.

Jonah watches her, bit of a frown on his face, and then picks it up and takes a swig of her juice.

"Phwoar—" Jo pulls his head back. "You want some juice with that vodka?"

Magnolia looks over at him, eyes gone soft around the edges again.

"Oh." She nods. "Because you're saying the ratio of alcohol to mixer is disproportionate? How witty."

She gives him a tight smile.

I watch their exchange, and don't even really mean to do it, it just happens—I lean over, grab her glass, ignore all the eyes that are on me and take a mouthful of my ex-girlfriend's drink.

Cough a tiny bit.

Fuck.

I thought Jo was probably being a bit of a dick, but it's pretty much straight.

Parks is watching me. Watches me take a drink. Watches me react to it even though I don't say a word. Neither does she.

She reaches across the table, takes the glass from my hand—our fingers touch just a beat longer than they should—and then she takes a long drink, not breaking eye contact with me once.

And I know what she's saying without her saying it. Doesn't need to speak to be heard, she's saying it loud enough: This is your fault.

That's what her eyes tell me as she sinks it in one go and then flags down the server.

"Another, please."

FORTY-FOUR

Magnolia

Julian's leaning back on my bed in the black logo-print track pants from Off-White. No socks, no shirt—nothing. Rather the way I like him, actually.

He's just sitting there doing my rhinestone-embellished YSL Rubik's Cube insanely fast. Genius-level fast. Like, solves it under twenty seconds no matter how I mess it up. He gets cockier and cockier every time, simultaneously getting hotter and hotter every time also.

He tosses it back to me. Solved that one in under ten seconds.

"You're not even trying, Tiges." He grins down at me.

I make a cross noise as I begin to mess it up the most I possibly can but then I hear our apartment door open and close and the sound of a voice I love.

I sit up straighter, listening intently.

Julian frowns, confused.

"Gus!" I sing out and then leap from my bed, thrilled.

I gallop out towards his voice.

"Gus!" I round the corner to find Gus—and my father.

"Oh. Harley."

He rolls his eyes.

"It's good to see you also, first born."

I give him a tight smile as I walk over and hug Gus anyway. "That's the most paternal thing you've ever said to me."

I look between them. "What are you doing here?"

Bridget walks out wearing Danielle straight-leg jeans from Khaite, with a white shirt underneath Marni's argyle-pattern vest, her shoes are from—my eyes pinch. The shoes I don't recognise.

"Dad's taking me to lunch," Bridget tells me.

I pull a face. "I guess we know who the favourite is . . ."

He gives me a look. "She does call me 'Dad'."

"Well," I concede, "she is more desperate than I am, so—"

Gus tilts his head, looking at me. "Are you in pyjamas?"

"Yes," I tell him, my nose in the air. "They are adorable ones though."

The Mimi Martine floral-print satin-jacquard pyjama set from Morgan Lane.

"She doesn't leave the bed much these days—" Bridget gives me a tempestuous smile.

I roll my eyes at her.

Not a huge fan of Julian, though she's yet to meet him.

"Magnolia," my sister says and tilts her head at me. "It's good to see you alive and not murdered." Bridget gives me a smug and annoying look.

Our father frowns, looking between us. "Why would she be murdered?"

"Because she's sleeping with me." Julian rounds the corner, tugging on the grey long-sleeve cashmere hoodie from Brunello Cucinelli as he walks straight over to our father. "Harley—" Julian grins, extending his hand. He's wearing little black Moncler scuffs now, and I think it's adorable that he brought slippers to my house.

My father shakes his head—laughing, if you can believe it!—and pulls him into a hug. "Jules."

Bridget stands there looking between them, jaw dropped.

Julian and Gus shake hands.

"Waterhouse!" Julian clasps both of Gus's hands. "So good to see you, man—" He looks from Gus to Harley. "Boys, that Bieber song was fucking tight."

I blink a few times.

"Wait, hold on." All the men look at me. I stare over at my father with a frown. "Are we from dirty money?"

My father folds his arms over his chest and Julian snorts a laugh.

"I swear to God, Harley—you tell me right now. Are we?"

I glance at Julian, giving him a polite smile. "No offence. Dirty money is better than new money," I concede. "Imagine being from new money . . ." I shake my head and laugh. "Yuck."

Bridget covers her face with her hands, sighing.

I peer over at Julian, hands on my hips. "What is it that you do?"

"Yes, Julian," Bridget pipes up. "What is it you do?"

His eyes pinch playfully at my sister. "I'm an art collector."

"Oh, really? How do you collect it?" my sister asks, blinking brightly.

Julian squashes a smile. "Back channels."

"Oh." I nod, not really wanting more information than that. I suspect there's plenty and I suspect I shouldn't much like to know it.

"How do you know each other?" I wave my hand in the direction of the men.

"Mutual friends," my father says vaguely.

Julian wobbles his head around. "We've partied together."

Bridget pulls a face.

"Weird." I blink.

"Very weird." Bridge nods.

"Did you see him having affairs with other women?" I ask brightly. Julian nods casually. "Hundreds of times, yeah."

My father gives him a tight smile and Bridget nods to herself. "Lovely."

"Oh." I purse my lips.

"So how long's this been a thing?" Gus gestures between Julian and me, casting my father a look.

"Not long." Julian shrugs dismissively. "She's a fucking handful."

My father emphatically nods at the same time Gus says, "Yeah, yeah," all while my sister says, "Isn't she though?"

I frown at them collectively.

Julian extends his hand to my sister.

"You must be Bridget."

She eyes his hand before she cautiously shakes it. "I am."

Julian grins down at her, unperturbed. "Heard a lot about you."

"Have you?" She blinks, un-charmed.

He nods. "Your sister speaks very highly of you. Says you're the smartest person she knows, the funniest person she knows, and that you're not going to like me at all." Harley snorts a laugh at this.

Julian leans in and whispers loud enough for us all to hear, "But I'm hoping we can make her be wrong about one of those things, because I don't like it much when she's right."

Bridget's eyes pinch. "Well, we have that in common."

Julian points at her playfully. "You'll come around on me."

"I doubt it," Bridget sings back before glancing at Harley. "Should we go?"

"Hold on, wait—" I point at her feet. "What on God's great dance floor is happening here?"

Bridget frowns. "What do you mean?"

"I mean why are you wearing those disgusting no-brand loafers with a £1200 Raey cashmere cardigan?"

"*That* you know?" She blinks. "Yesterday you asked me how to spell 'manoeuvre'.".

Julian tilts his head, considering this. "Pretty hard word," he says and snaps his fingers in Bridget's direction. "But not for the smartest person Magnolia Parks knows!"

I roll my eyes at his showmanship.

She looks over at him with a reluctant smile.

He's hard not to like when he's like this.

"Anyway." Bridget glances down. "What's wrong with my shoes?"

"Oh God," I sigh. "Where do I begin? Are they pleather?"

She gives me a look.

"100 per cent 'other materials'?" I frown at them. "Where are they from even?"

"ASOS."

"What's that?" I ask and everyone stares at me. And then I crack a smile, breezing my hand through the air. "I'm kidding! I know it's Net-A-Porter for poor people."

("Oh my God." Bridget blinks wide.)

I shake my head at her. "Listen, I pulled a pair of Oxfords last week for a shoot—your size, black. Ganni. Chunky. Easy to clomp around in as though you never attended finishing school—"

"—She didn't," Harley says, rolling his eyes.

"Well," I put my hands on my hips, "that explains so much."

"Just give me the fucking shoes," Bridget growls.

I clap my hands, thrilled, and run off to get them with a squeal.

"You know," I hear Bridget say as I leave the room, "she can't spell 'parallel' either."

FORTY–FIVE

BJ

Hen and I got called to Mum and Dad's for lunch today.

With our girlfriends.

Without our sisters.

Mum said she gave them her card to go shopping to get them out of the house.

"Give Jordan a break," she whispered to me on the phone.

Henry's still not really speaking to me. Barely said a word on New Year's or at brunch. Guessing that's what this is about.

Mum said it was to get to know our girlfriends better, but Taura's not Henry's girlfriend yet and she knows Jordan just fine.

Mum goes twitchy when Henry and I are off, mostly because it's only happened a few times in our lives.

We're pretty shit-free brothers. When he found out I cheated on Parks, he stopped speaking to me for a bit. Same day I beat the shit out of Christian, so that might have also factored into it. When he found out it was with Paili he actually hit me.

And when I overdosed he was weird with me for a while. Fair enough, I guess. He's pretty level-headed. If he's off me, I probably deserve it. Don't tell him though.

We arrive at the same time, and the girls swap hellos.

I nod him hey, but he doesn't say anything.

"Don't be a prick." Taura flicks him.

"Nah, that's his job," he says as Mum opens the door, throws her arms around us.

"Darlings!"

She kisses both our cheeks, then Jordan's cheek, then Taura's.

"Darling's darlings. Cornish hens are in the oven," she calls back to us as she leads us into the house. My favourite. "With potato gratin." Henry's favourite.

She leads up into the company-only living room. Henry and I catch eyes. We're (nearly) twenty-five and (nearly) twenty-six respectively and could count on one hand the amount of times we've been allowed in the posh living room. "Your dad's drumming up some cocktails in the bar. Talk amongst yourselves."

I wait till she leaves.

"The good living room!" Henry blinks. "What the fuck?"

"Don't touch anything," I tell the girls in a serious voice, only 50 per cent joking.

Tausie watches me, doesn't break eye contact as she pokes the antique Russian Fabergé silver gilt and enamel frame with a photo of the old tsar in it that someone gave to my mum years ago as a wedding present. Mum doesn't know why she was given it and it's become a family joke.

I roll my eyes at Taurs and she sits back, visibly pleased with herself.

Jordan peers between us.

"You two used to sleep together, yeah?"

Henry does a couple of big blinks, leans in, says under his breath, "Here we go . . ."

"Sorry." Jordan flashes him a little smile then turns to Taura. "But you were, right? Sleeping with him?"

"I mean—" Taura catches my eye then rolls hers. "It was a long time ago now. But yeah, I was. Until I realised he's hideously in love with Magn—" She catches herself. Face freezes.

Henry's face cracks with delight, that little shit.

My eyes go wide. Henry snorts a laugh.

". . . azines. Magazines. Total fiend for them. Bit weird, actually."

I roll my eyes at her attempt to save that.

Fucking ridiculous.

309

Jordan nods, then looks back and forth between me and Taura.

"And now you're with Henry?" Jordan clarifies.

"Yep . . ." Taura nods. "Ish."

Jordan squints over at her. "And Jonah?"

Henry breathes in steadily through his nose. I can hear that one hurting him a bit.

It gets harder and harder to share.

"Yep." Taura squeezes Henry's hand.

She knows it's getting weirder.

We all do.

It's the elephant in the room now, and none of us know what to do about it.

"Have you slept with Christian?" Jordan asks, eyebrows up.

I can't tell if she's asking to actually get a hold of it all or just to make them uncomfortable.

Taura nods pleasantly and, actually, this is one of the things I admire most about her: She doesn't give a shit.

I think people might call her a 'sexually liberated woman', and she doesn't see people's judgement from it either, even when it's there like it might be now.

It could be a bit weird if you think about it, maybe. I'll give Jordan that, but find me a friendship pool whose dating lives aren't in overlap.

"What can I say?" Taura shrugs, breezy. "These boys were my Pokémon."

I sniff a laugh.

Jordan tilts her head, thinking. "Who's Pikachu?"

I jut my chin out at the question.

Fuck.

I glance from Tausie to Henry, who's looking at his hands.

"I'm Bowser," I announce just to break the tension.

"Wrong game, dipshit." Henry glances at me.

I blow air out of my mouth, stand up, go help Mum set the table.

Walk into the dining room, give her a bear hug from behind.

She turns around, touches my face with her hand.

"I don't like it when you're at odds."

"I know." I nod.

"He doesn't like Jordan?" she asks.

I take the cutlery from her hands, start laying it out.

"I don't think that's it. Could be a bit it, though," I concede.

Mum looks over at me, waiting for more.

"I hurt Magnolia," I confess.

"Oh." Her face strains. "Worse than before?"

I consider it, nod once. "Probably. Yeah."

Fuck, I miss her. Feel like I've been stuck missing her for five years now. Had her for a second and then it busted again. Or I busted it, I can't tell.

"BJ—" My mum frowns.

I give her a look. "I know, Mum."

Lunch is good.

Dad spends most of it talking about the day he met Mum. We obviously know this story like the back of our hands, Taus too at this point, but it's new for Jordan. She watches my dad with stars in her eyes—a bit like how my mum still does.

Met at university, first day.

He saw her, followed her to a bar after a lecture (weird, and we always tease him for that part) and asked her if he could buy her a drink. She said yes. They spent the night together, drove to the White Cliffs of Dover the next day because Mum had never seen them, and then he asked her to marry him.

In a day.

Never looked back.

They got married a few months later and they're the happiest couple I've ever seen.

When you know, you know, my dad says.

I think that's why he gets so angry at me about Parks.

When you know, you know.

We're meant to be, me and Parks. Right?

That's what this is about. We're fated. Woven into the tapestry of the universe, my name right next to hers. We're in the stars.

311

That's why whatever the fuck's happening right now is so fucked up. We're meant to be and everyone who knows us knows.

I've known since I was six. Known for nearly twenty years she's the only person I've ever wanted to be with, but I can't stop fucking up anyway.

"When you know, you know." My dad looks over at me. "Isn't that right, BJ?" He gives me a warm smile.

Try to return it, but it's weak.

He doesn't say that to be a dick—he's not a dick. He's trying to remind me, trying to tell me without telling me.

I'm with the wrong girl.

Can't look at Jordan, how much I miss Parks is at an all-time high and I reckon it's written all over my face; if she sees it and if she has a shred of self-respect, she'll leave me herself. And good for her. She should, probably. Do the right thing by herself, because I'm not doing the right thing by anyone, I don't think.

I start clearing plates because I don't know what else to do.

Henry stands, clears from his end. Follows me to the kitchen, puts the plates down on the bench. Watches me.

"You okay?"

I look over at him, eyebrow cocked.

"Oh, you done not talking to me?"

"Depends—" He matches my face. "Are you done being a dick?"

I roll my eyes. "Hen—"

"—Beej," he cuts in. "It's Magnolia."

"I know, but—"

"—No." He shakes his head, properly worked up. "BJ, it's Magnolia. My best friend since I was four. There's a photo of me and her on the first day of school on the mantelpiece in the next room. We've gone on vacations with her family for the last twenty years."

"I know, Hen."

"In high school you got her pregnant."

I give him a look. "Come on, man."

"No, bro," He frowns at me. "You slept with her. You told her you loved her. And then you went home and fucked Jordan? I—" He sighs. "What the fuck?"

I lean back against the sink. "I thought we were done?"

"So, what? You thought you'd fucking nail the coffin shut?"

"Yes!" I stare over at him. "Why wouldn't I?"

"Because—"

I cut him off. "Don't tell me she's not doing the same thing, she is. I'm fucking over it." I shake my head. "How's she get away with it and I don't? She fucks me around as much as I do to her and I don't see you fucking climbing up her arse about it—"

Henry pulls a face like he's grossed out and I realise what I said and we both start to laugh awkwardly.

He starts loading the dishwasher. "What do you want from her?"

I shake my head, give him a shrug like it's simple. "I just want her."

"Beej," he gives me a look. "You had her."

I stare over at my brother, her best friend in the world. Of everyone who loves her in the world I reckon the two of the top three are here in this room. They have the kind of friendship where if he wasn't my brother and I wasn't sure she was as loyal to me as she is that I'd feel uneasy about.

If we ever had fights at the weekend when we were teenagers, she wouldn't sleep in the spare bed, she'd sleep in his. He's held her through so much shit that I haven't been able to. I don't think anyone knows her like I do, but my brother's probably a close second.

"Do you think I'm good enough for her?" I ask him.

He looks caught off guard as he blinks over at me. "What?"

"Do you?"

He frowns. "Yeah."

"Do you really?"

"BJ." My brother shakes his head. "I don't know what you're talking ab—"

"I cheated on her. And then I fucked around. Did drugs. Partied harder than she liked. Then I cheated with her. I know she thinks I'm a fuck up—"

"She doesn't," he interrupts me. Looks sad.

"Don't lie to me." I roll my head back. "I am a fuck up."

"Beej," he sighs. "You fucked up. You're not a fuck up."

I roll my eyes, don't really want his semantics at the minute.

"Just tell me Hen, I want to know—as her friend, as someone who loves her how I know you do—if I wasn't your brother, would you think I'm good enough for her?"

And it's just for a second, the smallest pause—flickers across his brow, don't even know if he'd know it was there—but I see it: the truth.

I'm not, and apparently we all know it.

FORTY-SIX
Magnolia

"Push the X—" Declan tells me with urgency. "The X. The X!"

"I am!"

"You're not."

We're sitting on Julian's couch. Decks is trying to teach me *Grand Theft Auto*.

"The X!" he yells. "The X! The fucking X!"

"I am hitting the X!" I yell back. "—Oh wait. No. Sorry. That was the circle."

Declan groans as Julian sniffs a laugh from his armchair behind his paper.

"Fuck! How are you so bad at this?" Declan frowns at the TV.

"I'm not bad at it." I blink. "I'm not bad at anything. Julian—" I pout. "Tell him I'm not bad at anything."

He doesn't even glance up. "She's not bad at anything." Then his big blue eyes pop up over the top of the paper. "You're pretty shit at that, though."

I drop the controller on the couch and walk over to him. Pull the paper from his hands, climb onto his lap.

I'm quite fond of him, if I'm honest. I've always been, to a certain extent. Something about him, isn't there? You get it. Maybe it's how deep his voice is, or how big his hands are, or that his eyes are the most peculiar blue I've ever seen.

And do you know, it is the strangest thing—for all the ways that he's allegedly the most dangerous man in the country, I feel unbelievably safe with him.

He's different towards me than anyone else I've seen him with, even more so when we're alone.

There's still that rough edge, of course. He feels me up all the time, talks about sex a bit too casually for my preferences as well. He's a big fan of leaving love bites on me, tiny territorial markings of where his mouth has been, but he always pulls me onto his lap or rests his chin on my shoulder if we're sitting or on top of my head if we're standing—he's so tall. And, when he thinks no one's looking, he whispers things to me. Sometimes they're sweet nothings, sometimes it's about what he'd like to do to me later, other times he whispers funny things about other people in the room, but either way, every time, the way his mouth feels against my ear makes my toes curl and forces me to swallow heavy. I still get the feeling like I'm going down the biggest dip of a rollercoaster any time he puts his hands on my body—and his hands are always on my body. He's still rude to nearly everyone around us, he can be possessive and brash, and he's always obnoxious, but then he knows that I love someone else, so what leg have I to stand on anyway? And while he can be an absolute brute, he also can then be rather chivalrous—opens doors, puts on my shoes, carries me over puddles—things I think he'd die if other people knew about, like how he holds my hand sometimes just for no reason.

Like now, his finger is tracing down my arm absentmindedly. He's just gotten done touching my cheek, and before long his eyes wander over my face until they land on my mouth.

He presses his tongue into his bottom lip.

I know what that means. I know his little tells now.

He'd like to have sex. So would I, actually.

The front door slams and we all glance over at Daisy sulking in.

"Hi!" I call out to her merrily, still trying to win her over.

She stares over at me, says nothing and keeps walking to the kitchen.

I look back at Julian, frowning.

"What's her problem?"

"She hates you," Declan says from the couch. Julian tosses him a dirty look as I throw a plastic water bottle at him.

"Her and Tiller keep fighting," Julian tells me. Then he tilts his head before conceding, "And she hates you."

"Oh no—" I frown, ignoring the last bit. "Why?"

Julian nods, his face a bit strained. "Why aren't they doing good?"

"Because he's a fuckwit," Declan says, not looking away from the TV.

I glance back at Julian, whose face pinches a bit. "Conflict of interests. We've had our fair share of run-ins." He gives me a shrug.

"He doesn't like you?" I blink.

"Doesn't like what I do." He shrugs indifferently.

"Arms dealing?" I clarify.

Declan's face flickers in the background, amused.

"Yeah." Julian licks his top lip. "Amongst other things."

I frown thinking about it. He's impossible not to like, and I know there's more to it than that, but I shouldn't like to think about it all that much, the nuances of what he's not saying and what I think it means.

The truth is, Julian is so clever and so charming in that awful Hemsworth kind of way where you don't dislike him for being beautiful and charismatic, you actually like him more for some reason.

"That copper's had a death wish since the day he landed on this doorstep," Declan tells neither of us in particular.

Julian glances at him for a few seconds and then says nothing, which makes me feel a tiny bit nervous. His face turns to brooding as his sister's sadness weighs heavily on him and I start feeling like I'd like to make it lighter for him.

"So Daisy's upset then?"

"Mmhm." He nods, staring at my mouth as he fiddles with my hair between his fingers. I don't know if he knows he's doing it.

I sit up straight. "I'm going to fix it."

He shakes his head sternly. "No."

"No, no. I'm good at it." I nod.

He tilts his head and considers this, but the face he makes doesn't imply that he has all that much confidence in me.

"I am," I insist.

"I feel like you aren't."

"Well, I'm very subtle."

He squints at me. "Who's been lying to you?"

I pout at him.

"You are polite," he lists off on his fingers. "You are smart. You are the hottest girl I've ever seen. You're getting there in bed—"

("—Thank you?" I tilt my head, frowning a bit. "You're welcome." He smirks.)

"But Tiges—" He pinches my chin between his thumb and his index finger. "About as subtle as a brick in the face, you are."

My frown hits rock sulky bottom and he kisses me how he'd never do if we weren't behind closed doors and six layers of security.

I glare over at him playfully and then jump up. "Well, anyway, you're wrong. I'm going to fix it—"

His head rolls back. "Please don't."

"Let her be," Declan says from the couch, still not looking away from the TV.

"Yes!" I nod. "Thank you, Decks."

"Not you, you idiot—" He glances over, rolling his eyes. "Daisy."

"Watch it." Julian points at him with his eyebrows up. His face is a bit sharper than I'd like.

I push Julian's finger down as I walk towards the kitchen with a bright shrug. "Imagine if I were the kind of person who said 'live and let live'."

"Yeah." He nods, following me. "Imagine."

I glance back at him. "I mean, I'm not going to say that."

"No." He walks ahead of me, holding open the door as he sighs. "Didn't think you would."

"Dai-sy!" I sing.

"What?" She frowns up at me, leering over a Le Creuset pot in the printed silk-twill jacket and matching shorts from Gucci.

"I hear you're sad."

"Fuck you." She points at her brother with a wooden spoon covered in creamy sauce.

She gets a bit on my cardigan.

I laugh uncomfortably.

"Daisy," Julian growls.

"That—it's fine—" I shake my head. "It's just my Juliet cashmere cardigan from Khaite that was about £4000, but it's fine. Accidents happen." I give her a cheery smile.

She looks over at me as annoyed and unimpressed as she always seems to be around me, then flicks her terrible little spoon in my direction again, this time on purpose.

Lots of sauce now.

Fantastic.

"Oi!" Julian barks as he stands in front of me. Daisy rolls her eyes. "Tell her you're sorry."

She rolls her eyes. "Fuck off."

I peer around Julian, holding one of his hands with both of mine.

"I'm sorry you and Tiller are fighting . . . Relationships can be so tricky."

She looks over at me, eyes slits. "You'd know."

I ignore her and persevere like the emotional pioneer I am.

"Seen Christian lately?" I ask quickly before ducking behind her brother in case the spoon comes back out.

"No." She glares at her pot. "You seen BJ lately?" she asks her pot spitefully.

She looks up at me, and my eyes are probably rounder than I'd like them to be. It's probably more obvious that she's struck a nerve than you'd want someone who taunts you to see, and Julian doesn't do anything except reach around me with the hand I'm not holding and he pulls me tight against him.

She stares over at us for a few seconds and then her face softens.

"Give me your sweater." She wipes her hands on her apron.

"It's actually a cardigan," I correct her. I don't know why. She looks like she wants to kill me again.

"Hurry up and give it to me." She rolls her eyes for the fiftieth time and holds her hand out, waiting. "I'll get the sauce out before it leaves an oil stain."

I've been wearing it as a bit of a dressing gown around the house.

"Oh—" I hug myself. "I don't have anything on underneath it."

She rolls her eyes like I'm the biggest pain in the world.

"Go on," she tells her brother with a nod of her head. "Give her your shirt."

Julian turns around to face me. He's got two on actually, the black logo-print cotton-jersey T-shirt from Billionaire Boys Club that he's wearing over the white lyocell and cotton-blend jersey T-shirt from Tom Ford. He offers me the black one and watches unflinchingly as I undo the buttons of my cardigan. He tilts his head, smiling a bit, and then takes off the undershirt without saying a word.

Daisy makes a disgusted sound. "I don't want to watch you have sex."

"So leave then," Julian tells her without looking away from me.

He flings my cardigan at Daisy as I hold his shirt against me. I peer over at her as she walks out of the room, annoyed. I give her a small, grateful smile.

She rolls her eyes at me, but it's less aggressive than before.

He waits for her to leave and then smirks down at me. Still using his shirt to cover my body, he plucks it from my hands, casting it aside. "We won't be needing that anymore."

FORTY-SEVEN

BJ

Bridge and I are back on for our weekly lunches. I have been for the last few weeks. I think she thinks I'm good enough. If Bridget thinks it, it makes me think maybe I am. Or at least I could be.

Happy to see her again too, happy to have her grumpy, imposing commentary on our lives. Missed her—not just because of the Parks connection, but because I've known her since she was two and she's like my sister too.

We've been doing some variant of this since high school. Bridge started at Varley when I was sixteen, and me and Parks were pretty much already together by then. Once a week we'd eat lunch just us in the cafeteria. Magnolia said she hated it but she definitely loved it. She loves her sister more than anyone. Anyone who's good to Bridge is in her good books.

That's not why I do it, but it's a merry side effect for sure.

Bit of a straight shooter, our Bridge. Zero time for your shit or mine, and no matter what, even when I was a kid, after every conversation I had with her, I'd leave smarter or wiser or at least less dumb.

I take her to 45 Jermyn in St James.

She sips her gin and tonic, squints over at me. "You would have been a good dad."

This is the topic lately. The baby. She's obviously processing it. Scared to bring it up with her sister. I like talking to her about it. Makes me feel good. Makes me feel close to her sister. Makes me think all might not be lost.

"Yeah?" I sit back, chuffed.

"Well," she considers, "you have a good dad, so."

"I do," I concede.

"Can you even imagine what a little kid version of Magnolia would have been like?"

"I can, yeah." I nod. "I mean, we survived the original."

Bridge shrugs. "She was less ridiculous back then."

"Who was?" Magnolia asks, suddenly at our table with her hands on her hips, frowning down at us. Black sweater, black skirt, tall black boots and a Chanel bag from the '90s that I bought her one Christmas when we were together.

Behind her is my brother carrying about twenty-five bags from all over New Bond Street.

I glance up at her, my eyes more lit than I want them to be.

But I know all her looks. She's happy to see me too.

Me, no Jordan. Her, no Jules.

Just how it should be.

"So," she gives me the tall eyebrows, sits down next to me without an invitation. Turns my backwards hat back round the right way. "I see your little Wednesday lunch club is back on."

I flip my hat back the way I want it just because I hope she'll touch me again.

"Clearly." Bridget gives her a bored look as she smiles up at Henry.

He kisses her cheek. "Bridge." "Hen."

Magnolia sighs loudly to bring the attention back on her.

"My sister and my . . ." she trails. Our eyes catch and I give her an amused look as I wait for her to try and label me. She bites away a smile. I don't know what she's smiling at, just glad she is.

"My . . . greatest folly."

I roll my eyes.

Bit of a blow. Guess it's pretty accurate though.

I nod over at Henry, next to Bridge.

"And you're what? On a shopping spree with my brother?"

("Hey, man." Hen nods at me as we bump fists over the table.)

322

"Well," she shrugs, "one of the Ballentines should be buying me things."

I roll my eyes again.

"And anyway, what I'm doing isn't the point. What are you doing?" she asks Bridget, frowning.

Bridget gestures to herself. "What am I doing?"

Magnolia nods, impatient.

Bridge swipes her hand through the air.

"Honestly, Magnolia, I'm just trying to get this show on the fucking road—" She waves her hand between us.

"Excellent," Henry nods.

Bridget looks over at Henry. "How long are these growing pains going to last for, do you think?"

He shrugs. "Already been too long, in my opinion."

"Growing pains?" Parks blinks, pretending she doesn't know what her sister means.

"Yes." Bridget scratches her nose, indifferent. "It's very tedious watching you two be with other people."

Parks looks over at me, her eyes wide with embarrassment, but she's happy.

I lick away a smile.

"Then you should watch something else," Magnolia tells her.

Bridget folds her hands on the table.

"Oh, that I could, Magnolia. Oh, that I could."

Parks rolls her eyes in an over-the-top way and looks back at me. Wants me to pipe in.

My eyes fall down her face. Forget what I'm doing. Forget the day of the week, the month, the hour. What a face.

Her cheeks go pink, watching me watch her.

"Normal people don't look at each other how you're looking at each other right now," Henry says, gesturing to us. Fucking arsehole. "I'll just say, that—that was an abnormal exchange."

Bridge nods. "Totally weird, yeah."

"You two are insane. We just glanced at each other." Magnolia rolls her eyes, but her hands are pressed onto her cheeks. A dead giveaway.

Henry gives her a look. "This is a glance." He and Bridget look at each other with complete indifference for one second before returning to me and Parks.

Bridget presents with her hands. "A glance."

Henry drops his chin to his chest, lifts up his eyebrows. "What you just did—"

And then Henry and Bridget try to emulate however it was that Parks and I looked at each other. Heads tilted, eyes wide and swoony, Henry making kissing sounds.

Parks laughs quietly but the bridge of her nose goes so pink that she could have just been in the sun. I ball up my napkin, toss it at my brother's head.

Then Magnolia leans in towards me, peeks down my jacket at the T-shirt underneath.

I give her a look, waiting for her approval. She looks down at my hand, picks it up, angles my finger to see my ring properly. It's not her family ring—I wish it was. It's just a blue one that matches my jacket. It impresses her though and that's enough for me.

"I've got an idea," Bridget says, clapping her hands together.

"Oh, good," Parks says dryly as she reaches over and takes the negroni out of my hand. Our eyes catch.

She has a sip.

Has another.

I know she does this just to feel close to me. She hates Campari.

One more sip.

She hands it back to me.

Our hands touch.

Not lost on Henry, smirking away from across the table. Smarmy git.

"Lets do a mini couples therapy." Bridget grins.

"No." I shake my head.

"Yes!" Henry claps enthusiastically. "Hundred per cent in."

"Not happening," I tell her.

"Okay," says Magnolia and I snap my head in her direction. She's just staring at Henry. "BJ and I will do a couples therapy right now if you, Jonah and Taura will do one and we get to watch yours."

I bite down on my bottom lip to temper the smile. My girl.

"Er—" Henry's face scrunches. "Nah." He shakes his head.

"Actually," Bridget nods, "that sounds great. Let's do that! Are you free Friday?"

"Nah." Henry keeps shaking his head.

"Oh, go on, Henry—" Magnolia pouts. "Bridget never has plans on a Friday, don't take that away from her!"

Bridget flips her off, rolling her eyes, and Henry keeps shaking his head.

"No. They're fine." He gestures vaguely towards us. "They're fine. They'll work it out. One day they'll just . . . you know, like . . . round a corner and be together forever."

Magnolia goes still. Looks over at me. We've rounded a lot of corners. Her heart breaks in her eyes like a dropped egg and I don't know what I'm doing anymore without her. I hate being without her. Rummage through the drawer in my mind as fast as I can to find the words to tell her that I'm coming for her, I'm on my way back, that this is just the long way home. But the drawers are a mess, the words are all jumbled—I love her and then what?—then she pushes back from the table.

"Anyway." She blinks a lot. "We've got to nip over to Bottega."

Henry stands, looks a bit sorry. I give him a small smile.

"Have fun," I tell them.

"Love you." She kisses her hand and smacks it into Bridget's forehead.

Then she walks away, doesn't say goodbye to me, does flip my hat again though. Suppose that's better.

I catch my brother's eye, toss him my Barclay's Infinite card and nod after her.

She's right. One of the Ballentines should be buying her things. Should be me.

Henry gives me a small wink, kisses Bridget's head and goes after Parks who's speed-walked out of here.

I watch them go, can tell I look sadder on the outside than I want to.

"Do you think that's true?" I ask eventually, looking back at her.

"What?" She pours us some water. "That you'll just be together again one day?"

I nod.

"No." She shakes her head.

I swallow, drop her eyes. Fuck.

"But—" She ducks her head to see me. "I do think probably one day you'll both just . . . decide to be together and it'll work." Kind of says that like it's just a confusing truth.

I squint over at her.

"But you're not there yet," she tells me with a sharp smile. "Neither of you are willing to do the things you need to do to make it work yet."

Gives me a dismissive shrug.

I frown at her.

"I'd do anything for her."

She nods once, watching me closely.

"Except lose face."

I open my mouth to say something back but nothing comes. Fuck.

She gives me a look that's wiser than a twenty-two-year-old should be capable of.

"Pride suffocates relationships, Beej."

"She's proud," I say back.

"Yeah." She nods. "She is, insanely so. Probably the only thing she is more than proud is afraid, though. Don't you think?"

That one sinks me like a fucking stone.

Afraid?

Fuck.

I hate the thought of her being afraid.

I hate even more that I'm the one making her like that.

326

FORTY-EIGHT
Magnolia

We head to one of the boys' clubs later, for no real reason other than Julian feels like it.

I go find my friends because he needs to speak to Jonah in his office.

Seems precarious. I don't like it much. It reminds me that Jonah does what Julian does.

I don't even know what Julian does. He's good at keeping those facts at bay, and I'd rather them be there, because without them he feels rather like a knight in shining everything, but I suspect that were I to receive confirmation from someone that, say, the immaculate print of *Beach at Scheveningen in Stormy Weather* in his office is in fact not a print, it might tarnish his image in my mind. Or maybe it wouldn't, because something about him is a bit like Teflon, and all the bad slides right off him, no matter what it is he does.

I swan over to everyone assembled in the roped-off area.

I dive and half-sit next to/on top of Taura, squeezing her, grateful her chosen seat is next to BJ so I can be close to him too.

I lean forward to smile at Jordan and, as warmly as I can muster, say, "Hi."

"Hey—" She smiles back. "Cool skirt."

It's the very short, very green sequin-embellished miniskirt from The Attico.

BJ's eyes wander over me and the corset I'm wearing more than they should. "You're in a lot of black these days."

It's because I'm doing a lot of mourning these days.

"I like your jumper," I tell him. I rub the material from his sleeve between my fingers.

He smiles at me like no one else is around us—and I miss him so much. More than I can say, more than I can process really, because I'm not only in love with him—he's also my best friend. And I wish I could crawl into his lap, curl up, face in his neck, tell him about all the ways this stupid boy broke my heart a few weeks ago, but I can't because it's him—so I tell him I love him with my blinking and he tells me he misses me with his question:

"What is it?" he asks, covering the logo on the front like I don't already know.

"Oh, come on." I roll my eyes. "Versace La Greca-print sweatshirt." I feel its hem as though I don't already know the answer. Graze his stomach as I do on purpose. No one knows but him. Want splinters up my arm like a broken bone. "Cotton."

He gives me a sad smile. "Very good."

Jordan leans over BJ a bit obnoxiously.

"What's Julian like in bed?" she asks curiously as she stares over at the boy I'm sleeping with.

I suspect it's an intentionally timed question.

She can't see BJ's face because he's just watching me, but his eyes close like the question hurts him too.

I catch his eyes, try to tell him I'm sorry before I start, but then I remember that he did this.

Told me he loved me, had sex with me four times before we left that hotel, and then went home and had sex with this girl who's asking me about the sexual prowess of the man I'm using as emotional Scotch Guard.

"An Olympian." I nod.

BJ rolls his eyes, looking annoyed—all the softness between us a moment ago up in flames. "No."

"Yes." I nod.

Taura leans in, nodding too. "Yeah."

"Really?" Jordan glances from me to Taura.

"Yep." Taura nods firmly.

"It's very athletic," I tell Jordan solemnly.

BJ picks something out of his teeth. "How?"

"We did it on the stair climber the other day," I offer him, thinking back to it. "It wasn't extremely arduous for me, but for him it was quite the workout."

Jordan leans back in her seat with the giggles and BJ looks so cross, if I could, I'd pour his expression into a Martini glass and take a big sip.

"Yeah." I twirl some hair around my finger. "One time I blacked out a little . . ."

BJ blinks a few times as though he's rejecting the information he's receiving. "What?"

"Yep."

He gives me a look. "You blacked out?"

"Mmhm." I nod.

His eyes pinch. "Why?"

"I don't know." I shrug. "It was just too much, I suppose?"

He scowls a bit.

I can scarcely believe it when he asks, "What were you doing?"

I pull back, surprised.

"Stuff."

He gives me a look. "What kind of stuff?"

I frown at him. "Normal stuff . . ."

"Like what?"

"Like specifically what?" I ask him, my eyebrows up, a bit annoyed.

Taura is watching on in baffled horror.

BJ nods, daring me.

"I was standing up, he was doing . . ." I trail. Cheeks go pink and I think I could throw up if I let myself. Me telling BJ about the sex I'm having with someone else? It's my worst nightmare. And I'm telling him like it's nothing, like it means nothing to me, like it's not going against every fibre of my being, telling him how someone else touched me and held me in all the ways I've only ever wanted him to.

"Something—" Julian was doing something, that's all I can give him. "And I suppose all the blood went from my head to . . . somewhere else and then I fainted for a minute—" I shrug. "And then I came to . . . And then I came."

That's an oversimplification. What I'm leaving out is that between blacking out and coming to, Julian called Daisy to check that I was okay. I woke up to both Haites hovering over me and Julian's face was so cute and so worried that sometimes I think about it for no reason—it's just a face that floats into my mind sometimes.

Beej pushes his tongue into the side of his mouth, squints at me like a stranger.

"Are my ears burning, Tiges?" Julian says, walking over to me.

Black Gothic Bomber Jacket from Raf Simons, Balenciaga's distressed logo-print washed cotton-jersey T-shirt and the elastic waist straight trousers from Y-3 in black. He takes me by the hand, pulls me up off Taura's lap, hooks an arm around my neck, pulls me back against him so he can watch BJ.

"Maybe."

I nod.

"You don't look too happy, Ballentine." Jules nods at Beej. "Knickers in a bunch?"

I look back at him, frowning. "Be nice."

He whispers loud enough for everyone to hear, "That's not what you said last night—"

"Okay—" Beej rolls his eyes. "We get it, you guys had sex."

Julian's face falters.

"Are you talking to me?"

BJ looks up at him indifferently.

Shit.

"Yeah, I am."

Julian cocks his head to the side. "If you've got something to say, big man, say it."

330

Beej nods his head towards the door. "You want to take this outside?"

I shake my head at him, staring at him in disbelief. "BJ—"

Julian gets a dangerous look in his eye. "Love to."

BJ stands.

I turn around to face Julian—plant my hand on his chest. "Julian."

"Woah, woah—" Jonah jogs over. "What's going on?"

BJ waves his hand invitingly. "Go on—"

"Beej—" I whip my head around to scowl at him. Julian shakes his head, grinning in a way that makes me nervous. He points at him.

"You better check your boy, Jo. That didn't not sound like a threat."

BJ cocks a smile he shouldn't and shrugs. "You know what? I think you're all talk, man."

"Do you?" Julian licks the corner of his crooked smile. "Are you willing to stake your life on that?"

"Easy—" I turn around, holding his face in my hand. "Look at me." I give him a look. "In no world. Do you understand?"

Jonah grabs him by the shoulders, shakes them jovially. He's playing it off well but he's nervous. "Let's go to my office, lad." Jonah nods back to it before looking over at BJ. "And you, pull your fucking head in, you git."

Julian clocks me, lifting an eyebrow. He knows I don't like drugs. "You mind?"

I do mind, actually, but I shrug like I don't because I'd do anything to diffuse this. He grabs me by the waist and kisses me more than he needs to. "Be back soon."

I wait about three seconds before speed-walking to the bar. I can feel a bit of a panic coming on. A shot. Something to take the edge off.

I get to the bar, lean over it. Pour myself a double in a tumbler. A bartender clocks me but they know I'm with Jonah. I look back at BJ, watching after me. Henry's speaking to him—yelling at him, maybe—but he's just locked on me.

I drink the drink quickly. Pour another and wait. He'll come to me. I know it. I can feel him like a fishing line in the water I can't see.

He stands next to me. "Oi—"

I steady myself and don't move my arm from how he's brushed his up against it. I look up at him. "Hey."

He grimaces. "Sorry about before."

I shake my head at him. "What were you thinking?"

His eyes hold mine. "I wasn't thinking."

"It'll be fine." I nod and wonder if I'm a bit saying it for myself. "I know he can be . . . tempestuous."

Beej licks his bottom lip. "He can be a fucking twat, is what he can be." I check over my shoulder to make sure we're safe with those fighting words he's saying. "He's not here. He's doing drugs in Jonah's office—which I don't do anymore, by the way."

He tells me and I can tell he's proud.

I smile up at him. "Really?"

He nods once.

"For how long?"

"Clean for . . ." He purses his perfect mouth as he thinks. "Since May. What's that? Nearly eight months."

"What happened in May?"

"I don't know—" He shrugs, looking a bit embarrassed. "Kind of felt like I was disappointing you."

I stare over at him for a few seconds. "You were."

"Knew it!" He laughs. "I knew it."

He grins at me and I'm smiling back but my smile feels like a sun's rising on my face. Nervous, cautious, light-bearing, hopeful.

"You got clean for me?"

He looks over his shoulder, checking who's listening but it's just us in all the world again. "And me."

My heart cracks open a bit with how much I love him, like daylight breaking through a boarded-up window. I smile up at him, beat down the urge to kiss him. I squeeze his arm instead.

"I'm proud of you."

"Thanks, Parks." His cheeks go a bit pink.

I move my hand down to his and squeeze his index finger. "I mean it. I'm really proud."

He rubs the back of his neck, swallows nervous.

"How are you, anyway? Good?"

He's asking sincerely.

"I'm fine." I nod.

He tilts his head. "Yeah?"

"Mmhm." I nod. "Are you?"

"Yeah, good, I guess." BJ nods his head towards the offices. "So it's going good with Jules then?"

"I mean . . ." I bite down on my lip. "It's a very base-level relationship."

"Right."

"It serves its purpose."

"What's its purpose?"

His heavy eyes catch mine.

An oxygen mask, is what I don't say. Also what I don't say is that I haven't left Julian's side barely at all. Nor do I say that he might be my favourite oxygen mask to date, that I don't get tired of breathing him in, and actually whatever Julian's atmosphere's made of, a small part of me likes how it feels in my lungs. I can't say any of that though, so I just raise my eyebrows a fraction.

"It's just sex," I tell him.

BJ watches me quietly, a hint of a frown present before he shakes his head. "I don't believe it. You can't do casual sex."

"I don't know—" I shrug. "Maybe you had a point all these years . . ."

He sighs, shoulders falling like I threw a weight on him. "I didn't." He shakes his head.

I flash him a look that's a delicate mix of hurt and trepidation. "We shall see."

His face pulls, sort of grimacing at the thought. "Just sex, huh?"

I nod.

333

"Does Julian know that?"

I give him a little look. "I don't suspect he'd care . . ."

BJ looks over his shoulder and he cringes.

"You might be right."

I follow his gaze to Julian at the side of the club, an awful girl on his lap.

Orangey blonde with Marilyn Monroe curls, stroking his face.

The skin on the back of my neck prickles and my chest goes tight.

I don't know why. I know what Julian is to me—Julian knows what he is to me. I'm in love with someone else so maybe it's a terrible thing to have thought—maybe even hoped—that I meant something more than that to him.

Which I mustn't. Your mind can play tricks on you when you're having a lot of sex with a person, it'll make you feel closer than you really are.

I had thought he liked me more than that, more than how little he must actually care about me to do this—hooking up with some stupid girl on a couch in the middle of a club when I arrived here with him forty minutes ago holding his hand, when the papers have been writing about us, when I've spent every day of the week in his bed, after he's told me time and time again not to go home—and now he's here, doing this right in front of me.

In front of BJ, which is worse, I think, because I have a quiet but prevalent worry that BJ might see me as a tiny bit disposable and the very idea of him seeing someone else perpetuate that makes me want to cry more than I already wanted to cry from just seeing Julian do this in the first place.

All of it spirals me too quickly, in a way that I lose all footing on all my thoughts.

In the same second I see Julian with his hands on another girl's waist like he had them on mine this morning, I lose BJ too. Again. Twice. Once to Paili, once to Jordan—never mind the thousands of times in-between with a million girls whose names even he doesn't know.

For all the ways BJ hovers around me, all the ways he shows up and says all the right things after doing the wrong ones, all the times his eyes find mine no matter what room we're in—none of that matters because he never can manage to love me more than he loves an orgasm.

And I hate him for that.

That's my mental process in two and a half seconds. Foot to the pedal in my mind that speeds me to the conclusion that Julian's stupid hands on that stupid girl's body is somehow my stupid ex-boyfriend's fault.

I don't even look back at Beej as I march over—I can feel that he's close behind me anyway.

I stand in front of Julian, waiting for him to take his hand out from under the dress of the girl he's with.

Declan elbows him a bunch of times.

Jules looks up at me, his eyes look funny. Almost as though he's annoyed at me for the interruption.

"Oh—hey?" He blinks up at me, innocent.

"Oh, hey?" I repeat back.

He blinks more.

"Listen—" I give him a look. "I don't care what you do when I'm not here, which is this, I presume."

He rolls his eyes.

"I'm not done talking." I put my hands on my hips and he pulls his head back, amused. "You want to feel up random girls who are substantially less attractive than I am? That's your prerogative. But when I'm in the same room as you, I am all you see."

Julian lifts an eyebrow, paying attention.

"Is that right?"

"That's right." I nod.

He cocks an eyebrow. "Or what?"

"Or we're done," I tell him without missing a beat. "Which is fine with me, by the way." I give him a half-hearted shrug. "You've wanted me for—ooh—" I catch eyes with his body-guard. "What would you say, Kekoa—four or so years?"

He shakes his head. "More like five."

I give him an appreciative nod and my gaze settles back on Julian.

"You've wanted me for about five years and I've sort of wanted you maybe for, like, three weeks, so it's no skin off my back."

Julian Haites snorts a laugh.

"So." I arch my eyebrows. "What's it going to be?"

Julian sighs, annoyed.

"You heard the boss," he says as he unceremoniously shifts the girl from his lap.

He stands up, stares down at me, then slips his arms around my waist.

"Don't you do that again," I tell him, gaze unflinching.

He laughs a bit, shakes his head.

"Fuck me, you're demanding . . ."

"Oh—" I nod. "You have no idea. But you're about to."

He flicks his eyebrows up playfully.

"Come on—" I nod my head towards the exit. "You're going to take me home and put me to bed."

He pushes some hair behind my ears, tilting his head as he looks at me. "Am I?"

"You are."

He squashes a smile. "In what way am I putting you to bed?"

I catch my ex-boyfriend's eyes for a second before I stare straight into Julian's. "Any way you like."

He smirks at BJ as he takes my hand in his, pulls me out of the club.

I don't look back.

His security team is waiting downstairs. They open the car door for us. He lifts me up into it. Unnecessary, but I'm happy to have his hands on my body. They distract me well.

I look over at him as the car pulls out.

"You know, if you ever hurt him, I'd kill you."

His jaw sets, amused and annoyed. "Was that a threat?"

I nod once. "Yep."

He presses his lips together.

"You know I don't respond that well to threats . . ."

"That's okay," I say, looking out the window before flicking my gaze back to him. "I can think of a highly functional way for you to take out your frustration on me."

11:17

Bridget 😴

True or false: BJ nearly fought a gang lord over you?

True adjacent

Holy shit

Would Julian actually hurt him?

No

He'd punch him, absolutely—

No two ways about that . . .

Yeah but who wouldn't these days?

Completely...

Massive pain in the arse . . .

That's what I'm saying

Great arse though . . .

Whose?

Both

Yeah but whose is better?

Goodbye Bridget.

BJ's?

Goodbye.

Should we talk about who's bigger at least?

We should not.

So Julian?

Bridget!

BJ?

Bridge.

Throw me a bone!

honestly Bridge, I'm fielding bones
left and right at the minute

HAH.

Parks

You good?

You went weird at the end there.

I'm fine.

You're never fine when you say you're fine.

Well, I'm fine now.

. . . you seem fine.

That's because I am.

Clearly.

. . .

Right.

Have fun tonight.

Try not to black out.

Fuck you

Julian's seconds?

Pass.

FORTY-NINE

BJ

"Been meaning to ask you something," Jo says without looking away from the TV.

We're on the couch playing *Madden*. About as normal as life has felt since I accidentally got a live-in girlfriend and the love of my life started fucking an international art thief.

"Alright—" I glance at him. "Go on then."

He hits pause.

"Who was going to be the baby's godfather and don't you fucking say Henry."

I start laughing, shake my head at him.

"I'm serious." He stares at me.

He is being serious, actually.

I glance at him, a bit amused. "Why not Henry?"

"Because he would have been an uncle."

I roll my eyes, unpause the game. "You would have been an uncle."

"Yeah." Jonah looks annoyed. "But he's blood."

I pause it again, look over at him. "You might as well be."

Jonah watches me for a few seconds. "Is it weird you're as okay as you are?"

Jordan's not here, glance around for her anyway. Just in case. She's out with her work friends, she said. Wouldn't be dead surprised if she was out with that DJ. Saw his name pop up on her phone. I didn't say anything. What could I say anyway that wouldn't cut my own legs out from under me?

I peer at Jo out of the corner of my eyes.

340

"I wasn't okay for a bit," I tell him with a shrug. "But Parks and I went through this all already like ten years ago. New information for you. Not for me."

He nods slowly.

"You were my pick for godfather," I tell him, looking back at the TV.

"Yeah?" He grins over at me.

"Yeah." I flick my eyes between him and the screen. "Parks was pretty hellbent on trying to get Jennifer Garner to be godmother though."

Jonah starts laughing.

"Garner or Bridge . . ."

"Does she know her?"

"No."

Jonah's face flickers, amused. "Does her dad?"

Our eyes catch and I smirk. "No."

We both chuckle and I miss her. Feel angry at the her-shaped hole there is in my life.

Increasingly hard to stomach, Parks and Julian. Sits weird with me. Makes me angry whenever I think of it. Don't know why—I do—but it's more than just the obvious.

The obvious being that I love her and I'm trying to fix what's broken, the less obvious is that she's breaking us more. I am too, I guess.

Shouldn't have sent her that text the other night though. That was shit of me. We haven't spoken since. Not like us. I breathe out my nose louder than I mean to.

"What?" Jo glances at me.

I shake my head a bit.

"I don't know." I shrug. "I kind of can't believe you're letting him just fuck around with her."

He pauses the game. Looks over at me, a bit surprised.

"You think that's what he's doing?"

I shrug again. "He was all over that girl the other night."

"What, like you used to be?"

I roll my eyes.

"I mean, he hasn't had a girlfriend since high school." Jo shrugs. "The other night, I don't reckon it would have crossed his mind that him touching that girl would have annoyed Parks."

I eye him. "Is he an idiot?"

"Are you?" he shoots back.

My jaw goes tight.

"Come on."

He gives me a look. "Beej, he's wanted Parks since she was sixteen."

Fuck.

Fuck!

"So they're together?"

"No." He sighs, thinking about it. "But probably about as together as he can be with anyone."

"What do you mean?"

"Like, not fucking around with anyone else."

I stare at him a few seconds. "He's not sleeping with anyone else?" Feel my face freeze.

"That's what he told me." He shrugs. "Under the guise of 'she's such a fucking handful. Who has the time?' But, I mean, it's Julian, so if he wanted to, he would be."

Shit.

"You think he'd date her?"

Jo shakes his head, sure. "No. No relationships."

I roll my eyes. "They're in a relationship."

"No labels then. He'll never call her his girlfriend." Shrugs. "It'd never be enough for her."

I stare at the controller in my hand. Roll the analogue buttons under my thumb.

"Do you think she's falling for him?"

He can hear in my tone that I'm worried.

Fuck.

Hate that about myself. Hate that she gets me like this.

"Nah, man. Not really. I mean, you know her." He shrugs. "Gets attached to her baristas. Remember that poor bastard

342

from PAUL who took a flu? She made us all sign a card. And she gave him a five-thousand-pound get-well present?"

I start laughing. I think he took a restraining order out for her after that. She's such a fucking idiot and I miss her so fucking much.

"She just gets attached to people. Abandonment issues, man . . ." Jo shrugs it off like it's just a flesh wound, not this big, shitty monster in my pocket. "If she's like that with the guy who gives her an oat milk latte every day, imagine what she's like if someone's giving her an orgasm—even if it is all just to get back at you." He gives me a bit of a look, sort of wry, sort of wary. "But honestly, man—and I hate to tell you this—but I reckon she was kind of attached to him before anyway. There's been a vibe there the last few years."

"I feel sick." I drop my head in my hands.

He smacks me on the back. "Beej, it's gonna be fine."

"What if she becomes the neck that turns the head of the Haites dynasty?"

Jonah chuckles. "Could you imagine?"

"Yeah. I can, Jo." I stare at him. "That's the problem."

Jo shakes his head again. "Julian thinks that loving people makes you weak. Thinks that it gives his enemies an extra thing to hold over him or some shit. So, set you aside—and you're a big aside—" He gives me a look. "It won't last. He won't let it."

15:49

Julian 💜

Oi

Hi

Where are you?

343

Just finishing up at the office

So you're on Bond Street?

Hahaha

Yes. How did you know?

Lucky guess.

Come over?

Really?

Yes

I just left this morning?

Don't be a fisher of men.

That's Jesus

And Magnolia Parks, apparently.

Want me to come get you?

Will you take me shopping?

Sure

Digger of men.

I have more money than you.

It's so cute you think that.

344

I'm a dick.

Yes you are.

I got jealous.

I know.

Still feels weird sometimes.

Yeah.

I know.

Plus you're dating the world's biggest fuckwit.

As you so eloquently articulated last night . . . I'm not dating him.

Sorry.

I'm also not convinced he's the biggest one . . .

I know this guy . . . told me he loved me. Slept with me. Slept with some other girl that same day. Initials for a name . . .

What a wanker

Tell me about it

Is he hot?

He's pretty hot.

Good kisser?

Great kisser.

Best one out there.

Best friend?

Mmmm. He used to be.

Fuck, Parks

Just kill me why don't you.

Hah

Sorry

<3

Me too x

FIFTY

Magnolia

I don't much like going to the bathroom in front of anyone. Call me crazy—it's just not for me.

Gun to my head, if I absolutely had to, I could have a wee in front of BJ. But Julian? I can't. Could never.

He asked me about it once. "You can't piss in front of me?" Piss. He said the word piss to me, can you even believe the nerve of that boy? Anyway, I told him no and he said, "Why? I've seen you in much more compromising positions," and I said, "I BEG YOUR PARDON, LIKE WHAT?" And then he said—well, actually, never mind what he said—but anyway so it's about 2 a.m. and I've left his room to use the hallway bathroom because I don't want him to hear me wee and we just had sex so I have to wee because I don't want a UTI.

It's very dark in here. People come and go. I presume it's quite safe, what with all the security about, but then sometimes I wonder what they're securing it from.

Anyway, it's not necessarily my favourite place to be without Julian. Julian makes everything feel safer, but this house without him—even with him down the hall—frightens me a bit. But lots about my life right now frightens me a bit so I venture on.

Julian is so strange. There have been a few times where I started to wonder whether he liked me—like properly liked me, do you know what I mean? Like-like. And then Jonah told Taura who told Henry who told me that Julian said he can't get rid of me? As though he tried to and I wouldn't budge. Like I'm the one telling me not to leave, like I'm the one organising myself private masseuses to his house, like I'm the one making Alexia Clark come in to give me private training.

It annoyed me when I heard that because he's making me sound stupid. But also I guess I'm relieved because sometimes it's easy to feel like you're falling for Julian but you aren't really because he doesn't want you here and he just doesn't have the heart to tell you. I don't need to fall for another person. I don't need a repeat of last year's fiasco. I don't think any of us do.

Though, of course, there are some variables this round.

BJ has a girlfriend now, who I thought he'd have broken up with by now but he's staying with. Henry said it's because I'm with Julian, and I said, "I'm not with Julian," and then he gave me a look I didn't like. He said he thinks if I stop seeing Julian, BJ will call it with Jordan, but I don't think that feels fair. He should go first. It wasn't me who slept with someone else the second after we had a fight. I had the good sense to wait a full thirty-six hours after said fight before I went to find Julian. Henry also gave me a look when I said that.

I nearly didn't come by Julian's today at all. I filled my day with a terrible amount of work—really, really over-committed to several things—but my blasted laser-focus-when-sad kicked into gear and I finished everything I had to do disastrously quickly, so I stopped by and found Julian being straddled by a mostly-naked girl.

I thought I was maybe going to faint, actually. I won't tell him that. I think it makes it sound like something it mustn't mean, but I did feel sick when I saw it. Felt a bit as though someone threw a bucket of cold water over me while I'd been having a really nice dream, because I know who Julian Haites is. He is sexy and fun and apparently dangerous, though I've never seen the fruit of that. He's also a notorious womaniser. I didn't really think that I was the only person he was sexually involved with at the minute, but then, I just never really thought about how it would feel to see that. And they weren't doing anything more than kissing, but still it made me feel weird and as I turned on my heel to leave, I told myself it was good that he was doing that because it meant that he didn't like me and it's all pretend.

It's important to remind myself that how Julian makes me feel—like when he's holding my whole face in one of his hands—that it's not real. And I don't need it to be real, I just need the person I'm actually in love with in real life to come find me, get down on his knees, tell me he's an idiot and that he made a mistake—again—that it was just a misunderstanding, and please please please will I take him back? I'd pretend to umm and ahh about it for a minute but then I'd get down on my knees too because I love him and I always will.

Julian ran after me though and we had a weird exchange and he kissed me and asked me to stay. So I did and now it's 2 a.m. and I'm wondering if I should call my car to come and get me or if that's selfish to do to my driver?

That's what I'm thinking about when I walk smack-bang into an invisible person in the dead of night in the home of the sexy criminal-adjacent man I'm sleeping with.

When I tell you I screamed—my God. When I also tell you that the person clamping their fucking hand over my fucking mouth didn't help ease my concerns . . .

It wasn't until he practically somersaulted me over his arm to face him that I realised it was Christian.

"Motherfucker!" I cover my face. I never say that word. So vulgar. "Sorry!" I reach out and touch his face where I just clawed at him. He winces at the sting.

"I can't believe you just said 'motherfucker'."

"I know," I sigh, rueful.

"You fuck a gang lord for a couple weeks, Parks, and you get a real mouth on you."

"Well, I thought I was about to die." I clamp my hand to my chest. "Phewf!" I sing loudly as I bend over to catch my breath. It's then, in my bent over position, that I start mulling over some things.

It's 2 a.m..

349

Christian is mostly naked bar his little black boxer briefs from Calvin Klein. Cotton classics.

"Hold on—" I frown at his navel as the pieces land in my mind. "Wait. Are you just in—" I reach over and snap the black band of his Calvins and gasp.

"Oh my God!" I whisper rather loudly.

Christian gives me a look. "Magnoli—"

"OH MY GOD!" I whisper even louder.

"You love her!" I poke him in the chest.

"Shut up!" He grabs my finger.

"Just tell her!" I stomp my foot.

He shakes his head. "Fucking stay out of it!"

"You're being so stupi—" I shove him, he shoves me back.

"Well you're always stupid and I never say anything!"

"Then you're a terrible friend!"

"You're a terrible friend!"

My jaw falls open. "I was voted the best friend in the whole grade when—"

"—We were nine!" he whisper-yells and I'm annoyed that he's diminishing that for me so now I'm smacking him all over his stupid body.

"You act like you're nine!"

"What the fuck nine-year-olds are you hanging out with?"

"I don't hang out with nine-year-olds, you stupid idiot!"

"I'm not an idiot, you're an idiot!" Christian starts as he puts me in a headlock and then someone clears their throat and we freeze. Christian in his underwear, me in nothing but the angel sleeve robe and the tiger embroidery triangle bra and brief set, all from Fleur du Mal.

Julian and Daisy are both standing there. Daisy, who's barely dressed in a T-shirt that I know is Christian's (*J'accuse!!!*) and is as unimpressed with me as always. Julian, towel-clad, very handsome when wet, and his whole face pinched to perfection.

He squints over at us, eyes moving between us. "What's going on?"

I let out a nervous laugh. "This isn't what it looks like."

Daisy bites down on her bottom lip, annoyed. "And what does it look like?"

I give her a demure little shrug and Christian shakes his head about like an idiot. "I'm not still in love with her," Christian announces rather unceremoniously as he gestures towards me. "At all."

"Right." Daisy's eyes pinch. She looks suspicious and I feel a pang of guilt.

"No, he's right. He's not. At all," I jump in. "I just think Christian's being a bit of a ninny."

"Why's that?" Julian asks, staring me down a bit.

"Because he won't just tell D——"

And then fucking Christian Hemmes clamps his stupid hand over my mouth, laughing loudly to shut me up.

"She's drunk!"

"I am not!" I try to say but it barely comes out.

"Don't listen to her!" He starts shaking his head, looking between the Haiteses before realising he's still holding on to me.

And—you're not even going to believe this—he makes this sound like he's grossed out by me and—get this—flings me away from him over to Julian who—by the way—isn't even looking at me. He's staring at Christian with this bemused, baffled combination but catches me nevertheless.

There is something sexy in the way he does it.

Terribly unfazed at me being flung towards him, he steadies me on my feet with ease. And the way he grips me is so mindlessly strong. I stare over at my ex-second-best male-friend and give him a sharp look. "I did not care for that, Christian."

He keeps shaking his head. "Everyone just ignore her."

Julian parks his chin on top of my head. I don't know why, sometimes he's just like this. Not usually in front of other people though. For some reason it calms me an inch.

"And what the fuck is this, then?" Julian nods his chin towards Daisy, moving my whole head with him. "Where the fuck are your pants?"

Christian gives him a proud smile.

"I took them off her," he tells Julian and I wonder if he has a death wish, but Julian just blows some air out of his mouth.

Daisy rolls her eyes, turns on her heel and walks back into her room.

"Goodnight!" I call after her. She says nothing but her brother slips his arms around my waist.

"We're good yeah? Parks?" Christian looks for my eyes. "We're fine. Like, we're not gonna . . . you're gonna . . ." He tosses me this little desperate look, begging me to shut up. I think about telling him he's being stupid, because he is, he's so in love with this girl that sleeping with her feels like a drug addict just doing a casual bump, but then I'm stupid too, so who am I to talk?

I give him a little scowl. "We're going to have a little talk about that shove."

"Ohh." He rolls his eyes sarcastically. "I'm shaking in my boots."

"Fine." I stand up taller. "Julian's going to talk to you about that shove."

Julian starts shuffling us back towards his room, arms wrapped around me.

"I'm not," he tells me as he's closing the door and I spin around in his arms, hands on my hips.

"You're not going to defend me?"

He rolls his eyes. "You didn't really need defending."

"He pushed me!"

"Yeah." He scoffs. "Into my arms."

I glare up at him a bit. "BJ would have fought him for that," I tell him but I don't know why. I feel a bit indignant about it now. I didn't a minute ago when in my imagination Julian might have defended me over it, but now in reality that he's saying he wouldn't, I do. I'm cross that the shove happened and no one is here to fight for my honour.

Julian doesn't like it when I mention BJ though, I can tell. It's one of the reasons I initially thought maybe he like-liked me but he keeps proving that theory incorrect.

His eyebrows arch up unimpressed all the same at the mention of his name. "Would he?"

"Yes," I tell him proudly. A bit to bait him and a bit because it's true.

Julian juts his chin out a bit and nods. "BJ's also probably fucking that girl of his. Ooh—" He takes a fake glance at his watch. "Right now. So if you want to give him a call and ask him to swing by to fight your fake battles, be my guest."

"Maybe I will," I tell him, my chin in the air.

Maybe he'd be relieved that I'm calling him, maybe he'd come. Use it as an excuse to be close to me, to save me from a thing I don't really need saving from.

And then, without my permission, my eyes start to well up a bit so I drop the glare I'm giving Julian and spin on my foot.

Over in the corner of the room I spot the white Charles bouclé coat from Gabriela Hearst that I arrived in and dart towards it and pluck it up from the floor.

"What are you doing?" Julian sighs.

I ignore him because my cheeks are hot and I look around for my shoes. Brown Franne sock ankle boot in matte calfskin also from Chloé. I lost them somewhere in the house during this afternoon's shenanigans.

"Parks, what are you doing?" he asks again, sounding annoyed.

I find one shoe on his bedside table and hug it to my chest like it's my ticket to escaping a room I don't even want to leave, but it's a drum I'll beat to save face.

"Magnolia—" He speed-walks over to me and spins me around, frowning down at me. "Would you stop fucking ignoring me?"

I think my bottom lip might be going a little bit because he stares at it for a second and he breathes out like he's sorry and tired of me all at once. Then he slips his hand up to my face and holds it.

"Want me to go smack him around a bit?"

I wipe my nose and sniff. "Which him?"

He tilts my chin up with one finger and looks for my eyes. "Any him you like . . ."

That makes me smile a bit and as soon as I do his arms go around my waist and he pulls me in towards him, looking down at me, eyebrows up.

"You a bit bored tonight, Tiges?"

"No?" I frown.

"You're out here looking for drama. I'm just wondering why." He gives me a look.

"No, I'm not—" I scowl up at him. "Just . . . what's the point of dating you, if—"

"—We're not dating," he interrupts.

"Oh." My mouth snaps shut and my cheeks go that stupid pink all over again. "No. Right. I didn't m—"

He grins down at me, not shifting a muscle. "You want me to go across the hall and hit Christian?"

"A bit," I tell him, still mildly disgruntled by the entire thing.

Julian nods once, accepting this. "Alright." He starts moving towards his bedroom door.

"No!" I laugh.

"Nope—" He shakes his head and opens his bedroom door. "I'll defend your honour," he tells me gallantly before glancing back at me playfully. "And then I'll take it later."

"Julian!" I run after him, grab his wrist and pull him back.

"I've got to, Tiges. I don't have a choice. The drama's calling me," he tells me and steps out into the hallway. I keep pulling but he's very strong so I jump on his back.

Not because I think he'll actually hit Christian, but because I feel like being close to him again.

And I don't quite know how he does it, but he reaches behind himself and pulls me around him so I'm wrapped around his waist, eye to eye.

He stares at me for a few seconds then sighs again. "Well then, I guess you're coming with me." He keeps walking across the hall and I start laughing and he's laughing and so I kiss him because I want to.

He carries me backwards before tossing me down on his bed. He lies down beside me.

"So what was that all about?" He nods his head towards the hallway.

I prop myself up a bit. "How good are you at keeping a secret?"

"I'm a gang lord," he tells me and I frown.

"Is that the job title we're sticking with, then?"

"Yep."

"Really?" I frown.

He nods.

"Well, that doesn't work that well for me as a measuring stick for how good you are at secret-keeping because you're the only proper one of those that I know."

"I'm not." He shakes his head. "For an absolute toff, you have a surprising amount of friends linked to the criminal underworld."

That makes me feel nervous so I shake my head.

"Well anyway, they're back to sleeping together again—did you know?"

Julian blinks a few times.

"Did I know my sister and her ex-boyfriend are sleeping together again right after we just bumped into them in the hallway at two a.m. and neither were dressed?" he asks, eyebrows up. "I can't say I'm conclusively positive, but empirically, yeah, I had taken a guess."

I roll my eyes at him. "Well, he's terribly in love with your sister."

He shakes his head. "Not a revelation."

"And!" I announce. "I think she's in love with him!"

He keeps shaking his stupid, beautiful head.

"Literally nothing you've said yet is a secret," he tells me as he runs his thumb over my mouth.

"And they're idiots." I shrug my shoulders.

"That is true." He nods conclusively.

"Because they're just doing what they used to do and he won't tell her he loves her because he thinks she'll reject him, but she won't because she loves him too."

Julian nods along and shrugs like it's all inevitable and the chips will fall where they may, which is entirely unacceptable, so I give him a look.

"We should help them get back together."

"No," he says immediately.

"Yes!" I sit up a bit.

"No."

He props himself up a bit too.

"Yes! Absolutely we should—"

Julian pulls a dismissive face as though he thinks I'm being silly. "We should probably just give them some space and time to figure it out."

I look at him like he's an idiot.

"Dastardly un-proactive . . ."

He tilts his head. "Just a bit of time, Tiges."

I cross my arms over my chest and have a bit of a huff for a few seconds before I peer over at him out of the corner of my eye. "Do you want to know another secret?"

"An actual secret or, like, a fucking plain-as-day 'secret'," he uses quotation marks, "like those two being in love."

I play-glare at him. "A real one."

He squashes away a smile. "Tell me."

"Christian and I nearly had sex in New York."

He stares at me for a few seconds. Two, to be precise.

"Yeah. I know."

"You know?" I frown.

"Mmhm." He shrugs.

I make a sound that's sort of a scoff, sort of a weird babble of disagreement. "How do you know?" I ask, sitting up all the way now, my hands on my hips.

He shrugs again, this time totally indifferent. "We talk."

I stare over at him. "Christian told you?"

"Yep." He yawns as he leans back on his bed.

I frown as I watch him. "You're not jealous?"

He gives me a look that is basically rolling his eyes without actually rolling his eyes. "Do you want me to be?"

"Maybe?" I shrug, nose up in the air again.

"Alright—" He launches himself up. "I'm back to hitting Christian again . . ."

"Julian!" I laugh, grabbing his hand and pulling him back down on top of me.

He touches my face and gives me the eyes that before made me think he liked me.

"You're trouble, Tiges. Do you know that?"

"I've heard it before, once or twice."

I bat my eyes at him.

He licks away a smile. "Yeah, right."

16:36

Johah

> You said it was nothing.

I said it wouldn't last.

> don't do fucking semantics with me.

> Christian said they're good together.

What do you want me to say, Beej?

That they're not?

They are.

Why don't you try calling time with your girlfriend and see if that changes anything?

> I'm not calling shit.

> Not while she's with him.

FIFTY-ONE

BJ

Me and Parks used to take trips all the time.

Not just our drives up and down the Isle but everywhere, things for her "work", also things for her actual work.

We flew all over. Sometimes the others came, sometimes it was just us. Usually better when it was just us, but sometimes it was worse. Went to Bali once a few years back. One of those rare moments in time where she didn't have a fake boyfriend. It was just me and her away, just how I like it.

Got into it though. We'd been there a few days—I was drinking, she was drinking—and I don't know why girls do this sort of shit, but out of the blue she just goes, "How many girls have you been with?"

I pulled back. "What?" Wondered if she was really asking me what I thought she was.

"How many girls have you had sex with?" She lifted her eyebrows and waited for the answer.

"Ever?" I glanced around for an edge to hold on to.

"Well, ever—" She shrugged. "And/or on a weekly basis."

"I don't know." I shrugged, felt all jammy inside.

She frowned. "To which part?"

I shook my head, hating it. "Both?"

Her eyes went wide. "You lose track on a weekly basis?" I shook my head.

"And why is that?" she asked me even though she knew.

I gave her an exasperated look. "Why do you think?"

We'd get like this—fighting and pulling at threads, picking fights with each other about shitty little things instead of tackling our one real issue.

What are you doing? I blinked.

Drowning, I think she told me.

Then I shook my head at her, looked away. "What do you care?"

"I don't care!" she told me, lying through her teeth. All spite. "So tell me. What's your number? Ball park it." She waved her hand around impatiently. "What's your ball park!?"

"Why do y—" I frowned at her. "Stop saying 'ball par—'"

"—Fucking ball park it, Ballentine," she growled.

"I don't know!" I yelled, exasperated. "None sometimes."

"And other times?"

"Two? Three? More maybe, if I drink a bit." I shrugged quickly, feeling trapped.

"Two or three in a week?" she asked, her voice sounding a bit dazed.

I sniffed. "No, ever."

And then her face went really still and pinked up a bit like she was embarrassed.

"What?" I frowned. "How many have you slept with?"

She'd had a few boyfriends by then. Christian had happened, bunch of the other fake ones. I had assumed . . .

"One." She blinked and my heart fucking dove off a cliff.

"No." I shook my head, feeling scared, feeling like I was losing her somehow. "You've slept with more people than that."

She pressed her mouth together and dropped my eyes. "Just you."

"Christian?" I asked, but it almost sounded like a beg. Like I needed her to have fucked him so I wasn't such a fuck up myself.

She shook her head. I could tell she wasn't lying about it. Think she would have rathered she had. I would've rathered it.

I felt sick. Pressed my hand into my mouth, shook my head. "Well, I'm not telling you now."

"Why not?" she growled, drunk.

I waved my hand at her. "Because you'll cry."

"I will not!" She shook her head, indignant.

"No, Parks."

"Please?"

"No."

"Please!"

"No!"

"Why?" She banged her hand down on the table, knocking over a drink. "Why do you never tell me anything?" she yelled.

Now, in that moment—she didn't know yet that it was Paili, and—you might remember—that the mystery of 'who' was our number one issue. My biggest fear was her finding out that I did that with her best friend, and I would literally do anything to appease her enough for her to drop it. Anything. Even if I knew it would hurt her in different, new ways.

"Hundreds," I told her and pressed my hand into my mouth, trying to steady myself. And then it was like she tried to take a breath she couldn't find. I'd winded her.

Deadlocked on each other's eyes, both our faces were portraits of grief.

Her losing me to hundreds of different people, me losing her to them too, I suppose.

"Are you okay?" I asked, a bit nervous.

"Yeah!" She blinked back tears. "Fine." She nodded, swallowing heavy. "Thank you for telling me."

She pinched her top lip as hard as she could—one of her anxiety tells. Done it since high school.

I said nothing and just watched her, trying to work out how to fix whatever I just fucked up.

"So." She scratched her hand absentmindedly. Another nervous tell. "You just pick up girls?"

"I guess?" I shrugged, uncomfortable. She nodded along. "Show me."

I did a big blink, couldn't believe my ears. "What?"

"Show me," she said, voice shaky. "How you do it? P—"
Couldn't even get the words out. "Pick up a girl."

"Here?" I looked around us, horrified.

"Yep."

"Now?"

"Mmhm." She nodded.

"No." I shook my head.

"Why?"

"Because this is weird and you're acting insane."

"I'm not insane, I'm curious!" She shrugged like it was
nothing, like she wasn't asking me to act out both our nightmares in front of her.

I glared over at her. "Curious about what?"

She mashed her lips together. "About who you really are."

I blinked, taken aback. "You know who I really am."

"Do I?" she asked, bottom lip trembling.

I looked away from her, shook my head, bit down on my
bottom lip. Felt like crying myself. She didn't know me? She's
the only fucking person who ever has.

"Show me." She drummed her fingers on the table impatiently.

I stared over at her, pretty hurt myself by that point. "Why
are you asking me to do this?"

"Because it doesn't mean anything! Obviously!" she yelled.
"To you and to me. I don't care. Okay? I want you to know
that I don't care about you. Like that. Anymore." She took
a staggered breath. "Fuck whoever you want as much as you
want. Don't not do it for me."

She was crying when she said it. "Because we're just friends—
if that!" She shook her head, wiped her face. "I obviously
don't know you how I thought I did, and I don't care about
you like that, so show me."

Her chest was heaving. It was a fucking lie—I knew it, she
knew it—but holy shit it still hurt.

I sucked on my bottom lip, nodded over at her and then
smacked both my hands down on the table, pushing myself
up and away from her.

If I was a better man at the time, I would have just taken her home, told her I was sorry. Actually, if I was a better man we wouldn't have had the conversation in the first place. If I was a better man I would have looked at Paili in the bathroom that night, and when she asked me if I was okay I would have said, "No, I feel like shit, can you take me to my girlfriend?" And I would have told Magnolia what happened and who I saw and she would have reacted how she did that day at Dunstan's and we never would have broken up, I would have married her, I would have knocked her up again, we'd be living Devon way, maybe in the south of France, and I wouldn't have been in Bali looking for a girl to fuck to spite Magnolia.

My eyes landed on a hot enough girl with eyes that were good but not as good as Parks's. Blonde hair. Big smile. I went over to her, positioned myself so Parks could see the whole thing.

I ducked apologetically into the conversation she was having with her friend, offered her my hand. She glanced at her friend before shaking it, smiling up at me the way all girls do.

"Are they real?" I nodded at her eyes, the start of my routine. Look into them in a way that makes her think I mean it. Then I shake my head like they're the best fucking eyes I've ever seen. Worked all the time.

I nodded at her mouth. "Did you have braces?" I asked. Sometimes I'll ask, "Are those your real lips?" to change it up, but it's all just so she'll look at my mouth. I have a good mouth. I'll bite down on it, give her a crooked grin. That's usually all it takes.

All it took that night, anyway.

The girl asked me about Magnolia—guess she'd seen me before I saw her.

"Just a friend." I shrugged. "If that," I added, just for spite even though she couldn't hear me.

"Can I buy you a drink?" I asked her. She said yes, and then, well, you know the rest.

She left after. I stayed up all night sick over what I'd done. Climbed out of bed before sun-up the next morning. Grabbed a blanket from the couch and headed for the balcony.

And there she was. My favourite person in the world. Tiny pyjamas, hair whipping around her face as she stared out at the Indian Ocean.

I slid open the door and stepped out onto the balcony with her.

She looked back at me, got a proud look in her eye. "How was she?"

I didn't say anything, just pressed my tongue into my top lip to stop myself from crying or vomiting on the spot.

Having sex with someone else while she was in the room next door?

Fucked me up. Fucked Parks up too, actually.

"She sounded like she had a great time!" Her voice dripped with sarcasm.

I shook my head, but only barely. "What do you want from me?"

She took a shallow breath. "A time machine?"

I didn't know what to do or what to say, so I just did what I wanted. Moved behind her wordlessly, wrapped my arms around her, the blanket around us both, and rested my head on top of hers.

"I'm sorry," I whispered into the back of her head.

She froze, turned around after a few seconds, buried her face in my chest and cried. Cried for ages. I cried too, don't know if she knew that. Screamed that I loved her as loud as I could without making a sound. Probably wasn't enough though.

We were fucked up back then, still fucked up now, I guess. I just loved her, that's all. And I was bad at it even though I used to be good at it. Nowadays I'm worried I won't know how to be good at it again.

"Come on," I said to her eventually. "Let's order up some breakfast."

"You and your Eggs Benedict." She sighed, looking over at my breakfast. She ordered the pancakes.

I sniffed. "What about me and my Eggs Benedict?"

She scratched the tip of her nose. "You always get it."

And I did my best to squash the smile I felt coming but she caught it anyway.

"What?" she asked, frowning a bit.

I shook my head, shrugged. Not a hill I wanted to die on that day. My faint smile started to get less faint though.

"What?" she asked, frowning.

"Nothing." I shook my head.

Her little fists balled up. "What?" she demanded.

I opened my mouth to say something, then shook my head. Not worth it.

"Go on," she demanded, drumming her fingers on the table impatiently. I sighed.

"I hate hollandaise sauce." I gave her a tight smile.

She blinked. "What?"

"I don't like Eggs Benedict."

She eyed my plate. "Then why—"

"—Because you like it," I interrupted her with a shrug. "And for some reason it makes you feel good when you order different breakfast meals, because you pride yourself on being unpredictable."

She straightened up, put the best nose in the world in the air.

"I am unpredictable," she said in unison with me.

Her face pouted.

"Honestly, Parks—" I sniffed a laugh. "You should have seen yourself the morning you ordered Bircher Muesli. You'd have thought you'd just landed the Mars fucking Rover the way you went on about new taste explorations."

Her mouth fell open, offended, and I remember wanting to kiss her then.

"I'm not predictable." She shook her head. "Do you want me to list off all the ways I'm unpredictable?"

"I really don't, no—" I yawned and shook my head.

"Number one," we said at the exact same time.

"Hey!" we both said in unison. I pointed at her and she stomped her foot at me.

I shook my head at her a bit. "Honestly, Parks, just when I think you're about to swing left, you swing . . . left."

Got cross after that. Had a proper strop the whole time she brewed her cup of tea.

"Is it a head thing, then?" I asked her gently.

"I beg your pardon?" She glared over at me.

"You know—" I shrugged. Gesturing to my head in case she'd forgotten where hers was. "Your head thing."

"My what?" Her cheeks started to go pink so I shrugged again, not wanting her to feel weird.

"Your obsessive compulsive thing?" I ducked my head so I could meet her eyes.

"Oh." She went pink. "Know about that, do you?"

"Yeah." I gave her a small smile.

"How do you know?" She frowned.

And I didn't mean to, but I let out a single laugh.

"What?" She sulked.

"Magnolia, I've known you since you were four." I gave her a shrug. "Of course I knew."

She swallowed. "How?"

"The clothes thing, for one," I started and she rolled her eyes. "You've kind of always had weird rules you live by, and if you don't follow them you get weird and antsy."

She cleared her throat. "Such as?"

I blew some air out of my mouth. "Like the shower thing. You can't go to bed without a shower, but you can have naps without one, even if your nap is in the bed." She squinted over at me.

"Or," I continued, "you stir you tea in multiples of seven. You need the mint taste in your mouth to go to sleep. Or how your food can't be touching. Or how once you get into bed at bed time, if you get out again, you need to wash your feet or you can't sleep." She just glared at me.

"Probably the one that really gave it away was—pretty early on, I guess—we were at school, we'd been together a bit by then, and you got a splinter in your wrist. Do you remember?"

I heard her breathing change. She nodded.

She brushed up against a wooden railing when she was sneaking into my dorm room and then she disappeared off into my bathroom for ages. Eventually I went to check on her and there she was, legs crossed, sitting on the edge of the bath with a safety pin in her hand and scratch marks all over her forearm. My eyes went wide. Worried she was doing something else for a second before she said in a quiet voice, "There's something under my skin." She tried not to cry as I knelt down in front of her. I nodded, brows creased, and dabbed the blood away from her arm with some toilet paper.

"I see it," I told her. She offered me a tight-lipped smile and wordlessly handed me the pin.

I remember that I grimaced at the idea of hurting her—it was such a foreign concept at the time. Little did I know that in a few short years we'd be masters at hurting each other, that causing each other pain would be the lynchpin of our relationship, the only thing more consistent than each other.

"No." I shook my head in that bathroom, nauseous at the thought.

"Please." She swallowed. "I can feel it just sitting there. I won't be able to sleep if you don't."

"Why?" I sighed.

Her mouth pulled. "Because I can't put the thought down."

I paused, gave her a long look and then took the pin from her—took her wrist in my hand and then dug the splinter out.

She flashed her wrist to me in that Bali villa. Two long, thin scars from where she'd unsuccessfully hacked at herself to get it out. I frowned, grabbing it like I was seeing them for the first time, like I didn't know her whole entire body like the back of my hand.

"Anyway," I sighed, not letting go of her wrist. "That night was a bit of a giveaway."

"Do you think I'm crazy?" she asked, quietly.

"No." I shook my head. "I think you're the best."

"Even though you know the worst parts of me?"

"I don't know the worst parts of you."

I ran my thumb over her scar. "I just know you, Parks."

I lifted the Room Service lid off my (her) Eggs Benedict and held the plate out for her. "Come on then."

She waited a few seconds, probably trying her hardest to prove me wrong, but I knew—as always—that she really wanted eggs for breakfast. Sheepishly she handed me her (my) plate.

I picked up my knife and fork, looked down at it, then flickered them back up over to hers. "Felt like pancakes today."

Pancakes were a lucky break, honestly. God help me if there was ever a fucking fruit parfait on the menu. Powerless before those, she is. Doesn't like them at all, even though she thinks she does.

So actually, do you know what? I don't care that the boys say that Parks and Julian are good together. Fuck them. I loved her first. I love her more and he doesn't know her like I do.

No one ever will.

FIFTY-TWO
Magnolia

Daisy had initially warmed to me after that night with the cream sauce. The other day she even asked if she could borrow my cropped wool-blend cardigan from Alaïa and I said yes, of course, but in the spirit of full disclosure, I admittedly had just had sex with her brother in it a few hours prior and she thanked me for my honesty and retracted her request. I'm now back in Antarctica because I assume that Christian told her we nearly had sex in New York.

So I'm following her around her kitchen trying to make her like me again, and because she's a control freak, I thought maybe if I let her boss me around in the kitchen, her hardened exterior would soften towards me. I'm going to crack her like a macaron. Julian said not to tell her that.

It's all a bit thrilling though. She's a bit like my own personal, meaner version of Gordon Ramsey.

"For fuck's sake, Magnolia," she growls at me. "You don't scramble the eggs, you fold them."

I stomp my foot. "That fundamentally does not make sense."

Julian and Declan glance up from the table.

She blinks at me a few times. "How's that now?"

"Because they're not called 'folded eggs'—they're called scrambled eggs."

Julian laughs and I scowl at him.

"Yes." She gives me a long look. "Do you not remember when we scrambled those in a bowl about, I don't know, forty-five seconds ago?"

368

I nod. "I do remember that."

"Is it possible that may have achieved the scrambling?"

I put my nose in the air. "Could have—"

"What's going on here, then?" Jack Giles asks, walking in. "Why are you making eggs at nine p.m. on a Friday night?"

"Because Magnolia can't cook for shit," Daisy tells him brightly.

"Hey." I frown.

Daisy ignores me.

"We tried pasta, a steak, ceviche—"

"Why did you even bother trying that?" Julian says to her.

She ignores him too.

"Cupcakes, cookies—"

"—Those were good!" I interrupt with a frown.

"You ate the dough," she snaps and I give up, leaving the spatula in the pan to go sit on her brother's lap.

She looks at the spatula and then over to me. "Did you just—" She stares wide eyed at the pan. "The stove is on."

"So?" I frown.

She blinks more. "Thank God you're pretty." She turns away.

"Did you hear that?" I lean into Julian's ear. "She thinks I'm pretty!"

He snorts a laugh and kisses me.

"So Daisy, when you get done with your fun kitchen adventure, which is very delightful by the way, and not at all reminiscent of *Hell's Kitchen* for me," she glares at me for that and I give her a big grin, "will you be ready to go?"

"I already told you I'm not going anywhere," she tells the pot she's scrubbing.

"Oh no!" I cry. "You have to. You'll be my only friend there."

"Not your friend," she says without looking up.

"Christian will be there," I say enticingly and she freezes momentarily before she goes back to scrubbing.

"I thought I was your only friend there?" she tells me, eyebrow up.

I match her look. "I thought you weren't my friend."

"Come on, Dais—" Jack groans. "I need a dance."

"Plus," I interject, "you're so pathetic over there with your cast-iron pan of folded eggs on a Friday night," I tell her before I duck behind her brother, lest she starts throwing things again. I slip my hand under Julian's black distressed logo-print washed cotton-jersey T-shirt from Balenciaga, run my hands over his stomach, think of deplorable things and hope we might do them later.

"We'll have fun!" I tell the girl who's intermittently glowering at me and a pot I may or may not have ruined.

"I never have fun with you," she tells me but I can tell that's at least a sliver of a lie.

"I'm easier to be around the more you drink," I tell her.

Julian nods. "That is true."

I smack him and he presses his nose into the back of my head.

"Fine." She lets out a frustrated groan and then stands. "But we're still not friends."

I lean in close to her brother's ear and whisper, "For now."

9:08

BJ 🐝

Jo said you came after I left.

Oh.

On purpose?

No.

Really?

Promise.

How's everything?

It's okay.

How's everything with you?

Yeah, good.

How's Jordan?

She's fine.

Still together?

Yeah.

You and Jules?

Sort of.

Yeah too, I guess.

Fuck.

Hahahaha

Are you with him right now?

Do you really want to know?

No

Yes

Fuck.

Yes.

Yes.

Fuck.

Sorry.

Yeah, me too.

FIFTY–THREE

Magnolia

The sound feels particularly offensive. The tyres of his Escalade screeching off as I stare at Julian's car speeding away from me before I even have a chance to put on my coat (the shearling-trim midi coat from Prada—so lovely, so evidently wasted on him).

I don't understand what just happened at all.

If I sound confused, it's because I am.

We were at a dinner, he and I. It was his friend Carmelo Bambrilla's new restaurant. We were there, everything was fine. Julian's security friends were there, but it was just me and him at the table like a proper date—he even pulled my chair over to be close to him. Put his hand up my dress because he's bad like that, and I told him to stop but I didn't really mean it, grinning away. I like how I feel around him. Something about him makes me feel quite brave. I like to feel brave. Loving BJ as much as I do, it makes me feel weak and stupid. Next to Julian, I feel quite powerful.

So we were fine, everything's fine and then there was a blackout.

He freaked out completely. Completely.

He threw himself on top me, practically tossed me into the arms of Kekoa and then was weirdly aggressive towards me in the car as we drove away.

All I did was ask him if he was okay and he flipped a switch, told me we were done on the spot, that he was sorry he cared for a minute, that he doesn't anymore and he won't again. Then he just dropped me home and drove off.

I stand outside for a few minutes collecting myself because I feel embarrassed. Sort of just staring after his car and wondering if he's going to come back. It felt so chaotic that I actually wonder if he might.

But he doesn't and its past nine on a chilly night in February, so I go inside.

"You're home!" My sister looks up from the couch and closes her journal. She's surprised to see me.

"Are you okay?" She frowns.

I nod again staring at the TV.

"Which one are you watching?" I ask her, walking towards the TV. I feel a bit woozy if I'm honest.

"Oh—" She shakes her head, annoyed about it. "The silly 1800s one."

I shrug as I sit down next to her. "I quite like that one."

Bridget watches me closely. "Are you sure you're okay?" She mutes it.

I stare at her for a second and then look back at the TV as I pointlessly try to flatten my dress. Oscar de la Renta, floral-embroidered minidress. Black.

There's a funny feeling of being discarded that I don't like but it feels familiar. BJ, Tom, after our fight (but I suppose I deserved that one), and now Julian.

It's quite a horrible feeling, like he used me how he wanted me, had his fill and threw me away. I don't really want to tell her. My cheeks go hot as I think about saying it aloud.

My iPhone dings and my sister cranes her neck to see my phone, that nosey little b-word, but my heart skips a beat because I'm sure it's going to be Julian telling me he's sorry and he's on his way back and I'll be glad I didn't tell Bridget because that would have been embarrassing too, but different.

Kekoa 🪙

> Did you get inside fine?

> > what?

> Did you get inside fine?

> > why?

> Yes or no

> > Yes.

Bridget looks at me confused. "What?"
 Also, why did my heart skip a beat just before?
 My phone dings again.

> Ok.

I frown down at the little screen in my hand and type something back.

> > He couldn't just ask me himself?

No response.
 I toss my phone down on the couch.
 "Julian and I are through."
 My sister snaps her head in my direction. "What?"
 "Mmm." I stare at the TV.
 She grabs my arm, shaking it to get my attention. "What happened?"
 "I don't . . . Nothing." I shrug. "It was weird."

375

"Are you sad?"

"No," I lie.

I am a bit, but that feels stupid and I don't understand why I would be.

"So you just broke up?" she asks, just as confused as I am.

"We weren't—"

"—Oh shut up." She rolls her eyes. "You know what I mean."

"We went to dinner, I think he thought something dangerous happened because the power cut, and then he sort of just . . . went weird." I shrug. "I tried to ask him about it in the car but then he got weirder and said he was done with me and told Kekoa to drive me home."

"Pancakes guy?" she asks, trying to keep up.

"Yeah."

"Right." She nods.

"And that was it. He just drove away."

Bridget's whole face scrunches. "That's so rude."

"I know."

"I was just starting to like him."

Maybe me too? I wonder.

Bridget breathes out her nose. "Are you going to call Beej?"

"Maybe." I tuck my feet under me so I'm in a ball. "Do you think I should?"

My sister rolls her eyes. "For the love of God."

23:01

BJ 🐝

Hi.

Hey

376

BJ 🐝

What's going on

Nothing.

Just saying hello.

Ok

Hello

Hello

How's the weather?

☁️

Alright then?

Alright then.

And for you? How's your weather?

Pretty average most of the day.

Got real sunny about 11:01pm though

Don't kill that one.

Never again.

FIFTY-FOUR
BJ

Jordan's friends from Australia are in town and she's having drinks with them. She didn't ask me to come, thought it was a bit strange because she usually wants me to come everywhere with her, likes the photos and the fuss, I think. But not today.

I was right the other day, about the DJ. She didn't tell me. Saw a photo. They were at dinner. Nothing sus, I don't think. Someone took a video of them out at Manteca and sent it to Loose Lips. They posted it on their TikTok, I got tagged in it about a hundred times. She was on the couch next to me when I opened it. She watched me watch it. I looked over at her and she stared back at me. Neither of us said anything. I put my phone away.

She got into bed last night and rolled over to face me and gave me a smile. Put my phone away—I'd just finished texting Parks—flashed her a smile.

"We have a weird relationship, hey?" she said with a funny look on her face.

I laughed. "What do you mean?"

"Just funny." She shrugged. "I don't mind it."

I fight off a smile. "I don't mind it either."

Thought of asking her about the DJ but decided against it. Didn't feel like my business. I know that's weird, she's technically my girlfriend, but it didn't. Doesn't still. Makes me wonder about all Magnolia's fake boyfriends, but did they know upfront or did they realise it over time? That I'd always be there and they just had a specific function which was exclusively to fuck me off. Me and Jordan kind of feel like friends who live together and have sex sometimes. Pretty solid arrangement if it was intentional, like we've come to some sort of tacit agreement, feels a bit like it. Even if we haven't, I don't want to rock the boat.

I walk into me and Jo's and find the living room full.

Jo, Taura, Henry, some girl I don't know—that's interesting—Christian, Parks. No Julian—also interesting.

"Ey!" Jonah grins.

I nod hello to everyone, reach out to shake the hand of the girl I don't know.

"This is Georgia," Henry tells me. "We go to uni together."

I nod at her with a smile.

She's outlandishly beautiful. Like Stephanie Seymour on the cover of *Playboy* in the '90s. I glance at Taura—super pissed. Parks catches my eye and I temper my smile with her happy surprise that she texted me last night. For no reason. She used to all the time. Missed it. She stands up—big puffer coat from Gucci and a tiny blue dress under it—she walks into the kitchen.

I wait a few seconds then follow her.

She's standing there waiting for me, leaning back against the bench waiting for me.

"Say sorry to me," she tells me as soon as I walk in.

I go stand needlessly close to her.

My face tugs, amused. "For what?"

"I don't know." She shrugs. "I just feel cross at you and feel like you should say sorry to me."

"Actually cross?" I look her up and down for clues. "Or you want attention cross?"

Her face pinches. "The second one."

I try not to laugh. "Well, now I feel like you should say sorry to me."

"Then you would be wrong," she tells me, nose in the air. What I wouldn't give to kiss that nose. Anything, literally anything except wave the white flag first.

"Do we need ten seconds?"

Her perfect eyes pinch again. "Fifteen."

Even better.

"Ready?" she asks, eyebrows up.

I nod once.

She nods back. "Go."

I over-stare at her, get to three in my mind before I feel my blinking starting to slow. Don't want to close my eyes, if I'm honest.

"You look pretty today," I tell her.

Her face goes soft for a second before her nose goes in the air. "We're not supposed to talk when we do this—"

"Sorry." I nod. "Start again."

She nods once to signal the timer has restarted and then I reach over to wipe an eyelash from her cheek that isn't there.

She blinks a lot and I fight off a smile.

"Sorry." I shrug, flashing her my finger. "Eyelash."

She stares at my finger for a second and then her eyes pinch, dubious. "There's nothing there."

"If you think I'm touching your face just because I felt like it, you're insane—" I squash a smile.

She drops her chin to her chest, glaring over at me like she's not pleased but it's all over her that she is.

She breathes out her nose. "Start again . . . Now."

"Do you not think I look good today?" I ask immediately.

She turns her head away from me. "I think you look good every day," she says quickly and then grabs the sleeve of my hoodie. She doesn't say what it is out loud but she mumbles it under her breath. "Logo chunky-knit hoodie. JW Anderson."

Then she breathes out her nose. "Now, no talking. Fifteen, fourteen—"

"You can't count out loud, that's distracting," I say just to annoy her.

"BJ!" She stomps her foot.

I lean in towards her and whisper, "I love it when you say my name."

She swallows, nervous. "That's my line."

"I stole it," I tell her and her eyes turn to puddles.

Best fucking puddles in the world

"Guess what?" I say quietly, just because I want to keep her looking at me like this.

"What?"

"Had my first tattoo removal session today."

Her eyes get bigger. "Really?"

I nod.

She reaches over and peers down my shirt, looking at the bandage over it. "Did it hurt?"

Press my tongue into my top lip. "Yes."

She bites back a smile. "Good."

"No talking," I tell her. "Fifteen and go—" I say and lean in towards her, staring wide eyed, trying to make her laugh.

"What are you doing?" Georgia, the girl Henry brought with him, asks.

"Oh—" My brother rolls his eyes when he appears behind her. "Ignore them. They've done it for as long as they've been together."

"Oh!" She nods. "Are you together?"

"No," Magnolia and I say quickly in unison.

"Well . . ." Henry muses.

"No," Magnolia says firmly, brushing past me and back to everyone else.

I smack Henry on the arm and whisper, "Thanks, man," before following after her because I have all my life and old habits die fucking hard.

She sits down on the one-seater couch but moves over so there's enough room for me. Barely.

It's the closest our bodies have been since we slept together and it got all fucked up.

I nudge her with my elbow.

She peeks over at me, gives me a small smile that feels like a secret. Wonder how long it'll take for us to get to the place where I can just throw my arm around her, let her be mine out loud, not just inside my head.

"Where's Jules?" I ask her under my breath.

"Oh, um." She pulls a little face. "I think we're . . ." She cuts her fingers over her neck.

My eyes go wide. Done? Holy shit. What the fuck?

"Really?" I try not to sound too excited. She nods. "What happened?"

She shrugs like it's a mystery to her.

"Just . . . nothing. It just—you know. It didn't. We . . ." she trails. "We weren't—"

She looks over at me, mouth pursed.

Us, is what she's not saying. They weren't us.

I nod once. Grab that soaring kite heart of mine and bolt it to the floor of my apartment.

"And where is your girlfriend?" she asks, looking around.

"Out. With friends." I swat my hand. "Are you okay?" I ask Parks as I shift a tiny bit closer to her.

She stares at me, eyes big and a bit nervous. "I'm okay."

I nod once.

Jo passes me a wine and tosses an arm around Taura while he stares down my brother. Henry's eyes flick from Jonah's to Tausie's and then he slips his arm around the girl he brought.

Fuck. This is getting messy.

"Henry was just telling us the weirdest spot he's had sex," Taura announces with pinched eyes.

"Oh." I nod and grimace at once. "Which was?"

"Um—" Henry blows some air out of his mouth as he thinks. He looks over at Georgia. "We stole a gondola the other day. On the canals."

Taura's eyes darken. "That sounds fun." Taura nods, mouth tight.

"It was," Henry tells her, staring her down.

"Christian?" I nod at him just to keep it moving.

"Julian's bed," he says without missing a beat.

Magnolia pulls a face. "Ew! When?"

"Ohh—" He shakes his head, winding her up. "You don't want to know."

Magnolia dry heaves dramatically.

"Alright, calm down." Christian rolls his eyes. "What about you, then?"

Her face pulls and she looks up at me.

I don't know whether it's for permission or she wants me to answer for her or what.

I shrug at her. "We used to do it in the little cupboard under the stairs at Varley."

Her cheeks go pink.

"Which stairs?" Jonah blinks.

"The main stairs up to Hunnisett." Parks's dormitory house.

"We did do it behind a statue in Carver Hall too," she reminds me.

Carver Hall, my dorm. Bit risky, intimacy on the school grounds, but I've got to say: high risk, high reward.

I shake my head at her, fighting off a smile. "We didn't do that, we did some . . . other shit."

The room erupts into immature sounds and Parks's cheeks are on fire but she looks happy.

"I'm confused about your relationship," Georgia says, looking between us.

"We all are." Taura nods solemnly.

"Parks has to go again." Christian nods at her. "That doesn't count."

"Cockpit."

Henry nods at her. "You and Tom."

Magnolia goes a bit still next to me and I can't help but glance at her.

"You had sex in a cockpit?"

She stares up at me, blinking.

Her face is weird, sort of uncomfortable but also a bit pleased.

"You and Rush did it in the coat room of that bar," Taura reminds her.

"You did it on a fucking stair climber!" Christian rolls his eyes.

"Alright!" She smacks her hands on her cheeks, embarrassed. "Can everyone please stop talking?"

"I actually walked in on her and Julian in my office the other week—" Jonah points at Parks, ignoring her request. "Which isn't that weird for them but was fucking weird for me."

"Jo's office?" Christian cackles. "You've gone Full Beej."

Everyone laughs but me and Parks.

She smiles over at me, weak.

("Wait," Georgia whispers to Henry, watching us. "Are they together?")

The conversation moves on, Taura's telling a story about sex at an aquarium, but I'm not paying attention.

My mind's going a million miles an hour trying to work out how to tell her I don't care. That it doesn't matter to me even if it does, that I still love her the same, that nothing could undo how much I want her. I want her in an unchangeable way, even if loving her right now feels like a foot pressing down on my throat.

And Parks, she's just staring at me, watching my face.

Before I even look at her, I know she looks nervous.

Sad, almost.

I can feel it on her.

I swallow—think quick—try to let her know it's okay without saying the words.

I lean over, breathe her in.

"You smell different—is it new?"

She glances over at me, eyes quiet.

"Heures d'Absence. Louis Vuitton."

I hold her eyes steady.

"I like it."

FIFTY-FIVE

BJ

After the other night I decided that I'm going to end it with Jordan properly. As soon as Parks said she and Jules were done I knew I needed to call it. She was waiting for me to offer to drive her home last night, I could tell. Took all my willpower not to do it too, but I knew I couldn't. Knew if I did I'd kiss her, tell her I love her, take her clothes off and do my best not to fuck us up, but I'd already be fucking up because I know that it matters to her that I'm with Jordan still. I need to call it with Jordan before I start it up with Parks, that much is obvious after how everything played out before. The birthday trip Jordan's planned, that's the only snag. She's never been before and she's so excited to go—not that that's a reason not to call it with her, just makes me feel a bit more shit about doing it. That and I think she's lined up a bunch of sponsors for the trip, so I just need a minute to work out how to tell her we're not going anymore.

I put it off for a day because I'm trying to figure out whether it'd be a nice thing or a shit thing to just tell her to go by herself anyway.

She could take that DJ, I don't care. Don't know if I can say that either though, because even though I'm pretty sure we're on the same page, I don't know it for sure.

The minute I walk into Math Club I regret not having called it. Legs up to her fucking eyeballs, white dress with a shoulder out, a little flower headband and a French 75 in her hand.

She's at the bar with my brother and Christian—and fuck—I should have called it. I nod my chin at her as I walk over and her eyes go soft at the edges. She's happy to see me. Or she was until she spots Jordan and her friend from work.

I see Parks sigh. Posture drops, shoulders slump a bit—I hate doing this to her. I'm ending it tonight. Shouldn't have brought Jordan with me after how me and Parks were last night, Magnolia might take it the wrong way. I wasn't planning on it, but she and her friend wouldn't take no for an answer.

"Oi." I lean in and kiss her cheek anyway before looking at my brother and Christian. "Boys." I nod at them.

Jordan reaches around me and hugs a frozen Parks.

"Hi!" Jordan sings as she gives her a squeeze.

"Oh." Magnolia blinks. "Hello."

Not much of a toucher, my Parks. Just with me.

I think she's just being friendly. Australian, you know? But Parks would have hated that.

Fuck. I'm ready for this to be done.

"This is my friend, Caitlyn." Jordan gestures to her and then Caitlyn tosses her arms around Parks and gives her a hug too.

"Right." Magnolia frowns as the stranger holds on a few seconds too long.

One look at Magnolia's face and Henry starts to cough hysterically to cover his laugh.

"So nice to meet you," Parks says, sounding very unsure and entirely unaware that she's brushing them off her body as she smooths out her dress. "Do they rather like hugs in Australia, then?" she asks Caitlyn politely.

Caitlyn shakes her head. "Oh, I'm from London."

"Oh." Magnolia frowns and glances over at me. "But we don't like hugs here."

I lean in towards her and say, "Some people do," and then nudge her with my elbow. Our eyes catch and she swallows.

Jordan's taking photos of herself with the bag I bought her the other day and her friend is chattering away to Christian.

I move in closer to Parks, nodding my head at Julian on the other side of the room. "You talked to him?"

She shakes her head.

"You going to?"

She stares up at me for a few seconds, then shakes her head.

Christian ducks his head in, grabbing my eye urgently with his. "I'm gonna—" Nods his head towards Daisy. Jordan's little friend is a little too starstruck with him. I give him a wink and he darts away. I toss my head subtle as I can towards the table in the corner. Julian and co.

"You okay though?" I ask Parks.

She flashes me a quick smile and nods.

"What happened?" I ask, just because I'm nosey.

She shakes her head and shrugs her shoulders, and I reckon I see a tiny bit of genuine sadness creep in there and it scares me, so I nod my chin at her.

"Tell me about this dress, then—who are we wearing today?"

She stands a bit taller, eyes go bright how they always do about clothes.

"Take a guess."

I tilt my head, taking the opportunity to check her out. She's unreasonably beautiful. Always has been but when she wears light colours she goes browner. I love her in white. She's been wearing so much black lately, bit unlike her. She is the personification of colour and light, so that's all she should be wearing.

"Gucci?" I take a guess after picking up the hem of her dress in my fingers.

She shakes her head. "Cotton-blend lace-trimmed stretch-jersey minidress by . . . Miu Miu."

"Ah."

I nod once. "Should have guessed that. Coat?"

"Gabriela Hearst—" Points to her boots. "Chloé." Points to her headband. "Jennifer Behr." Flashes me her bag.

"—Saint Laurent," I jump in because I'm not an idiot.

Magnolia's eyes flicker over to the other side of the room where Julian is. Think their eyes must catch because she looks away quickly and back down at the hem of her dress that I'm still holding.

Jordan notices. Stares at the material between my fingers, looks over her shoulder at Julian, then back at Magnolia. Looks at her.

"How's Julian?" she asks as I finally let go of Parks's dress.

Magnolia and my eyes catch and she gives Jordan a delicate smile. "We are no longer," she uses quotation marks, "'involved'."

"Oh," Jordan frowns a bit. Can't totally place the frown. It's not empathetic. It's not sorry for herself either. It's inconvenienced, maybe? "Sorry."

Magnolia shakes her head. "No, it's—" She swallows. "Fine."

This is it, I tell myself. I'm going to do it now.

"Hey, Jords—" I nod my head towards the offices. "Can we have a—"

And then this happens so quickly. Jordan's staring at me, so I know she heard me, but after she clocks what I said she looks back at Magnolia.

"We're going to Italy next week," Jordan says brightly, linking her arm with mine.

I go still. Shit. Why?

"Oh." Magnolia blinks a few times and looks instantly wounded.

"Yeah!" Jordan beams, eying her down a tiny bit. "For his birthday. It's going to be so good. Just the two of us at this—"

She keeps talking but I'm not listening. I'm trying to tell Parks with my blinks that Jordan's wrong, we aren't, that I'm going to end it in a minute, but Parks isn't looking at me. She's powered down, eyes gone glassy, gone inside herself how she does when I hurt her.

I feel unreasonably angry at Jords for this one. I don't know why she did it, why she said it. Didn't even feel like she was doing it to be territorial of me as much as she was just trying to get a rise out of Parks. Where was this initiative a month ago when we were sitting at brunch with Parks and Julian with his hand up her fucking skirt? Where was this gumption on New Year's when Jules was kissing Parks's neck right in front of me? It decides to rear its fucking head now? Now that Magnolia's done with him, now that me and Parks are on a good foot? Now Jordan decides to deliver Parks with some casually devastating blows?

And I know we haven't had those conversations yet so I know then that I am technically still Jordan's, but still, I'm not. In every quiet whisper, every subtle and nuanced thread in the fabric of time, all the tiny ripples in the universe will tell you, that I'm actually just Parks's.

I need her to know, wish she'd just look at my fucking face right now so she could see it, but she's not. Her eyes don't come off her champagne glass.

And then there's a scuffle.

Over at the boys' table, Julian's on his feet and he's—I do a double take with this—he's shoving Carmelo Bambrilla.

I blink a few times. That can't be. They're thick as thieves. Pun intended.

Carmelo shoves him and I pull back as I watch on. Then Julian grabs Carmelo by the neck of his shirt and I don't know, maybe starts choking him? I look over at Parks and I don't see it coming but I should, because what happens next is typical her.

She runs straight into it. Pushes her way through the growing crowd to get to Julian, climbs on a table so she's taller than him and then she grabs his face, turning it towards her.

You know when you're drunk how there's that point of no return, where all you can really do is embrace that you've fucked it, feel the sick roll up through you and chunder the night away?

I feel the sick.

How's she like this? I don't know why she does it. Runs right into the eye of storms like she likes it in there—likes the drama, likes the danger—and my whole life, I've run right in after her. But I'm not chasing her this time. Not with her looking at him like that. Like it's not just naffing, likes there's feelings there that she doesn't know about yet, like the flower's taming a new fox. She's standing there on that table with her hands on his chest, calming him down like you would a spooked horse and fuck it, I'm out of here.

I can't watch this. Not again. Can't call it with Jordan anymore either, because fuck Parks with her hands on his chest, with his hands on her waist like she's his and not mine, like she might actually be his and not mine. I can't fucking do it again.

So I grab Jordan's hand, tug her towards the door and slip out. Kiss her stupid up against my car. She doesn't stop me. Holds my face, kisses me back, escalates things more with how she does it too. Hand up my shirt, tugging at my jeans.

I grip her waist like I don't even want to, press my body against hers like it's the right one and we move it into the car.

And yeah, I'm falling back into the territory of old habits and revenge fucks, but Parks doing it again, so why can't I?

10:16

Gus 🖤

> Guess who I saw last night . . .

Who?

> Jack Giles

> 🥲

Oh yeah?

How was he?

390

Well.

He said you guys aren't dating anymore?

Yeah

Was he by himself?

He was with myself and Julian and Daisy.

. . .

He fucked someone else.

Shit.

I'm sorry.

It's ok xx

Did he look ok?

Better with you

Liar

Lunch this week?

Please please

Love to

I'll take every chance I get to ogle Julian Haites.

Honestly, me too.

FIFTY-SIX

Magnolia

It was peculiar that night in the club. Merciful timing, I suppose. Jordan announcing that her and BJ are flitting off for a sexy trip right as Julian started trying to strangle Carmelo.

It made it easier to walk away from BJ in the moment, because Julian needed me. But actually, quietly, I probably would have gone to Julian in an instance like that no matter what.

It's nice to be needed sometimes.

BJ doesn't need me, I don't think. I need him but it's not the other way around, it never has been. All my life, he was all I had in so many ways. More than just my boyfriend and my best friend and my protector and my confidant, I needed him because when he was gone I felt horribly alone. But he didn't. He's never needed me, not with his functional family with his loving parents and siblings coming out of his eyeballs, and all his aunts and uncles and grandparents who are sober and checked in, who love him very overtly and very loudly. All the time, at his rugby games, when he did well at school, on his birthday—they were there for him how you need your family to be. He didn't need much from me. Actually, I think the only thing he's ever really needed from me was—well—he met that need with someone else in a bathtub one night.

I calmed Julian down, stopped the fight. Jules asked me to leave with him. I looked for BJ—not for any real reason, mostly out of reflex—but he was gone. So I did leave with Jules. We walked past BJ's car in the alley behind the club. Fogged-up windows, movement behind them. Julian didn't notice and I didn't say a word, but I nearly started crying on the spot so I fucked Julian in the back of his car just to make it even.

"I see a psychologist," he told me afterwards with me still straddling him in the backseat. Just in his black elastic-waist straight trousers from Y-3, sitting there all shirtless and perfect. His off-white flocked cotton-jersey Fear of God tee and black appliquéd faux leather panelled wool-blend bomber jacket from Kapital cast behind us.

My hands were draped behind his neck and I moved them up into his hair.

"Do you?" I asked.

He nodded, put his hand on my waist and leaned back against the seat.

"What for?"

He shrugged. "Everything."

I shifted a bit closer to him and he watched me as I did, this new calm now over him and I wondered if I might be bringing it to him.

"Everything like what?"

"Like always worrying something's going to happen to my sister." He breathed out a breath I didn't realise he was holding. "Like my parents dying in front of me." He gave me a tired smile.

"Julian," I said as I put my hand on his face because I wasn't sure what else to do, and he held it against him and kissed my palm and didn't say anything else about it. Laid me down in the back seat and kissed me more.

A few days later, he and I go to brunch with my sister and Gus at the Athenaeum.

My sister is being her staunchest self and pretending she still doesn't like Julian, who is actually nearly impossible not to like, and I'm being sincere when I say that.

There's something about him, how he looks at you, how he speaks to you—instant and total buy-in—that's why I believe there are men that would follow him anywhere, right off a cliff with bullets in their chests, if he asked.

There's something wildly seductive about him and not even in an overtly sexual way, just in the way where, whatever he says, you're in.

Chinese for dinner? Sure.

Can he have the rest of my salad? Absolutely.

Wouldn't it be so fun if I went to get him a coffee? Of course it would.

And it's different from how it is with BJ where it feels like everything—even the worst things—are fun. But Julian just manages to make you feel like everything he says is the cleverest, best idea.

Did I think it was genuinely a good or hygienic idea to have sex in the men's room stall at Verona a couple of nights ago? No, I didn't.

Do I have any regrets? No, I don't.

But he's still working on winning my sister over, so he's talking about the dangers of China as an economic superpower and I'm a million per cent not listening.

"—no, but it's also their investment in overseas infrastructure." He nods at my sister. "You know what I mean?"

He's playing to her intelligence while she fiddles with her earrings—thread silver-plated hoop earrings from Jennifer Fisher—and then nods.

"Their soft power makes them dangerous, absolutely."

I elbow Julian and whisper, "Can we speak about something else? This is very boring."

My sister shakes her head at me. "The unprecedented succession of a country's position to power is boring?"

I hang my head. Boring. Very boring. "I stopped listening again. Perhaps we should instead speak about the democratisation of luxury? I'm sure it's an issue that's impacting each of us very deeply."

"Not really." Julian frowns.

"Never thought of it once," says my dumb sister.

"Bit of a bummer—" Gus shrugs. "But nice for them."

"Who is 'them'?" Bridget blinks.

"The aspirational class," I tell her brightly and Julian snorts into his drink.

My sister stares over at me. "How have you not been cancelled?"

I shake my head at her. "I don't adhere to cancel culture, I think it's anti-progressive and positively draconian."

Bridget squints. "Didn't you cancel Paili?"

I flatten down my pink high-waisted check skirt from Patou. "I did not cancel her. Britain canceled Paili," I say very firmly. I wasn't here, I had nothing to do with it. "It happened without my consent or my approval, but I won't pretend I'm not the least bit pleased because I'm only human and she is a gigantic ho, so—"

Gus laughs as Julian licks his smiling lips and throws an arm around me without a second thought. Gus is watching him with a pointed fascination.

"Right." Julian nods at him. "So fill me in—what happened with you and Jack Giles?"

Gus sways his head, looking both uncomfortable and sad.

"He's . . . complicated," Gus offers diplomatically.

Julian nods, jaw set. "He still not over that fuckhead?"

"Taj Owens?" Gus clarifies and then shakes his head.

He's good at pretending he doesn't care, but I know he liked Jack. He's never really committed to anyone, Tom told me so when we were together. Jack was a big deal. "Yeah."

Julian sits back in his seat and shakes his head. "I'm sorry, man."

He means it.

Gus shrugs, conceding. "It is what it is. Everyone has a person they get stuck on."

Julian glances at me and I feel dizzy for a second.

I jump up. "I'm going to the loo—" I take a few steps towards it before realising Bridget isn't following me. "Bridget?" I stomp my foot.

She growls and rolls her eyes but follows me all the same.

"You'd be so annoying to be friends with," she tells me.
I pout at her. "You are my friend."

She rolls her eyes but I can tell that she's actually pleased.
She follows me into the toilets and I run my wrists under the
tap just because.

"Do you like him yet?" I ask, a little bit nervous. I don't
know why.

She shrugs. "Why does it matter if I like him? He's just
pretend."

I feel myself frown a little.

"You're still in love with BJ, right?"

"Right."

She shrugs again. "So it's all for nought. Who cares if I
like him or not?"

"I do." I frown. "He's my friend, he's important to me,
I'm spending almost all my time with him. You're smarter
than me. I like to know what you think. I ask you to read
the ingredients on the packet of my bliss balls because I care
about what I put inside of my body."

She blinks. "You're putting a gang lord inside of you."

I give her a look and she rolls her eyes as a wordless apology.
She stares at me for a few seconds.

"You know this is called 'transference', right?" Bridget tells
me. "You're seeking my approval because we've never had
parental approval."

"Mum approves of some things. She likes my shoes or
whenever I wear a plunging neckline."

Bridge nods. "She is a big supporter of your décolletage."

"She likes BJ," I remind her.

"Yes."

My sister gives me a steep look. "If not all too much."

"Marsaili wouldn't like Julian, I don't think—" I shake my
head.

Bridget waves her head. "Well, she doesn't like BJ either."
She looks at me and then sighs, fixing her ponytail. "I do
like him," she tells me, her expression softening. "He's very

charming."

I pull back, all the sudden feeling tall and pleased. "Isn't he?"

I feel a bit proud of him, I'm not sure why.

We sit back down at the table and they're talking about the NBA.

Julian puts his arm back around me without even thinking and Gus's eyes pinch again.

"You good?" Julian asks, glancing at me. I nod. His phone rings. He pulls it out of his pocket, looks down at it with a frown and holds it against his chest.

"Be right back—" He kisses my cheek

We all watch him leave because he's hard not to stare at.

Balenciaga's Chinese Year of the Tiger oversized T-shirt overtop a white Rag & Bone long sleeve tee with the black Vetements tapered logo-print cotton-blend jersey sweatpants and a pair of the Mercurius lace-up boots from Moncler.

Gus waits till Julian's out of earshot and then looks back at me, frowning. "What the fuck are you doing?"

I frown back. "What do you mean?"

He shakes his head, annoyed. "You're doing it again."

I roll my eyes. "What are you talking about?"

"That man," Gus points in Julian's direction, "is head-over-heels in love with you."

I blink at him a few times. "Are you crazy?"

Gus shakes his head at me. "He can't keep his hands off you."

I sigh, annoyed. "He likes my body."

"He likes you." Gus gives me a look.

Bridget purses her lips. "He is protective of you."

"Yeah—" I roll my eyes. "He was really protective of me the other week when he dumped me and left me on the side of the road."

"I thought you weren't together?" Gus asks, eyebrows up.

"We aren't." I shrug defensively.

Gus shrugs petulantly. "Can't dump someone you're not with."

I roll my eyes. "You know what I mean—"

"Well," Bridget says with a gesture to herself. "I personally never know what you mean . . ."

"Well anyway," I say loudly, "I said something he didn't like and he said we're done. On the spot. Dropped me outside of our place in the dead of night—"

"—It was nine p.m.!" Bridget interjects.

"—Right on the street!" I ignore her. "That's not what you do if you like someone." I'm sure of this. Maybe before that night I might have wondered, but that was the answer. Julian doesn't like me. I am disposable to him too. Which is fine. I feel fractionally ill over the thought, but it's fine. Because I love BJ and it's fine.

Gus gives me a little look. "And yet here you are . . . at lunch with us. Together."

"Well, then we saw each other again, and I don't know—" I shrug.

"I do." Gus blinks a few times. "He loves you."

"August." I sigh, annoyed. "I know he doesn't love me."

"How?"

"Because he doesn't look at me like . . ." I trail off, give them both a tight smile. I don't know why saying his name felt rather difficult just then.

"BJ?" My sister jumps in. "Magnolia, that can't be the benchmark. No one is going to look at you like BJ looks at you."

"Although, Julian is surprisingly . . ." Gus trails off now, thinking of the right word. ". . . Tender towards you?" He peers over at me. "I've seen him with other girls. He's not like that."

That is true, I'll give them that. Sometimes Julian's tenderness with me takes me aback. And I might have worried about it before, but then he dumped me. And you don't dump people you want to be with completely out of the blue because they ask you a question you don't feel like answering.

He doesn't like me. He might like facets of being with me, he might like my body, he might like having someone he can be sweet to because who else could he be like that with? I think all people have this side to them, all people have this capacity for gentleness inside of them, but when does a gang lord who hates being in love ever get to explore it if not with me inside of the strange feelingless vacuum we've created?

"You love a wake of destruction behind you, don't you? Just a trail of forlorn and pining men."

"Gus." I frown, feeling picked on.

"What?" He folds his arms over his chest, unimpressed with me. "You do."

"It's not completely your fault," Bridget jumps in, defending me.

"No—" Gus nods. "They let you do it. You kind of siren them in with those eyes—" I roll them at him. "And then they love you, and then they're miserable because you've only ever loved one boy and one day you will—God willing—sort yourselves the fuck out and be together. And then you're going to break his little gang lord heart."

I laugh at that, shake my head at his ridiculousness.

"Are you kidding?" I push my hair over my shoulders the same way I'll push this thought away. "That's Julian Haites. I couldn't break his heart if I hit it with a sledgehammer."

"Baby girl—" Gus gives me a look. "You are the sledgehammer."

14:41

Jonah

Hey, you riding in with me and Tausie tonight?

Riding in where?

To BJ's.

What?

Fuck

399

BJ's having a birthday thing?

Yeah

But it's nothing

Jordan planned it

He didn't.

Right

It's a surprise. He doesn't know.

Ok.

You alright?

Yep.

Grand

We'll do something just us.

No

That's fine.

I'm sorry, Parks.

It's shit. You should be there.

It's fine.

FIFTY-SEVEN

BJ

For my birthday we go to Aqua Shard.

Think it was supposed to be a surprise, but she booked it on my card and they called me to confirm it. Dinner for seven on the 14th of February. It was nice of her. I didn't say anything. Did it herself.

When we arrive at the restaurant, Jordan's in this long dress that's patterned with too many colours. She looks pretty because she's an attractive girl, but really I just want to see what Parks is in.

Dressed to the nines for my birthday every year, even if we aren't together. Red or pink because she's not a saint and she'd never roll on Valentine's Day for me. Used to my birthday being as much about her as it is about me. Kind of like it that way too.

I wonder what she got for me.

We walk to our table, big smiles and Henry sort of yells an unenthusiastic "surprise". I roll my eyes that Magnolia's late to this.

Then everyone sits and I realise there's no chairs left.

Dinner was for seven. There's seven of us here.

I lean over to Jonah and whisper, "Where's Parks?"

He looks over at me, face ripe to cringe. "Jordan planned this."

I blink at him a few times. Can't believe it. "She wasn't invited?"

Fuck.

Jo gives me a look. "Did you think your current girl-friend would invite your ex-girlfriend to the birthday party she planned for you without prompting?"

I shrug at him hopeless. "Then why didn't you prompt her?"

Jo shrugs back. "Not my circus."

I drop my head in my hands before I look over at him. "Did she know there was something on for me?"

Jo grimaces again. "Yep."

My jaw goes tight. "Fuck."

"Yep."

He nods.

"She's going to kill me."

"Who is?" Jordan asks brightly from the seat next to me.

I turn to her, try not to look as stressed as I feel. Don't know how to say it without coming off like an absolute fucking prick, but anyway.

"You didn't invite Parks?" I say, eyebrows up. "And Julian." I add as an afterthought.

Jordan straightens up a little. "She upset you the other night. I could tell."

I frown, don't say anything. She could tell? When? I mean, she's right. She did. I was upset. I didn't know she knew that though.

"I didn't think you'd want her here—" She gives me a shrug. "I didn't think she deserved to be invited."

I give her an uncomfortable smile. I think she's trying to do right by me.

I mean, she's wrong. She's fucking off the planet wrong. But I think she's trying to be good to me. Punish Parks or something. Makes me feel a bit sick. Feel sweaty at the thought of Magnolia sitting at home thinking I didn't want her here.

I always want her here. I want her everywhere. Next to me, on me, all the time.

Haven't had a birthday without her in forever.

She makes them good even if she doesn't—even if she fucks them up completely. Rather have them with her than without her.

402

For my seventeenth she planned for us all to go to the Royal Myconian in Mykonos. Me and her, the boys, Paili.

No Lorcan. He'd just started dating a lad from City of London and felt like it was a bad omen to miss that hallmark occasion, what with it being Valentine's weekend. Parks did convince Arrie to chaperone the trip under the guise of a girls' weekend though. We have the funniest photos of us at the pool bar with Parks's mum, Jennifer Saunders, Posh and Helena Bonham Carter.

On paper, Parks and Paili shared a room and me and Jo shared a room. In reality, Paili and Jo definitely hooked up the whole duration of that trip and I stayed in Parks's room the entire time.

Her mum never looked in once—bless her checked-out soul.

We hadn't had sex yet, me and Parks, and we'd been together seven-ish months. Done other stuff, as you do. Loved the other stuff. Huge fan.

And I don't know why, but she was convinced that was the trip, that we were going to do it there. She'd built up to it happening on that trip. It was happening and it was going to be great.

The lingerie Magnolia packed with her was another level.

I wouldn't say—and don't tell her I said this—that being sexy isn't her strongest suit. I've never loved her because she's sexy, never wanted her because she's sexy. Don't get me wrong—she's beautiful and ridiculous and enigmatic and I'll be locked into her gravity till I die—but she's not overtly sexy.

Actually, if anything, the lingerie she brought scared me a bit. Would have made a porn star blush.

"Where the fuck did you get this?" I held up a thing with a lot of straps. She didn't think it was funny.

I dodged it for days and days. Don't know why—maybe now I do in retrospect, but I wasn't conscious of it at the time. Knew she wanted to, I wanted to too—just felt nervous about it all.

I staved her off with the other things, but on my actual birthday morning she was ready. Didn't come out wearing a big bow but she might as well have.

The short version of this story is that it didn't go to plan.

I said no, she locked herself in the bathroom, cried. Wouldn't come out. Not for my birthday breakfast, not to be on the yacht she booked for us all. She was shattered. Most hurt she'd been till recent years. First time I rejected her, I guess. Didn't take it well. Should have learned from it. Didn't, quite. Getting there, though.

Pails skipped the yacht too. The story's all downhill from there. Those two got shitfaced. The boys and I went on the boat anyway—Jo was a bit like, 'fuck 'em, it's your birthday, why's she making it about her?'—and we had a cracker of a time with Arrie and the girls. But while we were gone, Parks and Paili wandered off to a massive night club, got more shit-faced and got themselves into some pretty dicey scenarios.

Worth saying: Paili drunk has zero inhibitions and can't tell shit from shit. Magnolia drunk is a deer in headlights.

My deer though.

She tried calling me. Didn't have service out on the Aegean. By the time we got back that night a bit after sundown my phone had a bunch of missed calls and texts. Called her back, but she wasn't answering. The voicemails she'd left simultaneously got progressively more drunk and more chaotic as they went on. Could hear older men in the background. She was crying a bit. Something about Paili and a guy. Parks didn't want to leave her—someone was trying to get the phone out of her hand.

It was fucking scary.

Grabbed the boys, dodged her mum, did tell Helena though. Surprisingly responsible, that one. Looked everywhere for them. Jo put the call out, put his mum's people's eyes out. Searched for a few hours.

Found her phone by chance on the side of the road—it was bad. Thought the worst for a minute there. That maybe—because we're fated and all that star-crossed lovers shit—maybe the worst had happened.

We were by the beach, decided to just have a look in case and we found them. It was dicey as fuck. Older guys, four of them. Two on Parks, two on Pails. Parks was crying, Paili was frozen still. Both had sobered up by then, could see that on their faces. It was clear they knew they were in trouble. They were London boys, they knew who the girls were. Knew who Parks was at least.

Bit triggering for me, actually. Fucked me up. I was frozen too for half a second.

He can be dangerous when he wants to be, Jo—even when we were kids that was true. Mostly just a good time, mostly fun. Could kill you if he needed to though. I guess that's what that life does to you.

"Oi!" Jo growled to get their attention.

Parks looked over at me—lying on the sand, body weighed down by a man who wasn't me—and she called my name.

How she called it—I still have dreams about it. Afraid and trapped and hurt and I can't get to her. In the dream I can never get to her.

She started crying more, squirming under him, trying to get out.

Then one quick and wordless look and years of rugby together paid off. Me and Jo charged them. Me on Parks's guy, Jo on Paili's. Knocked them off the girls. Henry and Christian took the other two lads. And then it turned to mayhem.

I reckon they thought it was going to be an easy fight, but they were wrong. You toss Christian in the mix of any brawl and shit gets pretty nasty.

Me, Jo and Hen, we're all raw energy and feeling, but Christian is controlled aggression. Still is now. You want to win a fight, you bring Christian. Didn't really need him that night though because I beat the living fuck out of the man who'd pinned Parks. He got in one good swing. Chipped the bone in my chin, I'd find out later. Little divot in the bone still there now.

She touches it when she kisses me sometimes. I touch it when I miss her.

It was rough, the whole thing was rough. Even back then we moved as a pack, and we've only gotten better at it since. No one would fight us now back in London anyway, but the four of us at that beach with those men touching our girls? We were out for blood. It ended with four unconscious men on the beach.

My hands were bruised and swollen, black eye, cut cheek, busted lip. Jo broke a rib. Henry broke a finger and had to get a stitch above his eye back in London. Christian had a bloody nose but he was pretty much fine. Kind of forgot the girls were there until Magnolia flung herself into my arms. I held her tight against me for a few seconds, my chest heaving. I pulled back to look at her. "Did they hurt you?"

She shook her head. "Not really."

"Did they touch you?" I asked, my words caught in my throat a bit. Didn't want her to feel like I felt. Didn't want hands on her that weren't mine.

"A bit—" She shook her head more. "Kissed me—grabbed me a bit—if you hadn't come . . ." She started crying again.

I held her face in my hands, held her against me, kissed her forehead till she stopped and then I turned around and walked away. She tried to hold my hand, wouldn't hold it back. We got taxis back to the hotel. I sat in the front so she couldn't sit next to me. Tried to hold my hand again as we walked back to our rooms but I smacked it away.

"No," I yelled—sounded a bit battered, I remember that.

"BJ—" She reached for me.

"No." I shook my head again, scowled at her. "Stupid."

She grabbed my wrist. "BJ, I'm s—"

I shook her off and shoved her towards my brother. "Sleep in his bed tonight because you're fucking not sleeping with me." I skulked off.

Henry said she cried for about three hours straight.

But here's the fucked-up thing, right? I couldn't sleep without her anyway. Forget that Henry was texting me, begging for me to come take her off him like she was a new puppy crying in the bathroom. I couldn't sleep without her because even before any of the shit that would happen to us happened, we'd managed to sew ourselves into one.

Whenever I could at school, I'd sneak into her dorm. Whenever we were home, I'd sneak into her bed. We weren't fused yet, but we were fusing, actively and in real time. And fuck her for that—fuck her for that then, fuck her for that now—but back then it was three in the morning and I was there knocking on my brother's hotel room to be close to her. She opened the door, eyes red and emerald as fuck. I was leaning against the door frame and kissed her as soon as I saw her. Pulled her out of the room, pressed her up against the wall, my head on hers.

"What were you thinking?" I ground my forehead into hers.

She held on to my shirt by the waist.

"I was sad." That's all she said.

"Magnolia, if we hadn't found you—"

"I know." She nodded solemnly.

I nodded back at her, kissed her again. And then her busy little hands started all over again, the same hands that started this whole mess in the first place.

I moved them off me.

"No." I shook my head at her, frowning a bit. "Not like this."

She went teary again. "I don't understand."

"Parks—" I shook my head at her, sniffed a laugh. "You're not ready."

"I am," she insisted. "I've never wanted anything how I want you."

I pushed some hair behind her ears. She wasn't ready though. And I wasn't. I knew that. But not being ready and not wanting to, they're not the same thing.

Neither of us were ready, but we still wanted to more than anything.

So we did it a few weeks later anyway. We went ahead and welded our fucked-up little hearts together for good.

407

Definitely my worst birthday to date, but at least at that one I got to be with her.

One birthday, after we'd broken up and she was with Christian, I came home after a night out with the boys and there was a little diecast DeLorean on my pillow. No card, no nothing, but I knew it was from her. We had watched *Back to the Future* a few nights before we broke up while she was sick in bed. She couldn't follow the story for shit. I thought it was so funny, but she was annoyed at me, annoyed at it. "How's a car going to be a time machine, then? What an absolute crock," she pouted at the TV.

Got it tattooed on my arm that same weekend.

At the end of tonight, Henry stands, throws his arms around me and covertly hands me a box.

"From her."

He gives me a tight smile.

I look over my shoulder, make sure no one hears me. "Tell her I didn't know."

"I'll tell her." Henry nods. Walks away.

I open the box in the bathroom at home. Lock the door, give myself a minute alone with her, even if it's not in person. A blank card reads: *I don't think I'll ever stop looking for a time machine. Until I find one, here's a time keeper instead.*

It's the Vacheron Constantin's 'Historiques' watch. On the back she's engraved: On borrowed time without you.

I press my hands into my face.

Swallow the sound my body tries to make.

Fuck, I miss her.

I could end it with Jordan now. Should, I guess. I've spent my whole birthday thinking about the girl that she didn't invite—but I know that girl. Know how Parks thinks, what she does when her heart's backed up against the wall. It was the other night and she didn't even give me a minute to fix it, she just legged it straight to Julian.

And you want to think that at this point, we're past it— that we're beyond the hurting each other to feel close to each other—but I don't know.

408

And I don't even want to think about what she's doing tonight if she feels like I've rejected her. But I don't need to think about it, I already know what she's doing.

I do it too.

20:16

Bridget 😣

I wasn't invited to BJ's birthday

What?

As if.

Jonah said Jordan planned it

You're his best friend?

Am I

Yes

Are you ok?

No, not really.

Where are you?

I'm on my way to Julian's.

Yeah good.

Fuck him.

I'm planning on it.

I meant BJ.

Oh, no—I won't do that. Might send a mixed signal.

I wasn't being literal.

Oh.

I was.

Yes, I know.

Well

Enjoy your sad-person orgasm 👍

Thanks, enjoy no orgasms for the billionth night in a row 👋

lol

Bitch

FIFTY–EIGHT
Magnolia

BJ's birthday night I show up at Julian's.

A tiny bit drunk and heart sunk, out for blood.

Jonah called me, told me Beej didn't know. That she'd planned it, that she didn't invite me and he had no idea, that Beej would be upset that I wasn't there, that he would have wanted me there. I don't know.

I bought him a watch before I realised I wasn't invited, but it felt too sad to keep it so I asked Henry to give it to him. Henry said I should've just come anyway, but I couldn't go from being the only person on the planet that he saw to being the girl who shows up to his birthday parties uninvited.

Not just because I'm proud, but because my heart couldn't handle the whiplash.

Anyway, the security guards let me in and I park my car—I barely ever drive myself places but I felt like it today. I walk straight to his office.

I mean business.

This is BJ's School of Questionable Coping and I've learned from the master.

Sex is a potent tonic for a broken heart.

Julian's at his desk. Decks is there too, on the couch in the corner watching football.

"Hey—" Jules frowns, standing up. "I thought you'd be at the birthday."

I walk around the desk and face him, toe to toe. "I wasn't invited."

"Fuck." He blinks a few times. "Are you okay?"

His hands are folded over his chest, eyes flicking around my face. He looks annoyed almost until his eyes land on mine and everything softens.

"Are you?" He tilts his head.

I'm in the red satin-trimmed metallic stretch-jersey midi-dress from Dolce & Gabbana, a black and white faux-fur vintage Chanel jacket from 1994 with the Dolce & Gabbana black satin sandals with floral embroidery.

All clothes I picked out at a store the other week while imagining BJ taking them off my body and I wonder for a few seconds what's wrong with me? How I can have gotten dressed thinking about BJ's breath dragging across my skin and then get in the car and run straight into Julian's arms? Something's wrong with me, I know it is, and I can barely get the sentence written down onto the page of my mind before the answer presents itself.

I love him too much.

That's the problem.

That's the only problem I've ever had, really.

The only reason I'm sad how I am, the only reason I've been hurt how I have been, it's all because I love him too much.

And I wonder how I've moved through life stuck on loving the same boy since I was fourteen, which is far too young to be in love, but I dare you to find anyone who loves anything more than I love him.

I lift my arms in the air, waiting for Julian to take my clothes off.

He stares at me for a few seconds, doesn't look away when he says, "Declan, leave."

Declan sniffs a laugh, rolls his eyes at us and closes the door behind him. Then Julian grabs me by the waist. My feet are off the floor and he bangs me into the wall.

He reaches behind my body, undoes the zip to my dress and it pools around my ankles.

I'm on my tiptoes trying to be close to him and this is a feeling I've begun to grow terribly fond of—how big he is, how much he shadows over me, how his arms feel like branches that are protecting me from a storm.

He's kissing me down my neck, behind my ear, breath heavy on me like a welcome fog rolling in on a winter morning. He pulls back to look at me and his eyes remind me of being alone somewhere quiet at midnight. Dark, inky blue. Somehow still a bit sparkly. They're too beautiful to be the eyes of Scotland Yard's most watched man. That's who my sister says he is. I think it's probably slander from a rival arms dealer.

He has intrepid hands and a wandering mouth and I unbutton his jeans and he lifts me up onto his waist and hangs me into the wall again and a bronze Fanghu Han Dynasty vase crashes onto the floor, smashing everywhere.

"Fuck—" He laughs as he moves around the shattered marble, walking us backwards into a display cabinet of antique plates and vases—at least half of which smash to the floor too and Julian looks at the ceiling and yells a million swear words and I'm laughing. My hands are in his hair when he shakes his head and looks at me. "I told you you'd be an expensive fuck." His eyes go softer.

"Worth it."

Then he kisses me more.

I'm grateful he's like this.

Sex with Julian isn't really like sex with anyone else. He makes it harder for my mind to wander off, which it tries to do sometimes.

He carries me back over and onto his desk. He takes his own jumper off (Stone Island's logo-appliquéd cotton-jersey sweatshirt) and I'm always so interested whenever his shirt is off—which is often. I try not to look.

There are quite a few scars.

There's one. It's round. Pinkish still, so I guess it's new. I run my finger over it and he watches me as I do.

"How?" My eyes flick from the scar to him.

He swallows.

"Cage fighting." He gives me a small smile.

My face falters. "Why?"

"It's fun."

"Getting hurt?"

He shakes his head. "I don't get hurt."

He pushes some hair from my face. "I'm sorry he didn't invite you." He's sincere when he says that.

"I don't want to talk about him."

He gives me a look. "You always want to talk about him."

"Julian—" I stare at him. "Do you think I'm lying here, half-naked, to talk to you about BJ?" He licks his bottom lip. "Stop talking and have sex with me."

"Yep." He nods and undoes my bra with one hand.

He pushes me down, spreads me out, stretches my arms up over my head. He hovers over me, looking at me way too tenderly.

"What are you smiling at?" He squints and then does it more but on accident. I shake my head at him. "Don't you go soft on me . . ."

And then it's gone. His eyes light back up. I feel the lead up before the rollercoaster drops off and he cocks a smile. "Never."

He pulls me back up onto his lap, slides his hands down my body, arches my back himself.

His breathing gets heavier, mine gets faster.

He pushes some hair from my face and I collapse in the deep curve of his giant shoulders and whimper.

"Magnolia," he pants breathlessly.

I pull back and look at his face, my hands knotted in his hair, and I don't for one second close my eyes in case I see the other.

Afterwards, we're lying on the floor behind his desk. I'm lying on his chest and he's wrapped me up in a silver-beige cow hide rug. My chin sits in the little valley of his chest and he pushes his hand through my hair, frowning a bit.

"You think of him when you're with me," he tells me.

It's not a question, it's a statement. One he's not angry about either. It's just a fact.

I suck on my bottom lip and drop his eyes.

I sigh. "I try not to."

He nods a little as he kind of shrugs with his chin.

"I can tell when you do."

"Oh." I don't know why that makes me want to cry a bit. "Sorry—"

Julian frowns as he shakes his head.

He shrugs.

"Who do you think of?" I ask him as he stretches his arms up behind his head.

"Pretty good at staying in the moment these days—"

"You think of me?" I blink, bit chuffed.

He nods.

"All the time?" I'm surprised.

He sniffs a laugh but he doesn't answer me.

I shift some hair behind his ear. "Have you ever been in love?"

"Can't—" He shakes his head. "It's why you're here. I'm no strings."

I rub my mouth mindlessly over his cheek. "There are some strings."

He gives me a small smile.

"In another life I reckon I could have loved you."

I tilt my head, looking up at him.

"In another life I would have let you."

Julian sits up, leaning back against his desk. Pulls me with him, resting my head on his lap.

He peers down at me.

"What's it like loving someone how you two love each other?"

I sniff a bit sadly. "Bad."

"Bad?" He's surprised. "Really?"

I nod. "I think so. I don't really belong to myself anymore."

He frowns.

"What do you mean?"

"I mean he's in everything—everything. I'm always thinking about him and I want to know what he thinks, I want to know what he wants. And I worry about how he feels and whether he's safe and what he's doing."

I shake my head, feeling a bit trapped by it all. "With him I think about all the hands that have been on his body that aren't mine—"

"—Fuck." He frowns.

"He's not my every second thought, he's my every thought." The way 'every' sits in my mouth, it feels like a burden. "He infiltrates all of them. All my decisions, all my feelings—"

Julian shakes his head. "I'd hate that."

I barely smile up at him but try my best to. "Yes, you would."

He stares at me for a few seconds and I think if I were to acknowledge the moment in the fullness it deserves it would weigh differently in my heart, but I don't.

I tell myself that he combs his fingers through the hair of all the girls he does this with.

"So, what's it like being a gang lord?"

"Hah—" He smiles without looking at me, amused by the question. "You've accepted it then?"

I shrug. "I think it's all lies."

He gives me a look. "I mean. You know what it's like. You dated Christian."

I shake my head at him. "He didn't tell me anything."

"Why?"

"I don't know—" I shrug. "Because I'm named after a flower or something, I think."

Julian sniffs and nods. "Yeah, the delicate thing, I get it. You're all bone china and we're bulls."

I sit up, facing him. "Tell me what's it like."

He gives me a long look. "Tiring."

"Do you like it?" I rest my chin on his knee.

He purses his mouth while he thinks about it. "Was never a choice. It's just the hand I was dealt."

I nod like I get it even though I never will. I watch him curiously, trying to place how someone who's so beautiful,

416

whose mouth is so pink and whose hands are so gentle with
me could possibly ever have blood on them.

"You don't actually hurt people, right?" I stare over at him.
"A bit, but not really . . . Do you?"

He reaches over to my face, brushes an eyelash from my
cheek that isn't there.

"Nah—" He smiles a bit sadly. "I'm all talk."

FIFTY-NINE
BJ

I was fucking gutted that Parks wasn't at my birthday.

And I know I love her. Even know that we belong together.

That should be enough.

I know it should.

But then she did exactly what I thought she'd do when she thought I rejected her.

She ran straight to Julian.

Daisy and Christian were over the other night, and Baby Haites said that she walked into her brother's office after my birthday and him and Parks were on the floor wrapped in a blanket.

Christian kind of looked at her like 'What the fuck?' and I sniffed a laugh, shook my head and played it off like it didn't feel like someone just dropped a goddamn anvil on me.

Don't know why, it's exactly what I expected. When I hurt her, she hurls men at me.

And I try my best not to do it, but you know, sometimes curiosity gets the better of me and I wonder about her with him like that. In that capacity. The worst is when I think about them having sex while I'm having sex.

That's a real mind fuck.

Till then, in my head though, if I was thinking about them having sex—I don't know why—I kind of just thought whatever they were doing, it was probably a bit quick and dirty in the back of a car or some shit. I don't know—whatever I thought it was, it wasn't sex that ended with them wrapped up in a fucking blanket together.

So I, once again, decide not to end it with Jordan. Because I can't. Not till she ends it with Julian, and she should. Because Jordan's just a warhead, but Julian is a nuke. She escalated this, not me.

Me and Jords are meant to be going away. Part of my birthday present—though I'm pretty sure I paid for it myself.

It sounded like a good idea at the time . . . She asked me about forty-five seconds after that night where Magnolia told Julian he could take her home and put her to bed however he wanted to.

Said yes to Jordan without even thinking. Trigger response.

And now I've got a trip in the pipe with the wrong girl. I'm going away with a girl I don't want to be with but can't not be with because it turns out I'm in love with a fucking emotional terrorist.

We're at Ametsa in Knightsbridge, everyone's here except for Parks and Julian. They're late. I used to be late to shit like this with her, so I know what they're doing.

She's so laser focused when she's getting ready, so indifferent towards you that she gets twenty times hotter, as if that's even fucking possible. We always had the best sex before we'd go out.

Actually, we just always had the best sex.

"Sorry we're late," Magnolia says, shaking her head as they walk in. "And sorry that I look so insane! We had a mishap in the car."

"A mishap?" Julian whispers to her but I hear it. He's smirking. Fuck him. She smacks him quiet. I hate it. Hate that she smacks him without thinking. She's too mindless in how she is with him around her body.

Scares me.

"Anyway, my shoe broke so these are my emergency pair."

Daisy frowns over at her. "You're in black heels?"

"Yes."

Parks nods, wide eyed. "I know, I'm so sorry—"

Christian tilts his head, looking at her feet. "What colour should they be?"

419

"Ooh—" Her lips make the shape. "I don't know . . . buttercream yellow, ideally. Navy would have sufficed." She glances down, looking at the colours in her dress. "Cerulean in a pinch, I suppose."

Daisy rolls her eyes. "Oh, and you didn't have a spare pair of cerulean sandals in the back of your car?"

"Well—" Magnolia shrugs. "Not this car."

I crack a laugh even though I don't want to.

She sits down opposite me, Julian next to her, and straight away his hand is in her hair. She doesn't seem to notice either, and I wonder how many times someone needs to touch you before their hands on your body stops being something you notice.

"We're going to Italy tomorrow," Jordan brightly tells the table at lunch.

Magnolia glances over at me, looks a bit wounded—that's a positive at least—I want her chest to feel heavy how mine does, watching her not noticing Julian touch her—but then I flash her the watch she gave me to tell her I love her anyway.

"Are you?" Julian sits back, a bit interested. "We've got a house on the lake." He nods his chin at his sister.

She nods. "We haven't been in ages."

He shrugs. "We should go."

He looks between Parks and Daisy.

"Yeah." I nod. "Come for sure."

Magnolia throws me a baffled look.

I catch her eye, try to tell her without having to say it that, at this point, I can't think of anything I wouldn't do to be alone with her for five minutes. Fly to another country, watch another guy feel her up in the pool just so I can stay up late to watch shitty documentaries with her, swallow heavy as her fingers graze mine when she passes me the remote.

"Where's your place?" I ask Julian with my chin, ignoring that fucking hand of his that's slipped under the table.

"Lake Como," he says, not looking away from me while Magnolia squirms and lets out small laugh. "Let's all go," he tells Jonah.

"Come, for sure!" Jordan looks between Daisy and Julian, and she doesn't look phased at all. "That sounds so fun."

I shrug, tossing my arm around her as I look over at Julian. "Do you have room for us all?"

Julian nods and Jonah tosses me a confused look.

I raise my eyebrows barely, just enough to tell him to come.

"Yeah—" Jonah shrugs like, fuck it. "I'm in."

SIXTY

BJ

The next morning we fly out on Parks's plane. Gulfstream G700. Ten-seater with a master suite. Bougie as fuck.

When we walk onto it Parks pretends like it's nothing and she's not frothing over it, but she texted me about it all week when she got it.

"What does your dad do again?" Jordan looks over at Parks, not remotely concealing her awe.

Gus, suffering from what he's described as the world's worst hangover, lays face-down on the couch. Magnolia sits down in one of the two-seater layouts. Tausie sits across from her.

"He wins Grammys," she says, adjusting her Versace headband.

Julian sniffs a laugh because he's the sort of person who'd genuinely appreciate how obnoxious she's being. I try not to smirk at it, do my best not to look at Parks or I'll start laughing.

Jonah, Julian, Daisy and Christian sit at the front, huddled around a table and talking about gang lord shit or something, I guess.

I sit down at another one of the two-seaters, pull on a hoodie I know Magnolia bought for me. Bunch of clothes on my bed when I came home the other day. She buys clothes for all of us, especially when she's feeling out of control.

Jordan sits on my lap instead of across from me even though the seat's free and I get the feeling she's doing it on purpose.

She gives me an eighth of a smile, leans back into me and Instagrams the take-off.

Nothing I can do about that. Why wouldn't she sit on her boyfriend's lap? Why wouldn't she Instagram it?

Magnolia is well pissed though. Watches over darkly as Jordan now chats away to Bianca Harrington, the girl who, in my humble opinion, Jonah is actually in love with but he fucking swears up and down that they're just friends. Friends who had sex once, I'm just saying.

Her and Jords get along well enough it seems, so I have all the time in the world to stare at the girl I love over there in that dress and cardigan. I watch her how I haven't been allowed to for too long.

Love fucks you up, man. In what world, what shit has to happen between you and someone that you miss just being able to stare at them, because I've missed staring at her.

I love watching her do nothing, love how she moves, especially when she knows I'm watching, which she does right now.

She's swallowing, nervous, and peeking over at me whenever she can squeeze it in naturally. I can't look away because I'm thinking about all the things I used to do with her on an airplane. Never wasted a minute I had alone with her, not an inch of her skin I'd have left untouched or a corner of this plane I wouldn't have kissed her in.

Julian's a fucking idiot.

"This is nice!" Magnolia says as we walk into the foyer of the Haites home and Henry and I stare over at her in surprise. Can't believe it, actually.

To put this into perspective for you, when I took her to Versailles she didn't say a fucking word. Didn't blink twice. Actually, I think she might have said, "It's bit gauche, don't you think? Rather gold heavy."

I've taken her to the nicest hotels in the world—Baur au Lac, the Mandarin in Doha, Rambagh Palace—and she thinks nothing of them. She's completely indifferent. Let that be a measuring stick for you of how insane this place is.

It is off the fucking chain.

"Wow, how good is dirty money?" Magnolia blinks up at an ornately painted ceiling.

Both the Hemmes boys snort a laugh.

"Well, I guess it's true—" She shrugs, flicking her eyes between the Hemmeses and the Haiteses. "Crime really does pay."

I swallow a smile. "The expression's actually 'crime doesn't pay'."

She looks over at me with a bit of a frown. "That doesn't even remotely make sense . . ."

Julian hooks his arm around her neck and smirks down at her for a second before he kisses her.

"You tell 'em."

I look away.

"Alright," Julian says. "Figure out amongst yourselves where you want to sleep. Daisy, you're in the Chinoiserie suite."

She frowns. "I want the master."

Her brother scoffs, amused. "Yeah, right."

She frowns more. "Why do you get the master?"

He gives her a look. "Because I am the master."

Daisy rolls her eyes and pulls Christian away.

"Come on." Julian grabs Parks, tosses her over his shoulder like a fucking caveman and carries her up the stairs. "I'm going to show you just how well it pays."

They disappear for a while.

I'm sick for a while.

Fucks me up a bit, watching him carry her away like that. I second guess the call on having everyone come to Italy. Him kissing her is shit enough, but having to be in the same house as them while they're fucking?

Don't really know what to do other than Jordan, so I do.

Hate it, think of Parks the whole time. Hate that. Hate myself for being like this again.

Thought I'd evolved past fucking girls to process how much loving Parks has fucked me up but I've not—clearly.

Old habits and shit.

I feel worse for it than I used to because I guess now I know better.

"You were mad," Jordan says, looking over to me afterwards, "that I didn't invite her to the party."

She looks away, thinking.

"No." I shake my head unconvincingly.

"I thought you'd like making her sad," she says as she reaches over, pushing my hair back. Makes me feel a weird kind of sick, Jordan touching me like this, talking about Magnolia.

I flash her a quick smile. "I never want to make her sad."

"Even if—" she starts but I cut her off.

"Even if nothing, Jords," I tell her firmly, but it's kind of bullshit. I'm a professional at hurting Parks, but over my fucking dead body am I letting anyone else do it.

She watches me, thinking as she does, then she nods. See a question rise to the surface of her mind like a dead body in a lake. She breathes out with her eyes pinched and her blinks sink it again.

She rolls on top of me and flashes me a smile. "Fancy round two?"

Few hours later I head down to the pool. It's lined with about a thousand heaters so we can lie out and pretend it's not a toasty 12° C.

Daisy, Christian, Henry and Taura went out on the lake; Gus, Jo and Banksy are playing spike ball on the grass; Parks and Julian are lying under a cabana in the worst way possible.

Blanket around him (what the fuck is with them and blankets?), her leaning back between his legs.

He's reading the paper, she's on her iPhone.

Only redeeming part? She's in a little seersucker lilac bikini.

She flicks her eyes up at me and then she glances at herself, eyes pointing to the colour she's wearing. She looks back over at me, sending me a message without saying a word.

I sit in the deckchair directly opposite her so I can watch her again how I did on the plane.

Jordan does a few laps in the pool then jumps into the spa. I just take in the sights.

Skin so much browner than the rest of ours, hair all wavy from the chlorine, emerald eyes so bright you could spot them from the lake.

Rub my hand over my mouth mindlessly, as she stares back at me over her phone.

My phone vibrates.

She texts me.

14:43

Parks

What are you staring at?

You.

She swallows, nervous. Cheeks flushed.

You know I'm dating a gang lord right...?

I glance up at her, amused. Cock an eyebrow.

Thought you weren't dating . . .

She glances over at me, face all deadpan and perfect.

Would you really rather me say what we're actually doing?

She's got me there.

No.

How was your party?

> Good, how was yours?

She stares over at me darkly.

> Intimate.

Fuck. I've struck a nerve.

> I didn't know, Parks.

> Did you think I knew?

She purses her mouth. Surely she knew I didn't know. Jonah
said he told her I didn't know.
I wouldn't do that to her.

> That was mean of her.

> Can you blame her?

I give her a look from across the pool.
She frowns at my text when she gets it. Types back
aggressively.

> I can yeah, I think she's a bitch.

That's her throwing the first punch and my jaw goes tight.
That annoys me. Feel defensive of Jordan. Pretty sure she's
actually just trying to be a good friend in a fucking weird way.

> Don't call her that.

> You're defending her?

> Yes.

Why?

Because—

I glare over at her for a second before looking back down at my phone and taking a swing.

we're dating.

I know.

Parks's eyes are pinched, waiting for my reply.
I deliver the next hit.

And you don't have a fucking leg to stand on because you're dating Julian.

And then, in true Magnolia Parks fashion, she delivers the fatal blow:

*Fucking.

Fuck me, I could nearly double over from that one. I blink wide a few times. Stare at my phone. My jaw's gone tight. I nod once at her from across the pool and her eyes already look full of regret and it gives me a tiny shot of relief that some things never change.

Right

Right.

It's about to get ugly.
She's digging her heels into the ground, ready for the push back. I'm winding my arm up like Popeye.
I can feel it in me.

We're about to go UFC on each other where there are no rules except eye gouging, only I know she'd eye gouge me any fucking day of the week to win. Christian was an eye gouge. Dating Tom was an eye gouge. Moving to New York was an eye gouge. Jack-Jack Cavan was an eye gouge.

Fucking Jules is a fucking eye gouge.

And I'm about to get up and go hook up with Jordan in the spa in front of her when Henry, Christian and the girls dander up from the lake.

"Dinner?" Daisy asks everyone brightly, and thank God for the only Haites I like.

Daisy cooks. Huntsman Pies, insanely good.

I'm going to enroll Parks into cooking classes.

Can't imagine that going down too well if I'm honest, but worth a shot.

Afterwards, everyone piles into (one of) the living rooms to watch something. Christian suggests a horror film and all the girls veto it, even though I love watching scary films with Parks, because she holds on to me when she's scared, but then I realise she'd be holding on to someone else.

We land on *Jurassic Park*, because it's pretty much the greatest film of all time.

We watch the film. I watch Parks.

After, everyone's falling asleep except for me and Magnolia, because we've done this before. Know the drill. Know how to be alone in a house where that should be an impossibility.

Everyone peters off to bed.

Parks gets up, catches my eye and goes to the kitchen.

She doesn't know how to clean. I know how to clean, though.

Julian follows her in.

Jordan looks up at me tiredly.

"You go up to bed, I'm going to give them a hand—" I nod in their direction.

"Okay." She yawns, stretching her arms up over her head.

"I'll be up in a minute," I tell her, hoping it's a lie.

I walk into the kitchen and Julian's in the doorway on the phone, holding up a finger at her saying he'll be one minute.

Picture of chivalry.

He glances over at me, nods with his chin, mouths, "You good?"

Parks looks up at me.

"I'll give her a hand." I nod towards Parks. "You take your call."

Julian looks from me to Parks, juts his mouth out a bit and then shrugs.

"Better you cleaning than me, man."

He walks over to her, slips one hand around her waist and the other behind her head. Kisses the shit out of her. She goes pink as he does it.

"Wake me up when you come up," he tells her.

She goes pinker. Nods.

He walks towards the door but turns back around.

"You watch those hands, Ballentine." He points at me. "I know how I left her."

She tilts her head at him, rolls her eyes embarrassed.

I give him one curt nod and he leaves.

I look over at her, eyes wide, heart racing.

"Wow."

She swats her hands, embarrassed.

"He's just territorial . . ."

I scoff. "He's an arsehole is what he is."

She gives me a look and I cock my head in his direction.

"As if that doesn't bother you."

"Not really," she says quietly, her nose in the air. And I can't tell if she's lying. "It's nice to be needed sometimes."

She moves a pile of plates over to the sink and my heart does the same.

I stare over at her, wonder what she means.

I bring over some cups. She's running the water, filling up the basin.

I give her a look. "You want to be needed for that?" I tell her as I move her by the waist away from the sink, taking over.

There's a dishwasher by the way, obviously. Don't want to use it. Want a reason to be close to her.

I hand her a tea towel, though I'll die of shock if she knows what to do with it. She glances up at me, frowning.

She gives me this weak shrug that crushes me for some reason. "Better than nothing,"

"Are you joking?" I shake my head at her. "Is that what all this shit is about? Fuck, Parks, I need you for that—"

Her face strains. "Ah, well, that's not strictly true is it, Beej?" She bites down on her bottom lip, looking serious. "Paili, Jordan—"

I lick my bottom lip. "You can't hold Paili over me forever."

"Says who?" She gives me a proud, defiant look.

"Besides." She shrugs as though the conversation's not killing her. "You've found lots of other people to fulfil that need."

I shake my head at her, solemnly. "No, I haven't."

I've tried. I've tried a thousand different people a thousand different ways. It's not the same. I pass her a plate to dry.

She wraps the towel around it. Holds it as she gives me a little heartbroken stare. "I'm sorry, but I don't believe you."

My jaw goes tight and I shake my head more. I don't know how to tell her that it's true, I don't want anyone but her, she's the only thing on this whole fucking planet that I need and I'd marry her right now here on the spot if I could work out how to be good enough for her.

But instead I pass her another plate to dry, and she blinks down at it.

"What do I do with this?"

I sniff a laugh, take it and the tea towel offer.

"Swap with me," I tell her. Then nod at the sink of dishes. "The goal is to wash the food residue off the plates."

She flicks her eyes at me, washes a couple of plates so badly I make a note of putting them in the dishwasher after she's gone to bed.

She purses her lips and peers over at me.

"I think about the stairs a lot. At Varley."

I look over at her. "Since the other night?"

She shakes her head. "Before that too."

Potter's bedroom, we used to call it. Pretty hard to find time alone in a boarding school, but the cupboard under the stairs up to her dorm room worked like a treat. No one ever knew.

I swallow.

"What about it?"

"About how we'd sneak away whenever we could and as much as we could. We were so in love, so doe-eyed about it . . ." She bites down on her bottom lip how I wish I was doing. "Feels embarrassing now, kind of stupid—" Her eyes fall from mine. "I would have done anything for you. Cheated for you, lied for you. I would have died for you. I think maybe I kind of did."

"Parks—" I barely say because I'm choked up.

"Did you ever imagine it?" she cuts me off. "That we'd be the ones who'd hurt each other more than anyone else?"

Fuck.

I shake my head. "No," I say too quietly.

She sucks her lip now. Nods.

"Sad, isn't it?"

I drop the plate I'm drying on the bench, turn her body to face mine.

"We could stop."

"How?" she interrupts. "Tell me how and I'll do it."

I sigh, give her a measured look. "Break up with him. Be the first to wave the white flag."

She shakes her head, looks at me like I've lost the plot.

"No."

"Why no?" I frown. Then she looks at me how a wounded animal might look at a person approaching it and I take a stab at it, nodding before I even say it. "You don't trust me."

Her face pulls tight. "How could I trust you?"

I shake my head at her.

"I'd die for you."

"That, I believe." She nods. "I too trust you with my life."

"Just not your heart." I sigh it out.

She nods slowly. "Just not my heart."

"What—fuck. Magnolia—" I shove my hands through my hair. "What the fuck are we supposed to do?"

She gives me a weak shrug, breathes out an old sadness she carries for me.

"Just keep on doing the dance, I suppose."

She walks towards me. Kisses my cheek. Properly kisses it, lips to cheek, hovers, breathes on me—what I would do to her on that dining room table in her boyfriend's house if I wasn't trying to be a better man . . .

I let her. Close my eyes. Let it make me feel everything Jordan hasn't made me feel ever.

Breathe her in.

Beg her to marry me fifty times in a second but I can't out loud because Parks doesn't trust me and I don't think I'm good enough anyway. I don't think there's anything I can do to make her trust me other than time, and I'll give her all of mine, I don't care about that. I'm not even worried if we never get off this track, I don't care, I'll stay on it forever with her. I am worried, though, that she'll figure it out and get off it without me.

She pulls away from me and as she does, I slip my heart in her back pocket.

That's a lie. She already had it. But I give it to her again for good measure.

She gives me a sad smile, nods her head up towards the bedrooms.

"Back to the salt mines."

I scratch the back of my neck.

"Do me a favour?"

She tilts her head, nods. "Yeah?"

"Don't wake him up."

SIXTY-ONE
Magnolia

Julian was a bit funny that I didn't wake him when I came up.

I suspect he knew the reason had to with BJ and not the reason I gave him ("You looked so sweet sleeping there.")

He didn't say much about it, he just gave me a look I didn't completely understand and kissed me and then jumped into the shower with me—making up for lost time last night, I suppose.

It was hard to do that with BJ in the house.

I feel like we're too connected, like he can hear my thoughts. He'd know what I was doing, feel it in the air, see it on me after.

And I have fun with Julian, and he's very good at what he does—but kissing BJ on his cheek last night was my favourite thing that's happened since BJ gave me my necklace back.

Julian went out for a bit after we were done. He said he had some work he had to do. I don't know what that means, but it did blow my afternoon wide open.

The house is quiet.

Christian and Daisy are off being the cutest couple in the world, Henry's on the lake with Taura and (weirdly) separately, Jonah's on the lake with Bianca.

I don't know where BJ is. Around, I hope.

We've always had a knack for stealing moments away with one another.

I wander downstairs and check the living room. Nothing. Then the dining room. Nothing.

I peer out to the pool. Nowhere.

Probably he's with Jordan, but I poke my head around a few corners just for good measure. And then in the corner of the house, in one of the more secluded living rooms, I find him—watching National Geographic.

I stand in the doorway and just gaze at him for a second.

Bare-chested and only wearing the harmony print knitted track pants by The Elder Statesman and the Dip Yosemite socks that match adorably well. One arm stretched up behind his head. On his iPhone, biting down on his lip. My whole stomach flip-flops just watching him. I love watching him. It's my favourite pastime. I used to lose hours just following him around from room to room at the weekends. How he'd butter his toast, how he'd drink from the carton, how he'd bite an apple, how he'd hug his mum. The way he'd hold his phone, the way he'd spin the remote on his index finger. The way he'd open a door. I loved the way he'd sit, the way he'd lean, where his hands would fall—and that was just the mundane things. Never you mind what it was like to watch him swim at school or play rugby. Him on a skateboard, him climbing things he shouldn't, him driving a car—

He glances over and sees me, the corner of his mouth lifting into a little smile.

"Hey." His eyes fall down me.

I'm not in much. Brushed leopard jacquard-knit turtleneck sweater from Dolce & Gabbana and the Cashmere In Love ribbed Mimie shorts.

"Hi." I stay by the door.

He pats down once on the couch next to him and I walk over.

"What are you doing?" I ask as I sit.

He nods his chin at the TV before peeking out the corner of his eye. "Where's Jules?"

"Working." I shrug.

He frowns. "On holidays?"

I shrug again. "Where's Jordan?"

He pauses the TV. "Shopping."

435

"Right." I nod.

He squints over at me for a second. "Did you wake him?"

I barely meet his eyes as I shake my head. "No, not last night."

He sniffs a sad little laugh. "An interesting clarification there."

I swallow. "I don't like lying to you."

His head falls back and he sighs as he covers his face. "You and me having sex with other people in the same house—who'd have thought it?" He looks over at me, tries to smile but just blows some air out of his mouth. "Worst sentence I've ever said."

It is. I hate it and I don't know what to say so I just look over at the TV. "Which one are you watching?"

"One of the ones on polar bears." He unpauses it.

"Oh!" I tuck my feet under me. "I love this one."

He looks over at me for a few seconds. "I know."

I let my hand fall down in the space between us, it's mindless and I rest it there, but BJ notices.

His eyes flicker down towards it and then he lets his own hand fall next to mine.

The backs of our hands touch and I freeze because touching him even in the smallest way is electric.

His hands are always so warm and I love his hands anyway, I always have. They've always been big but not grubby. Long fingers, not too skinny though, not too square, not too rounded, just strong hands that have held me through everything this life has ever thrown at me.

And then those hands that I love, that I think about touching my body every day, in my hair, on my face, under my pillow, those hands shift ever so slightly and his pinky finger links with mine.

I swallow heavy and clear my throat.

A smile breezes over his face as he stares straight ahead.

I purse my lips and don't move my hand an inch as I say, "Did we start watching these before or after we did it?"

Looks over at me, brows low, almost like he's offended.

436

"After."

"Oh." I nod at the TV. Then I look at him squinting. "Why was I talking about the bees then?"

His mouth cracks open into a proper grin and his eyes flicker over my face. "You were in the Congo the week before, remember? With your family."

"Oh! Yes—" I nod. "Mum's Jane Goodall phase."

My mother's been through many phases, as we all know. The Jane Goodall one was one of the more wholesome ones.

Beej's eyes go soft and he nods a few times. "Jane Goodall told you about the bees . . ."

I smile and make a little 'hm' sound, happy and content both to be here and to be wandering down memory lane.

It was the longest we'd been apart since we got together, that trip, and it wasn't all that long. Just ten days or thereabouts, but for me at the ripe old age of fifteen, being away from BJ for that long, I might as well have been a POW. I begged for him to be able to come and my mother actually said yes, but then Marsaili convinced her that BJ and I were spending too much time together.

"Every waking moment!" Marsaili said and I made a sound at the back of my throat and said, "That's hardly my fault, is it? I didn't send me away to boarding school to live with my boyfriend."

She rolled her eyes. "We didn't send you away to boarding school to live with your boyfriend! You don't live w— You go to boarding school and your boyfriend happens to be there also."

"Lily said BJ could come!"

"And I'm saying you need some space from him," Marsaili said. That was final.

It probably seeded in me then and there that I would instead, in fact, have anti-space. I cried when I told him she'd said he couldn't come, because I was dramatic like that but also because it felt unfair to me, that they'd force my hand to make me make my own family and then pull me away from him when they wanted me back.

He was sunny as always, it rolled right off him that he wasn't allowed to come. (Also filed under: because he doesn't need me.) He just kissed me a lot, told me it would be a breeze and I'd have Bridget and we'd have fun while we were away and then when we got back . . . he didn't say it, he just gave me a look.

Sex had been the topic for a while by then and when I went over to BJ's that Sunday night to tell him that Marsaili said he couldn't come, the Mandarin plan came to life as a bit of a 'fuck you' to her.

"What a bitch that she didn't let me come," BJ says sort of out of the blue and I crack up.

"I think she was just scared by how much I . . . you know?" 'Love him' is the end of that sentence. Present tense, not past. Always present-tense loving him. Marsaili always found it concerning. With good reason in the end, I suppose.

"Yeah." He nods, swallowing. "I don't know if I ever told you this—" He laughs once, shaking his head. "What Mr Kincaid said to me?"

I shake my head.

I'd arrived home from the Congo in the wee hours of Friday morning, so my mother had said Bridget and I didn't need to go to school, but I had one of the drivers bring me up anyway because I was just so excited to see BJ.

"You came to my last class, remember?" He smiles thinking about it. "You were in this sleeveless dress. Way too cold for March—"

I'd learned immediately upon dating BJ that were I to under-dress and be cold, he'd either be forced to hug me or give me his sweaters—sometimes both—and I loved both outcomes.

"Standing outside the classroom on your tiptoes to look through the window . . ."

"Mr Ballentine," Mr Kincaid said with a sigh, noticing BJ staring at me through the window as I waved excitedly. "Eyes up front, please."

Mr Kincaid was the boys' favourite teacher at Varley and the Housemaster of Carver.

"Can I just duck out for a sec, sir?" BJ asked brightly.

"No," Mr Kincaid said, flicking his eyes over at me.

"Sir, but Parks is outside. We haven't seen each other in, like, ten days."

"Mr Ballentine, you're hardly war-torn lovers, and this is science not social studies."

He gave BJ a little look.

"Is it . . ." BJ lifted his eyebrows playfully ". . . chemistry, by chance?"

"BJ, if you don't know the answer to that question yourself then I have failed you," he said and the class laughed as he tried to go on with the lesson.

'SAY YOU'RE GOING TO THE BATHROOM' I mouthed to BJ as he began mouthing back, 'JUST GO TO YOUR ROOM.' More pointing. 'I'LL SEE YOU IN YOUR ROOM.'

"Magnolia." Mr Kincaid poked his head out of the doorway.

"Oh—" I jumped. "Hello, sir."

He glanced down at me in my Spring 2014 RTW Chanel pastel-multi-coloured tweed dress. "And where is your uniform?"

I shook my head at him. "I'm absent today."

"Evidently not." Kincaid lifted a brow. "You are distracting my class by standing outside my door." He walked back inside his room and I peered in after him. "Do come in, Magnolia, and please be quiet."

I beamed over at him and then darted to BJ, who pushed back from his table and patted his lap just in time for Kincaid to turn on his heel and eye me down. "And do, for the love of God, sit in your own chair."

I gave him a curt smile and sat down next to BJ. He slipped his hand into mine immediately, kissed it three times, stole my heart forever with the quarter-smile he gave me, et cetera et cetera.

"Alright everybody—can anyone tell me what Newton's second law is?"

My hand shot straight up. Mr Kincaid's face faltered for a moment.

"Magno—"

"F = MA." He frowned at me even though I know I was right. "Force equals mass times acceleration."

"Correct." He nodded, smiling at me before turning to the class. "Multiplying MA in the equation means we're multiplying the units, so the units of F becomes—"

"—Kilogram metres per second squared," I jumped in again. BJ's eyes flicked over at me proudly.

Mr Kincaid titled his head. "Also known as?"

"KG times m/s/s."

He nodded once. "Also known as?"

"Newtons." I gave him a tiny smile and he crossed his arms over his chest.

"Aren't you in Year Eleven?" Araminta Bachman asked me, annoyed.

"Yeah, so?" I glared over at her.

She rolled her eyes, I rolled mine.

"Alright—" Mr Kincaid looked between us, still a bit amused. "Moving on."

After about thirty minutes, the bell rang and BJ was up on his feet and grabbing my hand, pulling me out of the classroom.

"Bye, sir!" I called back to him. "Thank you so much, excellent lesson! I really enjoyed how y—" And then BJ grabbed my face with both hands and pressed me up against the wall outside the classroom, kissing me in a way where the entire student body went balmy.

"Mr Ballentine—" Kincaid rolled his eyes, arms crossed again.

And BJ, he didn't stop kissing me, didn't slow down at all, he—if you can believe it, and I'm sure you can—held up a finger for his teacher to wait.

"And that's a detention." Mr Kincaid nodded.

BJ grinned against my mouth, one more big kiss that felt embarrassing because there was obvious tongue and then three little ones, and my cheeks were on fire but who was I to stop the love of my life kissing me like that?

"Yeah." Beej nodded. "Fair call. That's all good, just not this weekend, yeah?" He looked over at his teacher with a smile.

"Oh?" Mr Kincaid lifted an eyebrow. "Sorry, do you have other plans?"

"I do, yep." BJ nodded, throwing an arm around me.

"And what might those be?"

"Well, sir—" I stood extra tall. "We're going to have sex for the first time."

BJ smacked his mouth with his hand to stop himself from laughing.

"Oh." Mr Kincaid's eyes went wide, nodding. "Okay, right. I hate that. Hate it—" He shook his head. "Hate that you said it so merrily too, God." He pulled a face like he'd tasted something sour. "Are you sure you're ready?"

"As ready as I'll ever be!" I beamed.

Mr Kincaid didn't look so sure. "You strike me as a bit young . . ."

"Sir—" I snorted a laugh at him like he was crazy. "You're so funny. Anyway, I've got to go grab my Paddington Bear from my dorm room—"

Kincaid's eyes went wider as BJ nodded as I turned and walked down the hall.

"See you Monday, sir!" I called back to him with a merry wave. "Have a great weekend!"

"After you left," BJ smirks over at me on the couch in Italy, "he asked if I'd used a condom before."

My jaw falls open. "He did not."

"Yeah." Beej laughs. "Gave me a lesson and everything. He was like, 'Have you ever used . . .?' And I said no, and he nodded back into the room and sighed and was like, 'okay, come on then.'"

"Oh my God!" I laugh.

441

"He had me practise on a stapler." He laughs, shaking his head. "He was a good guy."

I like how his face goes when we talk about being young. Like all the pain and trauma and shit we've put each other through lifts for a minute and his face looks how it lives in my mind anyway.

"I was going to postpone it—" He chews down on his bottom lip, remembering.

"Postpone what?" I frown.

He shrugs. "Us. Doing that."

"Were you?" I pull back, a bit surprised. "Why?"

"I don't know—" He stares down at our hands still touching. "I was nervous."

"Really?" I blink. "Because of—?" My voice trails.

He shrugs. "Maybe. I wasn't thinking about it much then, buried it pretty deep, but I'm sure that was a bit of it. And then just, like, I think I knew. You know what I mean?"

I shake my head. "Like I had a sense that we'd do that and then we wouldn't be kids anymore."

"Oh." I feel a tiny bit sad at that.

"I loved being a kid with you." He smiles over at me. "I was going to tell you before I saw you that I thought we should wait. But then I saw you."

I swallow heavy. "What happened when you saw me?"

He shrugs.

"I saw you." He squashes a smile. "You were so brown. You know how I get when you're brown—"

"I do." I nod, blushing. "Though I'm sorry you did it if you weren't ready—"

"I'm not." He shakes his head. "Probably my favourite night of my life up to then—"

"And then after that?"

"Dartmouth and the lock." Beej nods his head towards my stomach. "And then probably us at the tree last year—"

"Are all your favourite nights with me?" I ask him.

"Yeah." He nods without thinking. "Why? What are yours?"

With him. Of course with him. All my best nights, all my worst ones, all are with him and I wonder if this is the point. This is what I'm swimming towards: not just in love with him but a whole wonderful, terrifying, beautiful, painful life with him.

I purse my lips. "I love the ones you said. I loved the day you gave me your family crest—" I give him an apologetic smile for throwing it away. "I really loved the night after we first had sex."

"Why?" He laughs, confused.

"Because we weren't nervous anymore." I shrug. "And it was so fun and new and I loved sneaking around with you." Our eyes graze and my heart casts a line out to him.

It catches and I swallow heavy.

He nods his chin over at me. "Want to make another favourite night soon?"

I straighten up a bit. "We could make one right now."

He gives me a gentle smile and shakes his head.

I nod once then move my hand away from his, placing it in my lap and his shoulders fall.

"You don't want me to, Parks—" He shakes his head. "That's not how you want me."

"I just want you, Beej." I shrug. "But my wanting you has never really been the question."

"Has it not?" he fires back and I sigh and stand up and start to walk out of the room.

"Off to find Jules then?" he calls after me.

"So what if I am?" I spin on my foot.

"You're so fucking predictable—" He looks away. "We fight for a second and you run off to someone else."

"Well, what would you have me do?" I ask, my voice a bit shaky.

"Stay, Parks!" he says loudly. "Just fucking stay."

I stare over at him and he over at me and it's like we're both lost at sea on different pieces of driftwood and the tide is pulling us in different directions.

"I'm back," Jordan announces from behind me.

I turn around quickly to face her, flashing a smile.

"Oh, hi." I quickly wipe a tear away.

She frowns a bit, glancing from me over to BJ and then back to me.

"Are you okay?" she asks, tilting her head confused.

"Yeah—" I shrug quickly. "Just, a polar bear died."

"Oh." She looks sad about that. "How?"

I purse my lips. "Drowned. It was far out in the ocean. It couldn't make it . . ." BJ stares over at me, eyes heavy. "I'm going to go upstairs and pack."

I hear Jordan say as I walk away, "Wow. She's really into polar bears."

SIXTY-TWO
Magnolia

"So where's the step-monster?" Julian asks brightly. My father frowns at me.

I laugh uncomfortably. "That's not—I don't call her that. That was a—he made that up, not me—"

Julian presses the tip of his tongue into his top lip to keep himself from laughing and Harley rolls his eyes.

"Believe it or not," my sister pipes up, "she's not all that excited to meet the gang lord who's shagging her daughter."

I grab his wrist and flash him a smile. He's so handsome.

"Don't take that personally." I wave my hand dismissively. "She wasn't over the moon when I was shagging Tom England either, and that's Tom England, who couldn't be less of a gang lord if he tried. Plus you're much more her cup of tea sexually."

My sister chokes on her wine a little and Julian frowns, saying nothing.

"How's that now?" my father asks.

"Well—" I give him an impatient look as I undo the buttons of Julian's Stone Island Shadow Project black bomber jacket because it looks better that way and tug at the Kiton white T-shirt underneath it so it sits how it should.

"Every time a swarthy man comes on a screen who has this sort of dark, golden-y hair with the deep-blue eyes she makes all sorts of noises."

"Oh. Good." Harley rolls his eyes.

I give him an uncomfortable smile. "That's unideal for you as her husband, as a black man with brown hair and brown eyes."

"Yeah, a bit."

I nod sympathetically and give him a shrug.

"You're pretty swarthy though, mate," Julian offers him and that sends Bridget over laugher's edge.

We're having dinner at Julie's in Notting Hill. My sister's suggestion, if you can believe it, and she's not in jeans for once in her bloody life. The Beatles Get Back intarsia cotton sweater from Stella McCartney and the Burberry vintage check tailored trousers—busy but good, actually. She's warming to Julian, I could tell when we walked in. For one, she's making an effort. When he kissed her cheek she flushed a little—which is hardly her fault, what with the sparkly eyes and the jawline I could grate cheese on.

Julian and my father catch up, talking about an American rapper they both know and dislike. Bridget leans over the table to me.

"These aren't terrible." She pokes my plaid-check print shorts from Philosophy Di Lorenzo Serafini.

"Holy fucking shit." I stare over at her. "Was that a compliment about my outfit?"

"I compliment you," she tells me with a frown that I match when I stare down at her feet.

"Why are the buckles on your shoes so large?"

"I don't know, Magnolia." She scowls. "I didn't fucking cobble them myself."

I keep staring at them. "Shoes are a real problem area for you, aren't they?"

She rolls her eyes. "I take it back, I hate your shorts."

"No you don't. They're lovely."

She ignores me. "How was Italy?"

I glance at Julian. "Good."

"Anything interesting happen?"

"Um—" I consider the question. "We did it in a steam room? I blacked out again."

She frowns at me. "What's the matter with you?"

"Nothing. I think it was just the combination of the heat and the mo—"

"No, you twat," she growls, gaze flicking from me to Julian and back to me. "You had sex with him while BJ was in the same house?" She shakes her head at me. "What the fuck are you doing?"

"He did it too." I give her a look.

Her face softens but she still rolls her eyes.

"He said we could stop," I tell her as I glance at Julian to make sure he's not listening, "if I waved the white flag first."

"What did you say?"

"I said no."

Her face falls.

I lower my whisper to a quieter one still. "I told him I loved him, I had sex with him—" I shake my head. "I waved the flag. He took it from my hands and used it as a blanket to have sex upon with Jordan."

Bridget sighs.

"How is this ever going to resolve?" She sighs.

I shrug, my nose in the air. "Maybe it won't."

Even the thought of that feels like a wave knocking me over and under the water. Like something in me is choking, kicking to the surface for an air that I can't reach.

"Sorry—" Marsaili sighs. My mother and grandmother in toe. Julian stands to greet them. He extends his hand to my mother.

"Well—" My mother's chin drops to her chest as she eyes Julian blearily. "Look at you!"

She takes his hand, yanks him towards her and kisses him merrily on the mouth. His eyes go wide and his face still.

"Mother!" I jump up.

Julian pulls back a bit, surprised, but mostly unbothered. "Alright."

"They're both drunk." Marsaili blinks. "Completely sauced."

I eye her. "I should think so—"

"My turn!" Bushka comes in with her two hands towards Julian's face.

"No, no!" I fend her off, shielding him from my grandmother's kissy face.

447

"Would you look at you!" Mum says, staring at Julian. She sloshes down into a chair. We didn't know she was coming so it's not her chair, it's just a chair she's pinched from the table next to ours.

I give them an apologetic smile. "Every family has one . . ."

And regrettably, all of England knows who ours is.

"You must be Julian—" Marsaili extends her hand.

He shakes it with both of his, smiling warmly.

"The infamous Marsaili." He gives her his best smile. "You're much less terrifying than Magnolia described you."

She gives him a pinched look. "You'd be surprised."

He chuckles. "No. Wouldn't fancy my chances with you in a dark alley—" He glances at my mum playfully. "Or you, but maybe for different reasons."

Harley and Bridge eat that right up. Mum's thrilled.

"God—" She shakes her head. "If I was a few years younger."

I give her a look.

"Or perhaps, you know, he and I weren't together . . ."

Both Bridget and Julian look over at me.

His eyebrows are a bit up, and his face is doing a terrible job of concealing his surprise.

My cheeks go pink.

"You know what I mean," I mumble.

"Anyway," Marsaili says, clearing her throat and trying to throw me a line, "you two know each other—" She points to Julian and my father.

"Through work." Julian nods.

I grab Marsaili's arm quickly. "Fear not—we are not from dirty money. Well, actually . . ." I think for a second. "You're not from any money, really, you just married in, so . . ."

Julian presses a knuckle into his mouth, suppresses a laugh.

"Do you know what I will say though, Harley." I look over at him. "Their house in Italy is much bigger than ours."

"We don't have a house in Italy," Bridget tells me.

I nod, unimpressed. "Much to my point."

She rolls her eyes.

Mum beckons over the waiter and waves her hand around the table.

"Should we get some vodka for the table?"

Bridget squints over at her.

"Table vodka?" My sister blinks.

"Mm." Our mother nods and smiles.

Jules watches her for a second and I think I see his face soften a little, like he's sad for her. Then he nods emphatically.

"Absolutely. A bottle of your best table vodka."

He looks over at me, gives me a small wink.

My mother bats her eyes over at him and I wonder if we should be worried. Mum's been quite a figure on the London party scene lately. It's not my favourite phase of hers. I much preferred it when she went through the Goop phase. It was more wholesome. There was a lot of hemp around the place, a bit too much flaxseed for my liking, but a lot of organic wine. That was nice. Always sandalwood burning.

This party phase, it's messy and it feels to me like she's trying to prove to everyone that she's having fun, but I suspect she isn't really having any. She's partying harder than the best of us. And she's always partied some, her and my father. The reason we even hired Marsaili in the first place was so they could party hard and not come home sometimes without being charged with parental negligence. Mum usually goes hard on her birthday weekend, maybe a few other times throughout the year, but this feels different. Constant. I have the niggling suspicion that this is all rooted in some kind of sadness about losing my father.

I don't really understand it.

I don't know that I'd ever have looked at them as being genuinely in love, but maybe I know less than I think I do. Or maybe she's reckoning with the fact that it just never stops feeling terribly impossible to watch someone who once was yours be with someone else.

After dinner, Julian comes back to my place. He sits on the edge of my Art Deco-style mid-century Italian bed I bought recently from La Maison London. I don't often like antiques, but I suppose Julian's been rubbing off on me so when we were wandering around their London showroom, I had to have it or else I might have died.

His fingers are pressed into his mouth. He's squinting over at me as I take off my Serpent Bohème ring from Boucheron and I press the bow necklace into my chest, try to feel closer to BJ than I am right now. Then take it off me too because I feel weird wearing it to bed with Julian.

I think about BJ's crest ring a lot still, the one I threw away at the Mandarin on that night. I shouldn't have done that. It was his dad's before it was his, I should have at least given it back to Henry to give to Hamish.

It wasn't mine to lose like that. And there are a million ways I could spin that, say that I wasn't BJ's to break and he broke me, but I was.

I was, I am. And he has.

"Together, huh?" Julian nods at me from my bed, interrupting my sad little reverie.

"No, sorry—" I shake my head, embarrassed instantly. "I know. You don't date."

He nods once. "I don't."

I shake my head as I press my hands into my cheeks, trying not to let him know I'm embarrassed.

"I didn't mean it like that."

His eyes squint and he glances over at me. "How did you mean it then?"

I shrink a little. "Sorry."

"You're in love with someone else," he reminds me.

"I know." I frown.

"So how the fuck might we be together, then?" He stares over, jaw all tight but rather sexy.

"Are you cross at me?" I ask after a minute in a very small voice.

"A bit." He glares over at me.

I cross my arms over my chest. "Why?"

450

"I don't know." He gives me a dirty look. "Because you're so fucking annoying. What do you want? Do you know what you want? Because it's everything and it's nothing." I say nothing and he swipes his hand through the air. "You're just a right fucking pain in the arse."

"That was a bit mean . . ." I pout a little.

And then Julian rushes me, grabs my face with both hands and kisses me backwards into my chest of drawers.

I make a little yelp because the draw knob digs into my back, but he ignores it.

"What are you doing?" I ask, not stopping him.

"This, with you," he says as he unzips my black and white, off-the-shoulder two-tone crepe minidress from Balmain.

I pull back to look at him quizzically. "Now?" He unbuttons his own C-embroidered cotton-poplin shirt from Celine Homme.

"Why?" I frown at him, confused.

He looks down at me, breathing heavy as he pushes his hand through my hair. "Because this—" he stares at me to make a point—"is what we do."

He kisses me again, hard. And then pulls back and points at me threateningly. "And don't you dare fucking think of me—"

I let out a confused laugh. "I'll try my best?"

He kisses me more as he lays me down on the bed.

"We're not together," he tells me as he looks down at me.

I give him a look. "This feels like a mixed message . . .?"

He shakes his head, hovering over me. "You love him. I love no one. Yeah?"

I shrug, a bit confused. "Okay?"

"Okay." He nods and drops his weight on me.

SIXTY-THREE

BJ

"How's it going, finding a place?" I look over at Jordan as she lies on my bed, feet kicking in the air watching the soccer with me.

"Good, actually." She glances back. "Claudia found a place she likes in Paddington."

"Oh, good," I tell her and she holds my eyes, an emotion flickering over her face that I can't place.

"You done with me?" she asks, smiling a bit.

Nothing on my face falters but my eyebrow.

"I'm joking!" She laughs, smacking my leg.

I shift on the bed, lie down on my side next to her, rest my head on my hand.

"We probably need to have a chat."

She rolls her eyes a little. "You're in love with another woman."

"Very much so." I nod once before I give her a grimace.

She gives me an amused smile. "It's hardly breaking news."

I sigh. "I wondered if you knew."

Her face pulls, unimpressed. "Did you also wonder if I knew that trees are green?"

I give her a look and she matches it.

"Jords, why did you stay? If you knew." I frown a little, trying to figure it out.

"Because you're fun."

She gives me a playful shove. "It was fun being your girl-friend—" She pauses and pulls a face. "Most of the time."

I roll onto my back, covering my face. "I've felt so shit—"

"You should, you wanker! Using me like that—" She punches me in the arm. "Lucky for you, I was using you too."

I give her a curious look and she shrugs lightly.

"My followers have tripled since we've been together."

I roll my eyes. "Henry was right."

She rolls onto her back too, staring up at the ceiling.

"Mmhm." She nods, flashing me a smile. "He's a really good judge of character," she says, tossing her phone up and catching it again.

"I felt had at first, but then I checked your iPhone's search history back in December."

My face pulls uncomfortably.

"I did like you—" She nudges me and I let out a bewildered laugh. "Like, when we first met."

"Oh, thanks." I toss her a sarcastic look.

She ignores me.

"I was running away from some shit that happened back in Sydney, and when I met you, I kind of thought—cool, this is probably it—we'll be together. You have like, a thing about you—" She stares over at me. I frown, waiting for her. "Like a, you save people, thing."

I sniff, a bit chuffed.

"And it was so fun being wanted by someone like you. It was such a good feeling. To walk into a room with you, the way people would look at me." She lifts her shoulders up merrily at the thought. "I loved it. And then I saw you with Magnolia—" She gives me a bit of a grimace. "And I thought—well, fuck. That's what it looks like when he loves you."

My face pulls sorry. "I should have just ended it the night I told you I slept with her."

She considers this. "I probably should have ended it the night you told me you slept with her."

I laugh.

"I had fun." She shrugs.

I nod. "Me too."

453

I eye her for a second. "What's going on with you and that DJ?"

She starts laughing.

"I don't know."

She shrugs. "We had sex once and then he was scared you'd find out and have him blacklisted from all the good clubs."

I cock an eyebrow playfully. "Might do. What's his name again?"

"Jett." She flicks me a look. "And you won't."

"Are you into him?"

She stretched her arms up over her head. "Don't know. We'll see."

I stare over at her, my head spinning a bit. A good spinning, but still spinning. "I'm sorry," I tell her. I mean it.

She reaches over and pushes her hand through my hair. "We're good." She rolls back onto her stomach and keeps watching the TV. "I'm also not moving out yet because I don't have anywhere to go."

"Right then," I laugh.

And then we hear the front door close. Voices fill the house.

"Oi," I say, flashing them all a collective smile as I get to the top of the stairs.

Magnolia looks over at me, eyes wide and bright, happy to see me.

I want to take her hand, pull her to the side, tell her I'm done, that we don't have to do this anymore, but then Julian wraps his arms around her waist and pulls her away from the window she's perched on and onto his lap.

Jordan sidles up next to me, catches my eye before she rests her head on my shoulder.

"We've been imagining how different our days at Varley would have been if Uber Eats had existed," Magnolia tells me, holding my eyes.

Julian rolls his eyes. "Not that fucking different, because what was there to Uber Eats out in Kent fifteen years ago?"

Magnolia eyes him. "Not all of us are practically geriatrics, Julian."

454

Jordan looks over at him, interested. "You went to their school too."

He nods. "Few years ahead."

Daisy rolls her eyes. "More than a few."

"You were in Upper Sixth when we were started Year Seven," Christian tells him.

Julian rolls his eyes, not loving the conversation.

I like it though.

I remember him from school. Felt a bit like a god. He was so good at rugby. People used to compare me to him when I started to play. That was a good feeling because he was the best. He *was* the best. Then I came along and I was better.

"Gross," Daisy says, recognising her brother's discomfort. "So when she was eleven, you were eighteen." She pulls a face.

"We weren't naffing then!" Julian says, proper annoyed now.

Magnolia laughs and stands up, points to the kitchen. "Wine?"

She doesn't wait for anyone to agree, she just walks on in. She's leaning against the kitchen bench when I walk in after her.

"Need a hand?" I ask loudly to cover my tracks. She doesn't. She knows where to find it.

She's not in here for the wine. She's in here because she knows I'll follow her. I'll always follow her.

She stares over at me, eyes heavy. I have this impulse just to tell her now, but it's not how I want to do it. I want to tell her by ourselves, just us. Dunstan's, maybe? I wonder if I could get her to take a drive with me this week? Maybe up to Dartmouth together. So I say nothing, even though I want to say everything and bite down on my lip to keep quiet. Shove my hands through my hair and walk towards her.

Pull out her favourite rosé from the wine fridge that she's standing in front of, have to move her legs to the side to get to it. Grateful for the chance to graze them, even if it's just for a half a second. Pour her a glass. Hand it to her.

"Good top." I nod at the grey one she's wearing.

She looks down at herself, pleased. "You like it?"

I nod once. "Love it, actually."

She looks up at me, eyes a bit startled but I hold them anyway. Hope she gets my point.

Her mouth falls open a bit. I think about just kissing her—I could do it. She wouldn't stop me. I'm in the clear. Maybe I will. I take a step towards her—

Then there's a knock on the doorframe. Both of us look over to Julian filling it.

He glances between us, frowning. Doesn't look angry how I thought he might. He does look something though.

"Hey—" She smiles big, pushes past me to get to him.

"I gotta go," he says, waves his phone. "Work thing came up."

"Oh." She frowns. "Okay. I'll come?"

"No—" He shakes his head quickly. "No, um, you stay here. I'll leave Kekoa. He'll take you home."

Kekoa. Julian's main bodyguard. That's weird.

"Oh, no." She shakes her head airily. "I'll just grab a taxi."

"No," Julian says, sharper than he meant to, I reckon. Catches it, touches her face in a way that I hate. "You stay here. Have fun."

Jo walks into the kitchen, clocks me, smiles down at Parks. "I'm going to come stay at your place tonight anyway," he says.

"Oh." She nods.

That's not a weird thing. Jo stays there all the time but Parks isn't an idiot and something's clearly amiss.

"I might come to yours later if I can get away," Julian says and kisses her. Then he turns and leaves.

Parks pauses—thinking, trying to figure it out. She glances back at me a bit confused then gives me a small shrug and goes back to the living room.

"Oi," I call to Jo, nodding him over to me. "What the fuck's going on?"

"Nothing, man." He's being dismissive. He's also lying.

I stare at him for a few seconds. "Is something wrong?"

Jonah shakes his head but I don't buy it.

"Is she in danger?"

Jonah rolls his eyes. "No, bro. You think I'd ever let anything happen to her?"

"Jo—"

"I'm gonna stay at theirs, Jules is going to leave some boys out front."

"What the fuck is going on?"

He shakes his head again. "Precautions."

I stare at him. Precautions for what?

Fuck. I feel sick.

"Should I go with her?"

If she's in danger I need to be with her.

He shakes his head at me. "I'm handling it, Beej. It's fine."

SIXTY-FOUR

Magnolia

"Is everything okay?" I blink up at Julian a few nights later.

We're standing outside the Connaught and it sort of dawns on me what I'm doing, who I'm bringing to Allie Ballentine's twenty-first birthday.

He frowns a little at my question. "Yeah, everything's fine. Why?"

"I don't know—" I shrug. "Keys stayed outside my apartment the whole night."

Julian nods. "Got confused. He thought I was coming back to yours."

"Oh." I nod. "Right."

He brushes his mouth over mine.

"Did you sort everything out?" I ask him, eyebrows up.

"Hmm?" He tilts his head.

"Your work thing?"

"Oh—" He nods, scratching his chin. "Yeah. Sorting."

He slips his hand around my waist and pulls me tightly against him, kissing me more than he should around other people.

I give him a look. "You behave."

"Yeah, right." Julian snorts.

"I'm serious." I give him a small scowl. "I love Allie. I love BJ's parents."

"You love BJ," he tells me, rolling his eyes. I ignore him.

"They've never been anything but good to me and I don't want to make them uncomfortable, so you will be on your best behaviour—" I point to him. "I mean *GQ* Julian. *Vanity Fair* Julian. Julian in front of Julie Andrews."

"Fucking love Julie Andrews—" He nods appreciatively. "Top notch broad."

"You'll answer the questions, you'll smile for the photos, you'll keep your hand off my arse—"

He eyes me playfully. "No promises there."

"You will be respectful and charming and you'll delight the pants off of everyone in there, and I do mean that in a strictly metaphorical sense. All pants are to stay on all bodies at all times, thank you very much."

He looks down at me, eyes pinched, a little annoyed. I can tell he wants to kiss me though.

"You realise you're talking to one of the most powerful men in the country?"

I blink up at him. Very sexy. White slim-fit bib-front double-cuff cotton tuxedo shirt with the O'Connor-fit wool and mohair-blend tuxedo, all from Tom Ford. Bit of a megalomaniac but very sexy.

"I realise I'm talking to a man who I had on his knees last night, telling me he'd do whatever I wanted . . ."

He squashes a smile into a smirk.

"Pain in the arse."

I kiss his cheek.

They've rented out the Mayfair Room for a small dinner of a hundred of Allie's closest friends. I could cry that she's twenty-one.

My favourite of BJ's sisters, easily.

Rather bright-eyed, very clever, very sweet. Same age as Bridge and her closest friend. I love her a lot.

We walk in and BJ spots me straight away. Hardly his fault. I'm in the crystal-trim velvet-bow embroidered tulle gown from Jenny Packham, Manolo Blahnik's black velvet jewel buckle pumps and the Ellerie crystal-embellished silver-tone headband from Jennifer Behr. I am dazzling.

Intentionally so.

He stares over at me. Throws back his whole negroni.

He looks so handsome, my heart drops a foot in my chest.

White slim-fit satin-trimmed wool- and mohair-blend tuxedo jacket and the black Shelton slim-fit satin-trimmed Grain de Poudre wool-blend tuxedo trousers, both from Tom Ford. White shirt underneath, black buttons. Paul Smith, I'm guessing. Black velvet Saint Laurent bow tie and the Grosgrain-trimmed velvet loafers from Christian Louboutin.

We match. We completely match. It's hilarious and accidental and I love it because it makes me feel sure our brains are still connected and I wish all of me was connected to him, but I guess I'll take what I can get.

Jules spots Jonah and nods his head to the side.

He kisses my cheek. "Be back—"

I glance around, looking for someone familiar. Can't spot Tausie or Bridget. No sign of Henry.

And then I'm swallowed by a group hug.

"You came, darling!" Lily Ballentine pulls away, touching my cheeks. "My God, look at that face! Hamish, look at her face."

"Yes, darling. Lovely." He rolls his eyes fondly at his wife.

I nod at Lil. "Nothing on hers though."

"Oh." She rolls her eyes, swanning.

"How are you doing, sweetheart?" Hamish asks with a paternal head tilt. "Heard you're seeing someone?"

I nod. "I am, a bit."

"Is it true he's a gang lord?" Lily asks loudly.

Hamish elbows her. "Lil—"

I laugh, waving my hand through the air, not wanting them to worry about me. "He's one of Jonah's good friends."

Lily gives me a look and I miss them so much.

I press my lips together demurely.

"Does he abide by all rules all of the time? No. But—" I concede.

Hamish's face falters a little. "Are you being careful?"

No. No is the answer, Hamish. But I'd rather not be careful and not be alone than be careful and have to watch BJ with the girl he picked over me.

460

"I am," I lie with a nod.

BJ walks over towards us a bit gingerly with no Jordan in tow.

He stands next to me and my heart swings on a vine back to the days where it used to be me and him and his parents. We used to talk all night and laugh. BJ would be so embarrassed of how in love they were, but I think we're like them.

We used to be anyway.

Beej smiles at his parents and Lily nudges Ham excitedly.

Hamish winks at his son—it's hereditary, their capacity to wink all amazing like that.

"So happy to see you, sweetheart." Hamish kisses my cheek before they walk away.

Beej faces me, looks down at me a little.

"You brought your gang lord boyfriend to my baby sister's birthday?"

"Not my boyfriend," I tell him with tall eyebrows.

He eyes me. "Not my point."

I poke him in the chest just for a reason to touch him. "You bought your gang lord best friend."

His face twitches a little, trying not to smile.

"Also not my point."

"Is your point that you wanted me to come here alone so that you could flaunt that girlfriend of yours—who you don't love—in front of me?" I ask, eyebrow cocked. "Make me feel sad that you're here with her instead of me?"

His face goes serious. "Parks—"

I shake my head at him, cut him off. "You don't need to try, Beej. I'm always sad you're with her."

"Listen, we need to talk ab—"

"Magnolia!" Allie throws her arms around my neck excitedly, Bridge standing behind her.

BJ sighs at the interruption, flashes his sister a smile, his eyes tired.

"Allie B!" I force a bright smile as I throw my arms around her. "Happy birthday!"

461

"Do you like my dress?" She gestures to herself in the embellished velvet-trimmed silk-crepe and stretch-jersey gown from Gucci.

I nod approvingly. "I do."

"Thanks." She shrugs. "My big brother's ex-girlfriend with whom he truly belongs gave it to me."

I smile at her fondly, adjusting the belt a little bit on her. "She has great taste."

"She does." She smooths her skirt.

"Big head too," my sister chimes in and BJ laughs.

"And where's the sexy gang lord?" Allie looks around. "I'd like to meet him."

Beej makes a noise in the back of his throat and walks away.

"Fuck him." She nods after him, resolute.

"Honestly, I'd love to. Though last time I did that it ended quite poorly, so—" I give her a look. Allie laughs and smacks my arm and my sister rolls her eyes as she says my name.

"Come on." Bridget takes Al's hand, leading her over to Julian.

I trail after them, looking over my shoulder to find where BJ is in the room. He's standing in the corner with Henry, Henry's talking to him, voraciously using his hands to make a point and BJ's just watching me.

"Danny Ocean," my sister says to the boy I'm sleeping with. "This is my best friend, Allie."

"Hello—" Allie extends her hand out to him. "You must be the sexy gang lord."

Julian grins at her. "That is what my friends call me." He takes Allie's hand, kisses it. "Happy birthday—thank you for having me."

"You're very welcome." She nods.

"For your birthday gift, is there anyone you'd like me to off for you?" Julian asks playfully.

"Julian!" I smack him and Bridge rolls her eyes, swearing under her breath.

"I'm kidding—" He laughs, then covers my ears as he mouths to Allie. "I'm not kidding."

I squirm out of his hold. "He's kidding, he's kidding—" I tell Allie and the man Julian's with who I didn't notice until now.

Allie laughs, delighted, before Bridget yanks her away.

"I told you he was handsome," Bridget tells her. "But what a git!"

I look up brightly at Julian, waiting for him to pay attention to me.

He holds me by the waist and gives a bit of a strained smile.

"Tiges, could you just give me a couple more minutes?"

"Oh—" I pull back a bit surprised. "Yeah, of course—"

He flashes me a smile and kisses my cheek.

He nods his head towards it. "I'll meet you at the bar."

I wander over towards it and find BJ there.

I stand next to him.

"Where's Jordan?"

"Couldn't make it," he says, watching me.

"Really?" I give him a look. "To your sister's twenty-first birthday. Not a very good girlfriend." I eye him to make my point.

His face pulls. "You'd like her more than you think."

I don't like him defending her so I lean over the bar.

"Martini," I tell the bartender. "Wet and dirty, please."

BJ chokes on his drink and I peer up at him, eyes wide and innocent. He looks down at me, trying not to smile as he shakes his head. "You're ridiculous."

"You used to love that about me," I tell him in a quiet sort of proudness.

He stares at the back wall lined with different spirits. "Still do," he says without looking at me. He nods at the bartender. "Negroni please, man. Thanks."

He turns to me, presses his hands into his mouth, face strained.

"I've got to ask you something."

I swallow. "Okay?"

"Have you forgiven me?"

"For what?" I face him.

463

"For Paili," he says and it's like he drops my heart from the thirty-fifth floor.

I breathe out of my nose, take a long sip of my drink. "No."

He shakes his head at me. "But you said you loved me."

I look up at him, frowning a bit. "Do you think I can't love you and be angry at you in the same breath?" I shake my head at his ridiculousness. "If I can't, I've never loved you."

He sniffs a laugh. He rubs the back of his neck.

"You and me hooking up—"

"—We've never hooked up." I stare at him as I shake my head, eyes round with hurt. "You and I, we've never hooked up. We were never like that."

He sighs and tilts his head. "You know what I mean . . ."

"I know what you mean." I nod at him defiantly. "And I want you to call it what it was."

He pauses.

His mouth looks for the words. "You and me sleeping together that night up in Wales," he says instead. "Did it fuck us up more?"

The question winds me a little, but I know the answer. "Yes."

He nods to himself. "It pushed it back."

I frown.

"What back?"

He gives me a solemn look. "Trusting me."

I gnaw down on my bottom lip, thinking. "Not what we did, so much as learning that it didn't matter to you."

His head rolls back. "Of course it mattered to me."

"You said it didn't!" I yell and he touches my arm to quieten me, giving me a look to remind me that there are eyes and ears everywhere.

"Parks." He sighs. "I would never had done it if I knew you'd go how you went—"

"How I went?" I stare at him defiantly, shoulders squaring back.

"How you went, yeah." He nods, annoyed again. "How you're going now."

464

I do a big blink and glare at him. "How am I going now?"

"You think I can't see it on your face, how you're looking at me?" He gestures to my face.

My head pulls back.

"And how am I looking at you?"

He gives me a smile. It's sad and quick. "Like I'm not good enough."

"BJ." I blink at him and my mind floods with a million memories and thoughts I have to prove him wrong.

"—You ready to go?" Julian appears, tossing an arm around me. "Oh."

I glance up at him with a startled smile. "Sure. Yeah—"

BJ gives me a tight smile. "See you." He nods his head at Jules.

I swallow heavy, barely holding his eyes. "Bye."

Julian takes my hand in his and we walk out into a waiting car of his.

I'm quiet as we drive and he doesn't say anything for a while either, just watching me.

"You okay?" he asks eventually.

"Yeah." I nod.

"What happened?"

I give him a weak smile as I shake my head. "You don't want to hear about it."

He stares at me for a few seconds. "Tell me."

I swallow. "We slept together."

His head pulls back in surprise and his whole face tenses in a quick but genuine anger.

"In Italy?"

"No." I roll my eyes, touch his arm. "No, remember ages ago . . . before we—" I gesture between us. "You and me . . . you know . . . whatever. He and I slept together, he told me he loved me—"

I don't want to keep going.

"Oh." He nods. "Right. I remember."

I purse my mouth. "But he was with Jordan at the time still. So he cheated on her—"

"—With you." He nods.

I nod. "Yes."

"You think he's going to do it again?" Julian guesses.

"I don't know," I say, not meeting his eyes.

Julian shrugs a bit, indifferent to all of it. "Maybe he will."

I look up at him. "Do you think?"

"People who love each other hurt each other all the time." He elbows me. "You should know, you're a fucking pro at that."

I give him a dark look before asking in a small voice, "So you think he'll do it again?"

"I didn't say that either—" He scratches his jaw, tired. "Listen, boys like Ballentine are born into families where they're taught that they have to do the right thing all the time for him to be accepted."

"How odd." I roll my eyes sarcastically.

"Shut up—" He gives me a look. "That kind of thinking, Magnolia—it fucks people up. It's all wrapped up in his self-worth now. Do good to get good. He did shit and he's scared he's gonna get shit. He can't help it. But people are people, and people hurt people—" He shrugs again. "It's just the nature of being human. We fuck up."

I give him a sad look.

"And his issue—" Julian gives me a look. "It's your fault, Parks." I pull back a little, offended, but he ignores me and keeps going. "You've got that thing about you that makes you want to be different or better." Julian shrugs a bit, all hopeless. "He's just trying to be good enough for you or some shit."

"He said that," I tell Julian quietly. "That I look at him like he's not good enough for me."

Julian tosses an arm around me and sniffs.

"Well, that is complete horse shit. You look at him like he's Michael fucking Angelo." He shakes his head. "He doesn't feel good enough for you, that's all that is."

"Oh, that's all, is it?" I give him a look.

"Yep." Julian nudges me as he lifts me up into his car. "Joke's on him, though. Little does he know how much you enjoy a bad boy."

I roll my eyes. "You're not a bad boy, Julian."

He scoffs.

"You're not—" I shake my head at him. "It's your greatest rouse."

I give him a defiant look and he gives me a pinched one.

Then he sniffs and looks out the window and I hope he knows I'm right, because I'm very sure that I am.

SIXTY-FIVE

BJ

Henry and I are sitting at The Guinea Grill over on Burton Place.

Our favourite pub, but we don't get here much because Parks says she can't be seen in anything close to a public house. The last time I took her to one she just sat there disinfecting her hands and all nearby surfaces with a little bottle of Carex.

"How's it going with you and Taurs?" I nod at him with my chin.

He flops back in his chair a bit. Exhausted.

"I'm over it, man." He shakes his head. "It's too much."

"What happened to that Georgia girl?"

"Yeah." He shrugs. "She's cool. Super smart. Obviously crazy hot. She reads people, she's like a little wizard with people's faces—which is fucking sick except that she knew the night I brought her to yours that I was in love with Taura."

"Ah." I nod. Sniff a laugh.

"Said she didn't mind and kept hanging out for a bit, but I don't know. It's not fun to feel see-through."

"Are you and Jo okay?"

Henry tilts his head, unsure.

"Yeah? I don't know." He shrugs. "It gets weirder and harder by the day."

"Have you talked about it at least?"

My brother shrugs. "A bit. Mostly that we just don't want to be you and Christian 2.0."

I sniff a laugh. "These girls, man."

He shakes his head and gives me a look. "We've gotta get out of London."

Henry runs both his hands through his hair, stressed. Shakes his head like he can shake it off.

"You and Parks, what's the go there? Anything new?"

I give him a rueful look. "Still haven't told her."

Henry smiles but it's annoyed.

"I love you, man," Henry tells me. "You're my best friend—don't tell Christian."

I sniff a laugh.

"So when I say this, I'm saying it because I love you—"

Here we go. I roll my eyes.

"But what the fuck are you doing?"

It's a fair question at this point, actually.

Been waiting on it a while. Wondered when my little brother would go big brother on my arse. Try to straighten me out.

"I tried to tell her at Al's." I drum my Young's London Original. Fruity on the top, bitter at the end.

"And?" Henry gives me an impatient look.

I shrug. "We were interrupted."

"Bullshit." He sits back in his chair. "If you wanted to tell her, you'd have already done it."

I give him a look. "That's not true."

"Oh yeah." He rolls his eyes. "I forgot how good you are at being restrained when it comes to Magnolia."

He gives me a look and I flip him off.

I put both my hands behind my head and crack my back.

"It's got to be different this time, man."

My brother gives me an exasperated look.

"Agreed."

"I haven't figured out that part yet." I bite down on my bottom lip, shake my head a little helplessly.

"Pretty in my head about it, man."

"About what?" Henry sighs. "She'll call it with Jules the second she knows you've called it with Jordan—"

I shake my head at him. "That's not what it's about."

"What, then?" Henry asks impatiently before he sinks his beer.

I breathe out. "That day, up in Angsley, you didn't see how she looked at me."

"Fuck, Beej." Henry breathes out, tired. "You don't see how she looks at you—this is in your fucking head."

"No, it's not." I stare at him. "You all but said it yourself—"

"Listen." Henry bangs my forearm with his fist. "Do I think, objectively, that she deserves more than the way you've treated her in the past? Yes."

My head drops, but he keeps going.

"Do I also objectively think that you deserve more than the way she's treated you?" He lifts a brow. "Yes."

I look back up at him.

"You've both fucked up," Henry tells me, both eyebrows up now. "Doesn't mean you don't belong together."

I swallow, press my tongue into my bottom lip. "She's not forgiven me, Hen."

"I know." He nods slowly. "Give her time."

I lift my shoulders, feeling beat. "How much?"

Henry shrugs back. "Does it matter, Beej? It's Parks."

I drop my head in my hands and rub my eyes. "It's been years."

Henry pulls a face like he's unsure. "Has it?"

I look up at him, confused.

"She found out it was Paili a little over a year ago, yeah? Then she left for a year. She didn't think about it, she ignored it, she avoided you and it at all costs."

I cross my arms over my chest, staring at him.

"Then she comes back, sees you again, loves you again—or still—depending on how you look at it." He shrugs to himself. "And is just now, for the first time since it happened, actually dealing with you fucking Pails."

I stare at him.

"Now, with that timeline in mind—she's really only been dealing with it for about five months."

470

I frown over at him, but I'm tracking. I guess it makes sense.

"Someone should tell her that's not really how time works." I eye him as I toss back my beer.

Henry pulls a face. "Feels like a you problem."

SIXTY–SIX
Magnolia

Julian and I went to dinner tonight at Maison Francois in St James, and the dinner was bizarrely date-ish. But it always kind of is with him, I suppose. He's so charming, troublingly so sometimes. He could talk his way into or out of anything.

He sat across from me at the table after sampling away at everything he ordered, just staring over at me.

It was a funny kind of stare. A bit far off.

"What?" I frowned.

"You're just . . ." He trailed off.

"What?" I frowned more.

He stared at me a few more seconds before a frown of his own appeared.

"Hot—" He grumped. "Fuck."

I sniffed a laugh.

"Hot?" I blinked at him. "That's what you were going to say?"

"No." He gave me a sharp look, shoving his hands into the pocket of his black logo-print cotton-blend jersey hoodie from Vetements. "What I was going to say was you're the most beautiful girl I've ever seen but you're a fucking pain in the arse, so now that's what I'm saying."

I still felt taller anyway because there was a compliment buried in there somewhere.

When we pull up to Jonah's club, Julian looks down at me before we walk inside.

He gives me a funny smile. His eyes are uneasy, his mouth's turned down.

Stupid Bridget.

Don't know why. Just feels like it's her fault somehow.

He walks me inside and kisses me halfway up the stairs.

It's a big kiss.

Obnoxious but not necessarily in a showy way. Just a blatant disregard for everything and everyone around us. A kiss at all costs.

It's a good kiss too.

A hand on my face, a hand in my hair. His body pressing mine against the wall. He pulls away a little, hovers over my face.

I look up at him quizzically.

"What was that for?"

He gives me a bit of a shrug. "Just cause."

Then he takes hold of me by the waist, pushes me up the stairs, holds me like that till we find Jonah and Beej.

Jules nods hello to both of them and I instantly feel self-conscious about his hands on my waist in front of BJ.

I don't know why. BJ's looking at me funny. His eyes are rounder than usual.

He swallows. I swallow.

The canary that lives in my ribcage jumps onto its bird swing and starts to chirp away and the loudest room in London can feel like a slow river running over small stones at a quarter past midnight when he zones in on me, when he turns down the volume of the world with eyes I'll never get past.

Hi, I mouth.

He gives me a barely there smile and a blink-and-you-miss-it wink.

"Oi." Julian nods his chin at Beej. "I've got some shit to do—can you grab her a drink?"

I look at Julian a bit perplexed. He just glances at me with a face I can't totally place.

Beej nods. "Sure?"

Jules nods his head at Jo to follow him and I guess that makes sense. Julian tries his best to keep this part of himself separate from me.

473

Beej glances at the couch and I follow him over.

"Where's Jordan?" I ask as I sit down next to him.

He leans over and almost grimaces. "We really need to have a talk, you and me."

I feel nervous immediately. I swallow, nod, wave my hand permissively. "Go on, talk."

He squashes a smile, looks around and then shakes his head. "Not here."

I look at him, confused. "Where, then?"

He nods his chin at me. "What are you doing tomorrow?"

My heart leaps up into my throat.

"I don't know," I tell him in a quiet voice.

He pokes me in the ribs. "Now you do."

My cheeks go pink immediately and I don't care for it, so I cross my arms over my chest. "Actually, I don't know a thing. That was all horrendously vague."

"You'll live." He gives me a small smile before he nods over at me." What did you do today?"

I shrug. "Lunch with Bridge at Annabel's."

He smiles. "She good?"

"I don't know. You tell me, you with your weekly lunches."

He gives me a look. "You live together." And then he leans back on the couch a little, rests his head back, smiling over at me.

"Who'd have thought it, you and Bridget living together . . ."

I laugh and shake my head at him. "She's my best friend."

"No, I know, but I can't really believe she agreed to it. You'd be a nightmare of a housemate."

I play-frown at him and he lets out a laugh.

"You would," he insists.

"I'll have you know that I am a breeze to live with."

"She told me you put all her vegetables she just bought into the dishwasher."

"I was trying to clean them!" I yell a little bit and he starts laughing. "I didn't want her to catch E. coli. It's not my fault vegetables wilt."

He smiles over at me, looks at me in this way that makes me feel like we're at school again. I'm fifteen on a yacht in the Balearics and his nose is pressed up against mine how I wish it really was now and he's promising he'll love me forever.

BJ clears his throat. The memory fades away.

"Like that." He juts his chin at my dress from Rodarte. "Always fancied you in polka dots."

I look cute as a fucking button tonight.

Black ribbed-knit cropped cardigan from Versace, the embellished polka dot silk-twill midi-dress, and the fire engine red 105mm lock stiletto sandals poppy from Tom Ford.

He licks his bottom lip and eyes me as he smiles over.

"You know what I was thinking about?"

I face him a little more, touch his shirt because Julian's not here and I can.

Blue hooded flannel jacket from Greg Lauren, Saint Laurent 50's Signature Destroyed T-Shirt and the light blue Cutoff 874 work pants from Dickies.

"What?"

"The night you and Christian called it?"

My face falters, confused. "Why?"

He shrugs. "Just been on my mind."

He gives me a look, squinting as he does.

"You think she did it on purpose?"

"Paili?" I pull back, surprised.

He nods.

I shake my head at him. No way.

He shrugs in tacit disagreement. "I don't know anymore."

We were at Perry's birthday dinner. BJ and I hadn't spoken since the night he beat Christian up at Box. I saw him up at the tree on December 3rd but that was it.

I didn't say anything to him then either.

Just, leaned on his shoulder. Wrote $E = MC^2$ in the dirt with my shoe while he wasn't looking, prayed to whoever that they'd let me find my way back to him, and then I left and went back to Christian.

I've always been like this. I don't know how to be alone. It's all BJ's fault.

He's always been too good at making sure I never felt alone. So in his absence I'm petrified to sit with myself.

Anyway, for Perry's birthday we were all supposed to be going away all together. His insistence. At dinner that night Paili was going through room allocations in her mind at the table.

"Me and Perry, Beej and Jonah . . . Christian and Parks." All our faces froze.

"No. I mean—" She tried to backtrack but it was too late.

"Why would she have done that on purpose?" I give BJ a look.

"Maybe she wanted you to get caught?" He shrugs. "Level the playing field, ease her own guilt."

And maybe he's right. It was a fuck-up of epic proportions.

"It doesn't make sense." He shrugs. "No one likes sleeping with you. Everyone always would rather let you have your own room because you're such a fucking pain to share with."

I pout and he shrugs anyway.

"She had to know what she was doing," he says, sounding sure.

Then he nods at me with his chin. "Why'd you and Christian call it that night, anyway?"

"Mm." I twitch my mouth around, thinking. "Well, once it became apparent that he and I were still seeing each other, Jonah starting losing his shit. I was yelling at Jonah and you were sort of just sitting there, a bit dumbstruck, and then you shook your head and said, 'You know what man? It's fine.' When Christian told me you said that, my face fell. And he knew I still loved you." I nod to myself. "So he took me aside and told me he wasn't anyone's placeholder. He ended it."

Beej nods once, a bit annoyed. "And then held onto it for another three years afterwards."

I give him a look and he laughs again.

"I walked you home that night, do you remember? I could have thrown up I was so excited you let me."

476

"You said you'd drive me home."

We walked for miles. Literally miles.

We were almost back at my house when I looked up at him with a frown.

"You parked really far away from the restaurant."

He laughed. "I actually took a car in."

I blinked at him, frowning in disbelief.

"I'm parked out front on Park Lane." He shrugged apologetically. "I'm just not ready to be done talking to you yet."

"BJ!" I laughed, staring up at him—side-stepping my beating heart. "Do you know how sore it is to walk in these shoes?"

I flashed him my six-inch Louboutins.

"Sorry—" He sniffed a laugh and smiled down at me. "Here, I'll carry you the rest of the way."

"What?" I blinked. "Like a pack mule?"

He gave me a tender smile. "I'd be anything for you."

"Will you be my friend?" I asked, staring up at him, wanting so, so much more than that.

He nodded once on that street corner. "Whatever the fuck you need, Parks."

Under these club lights oftentimes things can look better than they are. We've all fallen victim to that, rose-coloured, strobing glasses—but not him. All golden even though he's not, my favourite mouth in the world on the face I see when I close my eyes. BJ presses his tongue into his bottom lip and I want to kiss him so badly—he's watching my mouth—he wants to kiss me too. I know the look. He's leaning in towards me, I think. I wonder if he's going to do it—leaning, leaning, leaning—and it's for a fraction of a second before he pulls back, shakes his head a bit but sort of not at all.

"Where's Jules?" He looks around. "We should find him."

"Oh." I blink a few times and nod. "Okay."

That throws me a little.

But I guess this is us now . . . BJ trying to do the right thing by everyone, even at the cost of moments between us.

He stands so I stand.

"The offices maybe?" BJ shrugs.

I lead the way. Kekoa is standing by the hallway that leads to the offices. A promising sign. I give him a smile, but the one he gives me is strained.

"Is Julian down here?"

"Yeah, but—"

I move past him as he's talking. I'm not being rude, I've never not been able to see Julian when I wanted to see him before, so I move past Kekoa, round a corner, and I stop dead in my tracks.

He's got a girl hoisted up around his waist.

He's thrusting.

I can hear the friction of material rubbing.

The girl is panting.

They're clearly having sex. Clearly. I know his sex faces well enough by now to know what's happening.

And then I let out a couple of breaths that sound like laughs. Julian looks back over his shoulder at me around the same time that BJ grabs him by the shoulders and slams him into the wall.

The girl stands there, startled for a few seconds, shifting her dress.

I know who she is. Bianca Harrington's sister. I've seen her around before.

Too much eye make-up and brown, choppy hair.

Julian looks over at me—looks me in the eye as he pulls his pants all the way up. Black Arrows-print loose-fit trousers from Off-White. I bought them for him. He presses his tongue into his bottom lip.

"What the fuck?" I yell at Julian.

He swipes his arms to get BJ off him but BJ shoves him again. I hear the dull thump of a hand hitting his chest.

"Yeah, what the fuck?"

Julian turns his focus to BJ and I feel nervous.

"Oh, you want to go?" Jules eyes him. Shove.

"Yep."

BJ nods without thinking. Shove. Julian gives him a grin that I'm a bit afraid of. "I've wanted to do this the last three months."

Jules pushes BJ again and then—bam—BJ hits him in the mouth.

Fuck.

"BJ—stop!" I yell, rushing to him at the same time as Julian's security team does.

Julian's doubled over for a couple of seconds before he straightens up, presses a hand into his bloody mouth, and looks down at it. He sniffs, clearly a bit amused at BJ and shakes his head.

Holy shit.

Julian presses his tongue into the wound, spits out some blood.

Julian points at me and Kekoa grabs me from behind.

BJ sees and his eyes widen to panic. "Don't fucking touch h—"

Then Julian takes a swing at him. BJ ducks it but then Julian under-cuts him and BJ falls backwards.

"Julian!" I yell.

BJ rams him, knocks Jules clean off his feet.

I'm bucking in the arms of Kekoa, trying my hardest to get to them. I can't see properly but I can hear the sound of them hitting one another. The sound of fist meeting face, the crack of a jaw taking a heavy swing. The horrible grinding a nose makes when it takes a blow.

There are fists flying, crunches and cracks, and I guess at one point I must have started crying because my face is wet now and I'm screaming for them to stop it, but neither of them are listening to me. I'm screaming for Henry, for Christian, for Jonah.

Jonah comes running eventually from somewhere deep in the belly of the club and pulls me from Kekoa's arms, hurling me into Christian's and then he dives between his two best friends who are trying to tear each other apart. He drags BJ away, holding him back.

Julian stands, chest heaving. His face is bloody. He eyes BJ, shakes his head. "You better get him the fuck out of here," he says through clenched teeth.

Jonah shoves BJ down the hall and our eyes catch as he passes me—he's bloody too—his eyes look sorry and heavy as they slip past me.

My breathing keeps getting caught in my chest.

"What are you doing?" I yell at Julian.

"How many times do I have to tell you?" Julian bellows at me, getting right up in my face. Christian's grip on me tightens. "We're not fucking dating! We've only ever been fucking."

I take a breath that sounds like a cry. Maybe it is.

I don't know why I would be.

Because I'm worried about BJ, maybe? Because I'm embarrassed? Because I'm sad that Julian would do that to me? How many times has he done that to me? Am I always right around the corner?

Julian waves his hand in my direction but he doesn't look me in the eye.

"Take her home," he tells no one in particular.

"Come on—" Christian pulls me away from Julian and as he does, Julian looks up at me.

His breathing is uneven and the edges of his eyes look frayed with a hurt I don't really understand.

And then I turn away from him.

SIXTY–SEVEN

BJ

"Are you out of your fucking mind?" Jonah shoves me. "Beej?" He shoves me again. "Are you insane?"

I shake my head, trying to push past my best friend to get back to him, to finish this once and for all.

"BJ!" Jonah yells again, pushing me hard. "What the fuck are you doing?"

"He was fucking some girl in a hallway and Parks saw it." Shake my head. Can't believe that fucking son of a bitch.

"I don't care, Beej." He shoves me again. "He is the most dangerous man in England. He can do whatever the fuck he wants."

I shake my head at him, jaw tight. "Not with her he can't."

"Beej—" He holds me by the shoulders. "I need you to listen to me and get this through your fucking head: He. Could. Kill. You."

Jonah breathes out, face pulling with stress. "He might already."

I don't give a shit, I look back up to the building I'm outside of now, wonder how I can get back in, get back to her. I can't believe we left her with him.

"We need to go." Jonah shakes his head. "If he walks out here and sees you—"

"Where's Parks?" I look around for her.

He shoves me towards his car, shaking his head.

"That's not your problem right now, man."

"She's always my problem." I glare over at him.

Jonah watches me from the opposite side of his Escalade.

481

"Do you need the hospital?"

I swipe my bleeding mouth. "No, I'm fine."

He turns my face to inspect it himself. Pokes a deep cut. "This could use a stitch."

I smack him off. "I said I'm fine."

I stare out the window, jaw set.

"Take me to her," I tell him.

Jonah shakes his head. "Beej, no—"

"Yes."

"He could be there."

"I don't give a fuck."

"Yeah, I know, man." Jonah eyes me. "You've got that look in your eye where you don't give a shit about shit, and I know you get like this about her, but you don't know that she's not with him. She might be—"

I shake my head at him. "—She's going to end it with him. Now."

Jo gives me an exasperated look. "How do you know that?"

"Because I'm going to make her."

Jonah presses his hands into his eyes, breathes out, tired, and makes a frustrated grunt. Shakes his head then turns to his driver.

"Change of plans. Grosvenor Square, mate."

When we pull up outside the girls' place, Jo gets out first and looks around. Checking for other armed cars, any of Jules's boys he recognises. He shakes his head at me, cocks it towards the door.

He calls Taura, checks Jules isn't there then we take the lift up.

Hate that I've not been here before, hate that it took this for me to come here.

Taura lets us in, gives me a little kiss on the cheek as she does.

"Proud of you," she tells me.

I peer around for her. "Where is she? Is she okay?"

Tausie nods her chin towards a room down the hall. "Ask her yourself."

I follow the sound of a raging Bridget down the hall.

"—Pricky bastard!" Bridget yells, stomping her foot. "Slimy, repugnant—" Sees me. "Oh." She blinks. "I wasn't talking about you, believe it or not."

I sniff a laugh. "For once."

Parks looks up from her bed, eyes wide. They're dangerous tonight, all red and extra green. She stands up quickly.

Bridget glances between us then backs out, closing the door behind her.

"Are you okay?" I ask her, not moving.

She rushes over to me, holds my face in her hands and moves my head around, inspecting it. "Are you?"

Split lip, bit of a black eye, cut-up cheek, bloody nose.

"Come on—" She takes me by the wrist, pulls me to her bathroom.

Wets a face cloth with warm water and starts clearing the blood from my face.

Fuck, I love being close to her.

Her eyes won't meet mine. It's on purpose. She's gone shy on me.

We're as close as we've been in months—our faces not even centimetres apart—and she won't look me in the eye. She inspects the cut on my cheek.

"That looks quite bad," she tells me.

I shake my head, watching her eyes, waiting for them to find mine.

"It needs a stitch, I think."

"Don't want a stitch."

"It'll scar."

I duck my head so our eyes catch. "Worth it."

She swallows nervously.

I lick my bottom lip.

"What the fuck are you doing, Parks?" Shake my head at her.

"Beej—" She sighs and I shake my head at her.

"No, I mean it. What are you doing with him?"

"BJ—" She covers her eyes with her little hands, shaking her head right back at me. "I am so in love with you. So

483

in love. And watching you with someone else is rotting me away. I don't kn—"

And then I kiss her.

Her hands are still covering her eyes. She couldn't see it coming. Just kiss her.

Wrap my arms around her body, pull her in tight against me while she goes to mush.

I give myself five seconds and it's a fucking freeforall. I'm so in love with her, there's so much more I want to do than kiss her, but I'm not fucking it up this time and we're doing it right. I swallow then pull away.

She looks up at me, cheeks pink. Blinking. Breathing fast.

I push some hair from her face.

"End it with him," I tell her. She nods. "Okay."

I press my mouth against hers one more time and then I leave.

SIXTY-EIGHT

Magnolia

I'm nervous as I head over to Knightsbridge the next day
And sad, I suppose, if I'm honest.
I know I haven't a right to be.
I am Shakespeareanly in love with another man and Julian
knows it, but I wouldn't have slept with BJ without ending
it with him first, and I know we're not the same. I know
Julian is Julian and he treats not just women like garbage but
all people like they're disposable, but actually—I had begun
to think that maybe he saw me differently. Clearly I'm just as
disposable to him as anyone else.
BJ kissed me though.
That softens all the blows.
I don't know what that kiss means. I don't know what
that means about Jordan, but he told me to end it with
Julian.
I probably would have anyway after last night.
I can't quite erase the audio in my mind of the little sounds
that girl was making with her legs wrapped around him—sex
sounds are so terribly invasive from a third-party perspective,
and I've never wanted to see other people like that—but I
saw it and now I can't unsee it. So now, even if I'm a bit
sad about it in a way that, quite frankly, I don't understand,
I will, nevertheless, end it.
I walk up to his bedroom and knock on his door.
"What?" he calls and I swing it open.
He sits up straighter when he sees it's me.

And then I spot Bianca's sister and another blonde girl, both in his bed.

"Leave," he tells them unceremoniously.

Both girls roll out of his bed, gather their clothes quickly and scurry out of his room.

I stand there watching him, not them, arms folded, brows low.

"Nice," I glare over at him when they're gone.

He rolls his eyes as he gets out of bed. He's fully naked. Grabs a pair of black track pants that are by his bed. Black Tiger Motif track trousers from Kenzo—pulls them on.

"You were fucking a gang lord. What'd you expect?"

"More from you," I tell him as I slip off my reversible Damier Azur hooded wrap from Louis Vuitton.

He sniffs annoyed and shakes his head at me.

"You got what you wanted."

I give him a look. "What did I get that I wanted?"

His head pulls back. "You think I don't know Ballentine went to your house last night?"

I blink at him in surprise, open my mouth to say something but I don't know what I'd say.

"I have eyes everywhere," he tells me. "I see everything."

I fold my arms over my chest and walk towards him, frowning.

"You got him back." He shrugs. "You're welcome."

I stare over at him and shake my head. "What?"

"What?" he scoffs. "You think I didn't know he'd defend your honour when he saw me shagging some girl in a club?" He rolls his eyes. "It's sweet—" He waves his hand dismissively. "How much he loves you."

I stare over at him, a bit incredulous.

No. Could he really have?

I squint at him. "Did you really do that for me or is this just a happy coincidence?"

He gives me this long look, the question hangs there and I don't know what the answer is. There's so much he's not saying in the silence, I can feel it all thick with things I don't

486

know. Whatever it is, it makes me feel a peculiar tenderness towards him that I didn't want to feel while I was doing this.

Julian clears his throat and gives me a tight smile. "You know what? I'm embarrassed to say that I've fallen into the ranks of men who find that there's very little that they wouldn't do for you, Magnolia Parks."

My face softens.

"Oh my God." I walk over to him, sit down on his bed. "Are you being serious?"

He shrugs like it's nothing. "He needed to feel good enough for you. Nothing ups a lad's confidence like fighting for the girl he loves—"

"Julian—" I reach for his hand. He lets me take it. "That is . . ." I trail. "Thank you."

He lifts my hand to his mouth and kisses it, runs his thumb over my wrist and under the sleeve of my white Maddy ribbed-knit sweater from Khaite.

"You're welcome," he tells me then he drops my hand. "And I'm relieved."

I blink at him, frowning a bit.

He gives me a look out of the corner of his eye as he shakes his head.

"I thought Daisy was a handful, but fuck me dead, you're an absolute headache."

I frown more.

He clocks my face and chuckles.

"Bit worth it though," he says with a small nod.

"So this is it?" I ask him. "We're done now?"

He nods. "Yep. We're done."

I look over at him fondly. "I'll miss you."

He nods, confident. "I'm sure you will. No way he is as good in bed as I am."

I give him a look.

He cracks a smile that looks a bit tender. "I'm happy for you."

"Yeah?" I smile up at him, my cheeks a bit pink.

He nods.

"Hey." I poke him. "Would you do me a favour and not put out a hit on the man I love?"

He considers this, nodding slowly before offering me a shrug.

"He's a Hemmes for all intents and purposes. Under their protection. So are you, so you don't need mine. But you have it anyway." He gives me a steady look. "You need anything ever—ever—I'm your man."

He gives me a solemn nod.

I lean over and brush my lips against his.

"Yes, you are."

I get up and walk to his door before turning back to look at him. He stares over at me.

"You are a very dangerous man, Julian. I know that." I give him a look. "But I hope you know that above that and before that, you actually really are quite a good man."

He gives me a small smile and nods once.

"See ya, Tiges."

SIXTY-NINE

Magnolia

"And where, pray tell, do you think you're going?" I ask my sister pointedly.

"To dinner with you." She plucks my bright green Ghillies limited edition Birkin bag from the third row of my tote bag shelf.

"Can I borrow this?"

"Yes."

I nod, staring at her with pinched eyes, making sure it goes with her outfit—Versace safety pin logo T-shirt, Danni cashmere cardigan from Lisa Yang with the black original cropped straight leg jeans from Totême. Technically it matches, quite well, actually. But also technically, I am underwhelmed . . . However, I'm always eager for her to branch away from that no-brand leather bucket bag she refuses to part with. She bought it from a street vendor in Kuta on a backpacking trip she went on in 2018. Backpacking! Yuck. Bridge loved it though. She said that's where she'll get married one day, over in Indonesia. I said I'd Skype in on account of my sensitive stomach and at any given moment I'm really only one stomach flu away from being considered clinically malnourished, so it's hardly worth the risk.

"It is worth twenty-five thousand pounds," I tell her. "So be a bit careful."

She blinks at me a few times.

"What the fuck, Magnolia?" She shakes her head, putting it back on the shelf. "That's enough to feed a whole village for a year."

"Seems racist—" I bobble my head around.

"No." She gives me a sharp look. "You seem insane and ridiculous."

"Don't blame me, blame Pierre Alexis Dumas. He's really got me by the balls here."

Bridge shakes her head. "He really doesn't."

"Are you coming tonight?" Taura asks Bridge cheerily, tossing herself onto my bed.

"Wouldn't miss it for the world." Bridge beams excited.

"Love the enthusiasm." I nod appreciatively. "Just to clarify—do we all feel good about you wearing jeans and a T-shirt to dinner? Is that what we've come to as people?"

Bridget looks down at herself, confused.

"What's wrong with what I'm wearing?"

I look over at Taura, confused. "Sorry—did I not say jeans and T-shirt out loud?"

"What's wrong with jeans and T-shirts?" Bridget frowns more.

"Nothing!" I shake my head at her. "Nothing at all if you're herding cattle or you're like a street urchin."

Bridget rolls her eyes.

"Would you consider changing into perhaps into . . . pwha—" I think on my feet, darting to my closet. "This little Bottega number?"

I flash her the black silk knitted shirt dress.

She shakes her head. "I would not."

"Right." I frown and point to her Air Force 1 clad feet. "I doth protest."

Bridget groans.

"The sneakers could go, Bridge," Taura concedes.

Taura jumps up to find my black chain-embellished Medusa sandals from Versace and passes them to my sister. "These'll match."

"Better." I nod.

"Are you being pedantic about what I wear tonight because you're nervous and you don't know what's happening with you and BJ so you just want to control something?" my annoying sister asks.

"No." I give her a look. "I'm being pedantic about what you wear because I'm the style editor of one of the biggest magazines in the country and you're out here trying to dress like a fucking farm hand."

Bridget gives me a look.

"Besides—" I look between them. "We don't know that something's going to happen tonight anyway. It could just be a normal night."

"He kissed you," Bridget tells me as though that moment hasn't been on active replay in my mind ever since.

It was the perfect kiss.

There's nothing I love more in this world than his mouth up against mine, except maybe his body.

I shrug nervously. "He hasn't spoken to me since."

"Have you spoken to him?" Taura asks.

"No."

"Not even to tell him you ended it with Jules?"

"Oh, 'Jules' now, is it?" I roll my eyes at her. "Going to start having Wednesday lunches with him too?"

"No," she mimics me in an annoying voice and gives me a dumb smile. (But says under her breath, ". . . Thursdays." I look over at her and I can't tell whether she's joking.)

"Something's going to happen," Taura tells me, giving me an encouraging smile in the mirror as she looks at the dress she's wearing. Ruched floral-print crepe minidress by Magda Butrym.

"Are you saying that because one of the boys has told you something's going to happen or are you just being a good-vibes girl?" Bridget clarifies.

"The second one."

"Fuck." I groan under my breath.

"What's happening with Jordan?" Bridget asks.

I shrug.

"Is she coming tonight?"

I shrug again.

Tausie purses her mouth which usually means she knows something she isn't saying, which isn't a quality I love in her but she's good at not telling other people's secrets, which I suppose is theoretically admirable but is also literally annoying, so . . .

"Come on, trainwreck." Bridget pulls me towards the door. "Let's go."

When we arrive at Annabel's, all the boys (and no Jordan) are sitting at the table.

I think it's supposed to be subtle but I see Jonah elbow BJ when I walk in and his jaw goes a little bit slack which is, as always, my hope and intent.

His head tilts a little and he stands, walking around the table to me.

He looks a bit shy and I wonder whether he's going to kiss me—if this is our big moment—in Annabel's in Mayfair in front of all our best friends and half of the London social set, if this is how we'll announce to the world that everything is as it should be and we are a we again—but then he just wraps his arms around me. He pulls me into his chest, gives me one of those cuddles of his that I love, that used to be my bread and butter. I take what I can get, breathe him in all familiar, press myself tightly against him, make that silk Hawaiian shirt with lion mix print he's wearing from Dolce & Gabbana smell like me, and pull back a little, looking up at him.

"Hey." His mouth twitches, his arms still around my waist.

"Hi." I bat my eyes at him, my arms still around his neck. He looks past me and his face lights up.

"Bridget Dorothy Parks!" He lets go of me to hug my sister. "Out on the town and in heels and shit! How much did she pay you to be here?"

Bridget gives him a playful look. "Not enough."

I roll my eyes at them as though it annoys me, as though how much he loves my sister isn't the most endearing thing in the world.

492

I sit down next to Henry, who tosses an arm around me. "I like your trousers." I nod at them. Sunset Army jacket, trousers from Greg Lauren.

He gives me a proud smile before he yanks my hair, pulling me in close to his face.

"Did you do it?" he whispers.

I nod.

He smiles and presses his forehead against mine.

"Good girl."

BJ nods over at us from the other side of the table.

"What are you two talking about?"

"Nothing—" Henry swats his hand through the air. "Just how Parks isn't shagging a gang lord anymore."

Beej does a terrible job at suppressing a smile. He bites down on his bottom lip, nods a couple of times, then points in the other direction.

He nods his chin at me. "Want to go have a chat?"

"Sure," I say quietly as I stand.

I walk ahead of him so he has to watch me because I look great and I want to remind him that I'm prettier than Jordan and that I have legs up to my eyeballs. I take off my black Ludmilla Icon from Max Mara so he can see the rest of my outfit. Belted leather-trimmed suede minidress from Saint Laurent, black suede knee-high boots from Gianvito Rossi and the 2004 Holy Bible clutch from Chanel.

We find a table out in the back of the garden. He pulls out my chair and then sits down across from me, pushing a hand through his hair.

I thought it'd be more firework-y, if I'm honest. Us getting back together. It felt firework-y the other night when he kissed me in my bathroom.

He bites down on his thumb, smile cocked. "Hey."

"You already said that."

He chuckles. "What would you like me to say?"

"That you broke up with Jordan?"

He squints over at me, playfully.

493

"Did you?" I ask again, my eyebrows up in nervous expectation. His face softens. "Yes."

He reaches across the table and picks up my hand, playing with my fingers with his.

"Okay." I nod a few times, my cheeks all pink. "Why aren't you kissing me then?"

"I want to be friends."

Holy shit.

I snatch my hand back from him.

My neck feels hot and my chest goes tight.

"I beg your pardon?"

He rolls his eyes and holds his hand out, waiting for me. "Give me your hand."

I feel a bit nauseous. I might start crying. Not in front of him, I need to keep it together in front of him.

"No." I shake my head.

He reaches over further across the table. "Give me your fucking hand—"

"No." I move away from him.

He breathes out loudly through his nose, glares over at me a little.

"Me and Jordan called it back in March."

I stare at him confused. "What?"

"We broke up weeks ago—" He shrugs and then he tilts his head, conceding. "But, I mean, probably we were actually over the second I saw you at the wedding."

I frown at him. "Then what now?"

"I want to be friends," he tells me again.

I shake my head at him. "I don't want to be your friend."

He sniffs a laugh. "I don't want to be your friend either, but this—" he waves between us—"is it now."

My face goes blank for a second before it flickers to a frown. "What?"

"I love you, Parks—" BJ rolls his eyes. "I've been in love with you since I was six and you told me you could kick a ball better than me, and listen, after being together in some way

494

or another for nearly two decades now, I've got to tell you, Magnolia, it's not true." He shakes his head. "Your hand–eye coordination fucking sucks."

I frown over at him, offended and a bit in awe.

"You can't kick a ball for shit. But I love you," he tells me. "I'm in love with you, have never stopped, will always till I die, love you. And this is it—" He shrugs like it's simple. "So we're not going to fuck it up by rushing it. Can I have your hand back now, please?"

He takes it anyway, plays with my ring finger.

My cheeks are pink and all my self-control is being channelled into not ripping those Theory tapered reversible cotton-blend jersey and fleece sweatpants off of him.

"We don't have to rush it," I tell him, batting my eyes a lot because I really want to rush it.

"Parks." He gives me a look. "If we don't consciously not rush it, I'll have you pregnant again in a couple of hours . . ."

I sigh. Would that be so bad?

I give him a dubious look.

"We've never been friends."

He cocks an eyebrow. "We've also only ever been together or tried to kill each other."

"Can't we just be together?" I shrug helplessly and he shakes his head.

"I want you to see that I can not be with you and not have sex with other people."

I open my mouth to say something but he cuts me off—

"—And I want to see you not need to date someone to feel safe."

"But—"

He shakes his head at me. "You can trust me, Parks. And I need to see that you can." He shrugs a little. "And you need to see that you can. You can't just life-trust me. It's got to be heart-trust me too."

"I do." I frown because I really want it to be true and we both know I'm kind of lying.

495

"You don't," he tells me. "But you're going to." He pushes his hand through his hair again. "You'll see."

I stare over at him, frowning as I try not to think about his eyes and instead focus on what he's saying to me, as stupid as it is.

"I don't even know how to be your friend."

He sniffs a laugh and considers this.

"Neither."

I grimace. "Friends?"

He nods once. "Friends."

"Will you spend time with me?" I ask.

"All my time." He nods with a small smile.

"Take me shopping?"

"Yes."

"Sleep in my bed?"

His eyes pinch. "Maybe."

"Maybe?" I frown.

"Maybe." He nods. "If you watch those hands . . ."

He gives me a playful smile and then tilts his head gently.

"It's just for a minute, Parks. While we figure out how to do this thing properly."

"As friends?" I blink.

He rolls his eyes.

"Stop saying 'friends' like it's a dirty word."

I lift my eyebrows up mischievously. "If I said dirty words to you would you stop trying to be my friend?"

He gives me a look. "Parks."

I match his face. "Beej."

He shakes his head a bit. "Parks, this is important to me."

I sigh and swallow.

"You promise you love me?"

He nods. "Infinitely."

"And you want to be with me?" I frown.

"Forever." He nods again. "And I'm gonna be. We're going to figure this out."

I press my lips together and growl a little from the back of my throat.

496

"Fine."

His face lights up.

"Yeah?"

I roll my eyes. "Yeah."

We head back to our friends who are all making stupid noises as we walk back into the restaurant. I roll my eyes dramatically as I take my seat next to Henry.

"We all good?" Henry asks brightly, looking between us.

I clear my throat.

"At BJ's request we are going to be . . . friends."

"What the fuck?" Bridget leans across and smacks BJ over the head.

"No!" groans Henry.

Jonah covers his face and lets out an exasperated moan. "That was an unsanctioned decision—"

Beej starts laughing, watching me from across the table.

Christian tosses me a cautious look. "Fuck, this sounds like a headache."

"Are you okay?" whispers Taura.

"He told me he loves me," I whisper back.

She pulls back and stares over at BJ. "You told her you love her and you're still going to make her be your friend after the shit you pulled on my birthday?"

I stare at her, incredulous. "I whispered that for a reason."

She swats her hand at me dismissively and looks around at everyone else. "Anyone here surprised to learn that Beej is in love with Parks? Quick show of hands—" ("No," "It's terribly obvious," "It's actually all he talks about," "I genuinely wish he loved her less," they all say at the same time.)

BJ looks over at me, eyes locked on mine, shaking his head at the ridiculousness of our friends.

He's grinning.

And I stare at him, trying to look annoyed but everything is better with him, everything is fun, everything feels special, even being his stupid friend sounds like the time of my bloody life, and I want to pout at him, try to get him to give me my

497

way, but he looks happy and I love him more than I love me, so I want him to be happy more than I want me to be happy.

Besides.

I give him a week.

SEVENTY
BJ

Best week I've had in a while, being her friend again.

Took her golfing. Shocking: she's rubbish. Which is exactly what you want from a girl you love and who you're trying to take shit slow with. I absolutely helped her with her swing at every hole, which was way more than necessary.

We've fallen back into step too easily.

Took a long drive down to our school the other day. No real reason, we got in the car, drove to Kent. Didn't really talk about anything, just shooting the shit which is something I feel different about now.

The ease between us is something else. Not everyone has an ease how we do.

It's not an easy relationship and she's not an easy person to be with. That's not what I mean, she's a fucking nightmare 900 per cent of the time, but the ease between us that's probably a once in a lifetime kind of thing. The result of boarding school and trauma bonds and her heart on my sleeve and mine in her back pocket.

I'm meeting Magnolia over at Holland Park for dinner with her family at No.25, and to be honest, I'm shitting myself a bit. Jo told me that Harley and Julian got along crazy well. Like, Harley told him he could marry her if he wanted, which seems like bullshit to me. Sure, yeah, Harley's been a lax dad, but who's sending their daughter down an aisle with a gang lord?

Bit hard to hear regardless.

Her family used to love me, but now (besides Bridge) I don't know what I'm walking into.

I knock on the front door. Weird. Haven't knocked on this door since our first date. It swings open and Magnolia's confused face fills the frame.

"Knocking?" She gives me a look. "You really are taking things slow."

I smile at her, step inside, grab her wrist and pull her into me. My dream girl to the bone.

What a fucking time to be alive. Girl I love in my arms, I haven't fucked up, she's not hooking up with anyone for the single purpose of shredding my fucking soul, and we're standing in the foyer of the house she grew up in, holding her how I used to when my mum would make me come home sometimes and Parks didn't want me to leave.

"Well, this is very full circle," Bridget says as she walks down the stairs.

Parks breathes out a little sigh and I press my mouth into her hair because I won't kiss her yet and then she pulls away.

I toss an arm around Bridge, following Parks to the dining room.

I nod my chin towards it. "What's my yelp rating like in there?"

Bridget grimaces. "Hard to say."

I nod, accepting my fate. "Anything I should know?"

Bridget nods. "New BOTM's in there—"

"What's that now?" I blink at her.

"Boyfriend of the month." Parks turns on her heel, rolling her eyes at her sister.

"Arrie's?"

"No, Bushka's." Magnolia rolls her eyes.

Toss her a look. "Wouldn't put it past her."

"This one's pretty hot, actually," Bridget tells Magnolia.

"Great." I roll my eyes.

"And young." Bridget eyes me.

Parks and I trade looks.

We walk into the dining room. Fucking love this room. Always have. It's weird, not like our dining room at home. Both my parents come from money, Dad more so than Mum (Dad's dad started the biggest supermarket chain in the UK, Mum's dad was a barrister and her mother was a pretty renowned artist) but money nonetheless. But still, the way we grew up was so different. Mum cooked everything, Dad cleaned up afterwards. The dining room at home feels like a family dining room. I carved my name into the table when I was eight. Mum kept it there. Won't let Dad get a new table.

The dining room here has always reminded me of that scene from *Beauty and the Beast* where they're eating at opposite ends of the table. Huge table, huge chairs, massive room. Theatrically opulent. They have different china for different days of the week. Today's the Wednesday set.

Parks's favourite. Old Country Rose from Royal Albert.

Hate myself a bit for knowing that but she's prattled on about it for years now, told me it wouldn't be our Wednesday but our Sunday china.

Can't wait for my Sundays with her.

Harley stands when I walk into the room, extends his hand. "You're back."

I nod once, smile. "For the long haul."

I shrug off my jacket—Burberry—and toss it down on the chair before I give Arrie a kiss, then one for Bushka, then shake the hand of the new boyfriend. (Nathan. Blonde, looks like a lifeguard. Very young.)

I turn to Mars and grimace a little. Her mouth pulls and she squints up at me before she takes my face in both her hands. She glares at me but the edges are soft.

"Never thought I'd be happy to see your face but here we are—"

Magnolia nods, sits down next to me. "My shagging a gang lord was a real eye-opener for Mars. Things could be a lot worse than you cheating on me with my best friend and breaking my heart."

I give Parks a look and she gives me a bratty smile.

"Could be worse, could be better," Marsaili says, considering this. "Could have not cheated on her in the first place."

"What?" I scoff. "And spare you the ride of a lifetime up on that high horse? Mars, I'd never."

Toss her a big grin and Harley gives me warning eyes.

"Watch it . . ."

Parks looks from her dad to Marsaili, pointing between them.

"I don't love this friendship."

"We're married," her dad tells her.

"Well," Magnolia tilts her head, "are you?"

"Yes," Marsaili says with a nod at the same time Harley goes, "Literally, yes."

Parks scrunches her nose up. "Perhaps maybe, technically, on some level, you are married—"

"The literal level." Harley nods. "Yes."

Parks ignores him.

"It's just that sometimes when I'm not totally on board with this, I find it easier to categorise your relationship in my mind as purely friends."

Harley flicks me a look, mostly amused, tiny bit alarmed.

He presses his tongue into his cheek for a second before he nods again.

"Yes, but darling, we're actually married."

Parks shrugs happily. "Agree to disagree then."

"Magnolia, darling." Her mum leans over to her. "Smashing dress, darling. I love it, really."

"Oh!" Magnolia lights up how she does, glancing in case anyone wants to pile on with the compliments. Bridget catches my eye, gives me an unimpressed look and I squash a smile. "Thank you! Isn't it so interesting?"

"It's a dress." Bridget rolls her eyes.

"Bridget." Parks frowns. "It's the leather scalloped cutout dress from Chloé from their 2021 Fall Runway. It's completely gorgeous." Magnolia gives Bridget a look like she's an idiot.

"Gabriela Hearst is a visionary. It's so simple but has such whimsical nods to broderie anglaise—"

"Those are made-up words," Bridget tells her with a brat look on her face. Parks meets it.

"Bridget, you're smarter than this. You know fashion is incredibly important and dictating. It's high time that you just embrace it for the important role it plays in our society."

Bridget rolls her eyes as she pours herself more wine. "Why are you like this? Like, why do you like clothes so much?"

Magnolia's face pinches to a little frown and she breathes out her nose. Definitely cross, she says nothing though. Then Harley leans back in his chair.

"I used to bring her back issues of *Vogue* from whatever country I was in," he says, watching her.

She stares over at him—glares over, maybe—looks like she's fifteen again and my heart goes like a spinning top in my chest because I love her and she looks sad and this is news to me. Do you know how rare it is to learn something new about someone you've known for twenty years? Had no idea.

She stares over at her dad how she never does, like she cares about him, like she gives a shit that he never did, and it occurs to me somewhere in the background of my thinking—like the way snow falls, quiet without you knowing, and then you look behind you and your entire backyard, everything you thought you knew, is blanketed all white. She just wanted his approval.

It's not a technically friendly thing to do, but I reach over and squeeze her knee. She stares at my hand for a second before she holds my thumb and gives her sister a look that's a heavy mash of sadness, defiance and scorn.

"So, Nathan," I say loudly, keeping things moving because I know she'd want me to. "How did you and Arrie meet?"

"We met in Ibiza." He smiles at the room. "And it was love at first sight. How could it not be?" He stares over at her. "Look at that mouth."

Nathan seems unaware that that was a weird thing to say in front of Arrie's ex-husband and daughters. To his credit, he seems completely unfazed that he's dating the ex-wife of Harley Parks, who's sitting there, looking annoyed at his presence and mildly irked by Nathan's appreciation for his ex's lips.

Can't tell whether it's big balls or a lack of awareness, but it makes me like him a bit either way.

"Locked eyes, locked lips—" Arrie grins over at him. (Magnolia makes a gag sound next to me and I elbow her quiet.)

"Spent the rest of the evening dancing under the stars and between the sheets." She giggles.

"Mother." Bridget scowls.

Arrie sort of just stares at him fondly, and I wonder if she likes him for real a bit?

I nod at Nathan. "How old are you, man?"

"Twenty-three," he tells me and then takes a sip of his water.

Harley about falls out of his chair and Magnolia's head pulls back.

"My God, Arrie—" Harley looks at her. "Twenty-three?"

"What?" She blinks.

"Our daughters are twenty-three—"

("I'm actually twenty-four, but that's fine." Magnolia shrugs as Bridget nods. "Twenty-two but yeah, let's average it out.")

"So what?" Arrie says, looking increasingly annoyed.

"So what do you have in common with a twenty-three-year-old?"

"Lots." Nathan shrugs.

Arrie gives Harley a smug look.

Harley goes to say something but Bushka interrupts—

"—Is not so bad." Bushka shrugs. "I date twenty-six-year-old."

Magnolia looks horrified. "Who?"

Bushka points to me. Marsaili rolls her eyes.

"I show you ver good time." She nods and then points at Parks. "She so small, she not know how to drink."

Parks frowns.

"Well," I consider, "she knows how to drink fine. Doesn't know how to hold it very well."

Parks frowns more and I smirk over at her.

"I be good lover." Bushka nods and Magnolia spits out a little bit of wine.

("Wow." Bridget nods as Mars shakes her head. "I'm not putting vodka in your juice anymore. No. I don't care how much you ask me.")

I give Bushka a playful look. "You know what? As tempting an offer as that is, I'm actually in love with this girl—" I deliberately don't look at Parks. "And we're taking it slow. Pacing ourselves. Never been so good at pacing ourselves, to be honest."

("I'll fucking say," Harley says under his breath.)

"And it's my job to not dick around." I give Bushka a rueful smile.

"How's that been going?" Bridget asks brightly.

"Yeah, good." I nod.

"—It's been a week," Magnolia interjects.

"I had a shoot today with some very pretty girls," I tell Parks, proudly. "Didn't even look twice."

"Really?" Bridget blinks. "Didn't look twice?"

"Nope."

"How'd you know they were pretty, then?" Bridget asks and I give her an unimpressed look.

"Would you like some wine?" Magnolia asks loudly over her sister, holding out the bottle to Nathan.

"Oh, no thank you—" He shakes his head. "I'm not drinking for the month of April."

Parks stares at him, face visibly confused as she tries to process the information. "But . . . that doesn't even rhyme with 'dry'?"

"I beg your pardon?" Nathan blinks, confused.

Me and Harley start laughing.

"I did Dry July once," Arrie announces, nobly.

And everyone gives her varying degrees of dubious looks.

505

Parks tenses up and flicks her eyes over to me. I shake my head at her subtly.

She leans in towards me and whispers, "We're really going to let her refer to the time she was in rehab as 'Dry July'?"

"We are." I give her a stern look and try not to show it on my face that I'm dizzy with her near me like this.

Magnolia clears her throat. "It was actually a September," she tells her mother curtly. "After a very, very wet August."

I flick her in the arm and she peers up at me with shit-stirring eyes and holy fuck I love her.

Fight the urge not to take her face in my hands and kiss her on the spot.

Remind myself that we need to take it slow, reel in the slack so we don't choke ourselves on it again.

My face softens more than I want it to, but I lean down and whisper to her, "Your mum likes him—"

Parks's face flickers a frown.

"How do you know?" she says right into my ear.

I give her a little shrug. "I can just tell." But that's a lie. I can tell for a reason.

Parks's cheeks go pink in a specific spot when I do 'certain things' to her, say things that make her heart go funny, touch her face, press my mouth against her ear—she's done it forever. Arrie does it too.

Used to see it on her face when Harley actually gave her the time of day. I don't think he ever really loved her, but I could always tell she loved him. Loves, probably, if we're being honest.

After dinner, I drive the girls home.

Bridget rolls her eyes at the two of us as we stall downstairs like the twatty idiots we are.

Shove my hands in the pockets of my jacket as I stand out front of her apartment, staring over at her, trying my best not to kiss her. She folds her arms over her chest. She's cold—didn't bring a jacket so I'd have to hold her.

Vintage Parks.

I pull her over towards me by the waist and her eyes go heavy in a way I know. I rub my hands up and down her arms, warming her up.

"I've always quite liked you in a raglan," she tells me, tugging on the hem of my T-shirt.

"Yeah?"

"Yes." She nods and then her eyes pinch playfully. "I love being friends, by the way." She nods. "Love it."

I smirk down at her. "Same."

"Good." She nods once and I keep rubbing her arms.

"Great, yeah—" I nod back. "It's easy. I never think about you without your clothes on . . . ever."

She presses her lips together, trying not to smile.

"Are you going to come up?" she asks with wide eyes.

I do a shit job of not smiling at her when she says that, shake my head, laughing with my mouth closed. ". . . Mmm, nope."

She frowns. "Why?"

I give her a look. "Because if I come up you'll make me stay."

"Make you stay?" She looks at me with tall eyebrows. "I'm a tiny ineffectual woman."

I tilt my head. Give her a look.

"You . . . are the least ineffectual thing in my life."

Cheeks do the pink thing. That butters her up a bit, just for a second though. Then it's back to pouting.

"So you aren't going to stay over?"

"No."

"You said you would."

I give her a look. "I said 'maybe'."

She frowns. "So why no now?"

I roll my eyes at her—gesture to her vaguely. "Because you have a face."

"I don't have a face," she pouts. "I mean, well, I have a face but—"

I give her a look. "You have bedroom eyes."

She pouts more. "These are my regular eyes."

507

"They are not." I tell her, even though they sort of are.

"This is how I always look at you," she tells me and I'm telling you—that, right there, is the truth. As well as the reason why we got pregnant in high school.

I swallow heavy.

"I'm leaving," I tell her.

"No!" She stomps her little foot.

I press my mouth into her forehead.

"Breakfast tomorrow?" I offer as a shitty alternative.

She sighs. "Okay."

SEVENTY-ONE

BJ

My Dad's on the board of a charity for a food poverty foundation and every year we throw this big gala for the donors and the sponsors to raise money.

It's a big deal both in my family and outside of it.

My mum becomes a complete melter every year in April in the lead-up to it.

Me and Parks are getting ready at my parents' place, which seems annoying and overcrowded to me, but Mum and my sisters like having her there to dress them, which she's done all afternoon. There was some chaos about how Jemima's dress was £14,000 and Madeline's was only £8,000 because Mads is a brat like that. Parks has been overseeing all their hair and make-up, loving the control. She's bossing everyone around and yelling about clashing colours and, to quote her, 'a ghastly lack of pigmentation', but I managed to steer clear of most of it. Only briefly dragged in when Allie made Madeline cry because she called her flat-chested. It wasn't a conversation I wanted to be brought in on, wasn't a conversation I ever wanted to have to think about. The look I gave Parks when she said, "No, don't cry, Madeline, you have wonderful breasts, doesn't she, Beej?"

So now Henry and me are playing GTA 2022 in our tuxedos. Me in Tom Ford, him in Givenchy; both of us styled by the girl lying next to me who is still in her robe.

"Ey." My brother elbows her and nods his chin at the TV. "This giving you sexy crime lord flashbacks?"

She glares up at him from her phone.

"He wasn't a car thief." She rolls her eyes. "He wasn't a thief at all."

Henry and me exchange looks over her head. Ah well, what she doesn't know won't kill her.

"Magnolia!" Mum scolds, standing in the doorway, hands on her hips looking at Parks like she's still fifteen. "You're not dressed!"

"Oh—" Parks swats her hand dismissively. "No, I know. I like to be the last one ready so when I walk down the stairs everyone goes, 'Oh wow, you look so amazing. Who are you wearing? You're so pretty.'"

Henry starts laughing, and from some other part of the house, so does my dad. I turn to her.

"Do you think there's a red carpet here?"

Mum points upstairs. "We're leaving in twenty minutes. You move exclusively at a phlegmatic pace." Magnolia pouts but it falls on deaf ears with Lil. "Go upstairs and get dressed immediately!"

Parks grumpily obeys her, dragging her feet up to my room. I follow her because I know my role here.

Whatever dress she's wearing, she'll need me. She'll have picked a dress that needs my help to get in to. And out of. Old tricks of hers that I hope never die.

I walk into the room—my bedroom from when I was a teenager, Mum's left it as it was. I still stay here sometimes if Jo's being particularly suspect.

Parks sees me walk in. She slips her robe off her shoulders and it pools at her ankles.

She's standing there in nothing but knickers. Close the door as fast as I can, steady myself against it.

I press my hand into my mouth to keep it together. Her eyes are amused.

"What?" She blinks brightly. "I get changed in front of my other friends all the time."

"What other friends? You have two friends—your sister and Tausie."

"And Henry," she tells me.

I give her a look. "You get changed like this in front of Henry?"

"No, but he is my friend."

I roll my eyes at her, try not to stare. Toss her a T-shirt of mine and she dodges it, laughing, and my resolve is weakening.

"Magnolia Parks, I swear to God if you aren't dressed when I open this door," Mum bellows from the other side. Then, without waiting even a second, she swings it wide open and Parks darts behind me.

"Mum!" I growl.

"BJ!" My mother gives me a stern look. "Are you distracting her from getting ready?"

"Yes," Magnolia peeps from behind me, eager to not get a bollocking from my mum. "He's being terribly distracting, Lil. He's throwing T-shirts at me and telling me I have no friends."

"Get out—" Mum eyes me as she points to the door.

"This is my room!" I roll my eyes at her.

"Not anymore, darling. This is going to be my craft room, I've just decided."

"Is it?" Magnolia asks, cheerily poking her head from around me. "Can I come and use it?"

"You don't like crafts," I remind her.

"But perhaps I would if there was a room for it? What kind of crafts are you envisioning, Lilian? Flower pressing? Maybe some candle making?"

I squint down at her. "I'll give you a million dollars if you can make a candle."

"Alright, smarty pants." She gives me a look. "Better call Zurich because tomorrow I'm making a candle."

"Not if you're not dressed within the next two minutes, you aren't." Mum points a warning finger at her before slamming the door.

"The one night of the year she's a total head case—" I sniff, checking my reflection again and taking advantage of the chance to watch Parks in the mirror.

Fuck, she's perfect.

Push my hands through my hair.

She unzips a big bag that says Giambattista Valli on it and pulls out the biggest, fluffiest yellow dress I've ever see.

"You kill Big Bird to make that thing?"

She stares at me like I just told her I killed her mother.

"This is Giambattista Valli's infamous 2017 couture, buttercream yellow tulle layer gown." She holds it against her chest, admiring herself. "It's heaven."

It's a pretty dress, I'll give her that. Bit like Belle's from *Beauty and the Beast*.

She turns around, smiles at me all perfect and bratty. She knows she looks too beautiful to be a normal part of the world. Everyone else on the planet is a pavement and she's the flower growing out of the crack in it.

I take a deep breath, suppress a smile as I stare over at her.

"Fuck." I shake my head a bit.

"What?" She blinks.

I give her a look. "You know what."

She ignores me and shows me her back.

"Do me up?"

I swallow heavy, walk over to her. Stand closer than I need to, but I need to.

Zip it slowly from the bottom up, one of my hands dragging up her spine with the zipper.

An Olympic display of willpower, a gold medal performance and first prize is fifty excuses to fuck this 'friends' shit and kiss her.

I take a step away from her. Take a couple of deep breaths.

"Anything else?" I croak.

She turns around and faces me, eyes shy. She's gone pink.

"Shoes," she barely says. Nods at them in the corner.

I grab them and hand her the box, but she doesn't take them. Instead she makes a nervous laugh.

"Actually." Purses her lips. "I can't bend over in this dress," she tells me as she lifts forty-five tons of tulle up into the air and I'm met with my favourite pair of legs in the world.

I give her a long look, shaking my head as I slowly get down on my knees.

Fuck me. I breathe out.

She lifts up one foot and I slide on this bright yellow strappy shoe that's covered in butterflies. Do it up at the ankle. Flop my head on her leg, groan a little. "You're trying to kill me."

She sniggers a little, drunk on power. Lifts her other foot for me.

I shove on the other shoe as unceremoniously as possible, do it up one too tight just to get even with her and stand up fast as I can, putting some space between us. Turn my back to her, breathe heavy. Remember all the reasons why being just friends is the right thing for now.

In it for the long haul, I tell myself. When we rush things, we fuck them up. She needs to trust me. I want to see that she doesn't need to be with someone—

Maybe she just needs to be with me though?

I look at her from over my shoulder, squint at her, a bit fucked up that she's so beautiful.

Annoying, actually. Kind of rude.

Shake my head. "Fuck it."

And then I rush her. Lift her off the ground, push her backwards, and in a single move (because all the moves I have were learned on her body) I've got her on my waist, pressed up against the wall.

It happens so fast. We know each other's body how you know your way around your bedroom in the dark. I know where to find the light switch, I know what corners to watch out for, I know where to step for the floorboards to creak.

"Knock, knock," Mum says, walking in once again without any space between her knock-knocking and the door opening.

"Oh my." Her eyes shoot to the ceiling.

Parks's hands are literally down my pants.

"Uh—are you both ready?" she asks the air-conditioner unit.

"Yeah," I snort, looking at Parks with a crooked smile. Her

face is frozen in a mix of delight and horror.

Mum nods and backs out of the room, never having stared at an appliance so intently in her life. She closes the door and Parks dissolves into a fit of giggles into my neck, holding herself against me tightly.

I lower her back down onto the floor, grinning at her as I do. Want to tell her I love her but I just push her hair behind her ear instead.

She stares up at me shy, still smiling.

I glance down at myself, do up my fly, then grin at her.

"You ready for the most uncomfortable car trip of your life?"

It's an excruciating ride to the Ballroom at Claridge's.

Mum can't make eye contact with me or Parks, which gets funnier and funnier the less she looks at us. I'm completely beside myself, doubled over in the stretched town car—which I fucking hate by the way, so uncouth. But Mum likes us to arrive at these things together.

"What even happened?" Allie asks, frowning curiously.

"Nothing happened!" Lily says, unable to stop looking out the window.

"She walked in on them . . . you know," Dad tells her.

"Hamish!" Mum yells, mortified.

Parks tilts her head. "We weren't exactly . . ."

"Well, not yet, anyway." I shrug and Mum lets out a despondent cry.

"Surely you must know they have sex, Mum." Henry stares at her.

"Henry," Mum snaps. "Please!"

"They've been sleeping together for ages," Allie chimes in.

I'm cackling and Parks is hiding her face behind my shoulder. We're fucking rubbish friends tonight.

"No, they have not." Mum is convinced though she damn well knows better.

"Darling," Dad gives her a look, "Magnolia told you she was on the pill when she was fifteen."

Mum shakes her head. "She certainly did not."

She certainly did. Sunday night dinner, in the kitchen—Allie was there.

"And maybe she needed it for her skin," Mum tells her fingernails, in completely denial.

"Skin, Lilian?" Parks glowers at her. "My skin is radiant. Always has been, always will be."

"I saw them doing it," Madeline announces to no one in particular.

"What the fuck?" I blink at the same time as Parks goes, "Oh my gosh, Madeline!"

Parks stares at her. "When?"

Everyone's staring at Mads, pretty horrified.

"Oh relax." She shrugs. "It's not like I'm a bloody voyeur. I was about thirteen. So you were, what?" She looks between me and Parks, thinking to herself. "Sixteen? Seventeen? Anyway. Mum and Dad were out. I went upstairs to get some lollies from Mum's bedside table and they were doing it up there."

"IN MY BED?!" Mum cries, hands on her face.

"Well, on it." Maddie shrugs, gesturing with her hands. "Like, on top. Like, not under the sheets or anything."

I close my eyes, annoyed at my sister. "Excellent, Madeline. Thank you."

"IN! MY! BED! Baxter James Ballentine! In my bed!" Mum keeps yelling.

"On, Mum." I offer her a smile and scratch the back of my neck. "On."

"Hamish! Are you hearing this? On our bed!"

"No, sorry, I missed it, sweetheart." Dad leans in towards her. "Was it in the bed? Or on?" He flicks me an amused look.

Mum stares over at me. "How many times have you done that in our bed?"

Parks purses her mouth and shakes her head. "Just the one time."

Henry shakes his head, thumbs in our direction. "These two? Are you kidding? Only place they did it more than your bed was Harley's poor car—"

Magnolia swings her clutch at Henry's head to shut him up.

We finally (finally) pull up to the venue and it's probably the happiest I've been in years.

Parks with my family like no time has passed.

Dad taps me on the chest. "I'm assuming you've got a plan here?"

I nod at him once. "I'm playing for keeps."

He gives me a little wink. "Good man."

I offer Parks my hand to help her out of the car. She takes it without a second thought and then keeps holding it for no reason. See it dance across her face, remembering that we're 'friends.' She stares at her hand in mine for a few seconds, laughs uncomfortably before taking it back.

Shake my head a bit, mostly at myself, because what the fuck am I doing?

"Do you do that with your friends?" she whispers to me as we walk inside. "What we were doing in your room?"

I give her a look. "No."

"Oh—" Her eyebrows go tall. "How interesting."

"God, you're disgusting," Bridget says, frowning at Magnolia. "Who looks like that?"

"The exquisite woman who put you in that pink, silk, belted-waist, V-neck gown from Carolina Herrera." Magnolia gives her a curt smile.

Bridget lifts the skirt of her dress to flash me her shoes. Pink Air Jordans. Magnolia's eyes catch mine and I beam at her. Deep cut shit for us, her sister in trainers.

"How's it going being friends, then?" Bridget asks us, pretending to be bored. She takes a big sip of her wine and Henry tosses an arm around her.

"Yeah, guys." He grins. "How's it going being friends?"

Bridge looks up at him. "What are you being smug about?"

"Oh, nothing—" Parks swats her hand. "Lil walked in on me and BJ nearly having sex, but the moment's passed and we're back to strictly platonic."

Magnolia bats her eyes at me.

Bridget squints. "How nearly?"

Parks squints as she thinks. "Hint of—"

"—Don't say penetration." Henry shakes his head. "Do not say it."

"Penetration," Magnolia says just to spite him. Flashes him a smug smile.

My brother pretends to dry heave.

"Vintage you two. Maserati vibes. Nice." Bridget nods.

"You two love an almost, don't you?" Henry sighs.

"How much did Lily see?"

"Oh, look—" I pluck two champagnes from the tray of a waiter, pass one to Parks and down mine quickly "More than you want your mum to see, without a doubt."

Bridge squints. "What are we talking here?"

"Having a bit of a dry spell, are we Bridge?" Magnolia asks her sister.

Bridget gives her a dark look and skulks over to the bar. Parks dashes after her, not done sparring with her yet.

Henry gives me a long look.

"Friends, huh?"

I press my mouth together.

"It's been, what, a fortnight?"

"A fucking long fortnight, man."

"Are you done now?" he asks, eyebrows up. "With this friends shit?"

I shake my head at him.

He flicks me a look and nods his head towards the bar.

Big guy from our high school's chatting up Parks.

Holden Carrick. Julian's year.

Me and Hen walk over. I sidle up behind Parks. Extend my hand out to him. "Holden, man—"

He looks surprised to see me. "Ballentine."

He looks from me to Parks. "Are you?"

"No." Parks shakes her head emphatically. "We're just friends."

And it shits me. Makes me go tight in the chest. Fucking hate being her friend. Whose fucking idea was this anyway?

"Oh." Carrick frowns, clocking me, confused. "So can I

get you a drink?"

"No." She shakes her head before gesturing to me. "He runs a very tight ship."

He frowns more but I knock back a smile.

"Thought you said he's not your boyfriend?"

"He's not." She shakes her head. "But we are in love, he and I." Gestures between us.

"Oh." Frowns more.

"But we have some toxic traits," she concedes all rueful and I just want to kiss her. "Mine is that I use cute boys to hurt him—and, actually, you really are right up my alley."

"Oh, thanks." He nods, a bit affirmed.

"You're welcome." She smiles up at him. "How tall are you, anyway? Six-one?"

"Parks." I give her a look.

"Right, no—sorry." She shakes her head and points at me. "He's actually six-three and we're in love and we are friends now, proving that we can be, you know . . ." She purses her lips, struggles to find the word. "Normal."

"This does feel normal," Bridget interjects sarcastically.

"Doesn't it?" Henry grimaces from the side.

Roll my eyes at both of them.

"Well," Holden tilts his head at her as he backs away, "call me if it doesn't work out."

I roll my eyes at him.

"It'll work out, mate," I call after him before giving her a look.

She stares up at me, a bit defiant and beautiful. "How do you know?"

I give her a look, squint a bit. "We're in the stars, Parks."

SEVENTY-TWO

Magnolia

Someone released a sex tape of Christian and Vanna Ripley and it is all over the internet. And when I say it's everywhere, I mean, it's on every news outlet, it's on the front cover of every newspaper, on TikTok, on Instagram, it's trending on Twitter—all of it.

And Daisy's not taking it well, that's what Christian says. I mean, no surprises there. How else is she supposed to take it? But Christian begged me to talk to her.

She's not answering his calls or his texts or his anything. He said, and I quote, "She took a leaf out of your playbook and ran to Romeo Bambrilla." To which I said, "I've never run to him, I don't know to what you're referring" and then all the boys (even Henry (traitor)) groaned, which felt rude but whatever. It's not about me.

The sex tape is very sexy, by the way. Very, very sexy. Like, I don't watch porn, it's not for me. It's not an industry I condone. I think it's unhealthy and I've always run a very tight ship with those boys about pornography, but I'm sorry to say that at word of a sex tape featuring Christian, Bridget, Taura and myself wordlessly assembled in front of my computer screen and watched it in a sort of befuddled wonder, and I realise I may have really missed out on a great time with him in that capacity, but I don't need another log on the fire.

"Did you see it?" he asked me on the phone.

"What?" I blinked. "Nothing. No. There—Pffft. I don't know even what you're talking. What sex tape?"

He breathed out, annoyed. "So you watched it."

I blew some air out of my mouth. "Bridget was watching it and I saw it for a sliver of a s—" and then my sister dived on me, smacking me mercilessly. ("LIAR!" she yelled and I kicked her off me. "You loved it!" I yelled back. "I'm not the one who said 'look at his back!' and paused it—" "HE HAS A GOOD BACK.")

"Magnolia—" Christian sighed, impatiently. "Hello?"

I wrestled the phone back from my squealing sister and kicked her away. "Hello—what? Sorry, Bridget was just— God, you know her. So impossible sometimes. Anyway, what's up?"

And then he said my favourite words: "I need your help."

Christian fundamentally doesn't understand why or how Daisy is angry at him. And then I got angry at him when he told me he didn't understand why she was upset about it, and I got angrier still when he said he told her it was—and I quote him directly again here—"Just sex." But then he went over to her house on his own volition and she was in bed with Romeo Bambrilla.

"Not doing anything," he says. They were just sitting in bed watching a film. And I said maybe they're just friends now and what's the big deal with that? And then he likened it to BJ walking in on Christian and I in a bed together and I said, "I don't think he'd care." And Christian said, "You're an idiot." And I said, "You're an idiot!" And he said, "You're so bereft from reality it's fucking insane." And I said, "DO YOU WANT MY HELP OR NOT?" And then he stopped saying mean things to me.

So I'm off on a peace-keeping mission, standing on the Haiteses' front steps, knocking.

The door swings open and Julian stares down at me. His face falls into a playful frown. We haven't seen each other since.

"What are you doing here?"

"What are you doing opening your own doors now?" I counter.

He sniffs a laugh and wraps his arms around me a bit how he used to, chin on my head and everything. I find myself breathing out a little, like maybe I miss him some. Or maybe he just accidentally became a safe place for me.

He pulls back to look at me. "You okay?"

I nod.

"You here to see me?"

I give him an apologetic smile and shake my head.

"Ah." He nods, knowingly. "You're here on behalf of the most streamed man in Britain."

I suppress a smile.

Jules nods his chin at me. "He doing okay?"

"Well, he was." I nod. "And then he came here to see her and found her in bed with Romeo?"

"What the fuck?" His head pulls back.

"How did you not know that?" I ask.

He shakes his head. "Why would she—"

"Oh, you know them." I shrug. "They're complete idiots."

He nods once. "They are."

I eye him suspiciously. "How checked out are you?"

"Just busy." He shrugs. "With work. I'm good."

"Good." I nod but then I look at him for a second longer. He doesn't look quite himself. "Are you good though?" I ask him once we get to her door.

He stares at me for a few seconds. "Yep." He smiles a tight smile. "Are you?"

I nod.

"You two idiots back together?" I shake my head and his head falls back in exasperation. "Magnolia—"

"We're working on it!" I protest.

He rolls his eyes and I smile at him.

"Do you miss me?" I ask brightly and his mouth twitches. I think maybe I see something breeze over his face but then it scrunches and he shakes his head.

"Nope."

I blink at his rudeness. "I beg your pardon?"

"Don't miss you." He shakes his head more. "Fucking glad to be rid of you, if anything—"

"Oh." I frown a little and maybe my feelings are hurt a tiny bit, so I push past him to tap on his sister's door before cautiously opening it.

"Knock knock—" I peek in and Daisy Haites glares up at me.

"What are you doing here?" She frowns.

"Be nice," Julian tells her over my head.

"Why?" Daisy shrugs, petulant. "She dumped you, remember?"

He says nothing, so I glance over at Julian, my eyes feeling timid and I wonder if he looks a little bit sad. And the thought rattles through my mind only for a second, but I wonder whether perhaps I've had more loves than I knew of in this lifetime. For a moment I worry that Gus was maybe right.

Then I shake it all off and give her a pleasant smile, eyebrows up.

She waves towards the door. "You can leave."

"I'm going to assume that this hostility has more to do with the fact that you just watched your boyfriend wheelbarrow another girl and less to do with me personally—"

"Then you're an idiot," Daisy tells me and Julian points at her.

"Watch it," he tells her with his chin and then skulks away without another look at me.

I cautiously go and sit on the edge of her bed.

"Well—" I sigh, straightening out the skirt of my green pleated lace midi-dress from Giambattista Valli. "What a week."

She blinks at me.

"Firstly," I give her an encouraging smile, "congratulations! Despite the persisting rumours amongst our friends that we had sex, we did NOT and it seems as though he's very good at it, so well done you—" She glares over at me. "Not the time? Okay, right, that's fine—" I shake my head. Such a tough crowd. "Listen, Daisy, those boys are absolute fuckwits."

She flares at me suspiciously. "He sent you here to apologise?"

"I suspect I was sent here as a diffuser." I give her a sweet smile. "I have a very calming presence."

"You definitely don't," she tells me and I frown a lot.

"Well, lots of people think I do."

"No." She shakes her head. "Literally no one thinks that."

"Lots of people—"

"—Name one," she tells me.

"BJ." I give her a smug look.

"That's called dopamine. He's high off of loving you." She gives me an annoyed look. "There's not one calming thing about you, you're obsessive and infuriating and weird."

I blow some air out of my mouth. "Well, let's agree to disagree on that."

I pick a stray piece of cotton from my dress and then lay my hands delicately in my lap. "Perhaps I was sent in because I'm somewhat familiar with the feeling of losing the person you love to somebody else—sexually—even if you haven't actually lost them?"

"What?" She rolls her eyes at me. "BJ has a sex tape somewhere out there?"

"Well, no—" I purse my lips. Could do though, I suppose. "Then you don't get it, do you?"

"I've walked in on him having sex with someone else at least once. He had sex with my best friend. He slept with a very slutty celebrity who gave a very vivid account of it. I've seen him hook up with girls in clubs, in cars, on boats, on planes . . ." Daisy's mouth falls open a bit. "When I asked him and he did the maths, we suspect that the amount of women he's had sex with is in the high hundreds."

Her jaw drops.

"That's people." I nod. "Not times. Which puts the times tally well into the thousands." I shake my head. Shake it like it doesn't slice me wide open and feel like poison shooting through my veins.

I look over at Daisy and her eyes are welled up all teary. Mine are a bit too because that's exactly what it is: a wordless kind of pain. Some sort of betrayal that goes deeper than words, the kind of ache that gives your heart's knee a limp that it can't ever quite shake.

I purse my lips. "So, now, I do understand that that's not exactly the same as a sex tape being released of your boyfriend and his ex-girlfriend, but I think I'm in the neighbourhood." I give her a gentle look. "Daisy, I can't even imagine how horrible that must have been for you."

I reach over and brush the tears from her cheeks and then tuck some hair behind my ears.

"Here's the thing," I tell her. "All of those boys are undeniably stupid and far too cavalier about sex. Except for when they're in love—" I give her a look. "Somehow they've managed to distinguish sex with other people from sex with us."

She looks up at me, her bottom lip a bit wobbly. "It looked the same. Him with her. It looked like us."

I sigh, sad for her.

"Maybe it did." I shrug. "But it isn't the same because he's never loved her, he just loves you. And to them that's the only part that counts."

She chews on the inside of her cheek mindlessly.

"Come on—" I nod towards the door. "I'll take you to see him."

She nods and gets up from the bed. I watch after her—scrunching my nose a bit.

"Sorry. Are you going to wear that?"

SEVENTY-THREE

BJ

Walk into Parks's office on a Friday afternoon. I haven't done this in years but I've always loved it.

Like picking her up is a public declaration that she's mine.

I ask the girl at the front desk where Parks's office is and she points me in the right direction.

Few squeals and I'm stopped for a few photos on my way through. Hope Parks sees and it's a freebie to piss her off.

But then I round the corner to her office and she's not there. Stand in it for a minute anyway because I'm proud of her. She's always wanted to work in fashion.

"Equally as established, respected and unapproachable as Anna Wintour but less sunglasses-y" was Magnolia's career goal in Upper Sixth.

I've never known what I wanted to do—much to Dad's dismay. Fell into the modelling thing. Elite signed Parks when she was thirteen, did it for a while through high school but she didn't like it. Through her they signed me. Then the Instagram thing took off too. It's never been a conscious thing, just a thing I did because it was in front of me. Made good money, wore sick clothes, kissed hot girls. Good deal, really. But sometimes I wonder how it'd feel to know what you want to do. The only thing I've ever been sure about is Parks.

I wander back into the hall. Hear laughing from Richard Dennen's office, follow the sound, poke my head in. Sure enough, she looks over at me, surprised I'm here.

"Hi—" She sits up a little straighter.

Black-and-white checked dress with puffy sleeves, black heels, red headband. Kind of looks how she did in school, back when I thought I couldn't love her more than I did at the time. Life is weird like that, how it lets you love to a breaking point but the breaking point is just more ways to love that person.

"Hello there!" Dennen grins, standing, extending his hand. "Ballentine, what a surprise."

I take it, grinning over at him. "So good to see you, man."

"Just passing through?" he asks.

I nod my head towards Parks. "Came to see if this one wanted to grab lunch."

"Care to join?" Parks asks him brightly.

"Wish I could." He tilts his head. "Got a call with Paris." He looks between us. "Are you two back on?"

Magnolia lets out a little laugh and our eyes hold for a long second.

"On the way." I nod.

"We're taking the scenic route," she tells him dryly.

He laughs. "Happy for you both."

"Don't be too happy for us just yet, Rich—there's still plenty of time for Beej to cock it up again." She stands up, flattening her dress.

He chuckles and tosses me a wink.

Follow her out of his office.

"Where are you taking me?" She spins around on her heel to face me.

I shrug. "Where do you want to be taken?"

"Roughly in the supply closet?" She gives me a playful look and I fucking blush. Shake my head at her, trying not to laugh.

She pushes her hair over her shoulders.

"Are you taking me to lunch or shopping?"

"Fuck that—" I frown at her. "Where's that supply closet?"

She laughs and tugs me by the jacket into the lift. Some kind of brown suede shirt jacket. She picked it. Salvatore Santoro.

"How are Christian and Daisy?" She looks over at me.

"Good." I nod. "Better. Fixed them, you did."

"Yeah?" She beams over at me, chuffed.

"Yeah." I nod. "You didn't use my preferred method of deduction solving that case, but it got the job done, I suppose."

"And she's not sad anymore?"

I shake my head.

"And he's not being a prick anymore?"

"No more than usual." I grin and she rolls her eyes.

Mews of Mayfair, that's where we go. Walk over to Chanel after. She's browsing the store, I'm buying the store. Watch her with more focus than I would a film. We could call it making up for lost time because we've lost a lot of it but I've never stopped looking at her.

"How many of your friends take you shopping?" I eye the bags we're both holding.

"Oh, mmm . . . just you." She shrugs. "And Henry."

("And sometimes Christian, Jonah and Rush," she says under her breath.)

"What?" I call after her with a laugh. "Gus doesn't take you?"

"No," she says. Grumpy about that too. "Unfortunately not."

She rounds the corner on to Regent Street and then stops dead in her tracks.

Freezes.

"What's wrong?" I bump into the back of her.

She's completely still.

"Parks, what?" I peer past her and my hands ball to fists.

Paili Blythe is standing right there in front of us.

"Magnolia—" Paili smiles cautiously. Then she looks past her. Sees me.

"Fuck," I say.

Parks is a statue. I hate it, hate how she's gone. I can feel it on her, the fear. Hate myself for it. That standing here on a busy street corner in the middle of the day in London with me and her childhood best friend is her worst nightmare.

I did that to her.

She might live with the betrayal, and I'm not saying mine is worse, but I have to live with betraying her.

527

Paili looks between us, brows furrowed. "You're back together?"

"Yes," Magnolia says defensively, staring her dead in the eye and straightening up. She shifts in front of me like she's guarding me and I get a surge of loving her.

Take a step closer, hook my arm around her body.

A barrier between her and Paili.

"That's amazing!" Paili smiles, glances between us. "I'm so happy for you both."

Magnolia's face falters. "What are you doing here?" Parks shakes her head. "I thought you moved to Spain?"

"It's my dad's birthday."

Magnolia nods once.

"I was actually hoping I'd run into you—" Paili starts.

"—Which one of us, Pails?" Magnolia asks sharply.

Paili's eyes fall a little, glances between us again.

"You," she says with a look at Parks.

"Well, I have nothing to say to you."

Magnolia shakes her head. Paili frowns. "You're back together now, what does it—"

"—Matter?" Parks jumps in. She lets out this sharp breath that sounds a bit like a quick cry.

Hold her tighter just in case.

Paili shakes her head, looking tired. "Magnolia, I lost everything when that came out—"

I blow some air out of my mouth.

"You?" Parks stares at her. "You gave it all away for one night with my boyfriend. I lost everything." She holds my arm against her. "You took it from me."

My jaw goes tight, hang my head. I hate myself more than I did before.

She sighs. "Magnolia, I—"

Parks silences her with a shake of her head.

"All those nights I stayed awake, poring through my mind, trying to guess who it was. Me laying on your lap and crying about what he did to me . . . And you did it to me too." I can hear she's crying in her voice now.

She shakes her head, wipes her face so briskly she practically smacks it. "And you made me think it was Taura—"

"That was Perry," Paili clarifies, pointlessly.

"And you didn't stop him, why?" Parks asks, angrily. "Did he force your hand?"

"No but—"

"—No. Stop talking," Magnolia tells her. I've never really heard her talk to anyone like this before. "There's nothing you can say."

Paili looks sad. Could almost feel sorry for her if the situation was different.

"Magnolia, you were my best friend."

"Yeah, well, you clearly weren't mine." Parks eyes her.

She shakes her head, not getting it. "You've forgiven him—" Gestures to me.

Has she? I don't know. The sadness she's wearing here in my arms feels too thick if she's forgiven me.

"He . . . is the love of my life," Parks tells her. "You? You are nothing to me anymore."

Paili's head pulls back. "How can you say that to me?"

"As easy as could you do that to me," Parks spits.

Paili shakes her head a little. "Did you know what it was like to be your best friend? To grow up next to you? The other girl with Magnolia Parks?" Paili sucks in her bottom lip. Shrugs. Doesn't look at me when she says this next part, keeps her eyes on Parks. "I loved him too."

Magnolia's physical countenance falls. Feel it collapse in my arms. Bit shattered.

"He was my first kiss," Paili tells her. "Seven minutes in heaven in Jonah's closet and he never saw anyone but you—"

That's true. That's all true.

"I knew you liked me, Pails." I tell Paili. "I should never have kissed you that night at my flat. I was fucked up."

Paili shakes her head defiantly. "You weren't drunk," she tells me and I reckon she's looking for a reason to think I might love her a bit too.

I shake my head at her. "Different kind of fucked up." Offer her a shrug. "It's always been her." I rest my head on Parks's head, try to steady her crumbling heart.

Paili's mouth pulls a little.

She looks sad, like that hurt her a bit. Seems weird that she doesn't already know that. Seems sad that she hasn't realised that already.

She nods.

"It was a mistake," I tell her.

She nods again. "I know."

"The mistake started with me," I tell her and Parks goes stiff in my arms, holds me tighter and something about it makes me want to cry. "I'm sorry," I tell Paili.

I feel Parks slump into my arms a little more. Like I'm deflating her on the spot.

"Magnolia—" Paili starts.

"Please just leave," Parks tells her, barely.

Paili swallows once. "I'm so sorry," she says and then she walks away.

Parks pushes out of my arms, walks ahead of me. Grab the rest of the bags, jog after her. She takes a sharp turn down Burlington Arcade. Chest is heaving, face looks pale. I pull her to the side, take the bags from her hands. Drop them. Hold her face, find her eyes.

"I'm so sorry—" I shake my head. "Parks. I'm so sorry."

I feel sick. Her face looks like she's seen a ghost. She has, I suppose. Her hands are trembling. People are staring. I want to kill them all. Last thing she needs is this on the internet too.

Of all the ways how what me and Paili did killed her, the world knowing that I fucked her over with her best friend was probably the part that stung her the most.

"Come on—" I nod towards an empty taxi, pushing her into the back of it. "Park Lane, please," I tell the cabby.

Turn to her. Hate myself. She can't keep her eyes up, they're all weighed down with tears. Nudge her chin up.

"Parks." I shake my head at her. "What can I do?"

Staggered breath. She's staring out the window, those green eyes all blue now.

"Tell me you love me," she says. She can't even look at me.

"I do love you." I nod. "So much—I'm so sorry."

"And that it wasn't about me."

I shake my head. "Wasn't about you."

She looks over at me. "That you won't do it again."

"I won't do it again." Keep shaking my head as I reach for her hand. "We can stop this friends shit now."

She snatches her hand back.

"If you felt like we could have stopped with your stupid friends charade you should have stopped before we saw her. I don't want her changing anything—" She scowls at me.

"Parks—"

"No! She changes nothing." She glares at me. "You can't just make me be your friend till you feel like it and whip out a relationship like a trump card to win me back when I'm sad."

That hits me in the chest. Breathe it out slowly.

I nod once. Push some hair behind her ear.

"What do you need to forgive me?"

"Nothing." She looks up at me quickly before she stares out the window. "What could you give me that would matter? You can't take it back, it's done. I just have to get over it."

She shrugs like the thought of doing that is a bug on her shoulder.

"Do you know how to do that?"

"No." She shakes her head. "But I love you more than I'm angry at you, so I need to figure it out." She sighs.

I don't know what to say so I grab her neck, pull her in towards me, kiss her forehead.

Wish I could kiss her mouth. I don't want to be her friend anymore. I'm done with it.

Not going to fight her on it at this moment, don't want her thinking I'm over it just because of seeing Paili—that would fuck her mind around a bit. She'd read into that, I know she would.

531

"Do you trust me yet?" I ask her.

She purses her mouth. "I don't know."

I hold her face in my hand, angle it so she's looking me in the eye.

"I'm out late one night—" I raise my eyebrows at her. "Later than I said I'd be. What's your headspace like back at home?"

She frowns. "Why aren't I with you in the first place?"

I give her a look. "Because you trust me and I'm allowed nights out by myself."

"Right." She nods but looks unsure.

"Right?" I ask, eyebrows up.

She pauses. "Sure, I guess."

"Parks—" I sigh. "You have to trust me. We're never going to work if you don't."

"Trust is earned, BJ," she tells me quietly, nose in the air.

"And I'll earn it! I've been earning it." Lick my bottom lip, shake my head. "Fuck—I've held you and protected you since I was a kid. I've fought a fucking gang lord for you. What do you need for you to trust me again?"

"A magic eraser?" She offers me a sad smile.

I sigh. Shove my hands through my hair. Nod my chin at her. "What do you do? When I come home after that accidental late night?"

"Why are you late?" She squints.

"Jonah . . . He fell on a table in a bar and split his chin open."

"Why didn't you call me?" she asks, suspicious.

"Because he broke my phone as he fell." I shrug.

Her eyes pinch. "Why didn't you call me on someone else's phone?"

"Because I don't know your number by heart."

"Why not?" She scowls.

"Fuck!" I snort a laugh. "Because I'm normal. Magnolia, I need you to trust me. I need you to trust me more than I need you to forgive me."

She nods. "I trust you," she tells me in a quiet voice.

"Yeah?"

"Yeah." She frowns, nodding once as she tries to convince both of us that she means it.

17:38

Jo

Hey

Just letting you know, Mum's in the hospital

Shit man. Is she ok?

I don't know. Heading there now.

What happened?

Accident.

Fuck.

Want me to come

Nah

Update you soon

So sorry man.

Love you

if you need anything

xx

533

SEVENTY-FOUR

Magnolia

Maybe I should have smelled it in the air. Trouble.

After Paili? How could I not?

That threw a spanner in the works of my heart. Made me hate BJ all over again. I haven't in a while. Loving him took over the driver's seat.

I made a year's worth of bad decisions when I hated him and Paili for what they did to me. Once I realised I only hated BJ as much as I did because I love him as much as I do, I continued to make a few more months' worth of bad (and arguably spectacular) decisions with Julian, and it takes all of my self-control not to run right back there, because I could.

How he looked at me the other week when I went to visit Daisy? I could.

But I don't and I won't. Because I love BJ more than I want me to be okay, and that's new, I think. Progress, some might say.

For now I think I'll just say that it's killing me.

Seeing BJ and Paili near each other felt like being knocked over by a wave and I can't kick my way back up to the surface.

It made me feel stupid.

For how many years had it been in front of me plainly and I didn't see?

There were clues. I can see that now when I think back on it—things she'd do and say when she was drunk, like how she'd go with him. But it was never overtly sexual, not dissimilar to how I was with the other boys. Boys who were just safe places to me. I thought BJ was a safe place for her.

I never thought, well, you know what I never thought.

I hate feeling stupid. I hate in particular that it's not just the three of us who know. For years Jonah knew, for years Perry knew. And then after that night at the Rosebery, everyone knew. The whole wide world got a front-row seat to me finding out the two people I loved more than anything didn't love me enough not to do that.

I had anxiety attacks over that. Bad ones. The kinds you get taken to hospital for. Usually at night time, usually after I had been with another boy, trying not to think about the only thing I think about. Tom, Rush and Jack-Jack—all of them had to take me to Mount Sinai at least once. Rush a bunch of times, actually.

I love BJ more than I want the right to be angry at him— and I want to be with him, properly, always. I know for that to happen, the forgiving and the trusting need to happen.

And actually, truthfully, I kind of thought I already had.

Stupid, I know, because it was never conscious. One day it just stopped being the first thing I thought of, stopped being this thing that sat in my throat like a lump of dry bread that I couldn't ever swallow down properly.

That only happened when I saw him again.

A face like that washes away a multitude of sins, believe me, I've committed many with him and he's committed many on me. That face covers them all. His cool eyes are like a cold compress on my busy, curiously masochistic mind.

But then I saw her and all I could see was my old friend, who saw my boyfriend, my person, my love of my life, naked. She ran her hands through his hair, had him inside of her. And him, his mouth dragging over her skin, her eyes squeezed shut as he pushed into her how he'd push into me.

I vomit again. I vomit every time I think of it. This is what BJ does to me. This is what loving him does to me. It ruins me. Makes me stupid, makes my body act like it's broken.

"Maybe you should just stay home?" Taura tells me.

Some night for some thing at one of Christian's clubs, I don't really want to go myself, but what, with their mum in hospital and them not wanting us to do anything for them, I figure the least I can do is show up to his events when he asks me to.

I love Rebecca Barnes. I'll never forget the secret she kept for me all these years. I'll always be grateful for her. Christian and Jonah both seem strangely calm. Bridget says it's because of their sister, that they're just internalising things, but the Hemmes boys have always been epically stoic.

I shake my head at Taura, even though I think she's probably right. On a personal level I perhaps should stay away from him. On a relational level, I need to be there.

Plus, in all honesty, I've avoided BJ since that day with Paili, which is bad of me, but I'm trying. I've answered his calls, I've answered his texts. I'm trying not to wear it, trying not to have it set us back sixteen months. If I don't come I know he'll worry, or worse.

I don't want him to worry and I definitely don't want him worse.

So I pull on the off-the-shoulder lace-trimmed sequinned crepe minidress from Saint Laurent and slip into the Dolce & Gabbana black satin pumps with bejewelled embellishment. Toss on the blackandwhite checked wool and cashmere-blend coat from Valentino and that should tell you everything you need to know about my mind space. I don't need him to keep me warm tonight. Even if I desperately do need him to hold me.

Hen offers to pick me up. He knows. I didn't tell him so I guess Beej did. He doesn't mention it, the whole way there.

"You okay?" he asks on our way up.

I give him a vague shrug and he gives me a cuddle.

"Hey—" BJ ducks into my line of sight when we arrive.

Eyes heavier than I like them, weighed down with his worries about me, cheeks pink. He's nervous.

He's wearing Pleasure's embroidered-logo shirt jacket with the naughty angels on the back of it, stone grey logo-print short-sleeve T-shirt from Balenciaga with the black Iron loose-fit trousers by Axel Arigato. Handsome like he always is and maybe extra because that T-shirt makes his eyes extra green.

He wraps his arms around me, feels nervous as he does it.

He pulls back, looks at me again—he looks worried. I don't want him to look worried.

I try my best to smile convincingly. Try to be finer than I feel. Try not to feel Paili standing between us, but I can't quite, so I have a big drink.

Beej hangs around me, but what can he do? We're friends.

I don't know why we're friends and I know we're bad at it, and even though there are certain aspects of him that I find difficult to trust, I do trust that he would only be doing this whole friend fiasco if it was for a reason, so even though I don't get it, I'm trying. Trying to respect it or whatever.

An outward expression of the inward trust I lied about having.

If we could kiss, all this would go away.

Everything goes away for us when we touch, but the hugs won't cut it with this. We need a complete recalibration. All my clothes off, his hands on me till we're back in sync, but then again it rolls through my brain that his hands were on Paili and I get up and walk to the bar. This time he doesn't follow me.

"Alright," says a deep voice and a pair of black Timberlands from next to me. "What the fuck is going on with you two?"

I glance over at Julian Haites and roll my eyes.

"Oh, you know what they say—strike while the iron is . . . tepid."

He gives me an unimpressed look, shoves his hands into the pockets of his Hayes leather-panelled wool-blend bomber jacket from Golden Bear. Cream cashmere half-zip sweater from Brunello Cucinelli underneath it. He looks handsome. I feel guilty for thinking that. I'm sure I shouldn't, so I just shrug.

"Nothing. We're figuring it out."

Julian cocks an eyebrow and looks over at Beej, who's watching us, brows low. He looks uneasy.

"Figuring it out?" Jules looks from Beej to me. "He just told me you're just friends."

I feel embarrassed. I shake my head. "It's a loose term."

"Oi," Julian puts his head closer to mine than he needs to, "I didn't stop having the best sex of my life so you could go off and be friends with Ballentine." I give him a look and he returns it with a steady one. "You deserve more, Parks."

"Julian—" I sigh. "What are you doing?"

"Nothing." He shrugs, innocent. Like he's ever been innocent a day in his life.

"You don't like me like that, remember?" I remind him. "You never have. Relieved to be rid of me." I give him a tender smile because that one actually hurt my feelings but never mind. "I love him . . . I think I've done a bad job of showing him that."

Julian juts his chin out a bit and nods. "And him you."

I peer up at him, my eyes heavy.

"Look at you—" He gestures at me. "That stupid face you've got, who's not with you if they can be?" I roll my eyes and look away but his head ducks after me. "I'm serious, Tiges. What's he playing at?"

I sigh because I don't know.

I actually don't. That's the truth.

I don't know why we're being friends, I don't know why it took him seeing Paili and me looking sad for him to say we could be more than that. And I think Julian knows that because he knows me. More than I wish he did, maybe. I think he was paying more attention than I thought he was all along, and I don't have time to rationalise what that actually means right now, because for about the forty-fifth time this year, I feel like the rug is being pulled out from under me.

I swallow and barely meet his eye.

"I don't know." My voice is softer than I wish it was because Julian's brows dip and his jaw sets.

"Is he cocking around?"

"No." I give him a cross look.

"How do you know?" Jules asks a bit with his chin.

"He's just not—" I shake my head once. "I know he's not."

Julian sniffs a laugh, shakes his head, squints at me. "I know he makes you go starry-eyed and shit, but Parks, honestly, if he loves you how he says he does, why the fuck isn't he with you?" He shrugs his shoulders once. "You've got to ask yourself that."

I throw back my drink and walk away. Down the hallway towards Christian's office. I need a minute to cry for a bit, probably vomit again. I don't want it on camera. I don't want Paili to see that she's shaken me.

I unlock Christian's office door. Pin code: 6969. Same as his iPhone. Idiot.

I perch on his desk for a grand total of four seconds before BJ bursts in.

"What'd he say to you?" he asks, closing the door behind him.

"Nothing."

He lifts his eyebrows. Doesn't buy it.

"It was nothing—" I shake my head.

"Nothing?" he repeats. His voice is sharp.

I glance up at him with fighting eyes.

"Nothing I wasn't already thinking."

He nods at me once. "Go on then."

I jump up to my feet.

"I'm over this shit, Beej."

"What shit?" He looks annoyed.

"Being your friend! I'm not your friend—" I shake my head. "I've never been your friend. I don't want to be your friend. We practically had sex the other night! It's bullshit. Whatever you're saying is bullshit. I don't believe you anymore." My voice is getting louder and my insecurities are like cracks in the varnish of us. "None of what you said is about me, none of this is about me trusting you. That's bullshit. You're just not ready to commit to me or—"

"—That's coming from him," he interrupts, pointing at the door. "That's not coming from you."

"Is he wrong?" I arch an eyebrow and his head pulls back.

"Are you fucking kidding me?" He blinks. "Magnolia, you are the only thing I've ever been committed to in my entire life."

"Then what are we waiting for?" I wave my hands in the air, exasperated. "I said I'll forgive you. I said I'll trust you."

And, admittedly, the measure of those are perhaps less than either of us originally thought, but anyway. He shakes his head.

"Yeah, but see, the thing is, Parks, I don't trust you," he tells me, face completely straight.

I stare over at him. "What?"

He presses his hands into his eyes and then looks up at me.

"I don't trust you, Magnolia." He shrugs. "It's not just about you and you being able to trust me —which you don't, by the way. Obviously. It's about me and how I don't trust you either."

I blink a few times and I feel a tiny bit like he slapped me.

"You left," he says with his chin. "You said you loved me, you said you forgave me, we said that was it—that was it for me, I was all in, done. Game over. Done fucking around, done playing the games, all the bullshit with the girls and the parties and the drugs, I was done with it and then you left—" He stares over at me with sore eyes.

I cross my arms over my chest, feeling attacked. "Because I couldn't look at you when I found out the whole truth."

"I know, Parks." He shakes his head. "I get it. I get why you left, but when I said that it was it for me, I meant it. And I thought you meant it too." He shrugs—his eyes look wet and I wish I could reach out for him, but I don't know what we are. "But you left."

He looks so sad. So sad. The kind where it crushes me to think that I caused it, and it occurs to me for the first time ever that there are two betrayed people in this room.

He bites down on his bottom lip. "You're not the only one here whose trust has been broken, Magnolia."

My feeling sad for him is overtaken by the indignation in my chest that he thinks what he did and what I did are comparable, and so even though I want to hold his face in my hands and kiss it, I don't. I stare at him instead.

"It's not the same."

"No, you know what—" He gives me a look I don't like. "It's not the same, Parks. I reckon what you did is worse. Because I fucked Paili once. And you've dated my best friend, you dated my favourite skater, dated my fucking childhood hero, and then, to round it out, you dated my nemesis."

"He's not your nemesis," I tell him. I don't know why.

His eyes pinch at me. "You're the worst, Parks." My face falls. "And I love you—and I will always love you—but fuck you for that." He shakes his head at me. "And I don't trust you for shit."

I think he regrets saying it the second it's out of his mouth. It flashes over him, this realisation that the shot he took made contact. I feel myself breathing. That's never a good sign. I don't feel it because I'm mindful, I feel it because I'm losing control of it.

"Parks—" He reaches for me, frowning.

I push past him. "Don't touch me."

He grabs me by the wrist and I shove him off.

"I said don't touch me—" I glare over at him.

His eyes are raw and I pray to God that these are just the teething issues of learning to trust each other again.

He lets out this breath that's too sad and too heavy for me not to sniff at.

I wipe my own eyes because there's no way in hell I'm letting him touch me.

He doesn't look away from me and I can see in the sky of his eyes a little plane fly by with a banner trailing behind it that reads, "I'M SORRY, FORGIVE ME."

I write in the sand of the desert between us that I am too and I miss him already. As I step towards the door, I wonder how far we'll get this time before we feel our way back around the darkness of everything back to each other.

It's further than I thought, because I turn to leave and he lets me.

SEVENTY-FIVE
Magnolia

I go back and forth about what BJ said to me for the next day and a half. A day and a half feels too long for us to not have spoken, all things considered, but I don't want to be the first to buckle because everything he said was so mean. Even if it was true. If it's true it makes it worse.

I hate the idea of betraying him, that he thinks that I did.

It's strange to me, and I don't know what it says about us as people, that he felt like me leaving him was a betrayal equal to him having sex with someone else. I feel like I've betrayed Beej before, by the way. I don't think I'm perfect—I've felt that sticky, gluggy, quicksand feeling of me doing something wrong to the person I care about most every time I had sex with anyone but him. It might have gotten smaller and smaller every time I did it with that specific person. Julian was rather adept at quieting down my heart's rhetoric that sex was a thing just for Beej and I—and I'd do it more and more often like he used to do, like me acting like him was a bridge back to him. Try to feel closer to BJ in that way, but it never worked. I'd just miss him.

I don't know how many times over the course of our lives we've sworn to love each other forever, and to be fair we've both been true to our word.

I've never stopped loving him. I might be a runner but I have always loved him.

I can see the betrayal in the leaving, understand how he's arrived there. How he's learned not to trust my word—my word is good though, I promise. I will love BJ Ballentine until I die, irreversibly—but he can't promise he won't hurt me so I don't know how to promise I'll stay.

"How bad is it?" Bridget asks me as I pull up outside of Bala Baya. Middle Eastern restaurant in Southwark.

I silence my phone as it starts to ring.

She was just here having lunch with friends from university and I wanted her to tell me everything was going to be okay because I might believe it if she tells me. I can't really tell you why I'm picking her up from fucking Southwark, like I'm her own personal driver—bit annoying because she actually has her own personal driver, she just refuses to use him.

Me, on the other hand, I'm practically a pauper, what with Simon on annual leave. I'm schlepping myself around like a normal person in my white Aston Martin DBS Superleggera. How annoying is driving yourself?

I love being driven, I love BJ driving me places.

One of his hands on the wheel, the other on my knee. I love being in cars when I'm in cars with him. I should just sell my car so he has to drive me everywhere.

"Bad enough." I tug feverishly at the brown GG-monogram leather-trim linen-blend dress I'm wearing from Gucci.

"His fault or yours?" she asks, silencing my phone again.

I purse my lips. "Both?"

I grip the steering wheel tightly, feeling nervous to tell her, like I'm about to walk into the principal's office.

"He doesn't trust me," I tell her, flicking my eyes over quickly to assess her disappointment in me.

"Right." She nods. "Because you leave him all the time."

"What?" I frown. "How do you—?"

"Oh—" She swipes her hand through the air. "He's been processing that one for a while. Glad it finally worked its way into an actual conversation." She whacks my arm merrily. "Well done, you two."

I frown at her more.

I stare over at her, annoyed. "Could you tone down the

enthusiasm, please? My relationship is falling apart." I give her a bleak look, eyes doing their best not to well up. "Again."

She rolls her eyes. "Magnolia, it's not that big a deal."

"How's that now?" I blink at her.

"So he doesn't trust you." She shrugs, dismissively.

"Sorry, I know." I shake my head. "Call me old fashioned, I'm just one of those girls who likes their boyfriends to trust them."

"Well," Bridget tilts her head, "he's not your boyfriend, so let's not get carried away."

I give her a look and she laughs, shaking her head as we pull onto Westminster Bridge.

"It's very fixable, Magnolia," she says and gives me a serious look. "You just stay."

She gives me a small shrug like it's the simplest thing in the world.

"That's all he needs from you. You know you're in, in that insane, undoable way. You're always going to be. You just keep staying."

"Even when—" I start but she cuts me off.

"—Even when." She gives me a look. "Even when anything, there's nothing you could put at the end of that sentence that would warrant you leaving."

I frown at her.

"This is what it is, Magnolia. Loving him no matter what."

"I do." I frown at her.

"You do." She nods. "You two do have the loving each other down pat. The rest of it is just showing up." She gives me a sweet smile. "And not running away and not sleeping with gang lords, et cetera et cetera."

"Julian took me home last night," I tell her.

"Magnolia!" She smacks me in the arm. "Did you? You didn't!"

"No!" I shake my head. "I said I couldn't."

"Because . . .?" Bridget stares over at me, eyebrows up.

"Because I love BJ." I frown.

My phone rings again and I sigh. "Answer that for me, would you?"

"Oh, hello—" My sister groans. "We were just talking about you—No, you can't, she's driving—What? Sorry, I can't hear you—"

And then there's a bang at the back of my car and my sister yells, "MAGNOLIA, LOOK OUT!"

I don't even think I ever took my eyes off the road. I didn't look at the phone, I didn't pass it to her, it was in my bag on the floor.

I don't swerve. I was in my lane and driving the limit.

There are none of the sounds your mind is trained to listen for—no screeching of tyres, no horn blaring a warning.

I'm driving like normal one second and the next someone has driven into the back of my car. Mostly it's just a big jolt. We both jerk forward. My seatbelt chokes me a little—and it happens so quickly, pushing us onto the other side of the road—I barely have time to glance over at Bridget before the next car hits.

This time it comes from the driver's side and I don't see the car itself but what's about to happen on my sister's frozen face.

"Magnolia!" she cries before the loudest sound I've ever heard in my life is wrapping around us.

Glass everywhere, the grinding of metal folding in on itself and wrapping around my body.

I'm still watching my little sister's face—it breaks out in a deep kind of horror. She's talking to me but I can't hear her because everything else is too loud suddenly. I know it's probably dramatic of me, like some terrible cliché, but I suppose this is how these things go, isn't it?

How many loves do you get in a lifetime? For me it's just the one. I've had more but as I float away there's only one I'm thinking of.

He is what I'm thinking of.

Not how he hurt me, not what he did to me, not what we've done to each other. Just him.

How his hair falls on his face, the dip in his top lip, how his mouth parts when he's thinking, the freckle on the right side of his mouth, the shape of his nose. I trace his jawline in my mind, count the colours in his eyes. I feel sad for the splittest of seconds because I always kind of thought they'd be the last things I'd see here on earth, that we'd get to Tobermory eventually, grow up and old together, but here I am now, grateful anyway that I got the chance to love him at all, albeit maybe badly at times, but at least I got to love him, and maybe now, I appear to be leaving him once again—I hope that he forgives me for this one because it wasn't my fault. The sounds are getting quieter now, even though they could be getting louder too.

My sister's mouth is moving, she's reaching for me. My face feels wet? The edges of my vision start going dark.

And my Ballentine-stained heart surges as it remembers every waking moment of our youth spent tangled up with each other, and a million blurry nights of tears and bad words and big feelings and messy kisses and grabby hands and choices we should have never made but I'm so glad we did. I love that tree. I love that door that he could never lock. I love that piece of sandstone that is so much more than a piece of sandstone.

I try to tell Bridget that I love her but the sounds come out muffled.

It gets darker and my head feels lighter.

It's pulling me under and I let it.

And I drift off into the infinite void thinking of him.

SEVENTY-SIX

BJ

I was with Henry when I got the call.

I'm her emergency contact, I guess.

There'd been an accident. That's all I knew.

They took her to St Thomas's, that was the closest hospital.

I haven't spoken to her in nearly two days to make a fucking point, and for what? To tell her without telling her that she hurt me? To hurt her back?

I wasn't doing anything, sitting at home playing Madden with Henry when the phone rang.

Went pale.

Hen's good in a crisis.

"What?" He stared over at me.

"Parks was in a car crash," I told him, voice sounded foreign. Far away.

He jumped to his feet. "Where?"

I shake my head. "I don't know."

Grabbed me by the shoulders. "BJ, think."

I frown, trying to remember.

"Thomas's." I blinked. "St Thomas's."

Henry nodded, grabbed his keys, flung a sweater at me. Pushed me out the door.

He called the boys on the way, told them. I think he called Tausie after that.

I should call her family, right? Someone should. Should be me—but I can't speak. Besides, I am her family.

I bang my fist on Henry's dashboard.

"Can't you fucking drive faster?"

He looks over at me, watches me for a few seconds. "Beej, she's going to be okay."

I give him a long look. "You don't know that."

"I do." He nods. "This isn't how it ends."

I state over at him. "How do you know?"

He swallows. Looks back at the road.

"Jesus, Henry—the last thing I said to her—" I shake my head at myself. Press my hand into my mouth. Feel sick.

"Yeah?" He frowns.

I lick my bottom lip. My eyes have gone weird, everything's blurry. "I don't trust you for shit."

He holds the wheel tighter. Can hear him breathing. He nods.

Press my hands into my eyes.

"If I lose her, Hen—" I choke. Stare out the window.

"You won't."

My mind waterboards me with memories of her.

Our first kiss on holidays, how she smelt like coconuts. Her coming down those stairs at Holland Park for our first date. Slow dancing to Billie Holiday. Her blushing cheeks and her wide eyes on mine the first time I got changed in front of her. The way she looks at me when I'm driving her places. The first time I snuck her up into my room at school, Jonah went for a walk to give us some space—tripped, dislocated his knee—went missing for hours. Barely cared though, because I touched her boobs for the first time. Took her top off for the first time that night too—lit a fire in me. Our tree. Her at my rugby games in my hoodies on the sidelines. How her face goes in the morning. Undoing the buttons of her school uniform, her watching me with round eyes swallowing heavy, still as a statue, breathing all quick. All the bread in her hands on our first date.

Back in the car my eyes can't see through the tears.

Remember all of it, I tell myself. Her hand in my hair. How she smelt before. How she smells now. Her lips on my skin.

Her little trembling body wrapped around mine under the stairs at Varley. Wrapping myself around her body that trembled differently that December 3rd that I hate and love all at once, and whatever happens I know I'm lucky to have had her.

To have gotten to love her how I have.

I wish I was better at it. Wish I could do it again, that I had more time. I'd change everything and nothing.

Where the fuck is that time machine when you need it? I'd fly to New York, bring her home with me.

Henry swerves in and out of cars, speeding up. Looks nervous. He's never nervous. That makes me nervous.

We're there in under twenty minutes. Record time for this time of day.

Hen pulls in and I barrel out of the car and into emergency.

"Parks—" I bang on the desk to get the woman's attention. "Magnolia Parks."

She stares at me for a few seconds. Weird look. I can't tell whether she recognises me or she's about to give me bad news.

"Just got out of surgery." She nods. "Room 305."

I can't get to her fast enough. Bolt to the lift. Push the up button forty times. Bustle past a slow-moving pregnant woman to run down the hall. Burst through the door.

Bridget looks up from the chair in the corner of the room, gives me a tired smile and I think I breathe for the first time since I left my place.

"How is she?" I walk over to Parks.

Asleep on her bed.

Bridget gingerly nods. "Okay."

Touch Magnolia's face. A few stitches on her left cheek. Some bruising around that eye too.

I shake my head at the idea of something hurting her.

Run my thumb over her mouth. Breathe out some relief that she's still here.

"She had surgery?" I ask without looking away from her. "Shattered her collarbone," Bridget tells me.

Fuck.

I look back at her. "Are you okay?"

She nods.

"Were you in the car?"

She nods again.

I frown. "But you're okay?"

She shrugs. "The car hit her side."

I shove my hands through my hair.

"What happened?"

"I don't know—" She shakes her head, looks confused. "We were driving, everything was normal. Then someone rammed into the back of us. I think we must have sort of spun into the other side of the road? And then this other car drove straight into her."

I press my hand into my mouth.

Hate that this happened to her. Hate that I wasn't there with her.

"Where are your parents?"

"On their way." She nods. "Mum's in Greece with the boy-toy and Dad and Mars are in America but flying back now."

I nod. Look at her properly. She's still in the clothes from the crash.

Walk over to her.

"Hey." I kneel in front of her. "Are you actually okay?"

She nods, teary. "Yeah, I'm fine."

I pull her to her feet, wrap my arms around her.

"They checked you out, Bridge?"

She shrugs a little. "Just a couple of scratches. A bump on the head."

"You look pretty shaken."

She nods. "I am."

"Go home—" I nod at the door.

"No." She frowns at me. "She's my sister."

"Well, she's my everything, so—" Give her a dumb smile.

She flicks her eyes, fake-annoyed but real-pleased.

"I've got this, Bridge. I mean it." I give her a look. "Henry's downstairs. He'll take you home. Shower, have a rest."

She frowns, chews down on her bottom lip.
"You'll call me when she wakes?"
I nod.
"You won't leave her?" she asks.
I give Bridget a long look.
"Never again."

SEVENTY-SEVEN

BJ

She comes to a few hours later. The world's best eyes flutter open and look down at me, tired and bleary, kind of how my heart feels.

I stand up and push the hair back from her face.

She gives me a weak smile and holy fuck, I love her.

Don't know what I'm doing with my life anymore with how much I love her. Don't know what to do with all the ways. I've got too many things I need to do with her, too many things I need to say, too many kisses for time—

Spent the last few hours since Bridget left sorting myself the fuck out—the next few weeks, what it'll look like looking after her. Cancelled my shoots, got Jo to move my stuff into her place, couple of other housekeeping things—figuring out how to best tell her I love her out loud and quietly as well for the rest of our lives.

"Hi," she chokes.

"Hey, Parks." I give her a gentle smile. My eyes are teary. "How are you?" I frown at her, don't move my hand from her face.

She takes a few slow breaths, looks around the room confused. "You tell me?"

I give her a small nod. "Four broken ribs, fractured clavicle, a concussion, couple of stitches in your face—"

She instinctively goes to touch her face with her right hand but winces when she realises it's in a sling.

"That's the side with the broken clavicle," I tell her too late.

"You're awake!" Bridget says from the doorway. She's got an armful of flowers and some balloons. She scowls at me as she walks by. "You said you'd call."

"She just woke up." I roll my eyes at her and she dumps a garden in my arms to fuss over her sister.

"What happened?" Magnolia asks, trying to sit up.

"Car accident—" Bridget frowns. "Don't you remember?"

"I remember." Parks nods. "Are you hurt?"

Bridge shakes her head.

"Your side was the one that got hit." Gives her sister an apologetic smile.

Magnolia sniffs a little. "I'm glad."

She means that too. She'd die for her sister.

"I hear my patient's awake . . ." Her doctor walks in. Male. Youngish. Mid to late thirties. Good looking. Frowns when he sees me. Flicks his eyes over to Bridge.

"Sorry mate, immediate family only."

Bridget grimaces.

Magnolia glances over at me wordlessly and I square my shoulders. Jaw set. Annoyed this fucking clown of a doctor is forcing my hand here before I even get to have the conversation with her myself.

"I'm her partner," I tell him.

"Ooh," Bridget coos. "What kind of partner?" That little shit.

I give her an exasperated look. "Life, sexual, dance, gaming—" I shrug and nod my chin at the doctor. "Take your fucking pick, Bridge."

"We don't play a lot of games," Magnolia says quietly to no one in particular and I snort a laugh, giving her a look.

"Parks, you and I play more games than anyone else I know." I stand over her, kiss her forehead. "But I'm done with that shit."

She looks up at me, swallows nervously.

"Okay." The doctor clears his throat. "The surgery went well. We performed an intramedullary fixation—"

Magnolia frowns.

"He put a pin in," I whisper to her and she nods.

"We're happy with your progress," he tells her. "But we're going to keep you in for a few nights for observation."

She nods.

"Your father's called, and once we're sure you're stable, we're going to be moving you over to Weymouth Street Hospital—"

("Oh, thank God," Magnolia says under her breath.)

The doctor hears her and frowns. "Sorry. Thank you for saving me, I mean no disrespect, it's just that these fluorescent lights aren't doing any of us any favours. I won't heal to my optimal self underneath them."

Bridget groans. "She's fine."

The doctor snorts, a bit amused, and excuses himself. Says he'll be back to check on her soon.

Magnolia stares over at me, eyes as big as they are weary, and I swallow heavy, grateful she's okay.

I give her sister a look.

"Can you give us a minute, Bridge?"

She glances between us, pretends to be annoyed as she rolls her eyes. Walks out.

I stare down at Parks, slip my arms under her body, shift her carefully over—she winces anyway—then I climb in next to her. Hold her as best I can without moving her too much.

She starts crying as soon as I do. I figured she would. Figured she needed it.

I kiss the top of her head. Kiss it a thousand times and down her face till she turns to face me.

Looks up at me with those eyes I love.

Nudge her face with mine till our lips almost touch.

My breath is hot on her face and for a few seconds our mouths just hover close. Brush mine against hers. She takes a staggered breath.

It's gentle at first, she sinks into me, feel her relaxing, feel the trauma melting off her broken body and then she

555

presses into me. She loses her breath a little from the pain but doesn't stop.

Kisses me like she thought she mightn't get to do it again.

"I'm sorry," she tells me, not moving her mouth from mine.

"No, I am." I hold her face. "I'm not your friend anymore."

She looks up at me, bright eyed with a tired smile.

"You'll be my boyfriend again?"

I press my mouth into her forehead.

"I'll be whatever the fuck you need, Parks."

SEVENTY-EIGHT
Magnolia

Once they moved me they kept me at Weymouth Street for another four days before discharging me and sending me home.

I had lots of visitors, the boys, Tausie, BJ's parents, the sisters (even Madeline), Gus. No Julian and no Daisy. I thought that was a tiny bit rude, but anyway.

Broken ribs are a pest but the painkillers are nice. It hurts to move and it will for a while, my doctors said, but I've barely had to do a thing because Bridget says BJ is processing the grief of almost losing me by not leaving me alone, ever.

That could almost sound annoying, but actually, I'd live in his pocket if he let me.

When we get back to Grosvenor Square the house is filled to its brim with flowers.

Beej is staying for a while, so it seems.

"Could have asked first," is what my sister said when she found out. "I don't want to have to hear you two going at it all night. You know, my room is right next to yours, Magnolia—"

Taura gave her a look. "Look at her little mangled body. What's he's going to do with that?"

"Are you kidding? Those two?" Bridget gave us a look. "Where there's a will, there's a way."

I have a little bell I keep by my bed to get Bridget's attention primarily because she hates it. Sometimes I just ring it to annoy her because the reaction is so fun.

A lot of eye rolls and sounds from the back of her throat. One time I rang it just so I could time her to see how long she took to get to me. She was so cross she threw her phone at me and it hit me in my ribs, which meant her and BJ had a row. He yelled at her so much and he never yells at her— he's horribly irrational when I'm hurt—but all's well that ends well because Bridget was so guilty about hurting me that now when I ring her bell I've calculated that her response time is 210 per cent faster than it was before.

Showering is hard between the clavicle and the ribs, so much so I've been reduced to once-a-day showers, which is completely barbaric, but every time I liken my current show-ering privileges to those of a Guantanamo detainee I'm not met with an overwhelming response of compassion.

That said, BJ takes his role as my personal bather very seriously.

Absolutely zero funny business (but quite a many few kisses)—the carefulness of him with me is very sweet.

The great tenderness he undresses me with only adds to the build-up of how much I want him, and the part where I can't have him right now—well . . .

It's a funny kind of boundary between us, this physical one. We've never had one before. He'd get injured playing rugby but that barely slowed him down in this arena, but not here, not with me.

And I think he revels in it a bit, that I want to be with him as badly as I do and I can't be.

I've suggested an array of ways to make it possible but he just rolls his eyes. Scoffs, "Yeah, right—" And then he kisses me anyway.

That's what he did after this morning's shower as he helped me pull on the bow-embellished strapless dress from Carolina Herrera. Things without sleeves and straps are the MVPs for me at the minute.

He's standing on the other side of the room, leaning back against the wall, watching me with a small smile on his face.

The windows behind him, illuminating him in the way I see him in my mind at all times anyway.

Today he's in the white My Name Is tag-print T-shirt from Vetements, black baggy, Dolce & Gabbana jeans from the '90s that I pulled for him from a shoot the other day, and the black Balenciaga Political Campaign hoodie around his waist. Vans. As always. He nods his chin at me.

"Like your place . . ." I glance around, pleased that he does. I like it when he likes my things. "Good ceilings." He nods appreciatively. "Very light . . . Bit of a shame you have to leave, isn't it?"

I frown over at him. "No, I don't."

"Yeah, you do—" He nods.

"What?" I'm confused. Did something happen while I was at hospital?

He gives me a little shrug. "You have to move out."

"When? Why?" I pout over at him.

He scratches the back of his neck. "Because I bought us a place."

I blink at him a few times. "What?"

"I bought us a four-bedder over in the Lancer Square complex—" A thought crosses his mind. "—Which reminds me—I've got some papers I need you to sign."

I keep blinking. "Why?"

He looks at me like I'm an idiot. "So both our names are on it."

"No—" I shake my head. "Why did you buy us a house?"

"Oh—" He nods. "Because I'm going to ask you to marry me in a minute, and married people usually live together," he says with a shrug and then danders over to me casually.

I swallow, blinking a lot. "Are you being funny?"

"No, they really do."

I frown at him. "BJ."

He drops to one knee.

"How's the weather, Parks?" He beams up at me.

"Oh." I stare down at him, wide eyed. "It's looking to be quite fine—"

"Just quite?"

I roll my eyes. "Eternally sunny, then."

"Oh—" He grimaces. "Can't promise that. Storms always come, they have to—brings balance."

"What can you promise, then?" I ask as I kneel across from him so we're level.

"That I'll love you forever."

I roll my eyes. "Well, that's hardly special, is it? You've done that already all your life."

"So fucking marry me, then, would you?"

I frown over at him but he's completely serious. His cheeks are pink, his breathing's a little fast, his eyes are nervous. And then he pulls out a ring from his pocket.

I glance at it then I frown at it.

My head pulls back. "Is that my ring?"

He gives me a look. "My ring, actually—" Cocky half-smile. Single eyebrow up. "—That I gave you, that you tossed away dramatically in the middle of a fight."

I give him an uncertain look. "Are we really referring to that particular instance as a 'fight'?"

He pulls a face. "Definitely wasn't not a fight, was it?"

I frown at him, snatching for it. "Give that back!"

He holds it out of my reach, squints at me playfully. "Are you saying yes?"

I press my lips together, trying not to smile too much.

I nod once. "Yes."

"Yes?" He bites back a smile. "You're going to be my wife? Have my babies? Spend all my money—"

I give him a look. "I have more money than you."

He snorts. "I'm sure you do after the house I just bought you."

"Put that ring on my finger," I tell him.

He takes my left hand in his, holds it with his eyes on mine. Slips my old ring back where it belongs.

"I love you," he tells me with a serious face and a few nods.

I stare down at my hand, smiling at it proudly before I glance back at him, watching me like he's been lost at sea and he's just spotted land. Like I'm the shore he's washed up against.

He's every solider pulling into the train station in 1945. We've returned from war.

That's how we love each other. That's what our love feels like. Battered and bruised, but the only thing in this world I've ever clung on to for dear life is the boy here in front of me. I can't quite believe it.

That we made it?

That after all the ways we tried to kill each other, all the different ways we tried to snuff loving each other out, we're here.

Here like this in my bedroom with my broken bones and him still on his sweet knees.

"Are you going to kiss me, then?" I ask him with tall eyebrows.

He gives me a half-smile as he moves in towards me.

"Yeah, Parks—" He nods. "Forever now."

SEVENTY-NINE

BJ

Asking her to marry me was the easiest thing I've ever done. Easiest decision I've ever made, if we're gonna call it that. It was more like the undertow of the universe pulling me back to her. She thinks we're in the stars but I just think she's the current of everything and I'm always just drifting . . . Floating home to her.

Sorry—annoying, I know. But you know me, I love her too much and a nautical metaphor always seems to be on the horizon.

Should have done it years ago, probably. Maybe everything would have been different. Done it fresh out of school—bit unusual in our circles, definitely—it worked for Sam and Clara England though. They got married when they were eighteen and were embarrassingly in love until he died, but when you know you know. And I knew when I was six that I loved her. Didn't know it'd be like this, didn't know that loving someone this much can be as good as it can be fucked.

There are so many things I wish I'd done differently, too many ways I hurt her that I wish I could take back. But then I wonder if things now are exactly as they're meant to me to be. Because we're meant to be.

Not a question in my mind. It's her.

It's always been her.

And tonight we get to tell everyone.

Dinner at Heston Blumenthal's with the Full Box Set and each of our families.

It's a good day. Exciting day.

Should be anyway, but Parks is about ready to murder the whole fucking world because her sling 'doesn't go with anything'.

"Waited to marry you all my motherfucking life!" she yells from inside her wardrobe. "And you—you big prick—decide to ask me when I have a fucking pin in my shoulder."

"It's in your clavicle, Parks," I call to her.

She pokes her head out of the closet long enough to give me a glare before huffing back inside.

"We can postpone?" I offer because it feels like the right thing to do.

Her head pokes back out. "Excuse me, what?"

I shrug. "Postpone if you want?"

She stares at me. "Postpone getting married?"

I roll my eyes. "Postpone telling them."

"Oh." She blinks a few times. "No."

"We should talk about a date though," I call to her.

"Yes, right." She walks back out as she puts in some earrings. "A long engagement or a short one?"

"Hate long engagements—" Shake my head at her. "I'll marry you tomorrow."

"Would you?" She beams, pleased.

I nod.

She considers it for the briefest second then waves her hand through the air dismissively. "Don't be daft. Elie doesn't even know we're engaged yet, how's he going to make my dress by the morning time?"

I roll my eyes.

"It's almost May—" She purses her lips. "I'd have liked to have been married in the summer if we're getting married here."

Frown at her a bit. "So you want to wait till a year from now?"

She walks over to me in nothing but her knickers. Pretty fun. The novelty of that still hasn't worn off. Hope it never does.

Hold her by the waist, tilt my head. Smile a bit.

She's hands me a big dress in a garment bag.

"What's this? We getting married right now?"

"Off the rack?" She blinks at me, then laughs and shakes her head.

Zips at the side, this dress. Bit of a pain to get into with that shoulder of hers and those ribs, literally a pain. But she perseveres all the same, swearing like a fucking sailor, but anything for a good dress.

I have these moments where I can't believe it. That we're doing this. Properly, finally.

I'm locking her down, putting a ring on it and all that shit.

My eyes go blurry with this weird new want I've got for her. Different from before, different from the other kinds that still live in me.

Do her up, kiss her big.

She presses herself into me. Peeps in pain as she does.

Sex is a while off for us, I reckon, with these injuries of hers. She's taking it worse than I am.

Looks up at me with big eyes. "We could . . . you know . . ." Gives me a look. "Before we go."

"For sure—" I nod and point at her. "You've experienced some sort of miraculous intervention that's healed your broken ribs and clavicle instantly, yeah?"

She huffs. "You like sex."

"I do." I nod. "Especially with you. Can't wait to have it."

"Then why won't you do it?" She pouts.

I hold her face in my hands. "Because you have literal broken bones, Parks—"

Her eyes go a bit round and she shrinks back a little. "You won't get bored of waiting for me?"

"Ah." I nod. Heart goes heavy. Hate that my fucking around fucked her up. Force a smile. "Been waiting on you all my life."

She shakes her head. "You know what I mean."

"Listen—" I push my hand through her hair. "We both did shit things to each other when we were trying to work out how to get back to each other. I know I cheated on you—"

Her eyes fall from mine. "But remember, that wasn't about you, that was about me." She squeezes my hand, eyes big how they go every time we talk about what happened to me.

I brush my thumb over her cheek.

"But every other girl I've ever been with has been about you." I shrug and she frowns at me, confused. "I know you think I'm, like, a fucking sex maniac but I'm not. I like it. I'm good at it—ask anyone," I tell her with a grin.

That one doesn't land.

She glares at me. "Not helping."

I bite back a smile. "But Parks, besides that one time with Paili, I'd be hard pressed to find a time that wasn't about you, or because of you. Because I missed you, because I wanted you, or because you were gone, because you were fucking Tom England or you flirted with a bartender. Sex for me, for the vast majority of my life, has been about you." I give her a look.

"Oh." She blinks. Cheeks pink. "Um—" Flicks her eyes to the ceiling. "I'm codependent—"

I whistle low because it's true and also an understatement.

Her eyebrows twitch a bit, annoyed, but she keeps going.

"—And when you cheated on me, I filled the void of you with other men."

"Yeah, I know." I shrug.

"Oh." She purses her lips. "I just thought we were confessing things."

I nod. "We were. Yours are just embarrassingly transparent."

She frowns at me more. "Rude."

I nod my chin at her. "Try to just love me from now on." Say it lighter than it feels in my chest. One of those half-truths you joke about because you don't know how else to talk about it.

Her face falls. "Beej—"

I tilt my head, give her a look.

"Baxter James Ballentine, you listen to me—" She reaches for me and I slip my arms around her waist. "I have, over time, tangled my heart up with other people's—"

I gnaw on my bottom lip. Nod.

"But I have, since I met you, deliberately knotted ours together."

I sniff a laugh.

"I've never loved anyone how I love you," she says. No smile, no frills. "And I never will. And I've known that all along."

Push my hand through her hair again, smile at her—wish we could do the thing we can't do right now.

She pulls back, looks down at me.

"Is that what you're going to wear?" She stares at me, frowning a bit. "To tell everyone in the world we love that we're getting married? The Life straight-leg jeans from the Bianca Saunders x ISKO collar, the Moisson floral-print linen shirt from Jacquemus, and I haven't looked at your feet but I swear to God, Beej, if you're wearing black vans—" She shakes her head at me, eyes not moving from mine.

"I am." I suppress a smile.

"So help me God, Ballentine, if you try to wear them on our wedding day, I'll—"

"—Parks. I look good." I look over her and at myself in the mirror. "Yes, BJ, but you could look good in anything. Or nothing. I love you in either."

Keep frowning at her. "I think we match."

"That's offensive because I'm in a persimmon orange strapless silk gown from Oscar de la Renta. I'm so much fancier than you."

"Always, Parks—" Give her the magic smile just to appease her.

Doesn't work. Shakes her head.

I gesture towards her. "Shouldn't you be in white?"

"I'm trying to throw them off our scent." She pouts. "Do you not like it?"

"No, I love it," I tell her as I drink her in.

"Good." She clears her throat before pointing to my feet. "You cannot wear black Vans to Heston's."

Jut my chin. "Beige ones?"

She makes a sound in the back of her throat. "If you must."

"I must." I nod once, before going and grabbing them from the closet.

"It's not made for two," Magnolia had told me when she found me hanging up some clothes in her walk-in wardrobe that's the size of a master suite.

I flicked her a look. "I think you'll manage."

She gave me a long-suffering one. "I think I won't."

"Oi, actually, speaking of posh shit, I got you something." I walk over towards her.

"What?" She looks up.

Shrug. "Just some diamonds."

I pull out a Harry Winston box.

She stares at it for a few seconds and then—if you can believe it—frowns. Shakes her head.

"I don't want another ring,"

I shake my head back at her. "Listen, I'm not running the risk fifteen years from now you throwing in my face that I never bought you diamonds in the middle of an argument because I forgot to pick up milk on the way home."

"What the fuck happens to you and I in the next fifteen years that we devolve so heavily that we're forced to buy our own milk?"

Shake my head at how ridiculous she is.

"Besides," she shrugs, "you've been buying me diamonds since we were fifteen . . ."

"So why stop now?" I give her a look.

"Because I don't want another ring." She holds her hand to her chest, keeping my crest ring tight against her.

She moves away from me and I open the Harry Winston box.

"No, put it away," she growls and then double takes. "What's that?" She peers over at it from afar. "Three cushion-cut diamonds in a row?"

"Yes." I nod.

"Custom designed?"

Roll my eyes at my living, breathing, pain in the arse. "Like you'd wear anything else—"

"Two carats?"

Give her a look. "Three."

She purses her lips. "Clarity?"

"IF."

She squints. "Colour?"

I scoff, offended. "D. Obviously."

She puts her hands on her hips, huffs a bit.

"How did you know that's my dream ring?"

I laugh once, shake my head at her. "Because I fucking know you, Parks. And I've thought about marrying you since I was six." I raise my brows. "And also your real subtle Pinterest board named 'dream engagement rings' was of some help."

"Ah." She nods, a bit embarrassed.

"A husband's best friend, Pinterest—"

She gives me a look. "You're not a husband yet."

"Well, if you'd just take this fucking ring I'd be one step closer."

She rolls her eyes and then her face settles a bit. Sighs, looking at the Ballentine ring.

"I wouldn't like to take this one off. It's the most important thing I own."

"Is that why you threw it at me in a fit?" I ask playfully.

She gives me a look. "Do you really want to pull at that thread right now?"

"I don't—" Shake my head. "Comment redacted."

"Good choice." She nods.

"Thank you." I nod back then kiss her, smiling on her mouth with mine as I do. Slip the ring on her finger and she gives me a glare she doesn't mean.

"Do you like it?"

She nods, gazing down at it. "How'd you get it made so fast? You asked me just yesterday."

I press my finger into my mouth, squint at her a bit. Give her a tight smile.

"Called the boys at Harry Winston on December 6th."

She pulls back, blinking a lot.

"What?" She laughs.

I shrug.

"December 6th?" she repeats.

I nod once. "As soon as you said you were staying. Been carrying it around in my pocket since . . ." I think back. "Christmas."

"BJ!" She lets out a bewildered laugh.

"Had it in my pocket when I walked you home—thought about it. Probably should have, thinking back now." My eyes pinch. "Would have saved us a bunch of time."

She gives me an exasperated look.

Give her a shrug because I don't really care how we got here, just happy to have arrived.

"It was always going to be you, Parks. Just a matter of when."

We rent out the whole restaurant for this. Not because there are that many people coming but because we didn't want the extra eyes.

We're running about twenty-five minutes late for our own dinner, so when we get there everyone's already arrived but Christian—weird, I'll check about that later.

I think everyone thinks we're here just to celebrate that we're together.

No one knows. Haven't told anyone. Not Jo or the boys. Parks hasn't even told Bridge.

Was fun having a secret just us again for a day, ready to tell everyone now though.

Ready for everyone to know we finally sorted our shit out.

I can't wait to see my dad's face. Can't wait to see Harley's.

Walk in hand in hand and everyone, especially Henry and Jo, cheers.

But Bridget—fucking Bridget—stares at us for a few seconds, pinches her eyes and nods at Parks's hand in mine.

"Are you wearing a ring?"

Magnolia's face freezes.

569

"Are you wearing a fucking ring?" she repeats.

Magnolia rolls her eyes, gives her sister a dark look and then flashes her hand.

My mum screams. Covers her mouth in an embarrassing kind of maternal delight and Bridget forgets her sister has broken bones as she bull-rushes her, picking her up off the ground, excited.

Parks squirms in pain but grins and bears it, then Bridge stares over at me for a couple of seconds then about knocks me over with a hug.

After that, Parks and me are swallowed up in hugs and kisses and congratulation-y shit from everyone. It's nice how happy they are for us. We put them all through the fucking ringer to get here.

Jonah grabs my face, kisses me on the mouth before smacking my face excitedly. "Fuck, man—" He grins. "About fucking time!"

My dad's off ordering the best champagne they have.

Henry's hugging Parks from behind while my mum's crying, holding her face, welcoming her back—like she was ever really gone. I guess she was for a bit. Never again, though.

Madeline is Instagram Live-ing the whole thing.

Taura, Arrie, Allie and Jemima are fawning over the ring and Bushka's not talking to me because she's miffed I didn't ask her.

Then Marsaili broaches me, squinting.

"You didn't ask permission."

Magnolia looks over, curious. God's honest truth is she wouldn't have cared if I had or hadn't, she'd have said yes either way.

Harley shakes his head. "That's not true actually, love." He looks at her, nodding his head at me. "He asked me when he was seventeen."

I cock an eyebrow at Mars because I love an unsaid fuck you.

"Seventeen?" Marsaili blinks.

Harley nods. "We were in . . ." He pauses, trying to remember.

"Saint John." I smile at him.

"Virgin Islands." He nods. "And I walked in on something—" He eyes me and then Parks, who uses my brother's hand to hide her embarrassed face.

"I blocked this out," Magnolia says quietly before she calls to my mother, "Lily, stop listening. You won't care for this story."

"I took him aside, tried to scare him a bit with 'What are you doing with my daughter?' and 'If I ever see you touch her again . . .' You know . . ." He smirks over at me, a bit amused. "And this cocky prick says, 'Sorry, but I'm going to touch her forever, Sir.' I pulled back, couldn't believe my fucking ears." He chuckles.

Parks is staring over at us, surprised and wide eyed. Never told her this story. "And I said, 'Will you now?' And he said, 'Mmhm, I'm going to marry her if you let me.' And I said, 'Is that you asking me?' And he shrugged and said, 'Suppose it is . . .'"

Magnolia's staring over at me, eyes back to heavy with that old want. Same want that was being met that day in Saint John when he walked in on us, actually.

Harley extends his hand to me. "I'm glad you finally asked her."

I shake it. "Me too."

("Fucking took you long enough," he says under his breath as he sits back down.)

Towards the end of the night, my dad makes his way over to me. Sits down, smacks me on the knee a couple of times.

"You played for keeps." He smiles proudly.

Love it when he's proud of me.

I nod. "Told you I would."

He nods, sitting back in his chair. "It's been a long time coming."

EIGHTY

Magnolia

"Do you like it?" Beej asks, looking over at me a bit nervous. We're standing in the foyer of the house he bought us.

A cute little four-bedder apartment on Kensington Church Street. He paid £16.5 million for it so Bridget says I have to stop referring to it as 'cute', even though it is cute, because four is a cute number of rooms. The apartment itself is perfect. Completely. Not a thing in the world I'd change. I like the backsplash, I like the windows, the balcony's even lined with lilacs. Not to mention the number one house perk, that boy in the foyer I'm marrying who looks like a statue at all times, from all angles with his perfect hair and his pillow mouth and those eyes that make my resolve dissolve with a glance. Baroque-print silktwill shirt from Versace, black elasticated-waist straight trousers from Jil Sander, and my nemesis, black Old Skools.

"I love it," I tell the boy sincerely.

"Yeah?" Beej steps over to me, looking up at the high ceilings as he wraps his arms around me mindlessly. I dressed like a homeowner today. Versace belted cotton-tweed minidress in lilac (cute), the cream perforated logo cardigan from Sandro, with the cream Saint Laurent La 16 bouclé-tweed mules.

"Yeah, me too," says Henry as he strides out of one of the bathrooms, hands in the pockets of his black logo-tape detail cargo trousers from Heron Preston. "Can I live here too?"

"Sure!" I smile brightly at the same time BJ scowls, "No."

Henry's shoulders slump.

Bridget stands in the balcony doorway, arms folded over her chest, shaking her head at us.

"I can't believe that you two idiots finally sorted yourselves out—" She does a big sigh and walks inside. "Never thought I'd live to see the day."

I frown at her, locking BJ's arm around myself like a seatbelt. "We weren't that bad."

"Yeah, you were—" Henry nods. ("We were." BJ nods.)

I frown more and stomp off into the kitchen.

"Where was Christian last night?" Bridget asks, walking after me.

"Oh, yeah—" I turn back to BJ. "I was going to ask you but I didn't want you to think into it."

He gives me a look. "In what way?"

I pull an awkward face. "In the, you know, in the old 'he loves me' way."

I clear my throat, toss him a sheepish smile.

"Yeah, right," he snorts. "I think we're all past that now."

"Right, great." I nod and run my fingers over the white marble countertop, admiring it for a second before scowling up at the boys. "Then where the fuck was he?"

"Did he just not come?" Bridget asks, annoyed on my behalf.

"That's so rude." I glower.

BJ shakes his head. "I think something happened with him and Daisy."

"Did they break up?" I snap my head in Henry's direction. He's already shaking his head.

"Well, is everything okay?" I look between the two of them.

"Yeah—" BJ nods but he's frowning. He's lying, I think.

"Did Julian do something?" I ask carefully.

BJ shakes his head dismissively. "Nah."

I bite down on my bottom lip because I think Julian might always do something.

"Christian sends his love." Henry nods with a smile. "Can't wait to celebrate soon."

"Okay." I frown.

"How about these light fixtures?" Henry nods at the ceiling. "Spiff, man."

He's trying to change the subject.

"Have you seen the pool yet?" BJ asks him, leading him away.

Bridget watches them leave before stepping over to me.

"You're worried?"

I purse my lips. "He's done something."

"Christian?"

I give her a steep look. "Julian."

"Have you spoken to him?"

I scowl at her for thinking that I just casually chit-chat with my exes all the live-long day.

"No." Then I give her a demure shrug. "He did send us flowers to say congratulations though."

She stares at me for a few seconds and then links her arm with mine, resting her head on my shoulder.

"I can't believe you're marrying him. Finally."

"I know."

"Remember your first date?"

I nod.

"And you were so miffed at him because I was wearing Sketchers to the party when you said I couldn't wear them and he said I was the kind of girl who could wear whatever I wanted?"

I nod, smiling at her. I was so mad.

Mad that she was in Sketchers, mad that someone fucking bought her Sketchers, mad that he took her side, mad that it made me like him more.

"Who the fuck wears Sketchers to the Four Seasons?" I scowl.

She raises her hand, all smarmy and annoying.

I glance down at her feet.

"And look how far you've come in those little Prada Monolith brushed leather boots." I beam at her.

"You don't need to say the rest of what I'm wearing—" She gives me a curt look as she walks out of the room. "It's fine. I don't care—"

I scoff at her.

"Logo-embroidered tank top from Marine Serre, RE/DONE Stove Pipe high-rise jeans and the slogan-motif cardigan from Stella McCartney," I call after her.

"You're ridiculous," she tells me without looking back.

"You're wearing an eight-hundred-pound cardigan," I say, scrambling after her. "Might be time to climb down off that high horse."

"No thank you," she tells me, nose in the air.

"I'm going to miss you when I move out." I purse my mouth.

She nods. "Yes, I'm sure you will miss the turn-down service I provide."

I shake my head. "BJ does the same thing and with much less of an attitude."

She rolls her eyes.

"I will miss you though."

She gives me a tender smile and shakes her head.

"No, you won't—" She shrugs. "I'm right around the corner and you're finally, for the first time in about five years, exactly where you're supposed to be."

EIGHTY-ONE

BJ

The next week goes by in a bit of a happy blur.

Word got out quick that we were engaged. The rags touted it as the epic conclusion to 'Britain's Longest-Running Love Saga.'

"Love that for us," Parks grimaced when she saw that article.

Rolled my eyes, kissed her a lot.

We did an interview with *Tatler*. Arrie's making us do a Parks and Ballentine spread in *Country Living* ("But none of us live in the fucking country," Bridget growled at the news). There's a bidding war currently about who gets exclusive rights to our wedding-day photos. Arrie says *Vanity Fair*, Parks says it should be *Tatler* out of loyalty, her dad says it should be split between *GQ* and *Vogue* because they're both owned by Condé Nast and we'll make double the money if we each do an exclusive with them, Bridge said it should be *Good Housekeeping* in the spirit of irony, and I'm shooting for *Nat Geo* but they've not taken the bait yet.

Mum offered me £200k to not let anyone take any photos. Said we need privacy.

I told her it feels unlikely since I'm marrying who I'm marrying, and she touched my face and told me to think about it.

Told my parents about December 3rd too.

Parks said she didn't want to tell her parents. Think she's scared Marsaili will be angry about it, like she could ground her in retrospect, but I said I felt like my parents should know and she agreed.

Mum just cried for the most part. Said she was sorry we went through it alone. Had a billion questions for Parks. All but pulled her into her lap to stroke Magnolia's hair. She wanted to know everything. How far along, how the procedure happened, how she felt after, how I felt after. She wept constantly but it'd peak every now and then, like when she found out her name. And Mr Gibbs.

I'll tell you what, Mr Gibbs is in for a lifetime of Christmas hampers from Lil now. Whipped out her phone midway through the conversation to send him a ham.

Don't know why a ham if I'm honest.

Grief maybe.

After we finished telling them, Dad just held my shoulder for ages, couple tears snuck out. Nodded a lot, put his forehead on mine. I think he was proud of me for some reasons I don't really get.

Told me he was sorry a lot. Sorry that we didn't feel we could come to them, sorry that I felt like I couldn't come to him, that I had to navigate it all by myself, but Magnolia frowned at him and said, "He wasn't alone, he had me." And my dad smiled at her and said, "I beg your pardon, he did too." And then he said he understood, he thinks, why we are how we are. Don't even know what that means anymore because all I know about us now is that we're together.

But maybe that's what he meant. Maybe that's how we've always been. Just together. Or trying to be.

There's something about the letting go of a secret . . . makes you feel new or clean or some fresh-sounding adjective. Used to worry telling people would loosen the ties that bind us, but now I know we're tied anyway. Billie knotted us together.

Mum wants to visit the tree. We're going up next week.

I've had to really hammer it home to Parks not to mention to my parents that the reason the tree is special to us is because it's where the baby was made, but we'll see how long it takes for it to slip out that their very first grandchild was conceived at a drunken party because of a faulty lock in front of some pervert ducks. Parks will tell a quarter of the story to get a rise out of Mum, I'll tell the rest because I'm proud of it and I wouldn't change a fucking thing about any of it. Mum'll probably have a nervous breakdown about us doing it on her bed again (still hasn't gotten past that) but who cares because I'm marrying Magnolia Parks.

Henry and I are playing at The Grove.

Just us. Jo's been a bit MIA. Haven't really heard from Christian.

I chip off at the fourth hole. Watch it land and then turn to my brother.

"What the fuck's going on with the boys?"

Henry's face pulls, shakes his head.

"I don't know—" Shrugs. "Some shit went down."

I eye him. "Yeah, I figured. But what kind of shit?"

"Christian won't say." Face pulls again. "Only that Daisy's gone now."

I frown. "Gone where?"

He shrugs again.

"Gone where?" I ask louder because I like Daisy and I worry about some of the shit those boys do. She's not a willing participant. She's never wanted to be part of it, always made that clear.

"She's not—"

"—Dead?" Henry guesses grimly. Shakes his head.

Thank fuck. Who knows with that lot lately.

The boys always sort of shielded us from it. Knew they were doing shit I didn't want to know about, but Parks being with Julian opened up the conversation.

"Julian took her away," Henry tells me.

I lick my bottom lip, thinking. "Why?"

Henry squares off. Sighs.

Chips the ball perfectly. Looks back up me.

"Jo ended it with Tausie."

"What?" I blink.

He nods.

Can't believe he didn't tell me. What the fuck is going on?

"Something happened." Henry nods to himself. "Has to have—he wouldn't have done it otherwise."

I nod, look over at him.

"I mean, that's good for you though, right? You and Taurs can figure your shit out."

My little brother breathes out heavily through his nose. Pushes his hand through his hair.

"I don't know."

I frown over at him.

"She never made the call—" He shrugs.

I breathe out. Fuck.

"And if we start dating now, I'll spend the rest of my life wondering if she's with me because Jonah called it for her."

I nod quietly.

"Fuck—" I stare over at him. "I'm sorry, man."

Some sort of emotion rolls over his face that he doesn't want to feel, so he hits another ball just 'cause.

"Yeah." He nods. "Me too."

EIGHTY–TWO
Magnolia

"No." Henry shakes his head. "It'd be a fucking travesty."

I nod in firm agreement. "An absolute nightmare, yeah."

BJ walks in with too many bags of Chinese take-out and frowns at us.

"What are you two talking about?"

"Babies with a monobrow," Bridget tells him, unimpressed. She's perched on the kitchen bench of our apartment in Mayfair. BJ and I move into our place next week.

"Because, I mean, what do you do with that?" I give Beej a serious look and let the gravity of the question hang there for a moment.

Henry shakes his head. "It's not like you can take a toddler in for a wax."

"But then . . ." I give Henry a look. "Do you have a choice?"

"You do." Beej nods.

"Do you?" I tilt my head.

"Definitely do." My sister nods, holding her hands out for my fiancé to pass her the Singapore Noodles.

"When we have a child I will be praying for two eyebrows," I tell them all.

Beej scrunches his nose. "What about praying for just, like, working eyes, some hands, some feet?"

Henry rolls his eyes and I make a sound in the back of my throat. "Don't be that guy."

My sister starts laughing.

Bridget looks between me and Henry. "How often do they talk about babies?"

Beej gives her a look. "More often than you'd think."

"Popular topics include: parents who don't know their baby looks like a tub of goo, parents willing to throw their baby under the bus for a good photo of themselves, parents with children where one kid's much, much cuter than the other . . ."

"Oh God." Henry sighs all rueful. "Remember that Le Strange debacle? Fuck me, that was a travesty."

"Which segues into our favourite topic of all: ugly babies."

BJ shovels some food into his mouth, shaking his head at me and his brother. "I hate it when you two talk about ugly babies"

"Listen," I scowl at him as I bite into an egg roll, "I don't rag on you when you're talking about things that you're passionate about—like golf, which is stupid by the way—"

Beej and Bridget trade looks.

"That's—" He shakes his head. "You're ragging on it— And—It's not the same thing."

"I know." I give him a look. "Golf is boring."

"It's not," Henry interjects.

"But ugly babies are fascinating."

Henry nods. "That is true."

"You know what we should talk about?" BJ points his chopsticks at me. "A date for the wedding."

"Who's your maid of honour?" Henry jumps in, nodding at me with his chin.

I glance over at my sister and pull an awkward face.

"I mean, she is my flesh and blood. And I love her more than all my other friends."

"Thanks." Henry nods.

"But then again, Tausie is a much better dresser than Bridge . . ."

Bridget rolls her eyes and rubs her temple.

BJ nods his chin at my sister. "You okay?"

She nods. "Just tired."

Bridge looks over at me. "Are you getting married in England?"

I squint at Beej. Never really thought about getting married anywhere else.

"I've just always wanted to get married in June."

"June?" My sister blinks. "Like, June a month from now?"

I frown a bit. "Well, no, I suppose not. I guess next June?"

"Next June?" BJ's head pulls back. "Fuck that."

"Why June?" Henry asks.

"I don't know." I shrug. "It's just always what I imagined."

BJ keeps shaking his head. "I'm not waiting for a year."

"But I want a June anniversary!" I pout.

"Why?" he asks, eyebrow all cocked and annoying.

I glare over at him. "Just do."

"I know why," Henry says, inserting himself.

BJ waves his hand permissively.

"Because his birthday's in February and yours is August and June is bag in the middle. Nice way to space out the gift giving."

"Yeah—" My sister gives me a glib look. "That's what she needs. More presents."

"That reminds me—" I point at her. "You haven't given me an engagement present yet."

"Nor will I," Bridget says, standing and rubbing her temple.

"Well, that's not very nice." I eye her. "I gave you a present last year to celebrate getting your tonsils taken out."

"You did," she concedes. "And I begged you not to."

"And yet . . ." I give her a look.

She sniffs a laugh. "I'm really tired. I'm going to bed."

"Night Bridge," Henry calls.

Beej nods his chin at her, watches her walk out of the room, waiting till she's out of earshot.

"I think you hurt her feelings," he tells me.

"What?" I scoff. "No, I didn't."

"She went weird."

I roll my eyes at him. "She did not."

He nods back at me. "She did."

I give him a look. "When?"

"When you said Tausie might be our maid of honour."

Our. Cute. I try not to smile at him for that because I don't like it when he takes Bridget's side over mine.

I let out a puff of air to make sure he knows I'm annoyed at him, and he stares over at me, smiling a quiet, steady smile that seems smug even though he hasn't said a word. I can't wait to have him make that face at me forever.

I get up and wander into my sister's room.

"Hey you big, fat cow—" I climb into her bed. "I need to talk to you about something."

She doesn't roll over.

Rude.

"Listen, even though you dress like a tree and have the stylistic sensibilities of, like, a blind child, you'd still be the best maid of honour in the world . . ."

She doesn't say anything.

I growl at the back of my throat. "Don't make me beg."

I look over at her. "Bridget, don't be rude—" Give her a shove.

Her body moves around limply.

I shake her again. "Bridget?"

Nothing.

My chest goes tight instantly.

I shake her more.

"Bridget?!" I yell.

I roll her over and the way her body moves is bad.

Flops.

Her mouth falls open a little.

Slowly, carefully, feeling like I'm being tricked somehow, I lower my ear to her mouth and listen.

Wait to feel a little puff of air.

Just a small one.

Anything at all.

There's nothing.

I scream, I think? I must because BJ and Henry run in.

And then it all drops into a strange kind of slow motion, like we're all living out the moment underwater.

BJ runs over to the bed, falls to his knees.

"She's not breathing," he tells Henry.

Hen's already on the phone.

"Grosvenor Square—Apartment 12—Unconscious—No, she's not breathing—We don't know—No—"

Beej is good in a crisis. He lays her flat, checks her airways. His chest is heaving as he leans over my sister. He looks up at me with fragile eyes before he plugs her nose, lowers his mouth onto hers and starts pumping her chest.

I can't breathe—my mouth's gone dry and my vision . . . I can't see properly. I can't think straight. All I can think about is being nine in Paris with Bridget and it was close to the twilight hours.

"Magnolia, slow down!" Bridget whined as she ran after me. "You're going to get us lost."

"I know Paris like the back of hand." I spun on my heel, frowning at her even though I was lying. "I know where I'm going."

"We're in a foreign country!" She blinked, exasperated with me even then at the ripe old age of seven.

"We can speak French." I shrugged, turning back, all starry eyed to the footpath of Avenue Montaigne.

"Where are we going?" Bridget whined, traipsing after me.

Our parents were at a late lunch a street or so back. They hadn't looked at us in well over an hour and, believe it or not, they hadn't brought Marsaili on this trip. I think it was during their singular 'we can be a real family' phase, but it lasted about a day and a half, because now that I'm older, when I think back to that day I'm 70 per cent sure my father was feeling up a French pop star underneath the table and 100 per cent sure my mother was drunk because of it.

"Céline!" I squealed, drunk on the excitement of it all.

"Why do you like clothes?" she asked, trying hard to keep up. "They're just clothes."

She's always been genuinely confused about why I love clothes how I do. She had never wanted dolls growing up, she was always interested in science sets and blocks, and I thought she was so weird and embarrassing and so much better than me.

I peered down at her, horrified by the question. "Because they're beautiful and when you wear them you turn beautiful too."

She frowned up at me and shook her head. "You don't need them to be beautiful."

She pushed her glasses back up her nose.

"I'll buy you something?" I batted my eyes at her.

"You don't have money." She frowned.

"I took Harley's credit card," I whispered as though he could hear me.

She gave me a look. "He doesn't like it when you call him that . . ."

I shrugged.

"Does he know you took it?"

"No." I grinned mischievously before running into the store.

That was my candy store. I picked about twenty-five dresses and brought them to the counter.

"*Bonjour*," I sang sweetly.

"*Salut—*" The woman smiled, unsure.

"*Parlez vous anglais?*" I blinked.

"*Oui.*" She nodded. "Yes. Ow ken I 'elp?"

I shoved the dresses towards her. "I'd like these in my size please."

She blinked at me a few times. Bridget shifted uncomfortably behind me. "You said you'd buy me something?"

"Anything you want, Bridge." I gave her a big smile.

I turned my attention back to the shop assistant, smiling up at her. "My size please."

"Erm, these do not come in your size."

I blinked at her. "Are you calling me fat?"

"Non." She sniffed a laugh as she shook her head. "I am calling you a child." She looked around. "Where are your parents?"

"We're orphans!" I lied, giving her a big grin.

The woman eyed Bridget and me suspiciously. "What zort of orpheens wear Dolce et Gabbana?"

Bridget frowned at her.

"There are lots of ways you can be an orphan."

The woman's face softened towards my sister and then she took the credit card from me.

"Did you steal this?" She peered down at me.

"Yes." I shrugged. "From my father. But he won't be cross, I promise. He won't have even noticed."

The woman pursed her lips then nodded, rang it all through.

By the time we left the shop, it was dark out and wet. Bridget glared over at me, arms crossed, one foot stomping in a puddle.

"Now you've really gone and done it!" she growled. "Where are we?"

I pursed my lips nervously. "I don't know." I looked around then pointed. "We came from that way."

She shook her head. "No, we didn't."

And then I felt it—I didn't know what it was at the time, but now I know it was anxiety. I started to breathe quicker, my palms went sweaty, my eyes were unable focus right. Then Bridget snapped my hand up in hers.

She shook her head sternly.

"It's going to be okay. Don't be scared."

She found a map in a corner store and pulled out the compass she always kept in her back pocket on vacations, which every day till then I had teased her for using, but she remembered the address of our hotel.

And she navigated us there, by ourselves, in the dark.

I said we should have caught a taxi and she said, 'Haven't you ever heard of human trafficking?', which was insane because *Taken* hadn't even come out yet, so how the fuck did she know about human trafficking?

We got back to the hotel and our parents weren't there.

No one was looking for us, no one was waiting for us.

They hadn't even realised we were missing.

We gave ourselves showers, got into robes that were too big for us, and climbed into the same bed even though we each had one. We ordered up room service and watched *Cheaper by the Dozen* and secretly wished we lived in a family as big and poor as theirs.

My whole childhood is littered with memories of being alone and lonely and abandoned and disregarded in our family, and the only part that makes it feel okay is that Bridget was there with me. Through all the ways our parents failed us, my sister did not. My sister is the lace trimming around all of it and I'm watching my fiancé do his absolute and undeniable best to give my sister breath again.

But he can't.

She's already gone.

Kekoa

Wake up

Miguel answer your fucking phone

It's 2 a.m.

Jules is shot

In London

Give me her address

Fucking now Miguel

Directions to:

50 Kensington Square gardens

Acknowledgements

First cab off the rank, I have to thank the knights of the round table of things no one cares about but me. Amanda, Madi and Molly. This book would have crashed and burnt without your patience, your kindness, your encouragement and your swear words. Respectfully, eat my ass.

But also, I love each of you. I literally couldn't have done this without you.

Emmy, how you topped the first cover, I'll literally never know. You are so wildly talented, and I have stared at this one in awe for months now, and like the first book's cover before it, I will continue to do so.

Thank you for being patient with me, thank you for actualising the vague and warty visions I have in my mind onto beautiful paper.

I am lucky for many reasons that you are my best friend, but this specific reason in particular has been very handy for me.

Bill and Viv, for those special few months where we were trapped in Ireland and I'd work all day and night and you'd mind our kids, thank you always for your kindness and patience towards me.

Camryn, Ashley, Lindsey and Kim, for looking after my babies in America when I can't. So grateful for you guys.

Tori, thank you for your patience when I try to understand the UK school system. Best conference friend I ever had.

To the dream team over at Avenir . . . Betty Luke, Jayboy, Maddi and everyone else . . . You are so good at what you do, so patient with me, so much fun to work with, have the best eye for detail, the best ideas. I have loved doing this with you. I'm grateful for everything you've done, how hard you work and how good you are to me. I love you 3000.

To Nicole, thank you for all your help. I was in a very chaotic place when we began working together, thank you for really seeing this project. I'm grateful for all your work on it. Euan and Frances, thank you both for all your hard work as well!

Benja, Juniper and Bellamy. I love you all the most.

And lastly, to all the sweet people who have embraced the MPU in a way that really felt like it could only be in my imagination, thank you. Thank you for loving my imaginary friends so fiercely and making them your own.
    It's changed my life.

PS: this is maybe the first time in my life I've ever gotten to use "post script" literally. I like not changing my thank yous, I like them being locked to the time I wrote them, I don't keep a diary but they feel like a very specific diary entry, but I need to add a incredibly large and eternal thank you to Hellie, my agent, for being the best ever and also so patient and gracious with me, I know I can be a handful. And Alyssa and Caitlin, I know we're just at the start of everything but thank you as well. I appreciate each and all of your work(s). Emad, all the Orion team and Celia especially, you've been such champions of Magnolia since day dot. Thank you for believing in us.

About the Author

An Australian-native, Jessa Hastings now lives in Sherman Oaks, California with her husband, two children, her cat and a a dog that she semi-regrets getting. She feels guilty writing that here but is fairy confident he won't read it. She is presently exasperated by the US medical system (but who isn't?), she's also knee-deep in *Stranger Things* theories and is an aspiring water-connoisseur. She still misses Australian breakfasts, tans very well and highly recommends the Coconut Cake from Erewhon. *Magnolia Parks: The Long Way Home* is her third novel and she still (obviously) struggles to write a topically relevant author's biography. Sorry for this.

Discover more addictive books
from Jessa Hastings in the
Magnolia Parks Universe . . .

MAGNOLIA PARKS

How many loves do you get in a lifetime?

She is a beautiful, self-involved and mildly neurotic London socialite. He is Britain's most photographed bad boy who broke her heart. But Magnolia Parks and BJ Ballentine are meant to be . . . Aren't they?

'If *Gossip Girl* and *Made in Chelsea* had a baby, it would be this book.'
★ ★ ★ ★ ★

DAISY HAITES

No guns at the dinner table.

All 20-year-old Daisy Haites has ever wanted is a normal life. But as the sister of London's most notorious gang lord, she knows better than most that in this life, everything comes at a price . . .

'I will never get over Daisy and Christian.'
★ ★ ★ ★ ★

MAGNOLIA PARKS: THE LONG WAY HOME

It's been nearly a year since everything happened between Magnolia Parks and BJ Ballentine on the steps of the Mandarin Oriental.

Now they must finally face the question they've been avoiding all their lives: How many loves do you get in a lifetime . . . and are they each other's?

'I never want to leave the Magnolia Parks Universe!'
★ ★ ★ ★ ★

DAISY HAITES: THE GREAT UNDOING

Daisy Haites thought she'd left everything about her old life behind.

But when her safety is threatened, she finds herself back under the watchful eyes of her gang-lord brother Julian and her ex-boyfriend Christian. Everything gets more complicated when Julian finds himself entangled with broken-hearted socialite Magnolia Parks. Because for Julian, falling in love it could be deadly for everyone involved . . .

'This series has consumed my whole life.'
★ ★ ★ ★ ★